Renato, the Painter

Renato, the Painter

An Account of his Youth
& his 70ᵗʰ Year
in his own Words

Eugene Mirabelli

McPherson & Company

ISBN 0-929701-96-8
Library of Congress Cataloging in Publication Data

Mirabelli, Eugene.
    Renato, the painter : an account of his youth & his 70th
year in his own words / Eugene Mirabelli.
        p. cm.
    ISBN 978-0-929701-96-7 (hardcover)
    1. Older men—Fiction. 2. Painters—Fiction. I. Title.
    PS3563.I684R46   2012
    813'.54—dc23
                                              2011051924

Printed on pH neutral paper.

The author thanks Andrei Codrescu, founder and editor of *Exquisite Corpse*, which first published sections of this story. Thanks also go to *Fantasy & Science Fiction* magazine for publishing an episode that was later anthologized in *The Year's Best Science Fiction and Fantasy*, and further thanks to the *Journal of Southern New Hampshire University* and to the *Drexel Online Journal* for opening their pages to parts of this novel as well.

for Margaret

& the children

& the children's children

PART ONE

In which Renato is Introduced
to his Parents,
the World,
&
the Woman He will Marry

Q. Who made you?
A. God made me.

—Catechism of Christian Doctrine

1

I WAS MADE IN THE USUAL WAY, THOUGH WHETHER
I came here head-first or tail-first I don't know, since
my mother didn't stay around long enough to tell me, and my
father, if he knew me at all, never came by to admit it, but
my life having turned out the way it has, I suspect I came out
tail-first and that my head still dreamed in the dark while my
legs went thrashing about in the light of this world. One way
or the other I got out whole and got my bellybutton neatly
knotted, and what happened over the next few days or weeks
I can't even guess at.

Then came the moment I've heard about over and over
again. It comes like this. It comes KNOCK KNOCK KNOCK.
Then Pacifico Cavallù pushes back his chair and slowly gets
up from the long table, his white linen napkin still tucked in
his vest as he strolls across the big square hall and pulls open
the front door. Outside it's all black sky and freshly fallen
snow and, down at his feet, a large oval laundry basket with a
mound of blankets and—"Good God!" he says. Now there's
a clatter of dropped silverware and the scrape of chairs and
everyone comes running to the door to get a look. Bixio begins to bark and Nora, the housemaid, has to climb a chair
to see over the heads of the grown-ups. For a moment everyone crowds the doorway but nobody moves—Pacifico is still
peering into the dark where a few silent snowflakes tumble
through the doorlight—then Marianna steps past him, wari-
ly lifts the basket and carries it on her hip to the dining room.

There were fifteen people in the Cavallù house that night. First of all there were the parents—that's Pacifico and Marianna Cavallù—Pacifico at this end of the table, a sturdy man with beautiful eyes and a short iron-colored beard, and big Marianna at the other end, a woman such as you might find carved on the prow of a ship, with her broad face and her hair in a black braided crown. Their children ran in age from ten to twenty-five and were known for being handsome, quick-witted and rash. They were seated on both sides of the long table—Lucia and Marissa and Bianca and Candida and Dante and Sandro and Silvio and Mercurio and Regina, along with Marissa's husband Nicolo, an aeronautical engineer, and Bianca's husband Fidèle, a stone cutter. And, of course, there was Carmela the cook and Nora the housemaid. That's two in the kitchen, thirteen at the table and me on the front piazza.

Mother Marianna shifted the wicker basket from her hip to her place at the table and everyone continued to speak at once, saying, "Look at those big eyes it could have died out there in the cold why our doorstep such big eyes for such a small little baby what kind of mother would leave her baby but why our doorstep could have died under these thin blankets came to the wrong house and so strong the way it holds my finger take a look take those off and that one too and my God swaddling clothes unwrap the poor thing and let's take a look. Sfasciarlo! Sfasciarlo!"—Unwrap it! Unwrap it! Then the women sang "Ah-ha!" And the men chorused "Oh-ho!" and Regina, the youngest, said, "Look at his little ucellino,"— birdic—while Mercurio, a year older, frowned and blushed.

"He's going to be strong," Pacifico said. "You can tell by the legs."

"A Calabrian," Marianna said. "They wrap them that way in Calabria."

"Mamà, they wrap them that way in Sicily, too," Lucia informed her.

"No. Not like that. That baby is Calabrese," her mother insisted. "He's been washed and rubbed with olive oil and then swaddled."

"It's terrible and I'm not ever doing that to mine," Marissa said.

"Anyway, he wasn't born in Sicily or Calabria. He was born right here in Massachusetts," Lucia said.

The naked infant was nested back on the blankets in the wicker basket, which was handed up over the espresso cups, crushed walnut shells and dried figs to Pacifico. The table quieted while he unhooked the watch chain from his vest, drew out the gold timepiece and lowered it delicately along side the baby's head, close by his ear. For a moment no one drew breath, then the infant turned toward the tick-tick-tick. Pacifico, his face still heavy with concentration, abruptly hauled the watch up and lowered it down the other side. Again the infant turned his head and twisted about to find the ticking. Pacifico, hoisted the watch once more and held it directly above the baby's face, rolling the chain between his fingers just enough to start the gold and crystal flashing. The infant stared up, fascinated. Pacifico slid the watch back into one of his vest pockets and looped the heavy gold chain across and then glanced up. "É bello," he concluded. "He's fine."

Marissa's husband Nicolo, a logical man, asked, "Did anyone look for a note?" Now everyone looked. They unfurled the blankets and gently shook them out, they went back through the big front hall and the vestibule to see if a little leaf of paper had dropped to the floor when they had trooped in, and they even went out onto the porch. There was no note. Regina had taken one of the blankets which wasn't a blanket at all, but only a cheap kerchief. "Look at this. Can I keep it?" she asked. It was a square of thin blue cotton printed with a fanciful map of Sicily, one of a thousand such kerchiefs. "How does it look?" she asked, pulling it around her shoulders and turning her head to see the effect. "What do you think? Can I keep it?"

"No. It doesn't belong to us," Pacifico told her. "And neither does the baby."

Marianna had taken the kerchief from her daughter and now she began to fold it. "Some poor confused woman didn't know which side of the church the parish house was on. If it wasn't so late we could take it over right now. Father McCarthy can find a home for it."

"Not Mr McCarthy," Pacifico told her. He refused to call any priest Father.

"All right. Father Basilio, then."

One by one they fell silent as they watched Marianna tuck the kerchief around the baby in the basket. Carmela came and set a pan of warmed milk beside Marianna, looked without curiosity at the infant and then hobbled back to the kitchen. Nobody spoke. Bianca's husband Fidèle lowered his little finger into the baby's warm hand, which closed tight around it.

"We can't give him back," Bianca said, breaking the silence. "We can't just give him *away!*"

"He belongs with his mother," big Marianna said firmly. "And his mother doesn't live here."

"But maybe the father is here," Candida said. "After all, it could be Dante or Sandro or—" She shrieked and ducked aside, as Dante lunged across the table to throw his wine in her face, Sandro already on his feet, his chair crashing backward. She swept the wine from her cheek with the back of her hand. "All I mean is —"

"Candida!" her mother cried.

"She talks too much!" Silvio said.

"You!" Dante said.

"Me? What about me?" Candida retorted.

"You know what about you," Sandro said.

"That's enough," Pacifico murmured, holding up his hand, palm outward.

The baby went on crying loudly in the sudden silence. Bianca swathed him in his blue map-kerchief and lifted him from the basket, cradling him in her arms, while her husband Fidèle brought up the pan of warm milk. He sat down beside his wife and sank a twisted corner of his napkin into the milk, saying, "He's hungry. Let's give him something to drink."

2

A ND HERE I AM, MORE THAN SEVEN DECADES LATER, a vulgar old man with white hair on his privates and no time to wonder where I came from or where I'm going, because I'm too busy trying to make a name for myself. The parish house was on one side of St. Brigid's Church, the Cavallù house on the other, and my guardian angel, she—for surely angels are sexed—steered me to the right place. I was adopted then and there by Bianca and her husband Fidèle Stillamare. When I turned thirteen my parents gave me a diary in the hope that I would learn to spell if I wrote a paragraph at the end of each day, but after a few entries I quit writing and used it for a sketch pad, and have never succeeded in keeping a journal of any kind. Yet here I sit, writing any which way—*scribble, scribble, scribble.*

When I was growing up we had two autobiographies in our bookcase, a square brown one by Benjamin Franklin and a fancy red-and-gold one in Italian by Benvenuto Cellini, since each man had done great things in his way, though wise and prudent Franklin, a friendly guy, had no fire in his veins and Cellini, a good swordsman and sculptor, beat his women and bragged about it. My father admired Franklin for his hard work and scientific curiosity, but my mother liked Cellini for entertainment, forgiving him his sins because he was an artist and artists were heroes to her.

So I had thought to write a book of my life and views after I had accomplished some great works and grown famous, which was an innocent thought with no vanity in it, for I was only a kid. We natural-born princes of the world, we work for the glory of the work itself and for nothing else, still I had thought I would be famous by now or at least better known. And I don't have forever like I used to. My friends have begun to die off and my best and closest and dearest Mike Bruno is gone, gone, gone. Anyway, I have sat down to write this chronicle and not about myself alone, for I've never lived alone for long and hope I never do, and now will get on with this.

3

I DON'T KNOW WHO BIANCA AND FIDÈLE HAD ENVI-sioned when they dreamed of their first-born child, but they got me instead. They named me Renato, which means reborn, and gave me my birthday that same wintry night in March, and so it has been ever since. Now in my book, in *this* book, your true parents are the ones who love you and raise you, sit up with you when you're sick, whack you when you misbehave, teach you how to walk and talk, set you on your way and weep when you leave home. My father's name was Fidèle Stillamare, but instead of Fidèle he was called Fred. He liked to say he was just a stonecutter, but he was many other things as well—a mason and tiler and glazier, a sign mak-er, carver of letters in stone or wood, designer of alphabets, graphic artist and sculptor. We lived on the edge of town in a farm house on a long five-acre lot that went down to the dry bed of the old Middlesex Canal. Seventy years ago you could drive the back roads of these little towns outside Boston and when you came to houses with a vegetable patch out back, two or three fruit trees and a grape arbor made of iron pipe, you knew you were among the Italians and, in fact, you might be passing my home. *Stillamare's Cut Stone & Tile Company* was in the barn out back and employed two or three work-men, depending on the jobs my father had gotten. In winter he ate lunch with his men in the shop at a bench where my mother had set a pot of steaming coffee, and in summer at a table with a pitcher of iced tea on it under the big maple tree by our kitchen door.

In my earliest memory I'm playing in the dirt at the edge of our vegetable garden—even now I can smell the damp gold dust on the underside of the tomato leaves and get the warm taste of the bright red tomato which a beautiful wom-an, one of my mother's sisters, has bitten open and sprinkled with salt and offered to me. In those days we spoke Italian in the kitchen and English when we walked down town. Italian sounded old-fashioned and worn out, like our pots and soup spoons, whereas English was modern and sounded cleaner, but whenever I said anything like that my mother would slap me across the top of my head, saying, "Senti! In paradiso si parla la lingua di Dante. In heaven the angels speak Italian. Not English, Italian! Non dimenticare mai."

By the time my brother Bartolomeo was born I was four years old and already prince of our five acres, and a few years later I became king of the fields and woods. I knew the route of hidden creeks and the whereabouts of old stone walls that had crept into the woods years ago and been forgotten. On a rainy day I could run all the way from the Common to our house and not get wet, because I knew where to cross the streets and backyards in a zigzag that went beneath an end-less canopy of jutting eaves and elms and lilac bushes. I knew a friendly gray boulder shaped like a throne and knew a huge beech tree that had been half-uprooted in the Big Wind of 1938 and now grew at a slant, so you could walk up the trunk through a colonnade of branches, and I loved certain maples in whose slowly swaying branches I would be happy to rest even now. I knew how to call to crows, and when I called, they came. I knew where to find wild apples, blueberries, pears,

Concord grapes, tadpoles, woodchucks, rotted stumps, quartz crystals, mica and clay, and I knew where snakes went to shed their skins.

My grandmother Cavallù, my Nana, had nine children and when all of them had married I had sixteen uncles and aunts, and when they had children I had lots of cousins. My cousin Nick and I were about the same age, and my cousin Veronica about three years younger, and we spent a lot of time together when we were kids. We saw each other on the holidays, of course, but also every Sunday afternoon when our families would congregate to talk or play bocce and then sit down to coffee and, if we were lucky, some pastries and gelati. Furthermore, the three of us were shifted from house to house whenever our parents, still young and hot, wanted to have a weekend alone, and each spring another uncle or aunt got married and soon we were joined by more cousins, so there was troop of us children. Nick and I were the ringleaders of this pack, and if Nick wasn't around it was me and Veronica.

In August our families drove to the Cape where we used to swim or go digging for clams or pick beach plums, and if we stayed out of the way we could watch my father and uncle Nicolo and uncle Zitti pitch horse shoes—the iron shoe would rise from my dad's hand as lightly as a bird, and from uncle Nicolo it would whirl on its way, but from uncle Zitti it would tilt and veer and tumble and you never knew where it might land, because he was a philosopher and thought so much. Or we could watch our younger uncles build huge kites of bamboo and colored paper which they would launch from the sand dunes while their women, in swimsuits on the beach far below, waved encouragingly and smoked cigarettes, or lay back to sunbathe with a magazine spread open upon their face. (And now my nose, all on its own, suddenly remembers the exciting sharp odor of the gun smoke when the men were shooting clay pigeons, the tangy smell of Veronica's rubber bathing cap, and the gentle scent of the kitchen olive oil we used for suntan lotion.) Back home in February we would skate across the frozen marsh and through the woods, or if it rained we would play indoors, sprawled on the floor, drawing pictures on those glossy white oblongs of cardboard that uncle Zitti let us ransack from his freshly ironed shirts. I thought that everyone grew up this way, and it was only later I learned that the kids I went to school with didn't have a bunch of cousins to play with on weekends, but had to make do with whoever happened to be living in the neighborhood, a terrible thin social life.

My father saved my report cards and when I looked at them just now (pale yellow cards with his strong handsome signature on the back six times each year) I was astonished at how badly I had done. *He is inclined to waste time, and gets mischievous with his neighbors*, wrote grandmotherly Miss Blodgett. The reports show that I didn't obey promptly, didn't use time and materials wisely, didn't cooperate and was only average when it came to working at a given task. I was slow with number facts and even slower with letters. I didn't hate letters, quite the contrary. My father, being a sign painter and carver of inscriptions, loved the shapes of letters and numerals and he inspired that same love in me. On any day of the week our backyard had parts of the alphabet strewn around, leaning against the maple tree or stacked in a heap by the barn door, so I learned the names of letters, learned how to draw them and got to know their different personalities, but I didn't learn how to read and never asked to. When the time came, my mother took me to Hancock School and introduced me to Miss Gosling. There were six grades (Miss Gosling, Miss Blodgett, Miss Ouellette, Miss Keane, Miss Tennyson, and Miss Shea) and reading was dinned into me for six years and eventually it took, though I never did learn how to spell.

The world was filled with things and each one had a face and a way of gesturing for attention—certain intricately carved chairs, house-fronts, waters that winked or waved, trees that beckoned, muttered, sighed—and each one waited to be read, greeted or listened to. It turned out you didn't pay attention to these things or to pictures of them, but only to printed words. And after I learned to read words, those other things withdrew with injured dignity and even the boulders clammed up, refused to speak.

I loved to draw. I loved getting down on the floor on my stomach with a pencil and a sheet of my father's design paper or my uncle's shirt cardboard. I could draw better than anyone else, but it didn't count because they didn't teach it in school. Instead, we brought autumn leaves to class and traced them, then colored in the outline with wax crayons. In winter we cut snowflakes from folded tissue, or drew snow trees with white chalk on gray paper, and in spring we traced the bottom of our ink wells to make the sun and flowers. Our third grade class made a mural about Hiawatha's camp, but I wasn't allowed to work on it, even though I was the best at drawing, because I was slow at numbers and reading. Of course, everybody knew that tracing and coloring were for children and we soon put that behind us and had Art Appreciation instead.

In Art Appreciation the teacher would show us a picture of a famous painting, like *The Angelus* by the famous French painter Jean Francois Millet, and she'd read to us about it. Then each of us was given a miniature picture of it with stickum on the back which you licked, then you stuck it onto a sheet of construction paper. *The Angelus* was about a man and a woman working in a plowed field when they heard the church bell ringing, so they bowed their heads, and if you looked closely you could see the church belfry on the horizon. That was Art Appreciation. We Appreciated a lot of pictures like *The Age of Innocence* or *The Blue Boy* or the one about a dog that rescued people who fell off the dock into the sea, but they weren't very interesting and when we were through I decided I couldn't be a painter after all, because it was so dull.

We did a lot of singing and that was a joy. The teacher

would blow a note on her pitch-pipe and we would hum it till her note and our humming blended together perfectly, then we'd sing. Also, we got a lot of poems by heart, which I still think is the best way, so I can still recite *The Ride of Paul Revere* and *To A Waterfowl*. And in penmanship we learned to lick a new steel nib just once before dipping it into the ink well, and we practiced the Palmer Method with an eraser balanced on the back of our writing hand.

Each time the teacher gave me my report card it surprised and frightened me how low the marks were, because I knew that my mother would read it and hand it back, saying, "You'll have to give this to your father yourself." And after my father read it he would shout, "Do you want to be a ditch digger? That's where you'll end up, digging ditches! Is *that* what you want?" That's where dumb Italians ended up. No, I didn't want that. Being a ditch digger would mean working beside people like that pig Norman Oldacre who liked to make loud farts and told bathroom jokes and who took me aside in the school yard one morning and beat me up so hard my eyes watered.

But I didn't feel stupid and I knew that the stupidist kid in my class wasn't me but fat Collins. The teacher told him he was the cow's tail because he always came in last, but Collins just sat there being fat and smiled and blinked his sleepy-lidded eyes and said nothing. He wasn't my friend but I thought it was cruel to call him the cow's tail and make fun of him just because he couldn't memorize. I felt I could learn anything and that I was as smart as everybody else and even nicer than some other kids—certainly nicer than Eddy O'Toole who said *fuck* even though he was an altar boy at St. Brigid's, or Betty Bender who talked back to the teacher, or Carol Shepherd who stuttered, and as good as Jack Sawyer or Sue Meadows or that too-sweet girl with the permanent raspberry stain on her cheek whose name I've forgotten. I used to watch the shadow of the window sash creep ever so slowly across my desk and my mind would wander.

It's hard to believe, but years ago the town pried all the slate from the classroom walls, sold our desks and turned the school into expensive condominiums with big windows. When we were there the janitor used to sprinkle green sawdust in front of his broom when he swept the black oiled floors, and the stair treads had scoops worn in from our shoes. The Boys' Room had a wall made of brownish copper with water drizzling down it. You peed against the wall and the water washed it down to a gutter where it drained away past a white cake of disinfectant that smelled so strong it made you hold your breath. The sign over the paper towel box said *Why take two when one will do?* There was a tall skinny kid, three years older than everyone else, whose father used to beat him in the street and he had to keep his head shaved because he got lice. This kid caught me by the woods one day, twisted my arm behind my back until I took off my clothes and went swinging on the vines with him, then he unfolded his jackknife and said he'd get me if I told, but happily he was killed in boot camp three years later. Just before Christmas all the classes came out to the hall and each grade sang its own Christmas carol. The first grade had little voices so they sang *Wind in the Olive Trees*, the second grade was stronger so it sang *O, Little Town of Bethlehem*, and so on up to the sixth grade which sang *O, Come, All Ye Faithful!* When finally we were in sixth grade we were the last to sing and we stood very quietly in the hall and listened to the carol floating up from the little kids downstairs, singing in their sweet voices, and the songs went from room to room, getting stronger and richer and closer, and I felt this is what they meant when they told us about the angel chorus in heaven, this was what it sounds like.

Before I leave Hancock School I should introduce Miss Keane, my striking fourth grade teacher. All the gentle ancients at the school wore droopy sacks in mottled purples and moldy browns, illuminated by a lace collar or a pale cameo brooch, but handsome Miss Keane liked to wear silky white blouses that looked good to touch and a narrow black skirt that hissed excitedly against her stockings when she marched —tap! tap! tap!—down the aisle to see what we were doing. If we all had performed well, she would smile and take off her Mexican silver earrings and tell us about her trip to Mexico. But when we misbehaved she would angrily erase the black-board, her bracelets jingling frantically, then snatch up her pointer and smack it to her white palm in rhythm with our chant, not ending till we reached *nine elevens are ninety-nine.*

From Miss Keane I learned the multiplication table and how to spell some words, not many, and about volcanoes and cave men. And I learned that in Europe they thought it shameful to work with your hands (as my father did) and they looked down on a person who wore mended clothes (as I did), but here in the United States all citizens were created equal and it didn't matter what your last name was, because you could go to a public school and learn things and grow up to be whatever you wanted to be. Later, when I was in old Miss Tennyson's fifth grade, Miss Keane would step into my darkened bedroom and tie me naked to the bed, my arms like Christ crucified, then she'd pull my stiffened thing—like this, and this, and this! *this!*—until it fluttered in a strange soundless thunderbolt of pleasure, and sometimes Sue Mead-ows and Betty Bender slipped in behind her to see what was going on, their eyes shining with curiosity.

4

I SEE THAT I'VE LEFT OUT THE WAR THAT WAS GOING on in the background and that had been going on for as long as I could remember. In the candy store the bubble-gum came in flat squares with nice cards underneath, colored pic-ture cards that showed Japanese soldiers shooting the Chinese families they had roped together for the War in China. As I understood it, Mussolini had asked my mother and my aunts to give him their jewelry for the War in Ethiopia, but they had laughed at him—because they were so beautiful, I supposed, and didn't want to give up their bracelets and rings—though later my mother explained that it was because we despised the Fascists and admired Haile Selassie. In the newspaper there was a photograph of young men lounging in the street with their arms around each other's necks and little Italian flags in their hands: *These young men say they would be willing to fight for Italy in its war with Ethiopia.* All my aunts and uncles were shouting at once and my grandfather slapped uncle Silvio because Silvio was in the photo, but later everyone sat down to spumoni and coffee and went back to talking in English. Uncle Silvio had made a mistake, and we shouldn't talk about it in English. My grandfather and aunt Lucia sailed to Palermo to see about the villa, then the War broke out in Europe, too, and they couldn't get back, but Nonno wrote to us how ashamed he was when Italy invaded France, "a stab in the back" everybody called it. Every Sunday during coffee uncle Nicolo would ask, "Do you think we'll get dragged into this one?" and uncle Zitti would say, "We're already in it, Nicolo. We're already in it."

I was eleven years old when the Japanese bombed Pearl Harbor one Sunday afternoon and that meant we were actually in the War. The next spring my father enlarged the vegetable garden. A lot of people began vegetable gardens, which were called Victory Gardens the way the new bicycles were called Victory Bikes and later the letters from my uncles (shrunk to the size of a post card and covered with tiny writing) were called V-mail. My mother put up blackout shades and made soap, because it was scarce. We had ration booklets, we had buckets of sand at the ready in case the house was hit by an incendiary bomb, and we had the car headlamps painted black on top, like sleepy eyelids, so that our coastal ships wouldn't be silhouetted against sky-glow. Nick and Veronica and I had fathers too old to be drafted, so each summer we still went to Cape Cod and stayed there while our parents came and went by turns, but our young uncles couldn't come and the Coast Guard patrolled the beaches and forbid trap shooting or flying kites, because you couldn't carry guns near the beach and the kite string might actually be the wire aerial for a secret radio which could be used to contact German submarines. At night Nick and I would lie in our cots on the screened porch and watch the searchlights and listen to the bam-bam-bam of the anti-aircraft guns striking sparks from the black sky during practice.

There was a rusty target ship run aground about a mile offshore and while we played on the beach we could watch the B-25s make solitary bombing runs at it and see puffs of white smoke. If we were lucky the last bomber would make its final turn shoreward and come at us low. Then Nick and I would scramble to the top of the sand dunes and watch as the plane roared gloriously along the beach, its wings on a level with the top of the dunes, the pilot with his hand raised in a slow salute to the women who had dropped their magazines and were waving as he thundered past. We knew that German submarines were stalking off the coast, because once in a while we could feel a subtle shuddering boom—it could be day or night—and once in a while the tide crept in black with diesel oil, bearing bits of charred rubbish, but we weren't supposed to talk about it. Aunt Regina's husband, uncle John, was lost in the North Atlantic where the sea freezes you to death before it fills your lungs with water, but his body never washed up on our beach. Little by little it became clear what the War was and how I was going into it, and like other boys I began to pick up this and that about combat, not about killing so much as about how to dig a foxhole and how to lie flat when the artillery rounds came in, how not to be afraid of fear, how to identify planes, how accurate the German 88s were, how to Breath, Aim, Sight, Shoot, how never to leave your rifle, no matter how heavy it got, because the M-1 rifle was the infantryman's friend. Uncle Silvio sent us *Yank, the Army Magazine* and there I read about army life and studied the full page pin-up photos of cheerful girls in bathing suits and high-heel shoes. On my bedroom wall I had a big map of Europe which I stuck pins into to follow the progress of the War. Uncle Mercurio's B-24 was hit over the Mediterranean and he bailed out, parachuting down past Monte Pellegrino and into the Via Imperatore Federico, so he was able to run down the street and vault over the wall into his father's garden and rush upstairs to hide until General Patton and the Seventh Army marched into Palermo. We saw pictures of the rubble in southern Italy; my father cleared his throat but didn't say anything, my mother wept and threw the magazine across the room. The Italians surrendered and later the Partisans caught up with Mussolini, shot him and trampled him and hung him upside down at a gas station, killed Clara Petacci and hung her upside down too, right there, you could see her underpants. The Germans retreated slowly, leaving Rome and then Florence, but they counterattacked in France, coming through the snow. The Germans were barbarians, but the Japanese were worse, barely human. We knew what the Japs had done in China and the Philippines and none of us kids wanted to fight in the Pacific. Uncle Silvio liked to go in with the first wave right under the naval bombardment and dig in before the Japs had time to come out of their bunkers. On Iwo Jima we had to crawl on our bellies over the sand and pumice, one inch at a time, and flush them out with flame throwers and kill each one separately, because they wouldn't surrender. But no one wanted to hit the beach in Japan, Silvio said. We felt such powerful joy when the atom bomb obliterated Hiroshima, the pleasure lingering for days as the smoke hovered over the city and later the black rain fell, felt it again when the next bomb erased Nagasaki, and felt relief when they surrendered. I was sixteen when we gathered on the Common and the ministers of the town gave thanks to God for our victory.

5

MY FATHER AND MOTHER REFUSED TO BELIEVE I was as stupid as my report cards said I was, and they still hoped I would go to college, so over the next six years I not only had to practice reading and writing, I also had to bang my head on algebra, chemistry, physics, more algebra, plane geometry, solid geometry, trigonometry, French and Latin. The geometries delighted me, but I did badly at everything else and terribly at Latin. I stumbled over *amo-amas-amat*, trudged into Gaul in the last rank of my class, straggling further and further behind Caesar, then drowned as everyone else sailed off with pious Aeneas to found Rome.

My grandfather believed *his* children were born with the talent to write a sonnet, drive a car, draw, dance or fight, the same as they were born with the capacity to speak and sing (that's my grandfather, standing hairy-chested at the wash-bowl, scissors uplifted to trim his beard, singing an aria while Caruso accompanies him through the graceful horn of the Victrola in the bedroom) and since his children did do those things—some things better, some things badly—they assumed that *their* children could do them, too. Now, as often happens with adopted children, I had come to look rather like the people who were bringing me up, most strikingly like my mother, and my ability as a draftsman seemed to be an inheritance from my father, which pleased us both, and when I turned fourteen he said, yes, I could take drawing lessons, for I had been pestering him about it for months.

I began with Mr Horgan, a very stout man with crank-ily brown hair and a large oatmeal face, brightened here and there with fresh razor nicks. He had come to live in his parents' empty house; they had died long ago and the house, a huge structure with two chimneys at each end, was falling apart—the gutters hanging from the eaves, the white paint peeling from the clapboards. Each Saturday morning I would grab a fistful of pencils, hug my biggest drawing pad under my arm and ride my bicycle one-handed to the edge of town to ring Mr Horgan's bell. One of his young housemaids— housemaids is what he called them—would come to the door in bare feet, wearing nothing but one of Horgan's big shirts, look at me and shout over her shoulder, *Hey, Frank, the kid's here!* Mr Horgan, his paint-smeared shirt tucked crookedly into his corduroy pants and those pants tucked unevenly into his boots, would begin muttering resentfully as he limped out the door, and he'd continue to drop sighs as we walked together down the rutted driveway to his barn and mounted the jittery stairs (Horgan in front) to the loft where he had his studio. He would hum and groan and mutter irritably as he groped under the eaves, gathering up things (a cracked pottery jug, a chipped bowl, a tarnished silver cigarette case with a broken hinge, a ratty shawl) which he would set on the round, elevated piano stool which he used for a stand. When he had arranged each object precisely as he wanted, his resentment—I assumed it was resentment at having me there —would evaporate and he'd fall silent. Then he would sit on a tall stool with his drawing board in his lap and I would sit beside him on a somewhat lower stool with my pad, and we would draw the assembled pieces. During those periods of friendly silence, defined by the soft scratching of our pencils, I used to tremble with bliss and anxiety as I struggled to get my drawing right. When we finished, he would give me a complete critique of my sketch, his thick fingers dabbing here and there at my pad (I'd erase his smudges when I got home), then he'd show me what he had done and we'd discuss his work awhile. When the lesson was over he would continue to talk, but more amiably now, asking a question or two about my school work as we went down the quaking stairs (Horgan in back) and out the gravel driveway to my bicycle.

Mr Horgan taught me three things. First, always look attentively at your subject. "And don't just look at it, *watch* it. You might see it do something nobody has seen before. Listen to it, and if you get a chance, touch it, smell it, bite it and taste it!" Second, block it in. "Get it down on paper all at once, no matter how. Get your hands and arms and legs around it! Be *passionate*. The rest is details." Third, show that the shadows and the shady sides aren't really black. "If you can see it, there's some *light* on it, and if there's *light*, there's *color*. Remember this, Renato, *God made colors, not lines, colors!*" And I would have showed the passionate colors, except that Mr Horgan made me use my graphite pencils until, after six months, he threw his heavy freckled arm around my shoulders and said, well, by God he could look at my black-and-white drawing and see the colors I wanted to represent, so why didn't I bring some paints with me next time.

One day Mr Horgan auctioned off all the antique furniture in his house and the next day he auctioned off the house itself and drove to Montreal with pretty Miss Dewey, the librarian, leaving his housemaids with no place to stay. My father rarely said a word against anyone and was especially reluctant to knock another craftsman, but after Horgan had gone he announced that I could learn a lot more from a commercial artist, so the following September I began to take lessons from Mr Quill, a small brisk man with wispy hair, bright eyes and perfectly circular glasses.

Mr and Mrs Quill lived in an old-fashioned house (tall turret, scalloped shingles) where they worked together illustrating children's books. Mrs Quill would open the front door— "Good morning, Renato. Did you have a nice walk?" —and after I had wiped my shoes on the doormat or knocked the snow from my boots, whichever it was she wanted, she would lead me up the bright oak stairs and down the hall to their studio, a neat white room with two drawing tables face-to-face, each with its own slanted drawing board and jar of pencils. There Mrs Q would vanish and Mr Q would take over, talking cheerfully about what we were going to do that day. Beside his drawing table he had placed a small desk for me and laid a few things on it, maybe a row of paper knives or a set of French curves. He began the first lesson by giving me instructions on how to sharpen a pencil properly. The Quill Method was to pare away the wood until there was a long spindle of bare lead which he then briskly filed to a point on a pad of sandpaper.

Mr Quill really enjoyed teaching me things, like how to use a T-square and triangle or how to draw a pen along a ruler without smearing ink all over the place, all of which was useful but gave me a headache. He knew all the rules of perspective— "Invented by you Italians, Renato!"—and in the subsequent weeks I drew dramatically foreshortened cylinders, cubes, pyramids and cones. Perspective enchanted me. Under his guidance I sketched a shoe carton, drew the plan view at the top of the paper, the elevation views at the side, then projected lines from those views so they crisscrossed in the middle of the sheet and magically gave rise to a perfectly proportioned three-dimensional box. Whenever Mr Quill would say, "Now you try it," I'd sweat about snapping off a pencil point or busting his screw press, but I was filled with satisfaction at knowing how to do so many things. By the end of the year I had incised linoleum blocks and printed them without smudging, had made monotypes, lithographs, serigraphs and dry point etchings—many of them of Hodge Podge, the Quill's sleepy orange cat.

I didn't take any drawing lessons senior year, because I was too busy with basketball practice and track and working on the school paper and acting in the senior play and fooling around with my friends and having a good time. I still have my high school yearbook, a tall thin volume bound in glazed blue cloth stamped with gold letters (our school colors: blue and gold) and the numerals 1948, but I'm not about to open it. I know the certificates awarding me my sports letters are tucked inside, along with the big photo of Debby Field and me at the Senior Prom (a gardenia corsage strapped to her wrist), plus the graduation program which lists four student speakers under the heading "The Outlook of Youth in the Atomic Age." And I've seen the gray photos, each face looking so young and at the same time much older than high-school faces nowadays, with our old-fashioned hair styles and our 1948 looks. I opened the book a few years ago and discovered that looking at those banal photos and reading the names of classmates I thought I had forgotten compressed my chest as if a gravestone were standing on it, made my eyes water, and left me confused that these ordinary people whom I did not love could make me feel such loss.

6

I'M SURE THERE'S NOTHING IN HEAVEN MORE FILLED with innocent wonder and delight than an angel with his first erection, but it might not look that way to us fallen mortals, for as the Catechism says, *Our nature was corrupted by the sin of our first parents, which darkened our understanding, weakened our will, and left in us a strong inclination to evil.* Those first parents were Adam and Eve, and my nature had come cascading down from them to me and only God knew what had happened along the way. My mother suspected I had been conceived out of wedlock in a blazing passion which had burnt my natural parents to a cinder and left me an orphan on her father's doorstep, so she worried and kept on the lookout for signs of the same pyromania in me.

Now one lazy summer morning my mother came to rouse me from bed, pulling the sheets into a heap to be washed, and discovered me with my ucellino as stiff and springy as a willow twig. For a moment she was shocked, actually turned to stone by the sight of it. Then she broke into a rage, bawled me out for wasting my strength and ruining my health, began weeping and swatting at my head while I dodged around the room, snatched on my shirt, my pants, hopped down stairs, pulled on my socks and sat outside on the back steps to tie my shoes. A few years earlier she used to interrupt my play to kiss my neck, would ruffle my hair or bite my ear, and she still loved to gather me from the tub and hug me in a towel, letting whole navies run aground at the drain while she rubbed my head till my hair was dry. But my mother prided herself on being a thoroughly modern woman and not some immigrant cafone who swaddled her baby and hung garlic around its neck to ward off the flu. She followed the latest theories on how to raise a boy and learned it's his spermy fluid makes him virile, so a boy who wastes it wastes himself, leaves himself with weakened muscles and a drained personality — meaning there's scientific and hygienic reason to stop his fun.

My father didn't have as refined an education as my mother, who had gone to Notre Dame Academy and Regina Caeli, but he had learned his lessons in Boston's public schools and public streets, which may explain why he worried less about my growing up. My mother, still striving to bring me up right, spied her old volume of *Getting Ready to be a Mother* under my school books and snatched it up, whirling around to whack me with it and then stumbling over the boots and ice skates in the back hall, her undone hair snaking out every which way while I scrambled into my mackinaw and ran out the door. That fascinating book (photos of woman milking her breast, pages 122-124) didn't reappear in its proper place in the upstairs bookcase, but while searching for it I discovered a sturdy brick-like volume that had not been there before,

Gray's *Anatomy*. The *Anatomy* pages were stunning. I was enchanted by the intricately detailed engravings by Dr. H. Van Dyke Carter: the bones, musculature, blood vessels and nerve paths —handsome bodies portrayed as if they had been flayed alive, and in some views the artist had even drawn little hooks to peel back and hold open the flesh, making me recoil with pain. Still it was very interesting, all of it. And I was hypnotized by a meticulous view of the labia wide open, the secret clitoris, and the mons veneris with each small wildly curled hair separately depicted. My father, guided by his love of craftsmanship and his pragmatism about my growing up, had chosen the book and put it there for me.

My fourth grade teacher no longer visited my darkened bedroom and neither did my classmate Sue Meadows, but Betty Bender, who talked back to the teacher, she came night after night. In class it seemed I was holding one end of a thin rope and she was holding the other end and the rope was stretched so tight that we could feel every tug and vibration. At night she would step barefoot into my bedroom and undress hurriedly on the braided rug in front of my bureau, because her own bedroom had been demolished by something —a flood, a hurricane, the whole town wrecked, trees every which way, power lines down— and our unwitting parents insisted that we share a bed, so I'd reluctantly lift the blanket and she'd slip into bed in her white cotton underpants and undershirt, her freckled shoulder brushing my arm. *You'd better not take them off*, I'd mutter, sore at being disturbed. *I can if I want to*, she'd hiss, pushing down her underpants. Then everything would rush together, thrilling up to a big pulsing jolt of pleasure. And I wasn't able to keep the stuff from spurting onto my hand like I had a year ago.

Nick and I were crazy about our aunt Regina who was as reckless as her brothers, more beautiful than her sisters and the youngest of them all, being only ten years older than we were. When Gina was fifteen she ran off, or was sent off, to live for a while with her married older sister, Nick's mother, so Nick always bragged he had been in love with her since he was five. Now that Gina was a war widow, she lived with her daughter Arianne over her café in Gloucester. One empty Sunday afternoon when everyone else was at the beach, Nick and I lighted up a couple of cigarette butts from the clam shell ashtray on Gina's bed table and, seizing the moment, began to explore her bedroom. We peered into the closet at the dresses. "Yum, yum!" Nick said, reaching into a bodice. I laughed. We wandered over to the bureau, lifted the stoppers from the perfume bottles to get a whiff, unscrewed the jar lids to dab at the cremes, peeked into the jewelry boxes, and then gently tugged open the top drawer, pausing whenever it squeaked. It held a clutter of ring boxes, gloves, menstrual pads, a hair brush, some loose snapshots, a pearl necklace, kerchiefs, and so on. The second drawer was a tumbled bed of silken cloth, white and pink and gold, that slowly resolved itself into bras, underpants, stockings and garter belts. We gazed in silence, then I choked on the cigarette smoke and began coughing and had to stub the cigarette in the ashtray. Nick had pulled a dusky stocking up his forearm and was wiggling his fingers inside it. I studiously untangled one of the bras, a satin thing with a filigree of lace, then shoved up my jersey and flattened a silky cup onto my nipple. "Look," I said, "We're kissing." Nick had unbuckled and stepped out of his pants and now he began to sort through the drawer. I threw myself on her bed, rolling my head in the faint scent of perfume that rose from her pillow. When I looked up, Nick was wearing one of Gina's underpants over his tense privates. "Oh, God, oh, God, oh—" he gasped, stripping the pants off. "I'm getting a hard-on!" Voices floated up from the back door, Nick grabbed his pants, we shot out of there.

Later that afternoon, while the grown-ups were lingering over coffee in the front room, Gina stepped into the kitchen and pinched my cheek so hard it made my eyes water, holding me that way and whispering in my ear "You kids do that again and I'll break your neck! *Capito?*" Then she slapped Nick on the head and walked out. "What did you *do?*" Veronica asked us. We didn't tell her. "Let's go out," Nick said. We went downstairs and sat outside on the back step and watched Arianne and Bart and Tulio and the other little kids playing in the alley way. Veronica came and sat beside me on the step for a while, toying with the charms on her bracelet, but she got bored because we wouldn't tell her what we had done, so she picked up a stone and went off to draw a hopscotch pattern for the other children.

"Veronica's all right," I remarked.

"Veronica's a *child*," Nick said scornfully. "She's too young."

I thought about that a while. "She has breasts."

We watched Veronica on her hands and knees, scratching the hopscotch lines on the pavement. She was wearing a pale yellow sundress that made her arms and legs look very brown. I liked Veronica.

"I like Gina better," Nick said. And, as a matter of fact, five years later Nick and Gina were banging each other on her bed, which is another story but not this one.

7

VERONICA'S MOTHER WAS MY MOTHER'S SISTER, Candida, a handsome athletic woman who had won prizes for archery and swordplay, being skilled at épée in her youth, and her father was Calogero Zitellone, called Zitti, a professor of philosophy, amateur philologist, author of the epic poem *Luna* and creator of an onomatopoetic language. Our families used to meet on Sundays, sometimes at Veronica's home and sometimes at mine, but most often at Nick's because Nick lived in the big house which our grandparents

the eaves, and it was under those slanted roofs that we came across the baby carriage with the little port-hole windows, the big leather suitcases and, best of all, the huge steamer trunks covered with stickers from the Cunard line and White line. The trunks had been upended, so that when we tugged them open the lid swung out like a door to reveal a cramped dressing room with flowered wallpaper, a mirror, a stack of drawers, elastic pockets and a shallow closet with an interior of watered silk. It was while ransacking these little boudoirs with Veronica—Nick busy with his skeleton keys at the next trunk—when she would laugh or try to elbow me aside, the sweet scent of her bath soap mingling with the odors of tobacco and perfume that rose from the drawers, her breath on my cheek as we tried to decipher the rapid Italian scrawl in some forgotten letter—it was then that I became more and more tensely aware of her.

At our house one Sunday afternoon Veronica and I sat on the floor in my bedroom and while the voices of our parents came floating up from the living room we worked together on a giant jigsaw puzzle. Tulio, Bart, Arianne and the other little kids kept dashing in and out, but eventually they went outside to play in the snow. We worked the puzzle in silence a while. "Remember what we talked about last time?" I asked her, pressing a piece into the ragged edge nearest my knee.

Veronica glanced up from the puzzle and looked at me a moment, a slight flush on her cheeks. "Yes."

"Well?"

"Turn around and don't peek," she said sharply.

I turned around, listening attentively to the rustle of her dress and the jingle of her bracelets—sounds which have aroused me wild ever since. "All right," she said quietly. "You can turn around now."

She smoothed the hem of her skirt down over her knee and watched me, her discarded white underpants lying rumpled at her edge of the puzzle, then she swept them into her fist. I stood up, my legs trembling, and sat down beside her. She turned to look at me again, smiled briefly and waited.

What can I tell you? That afternoon she was wearing a white sweater and a dark green plaid skirt, white ankle socks and black shoes with a strap. Uncle Zitti wouldn't let her wear perfume, so she used lavender-scented bath soap, fresh and sweet, which I had come to like.

After we had said our good-byes at the front door, I rushed to my desk with my head in flames, grabbed my colored pencils and—my prick stiffening in anticipation—began to draw that gentle cleft and mound fledged with hair. Her flesh tones were impossible to render and I had to compromise on pinkish ivory, and she hadn't much more hair than on the back of a man's hand, but it was fascinating and I got it all —some hairs in small, precise semi-circular lines and others merely suggested by thicker shading. I don't know what happened to that sketch. I suppose I burned it to get rid of the evidence and now there's a hundred of my canvasses I'd set fire to if I could have that scrap back again.

In the cottage by the beach I pulled on my swim shorts and looked up to see Veronica disappearing from my bedroom doorway. I grabbed a towel and followed her into the kitchen, saying, "You were *spying* on me."

"No I wasn't!"

"I *saw* you, Veronica."

"You left the door open and I just happened to be walking by," she said, ignoring me.

"You just happened to be peeking in, you mean."

She put her beach towel on the counter and began to pour olive oil from the big gold Filippo Berio can into a saucer. She was in her swim suit and around her neck she wore a leather string with a bit coral. Everyone else had started down the road to the beach and the cottage felt unusually hollow and quiet. She dipped her fingers into the saucer of oil and began to rub it onto her shoulders.

"Do you want some?" she asked quietly, trying to be friends.

"Nope."

"Do my back," she said, turning away. She pulled down the straps of her swimsuit, revealing the pale negative of the suit on her russet shoulders.

"Don't you ever say *please?*"

"Please," she echoed.

I caught the warm scent of her skin and dipped my fingers in the olive oil and spread it on the back of her shoulders. She turned and yanked her swimsuit straps down, pulling it all to her waist. Her breasts were startlingly white. I looked. She started to draw the suit back up.

"Wait!" I cried.

She dropped her hands to her sides and waited. I drew my fingers slowly across this breast and then that one. "Jesus, I didn't mean to mess you up with the olive oil. I'm sorry," I said.

"That's all right. I don't mind."

Her nipples had begun to stiffen.

"What does it feel like when that happens?"

She shrugged. "Watch," she said. She plucked gently at the nipple. "See. It gets hard."

I put my hand over her breast. "Something else gets hard, too," I muttered.

"What? What else gets hard?" she asked, beginning to giggle. "Show me."

"You, too."

"Oh, no! *You* first," she insisted.

"How far do you want to go?"

"No farther than last time."

"That's what you always say, Veronica. Come on."

"I'm not stupid, Renato."

I can still call up the secret pallor of Veronica's breast and the tender blurred pink hue of the corolla around the nipple —a color I sweated to reproduce again and again the following autumn, working the chalk broadside to the paper and then rubbing it around and around with my fingers, blurring it, grinding my hand into the weave of the paper in a futile effort to bring back the firm give of her breast beneath my palm.

One freezing Sunday Veronica led me down to the ice rink where we sat on a bench and watched the skaters going round and round while she told me about a kid she was dying over, a boy two years ahead of her who had skated with her one afternoon and when it got dark and the street lights came on he had walked her home. They had stood on the sidewalk in front of her house and looked at the black sky full of stars. He had said he was going to phone her, but eleven days had gone and still he hadn't called. She had seen him in the school lunch room twice since then, but he wouldn't look at her. Veronica sat beside me with her head down and watched her own boots scuffing back and forth at the snow, but I couldn't think of what to say and felt stupid. We walked back to her house talking about other things, about Nick's going to college and me off to art school. Just before we went inside I told her the boy was crazy not to call her and wasn't worth spit and there were a lot of guys who wanted to date her. "You're good-looking, you know," I added.

"Oh, sure. Tell me another."

"No. I mean it."

"You're just saying that because I'm your cousin."

"No. I mean it. I think you're good-looking."

"Since when?"

I shrugged. "Since always. I always thought so."

Veronica looked at me — she was wearing her Sunday coat, the red one with the black velvet collar, her cheeks red from the cold and her eyes glistening black. She smiled and said, "I'll make us some hot cocoa."

8

THE FIRST TIME I WENT ALL THE WAY I WAS SEV-
enteen, fresh out of high school and working on the
fish pier at Newburyport. I was in the hot sun stacking crates
of chopped ice and flounder when a girl in a swimsuit came
walking along with her arms full of flowers. I said Hi and she
said Hi, then she looked around and asked me did I know
the *Saint Rafael.* The *Saint Rafael* was a fishing boat, a drag-
ger. I pointed to where it was tied up and watched her walk
down and go on board. She had long legs, a streak of mud on
one of them. A while later she came walking back, her arms
empty, and she put a hand up to shade her eyes and looked at
me, frankly curious. "Renato Stillamare," I said. She gave me
a quick, open smile—she had sea-green eyes and the bridge
of her nose was sunburned—but she kept on her way, a kid
with long legs.

After dinner I went down to the breakwater to hook up
with some friends and saw her strolling with a couple of girls
her age, all in striped jerseys and white shorts, and I said,
"Hi." They giggled and nudged each other. The next evening
she was down there alone so I asked her how old she was. "I'm
going to be fifteen," she said.

I laughed and said, "Is that the same as fourteen?" She
blew the hair out of her eyes and looked off at the horizon
and started to walk away. "Please stay. I like you. I really like
you," I told her. Her family grew flowers to sell, but she was
good at languages and planned to become a diplomat and
travel all over the world. I told her how I was going to the
Museum School in the fall. She thought it was amazing that
I wanted to be a painter and asked a lot of questions about
the school and about Boston. That night we were sitting in

the field up back of her family's greenhouse and when she lay back I kissed her, put my hand on her breast. I could feel her heart hammering so hard she could barely get her breath, but she wanted to show she was a grown-up and no kid, so she didn't move or say a word, just watched my eyes. She had never made love and I let her think I had. I pressed in by inches while she winced and turned her head aside—I could see she was gritting her teeth, but when I hesitated she gasped, "*Do it!*" and I did it. Afterward we held hands and walked down the long field to her house while she raked her fingers through her hair, combing out the burrs and pieces of straw. She told me her secret Algonquin name which she had named herself, but I could barely hear because I was thinking over and over what we had done. When I got home I didn't wash my hand but lay in bed with my fingers on my lips, breathing her fish odor, then I pulled a towel under the sheet and beat off.

The next night while we were walking along the breakwater with our ice cream cones she said, "I'm still bleeding." I broke into a sweat. "Maybe it will stop tomorrow," I told her. I didn't know what to do. That night in bed I tried to pray to the Virgin for help and then to Jesus and God the Father and then to the Virgin again, but all I could think of was her and then I had to beat off into the towel. She stopped bleeding and we banged each other night after night after night. One of her eyes was ever so slightly larger than the other, making her face asymmetrical and beautiful in a way I couldn't understand. It got so when I'd see her walking to meet me I'd feel a terrible weightlessness in my guts, as if I had stepped off the pier and were falling, and I'd get sick with desire. I was afraid I was going crazy and I wanted to phone my father, but I knew he'd tell me If that's the way you feel, stop seeing her. But I didn't want to stop seeing her, couldn't stop myself from seeing her, and by the end of August it was a relief to get pulled away, to go home and head off to art school.

9

A ND LOOK AT ME NOW, A BALD OLD MAN WITH HAIR
sprouting from his ears and a face like a truck had run
over it. I have a nearsighted left eye and a farsighted right,
broad hands, short fingers, a hairy torso (inside there's a poly-
propylene patch for hernia repair), good feet and good legs
and this thing, this third thing with, alas, a prostate the size
of Middlesex County. If only my friend Mike were alive, we'd
have some great talks, for he was a man who understood these
matters. And I should add that my eyes are full of shadows
—not metaphors, but real shadows from a clotted vitreous
humor.

Now let me introduce this dark-haired critic with the
sweeping eyebrows and high cheekbones and that lovely narrow waist; this brainy, sensual and high-handed woman, my
wife—whom everyone feels sorry for, because she married
me. She claims she weighs the same as the day we married
and maybe that's true, but she uses henna on her hair and
a crayon on her eyebrows. "God dims our eyes as we grow
older," she informs me. "It's his way of doing us a favor." Her
outline has been redrawn so she now looks less like Botti-
celli's young *Flora* and more like Giorgione's *Profane Love*,
saturated with what she knows.

What are we that we should be so mindful of these things?
Half egg and half tadpole, that's us—at our best we're like
those Atlantic salmon we saw at dawn, leaping against the
falls on the Connecticut River. We marveled at their power
to hurl themselves skyward against that falling tonnage, but
it was sad to come upon those same old fish above the falls, in
the limpid pools and shallows where they lay emptied, dying.
I've felt that way after the children have returned and run off

again to their distant worlds, when the house has grown calm once more and I'm alone in the clear silence with nothing to do, moving these old fins now and then to steady myself.

10

I ENROLLED IN THE SCHOOL OF THE MUSEUM OF FINE Arts in Boston. My uncle Nicolo, knowing my love of drawing, yet believing in mathematics, gave me a book called *Descriptive Geometry*, a sorcerer's manual of graceful solids —hyperbolic paraboloids, helicoides, volutes—and stereoscopic projections which, when made properly, would pop up from the page and hang in mid air. When I finished that book he quickly gave me another on the geometry of René Descartes, showing how to pack the long trajectory of a falling star into the nutshell of a quadratic equation. "Descartes? *René Descartes?*" uncle Zitti cried. "Descartes is another French blockhead!" For Zitti despised everything French and believed that the few Francesi he did admire, such as Montaigne or Napoleon, were really Italian. But uncle Nicolo was already pressing me to read *An Introduction to the Calculus*, a cabalistic book whose pages were covered with beautiful symbols—sigmas and deltas, arrows, lazy infinity signs and tall, graceful summations. "That's no way to prepare for life," uncle Zitti muttered, frowning at the group of wooden balls that lay on the bocce court like a diagram of planetary motion.

"The realities of the world are reflected in words, in literature," said Zitti. He held a bocce ball at arms length and squinted along the top of it toward the little ball, the pallino, which lay off to one side about half way down the powdery gray gravel court. He yanked his arm back, ran two steps forward and shot underhand with a leap, hurling the ball so vigorously that it caromed off a side board and whizzed past the pallino. He cursed softly, the same as when he played horse-shoes down the Cape.

"You need geometry, you'd do better," Nicolo told him, mopping a squared handkerchief across the sweaty tanned dome of his bald head.

"Listen," Zitti confided to me. "I'll give you a reading list. A good list. Short but good. It will be based on my method, very practical."

My uncle's first list began with Emily Dickinson, followed immediately by John Locke and Henri Stendhal ("Stendhal was essentially Italian and had a miserable childhood because he was born in France," he informed me) and it concluded with Ovid's *Metamorphosis*. I've kept all twenty of his neat handwritten lists and I owe my liberal education to him.

One warm autumn day uncle Zitti and I were in the field back of the big old house to watch uncle Mercurio and Coral, his wife, take turns with the bird gun. I told Zitti I thought the books he had me read weren't practical at all. "Oh, yes. Very practical. Later in life. You'll see." We watched as Mercurio scaled an old dinner plate high into the air—Coral fired BOOM and the plate went SMASH, exploding to bits. Uncle Nicolo waved vigorously to Coral to put the gun down, calling out to her, "They don't allow shooting in town anymore! Too many houses! Too many people!" Mercurio scaled another dish up over the field and Coral blew it to pieces. "You'll see," Zitti told me. "The unexamined life isn't worth living," he added, quoting one of his favorite philosophers.

But I was living the unexamined life and enjoying it hugely. I found outdoor jobs every summer and indoor work in winter, so I bolted from home and rented a room in Back Bay, within walking distance of my friends and the Museum School, for we were making art and talking about it deep into the night over coffee and lousy French cigarettes at the Commonwealth Cafeteria where the avenue was like a boulevard and the buildings had mansard roofs and that was our Paris.

Furthermore, I had met a young woman named Sophia, a student across the river in Cambridge, and had begun to go out with her. I hadn't had much success with women, which isn't surprising since I wasn't able to separate my hunger for flesh from my craving to paint and was always confusing what I wanted to do. In fact, I had already spent a couple of drizzly afternoons trudging back and forth across the long bridge over the Charles, trying to nerve myself for a vault over the rail, in despair over some woman or my prospects for fame, I never knew which. I was mad for paint and it didn't matter to me whether it was oil or acrylic, so long as I could get the color I wanted, and I could draw with a crayon, a brush or my own stiffened prick, as I learned when I was so foolish as to dip it in ink and swab it on the wall, and that May one of my paintings won a prize and I got into a group show at the Upstairs Gallery in Boston just before the little place went broke.

11

ONE DAY I WROTE A LIST OF THE WOMEN I HAD made love to, wrote it not from stupid vanity but in despair and madness, for I was crazed with influenza, my head banging like a loose door when I lifted it from the pillow — lying there sweaty and unshaven and rank, I made the list to show myself that although I was nobody and might die in that stinking loft at least I had been loved by these women. I'm sure you would have done something finer and more spiritual for solace, but I was me at twenty-five and my brains were cooking in my skull: when my friend Max brought me a bag of food I snatched the drinking glass from my bedside table and threw it at him, and when he said, *Hey! Stop that!* I grabbed the aspirin bottle and hurled it at his head, which it grazed before exploding against the wall. When the list of women turned up a few years later at the bottom of a paint-box I tossed it out, but then added a few more names and tucked it away again, because I didn't want to be the kind of man who fucks and forgets, and long after I was married I came across it rewritten and folded as a bookmark in an old sketchbook, so I kept it. Yesterday I searched all over the place and couldn't find it, shook out every mildewed sketchbook and portfolio, and this morning I tried to recompose the list and was embarrassed to find that I had lost the names of some of those women or remembered only a nickname, and when I thought I had gathered everyone, two others turned up to remind me that there might be more I had forgotten. I hadn't thought of those young women for forty years and recalling them made me slump in my chair and grow melancholy, and I don't know why, because all I remembered was how trusting we were with each other and that's nothing to be sad about.

True, I did meet one or two cold bitches who would turn a man's heart inside out just to see what it contained, and I knew it instantly afterward, while still on my knees, pulling out and panting, "*What am I doing here?*" I confess I've been mostly fortunate, for God gave me this thing—this young prick, this old whatever, call it what you want—that knows when to hang back out of shyness, and shy privates have rescued me where my brains have often failed. But the women I remember best were good-natured and far more patient than I, which reminds me that I want to apologize to them, fi-nally, for my moodiness, my endless ranting about galleries, for implying that a bad time in bed was never my fault, for my sullen silences, for my throwing paints and brushes, smash-ing furniture, slamming doors, for destroying someone else's books or stealing their cigarettes or underwear, for my wak-ing a body at three in the morning just to talk, and a hundred other stupidities.

Now let me go back to when I was a student, grinding and polishing my talent till it was bright as the blade of an ax. In

Boston one winter day I ran into the girl from Newburyport, the one I had known in the summer, now buttoned up in a long black coat with a black beret pulled down to her ears. We stood on the arctic pavement, stamping our feet and beating our arms to keep warm, and I learned she was in her first year at Boston University and planned to major in comparative literature, a subject in which she could use her French, and she liked living in Boston. I felt so many different ways at once and I can't recall what I said. Afterward, as I was trotting away, I thought it would be nice to phone her and go out for a cup of coffee and a longer talk and I don't recall why it never happened.

Of course, by then I was going around with Sophia and that would have been reason enough. I wish I could give you Sophia as she was then, her looks and also her talk, for she had a way of talking that dazzled me like acrobatics. She enjoyed words, including dirty ones, the way another woman might enjoy oranges or cherries, and when we made love it was mostly what she said that brought me to a frenzy. She claimed to like the way I said whatever I was feeling—"I love you because you're so rash," she told me—but there were feelings I didn't have words for and whenever I tried to tell her about those things she would say, "If you don't have the word for it, you don't really have it." More than once I secretly had to look up a word she had used. One night after she had gone home I cut up my dictionary, took a scissors and cut out word after word until the pages were in shreds, then in a flush of embarrassment I stuffed them back into the book. The next time she said, "If you can't say it, you can't have it," we were naked, kneeling face to face on my bed. I wrestled her onto her stomach, a position she never liked, and while she thrashed and began cursing me I grabbed the dictionary from the bed table and shook it open over her so words swirled down in a blizzard, making a word-drift in the saddle of her beautiful back.

I saw the girl from Newburyport two years later at a big party. By then Sophia and I had broken up or, to be precise, Sophia had dumped me after some lapses on my part, after scolding me every other month, calling me a truant and a delinquent because I had gotten involved with other women, mostly during those times when Sophia said we should lead more independent lives. The party was in the West End, the old brick West End that used to be, for the neighborhood no longer exists, the people thrown out and their homes demolished to make way for the rich; anyway, the West End, the rooms small and so crowded it took me half an hour to edge into the kitchen and that's where I bumped into the Newburyport girl again, and we said *Oh!* and *Hi!* and I felt the same confusion as before. I put a few chunks of ice in my drink and asked if I could get her something. "Fill it with gin," she said cheerfully, holding out her glass. "Gin and what?" I asked. "Just gin," she said simply. We went out the kitchen door and sat sweating on the back steps under a hot copper sunset. She said she was still at Boston University, but was now majoring in art history with a minor in French and hoped to go to Paris next summer. She was waitressing this summer. I said I had finally finished at the Museum School, was working as a carpenter and waiting to get drafted. I wanted to talk about Sophia but decided against it, so we sat there not talking, just looking at the fading sky and the wilted flowers. She lit a cigarette.

"Ka-gi-gi," I said. "Just now I remembered your Indian name, the Algonquin name you named yourself. Ka-gi-gi, the raven."

She looked at me. There was a fine glaze of sweat beneath her eyes, like when we made love that first summer, and for a moment I thought I could smell her skin, which started a little panic in me. She let the smoke drift from her mouth and she said, "I was fourteen. I hated my real name."

"You have a beautiful name."

"Yes? Well, I didn't think so at the time."

"Did you come with somebody tonight?" I had come alone and thought maybe she, too, was single this evening and would leave with me.

"He's inside."

"You shouldn't drink that way," I told her, more sharply than I intended.

"What way?"

"You shouldn't drink so much gin so fast."

Abruptly she went and poured her glass into the flower bed and came back to sit closer beside me on the steps, where we exchanged phone numbers, and for a time that evening I kept her in sight, attempting to figure out who she was with, and I even trailed her out to the garden and listened to her throwing up in the dark, after which I began talking to a hefty young woman in a black sun dress, a badly drawn version of Sophia, and I ended up at her place. I was drafted that fall, did my Basic Training at Fort Dix and was soon discharged because of allergies which disappeared when I became a civilian again.

I spent the next six months in New York, painting and meeting people (Max, Karen, Sue, and Wilson, but especially Max—good guy, good painter), then returned to Boston and met Odine, a tall woman with swan-white skin. By then I was achieving great things in abstract expressionism and psychotherapy, I thought, and Odine didn't lecture me about other women, didn't call me names the way Sophia had, but was non-judgmental and told me I was *sick* and, she explained, I was *sick* because I had started life as a foundling and it was my insecurity about who I was that compelled me to seek out women, for under the guise of hunting for a fresh bedmate I was really searching for my mother. And her diagnosis was probably right, I thought, because I had all the symptoms, but my having this ailment didn't bother Odine and I was grateful for that.

people, and a couple of times I even went to the Cedar, which was supposed to be a great place for that crowd to drink and pick up a quick fuck, but I could never drink much or pick up a woman in a bar. I had hoped to get my work looked at by other painters and maybe by a gallery or a buyer, but after a few months I ran out of money and took a part-time job illustrating manuals and catalogs for a hardware company which, I told myself, was a good way to learn graphical precision and discipline, but it was soul-destroying work and I longed to be outdoors pulling lobster pots or stacking crates of fish, and though I had friends I felt lonely much of the time and used to press myself into the corner of my room to feel the walls embrace me while I wept.

I got sick and sicker: my head throbbed, my guts felt like they had been pulled inside out, I couldn't stand up at the washbowl or walk but had to crawl back to bed. Two days later my friend Max came by, took one look and came back with a bag of food, which is when I threw the drinking glass at him and tried to brain him with the aspirin bottle. Another afternoon he came around with a bottle of ginger ale and a box of crackers and he had with him a woman named Bena who returned alone the next day—simply to cook me a meal, she said. Bena was a large but firmly built woman— "Statuesque, Renato. The word you're looking for is statuesque," she said, seating herself slowly on the margin of my bed—with dark hair and dark eyes. Maybe she would have looked overweight if she had gained a pound here or there, but she never added even an ounce and remained properly large-bodied, larger than any woman I had known. When I had taken the straps of her slip from her shoulders, had rumpled the bodice down to her waist and had begun to push it further down, she stretched and smiled and murmured, "No. It can't get past my hips. It comes off the other way. Over my head—" and indeed it did. Even after I left the flu behind, got off my bed and began to get around, Bena insisted on coming over to cook a meal again and again. She didn't care for my drawings of some young women I had been going with a few months earlier—"Scrawny. Malnourished," she called them—but she liked my abstractions, talked about them intelligently, and also said she believed that my desire to paint was an unconscious stratagem, a way for me to remain a child forever and avoid adult responsibilities and, unwittingly, to destroy myself. "You like to draw pictures. You want to play with colors and shapes forever." She didn't think any the less of me for this, quite the contrary. "I admire you. Artists are eternally young," she told me one evening while I watched her unpin her hair and remove her blouse. "People have known this for a long time. Artists are children. They are children in their delight at the world and in their spontaneous creativity," she said, reaching behind her back to unhook her bra. "And what's important is to keep them from self-destructive tantrums." Her breasts had the largest and darkest aureoles I had ever seen.

Bena used to come by my place after her shift at Beth Israel where she worked as a dietician, and I'm sure her potato pancakes, her matzoh balls and all that chicken soup helped me get stronger. I was sorry she had that lunatic theory about artists being happy children, spontaneously drawing pictures and coloring inside the lines, because other than that she made sense, mostly. I hadn't gotten my full weight back, but I felt good and my mind was clear, very clear. I knew I wasn't destroying myself, knew also that the New York art business was rotting my soul and making me sick and I knew it would be good for me to leave. So, early one morning, before Bena arrived, I packed everything I wanted into my suitcase, broke up all my paintings and crammed them into the huge metal drum I used for a trash barrel, then I poured kerosene into the drum and set it on fire. It made a surprising lot of black smoke, so I shoved the drum over to the window and pushed open all the window vents. The flames crept up into the smoke and the ceiling began to blacken. I poked into the barrel with a broomstick, hooked one of the flaming canvasses and pitched it out the open window, then pitched out another and another and so on, letting them sail this way and that down to Greene Street. It was exhilarating.

"Hey, Renato!" somebody said, and she wasn't in Newburyport or Paris but here in my doorway.

"I thought you were going to Paris!" I said.

"I'm leaving tomorrow. What are you doing?"

"I'm getting rid of some rotten sick bad paintings."

She gave me a quick smile. "I was on the sidewalk hunting for your address when these pieces of fire began to fall out of the sky. I thought it might be you."

"Want to go out for breakfast?" I asked her.

She said yes, so I picked up my suitcase and my paintbox and we walked down to the street where she waved off some athletic guy in a chrome yellow sports car. I asked who he was and she said "Just a friend who gave me a ride down here. Let's eat I'm starved." We ate breakfast in a deli and I asked what had she been doing for the past nine months and she said she'd been waitressing around Newburyport and now she was going back to Paris to study art history. Her father had been ailing but he was better now. I was sorry to hear about her father whom I remembered only as a tall man who loved to grow flowers. I told her I was sick of New York and was leaving it for good, and that I planned to go home for a few weeks, then go to Cape Ann where my aunt Gina had a café and I'd work outdoors and not paint for a while. I started to tell her all sorts of things I had been brooding about, but I broke off for fear of boring her. "I have your parents' address," she said. "And here's where I'll be staying when I get to Paris." She wrote it on a paper napkin and slid it across the table to me.

"I don't know how to write letters very well," I told her, stuffing the napkin into my breast pocket.

"Send me drawings," she said.

12

I SAVED HER LETTERS AND HAVE THEM STILL, DOZENS of tissue paper pages covered with type which varies in hue from clotted black to foggy gray, lots of words xxxxxed out and others scribbled in the margin with long inky tails pointing to where they belong. In her first letter she wrote about the Parisian neighborhood where she was living, about her rooms and her roommate and the view outside the window and she signed with the name she had hated as a kid, Alba. *Alba is the ancient Celtic name for Scotland which is where my parents came from*, she added. I replied with a plain, unshaded line drawing of my bedroom and the window that looked into the old maple tree, and I wrote around the margin *Alba means dawn in Italian and I've always liked your name and my last name isn't Stellamare it's Stillamare.* Her next letter was about her classes at the institute and about her roommate, Dolores, known as D, and she concluded by saying that she had always thought my name was Stellamare because that would mean star-of-the-sea, which was a beautiful image and, frankly, Stillamare looked like a misspelling to her. I made a line drawing of my father's shop front, Stillamare's Cut Stone & Tile Company, and on the back I wrote that *stilla* was the Latin word for drop, like a raindrop, and Stillamare means drop-of-the-sea, and as a kid I had been called Trin, which was short for Trinacria, which is the ancient name for Sicily. I left out the part about my being found swaddled and wrapped, one of the wrappers being a cheap kerchief which had a map of Sicily printed on it. Alba's letters continued to arrive at two- and three-week intervals, and I learned more about her studies for the "doctorat," which wasn't a doctorate but a master's degree, about her roommate D, and about a scruffy bookstore near Notre Dame with an espresso machine at the back. The bookstore was a meeting place for all sorts of down-and-out artists and poets, including a scornful writer from England who sounded bogus to me. The writer was forty years old, a savage intellectual who held all social conventions in contempt, and although I wasn't surprised when Alba moved in with him I was sore at her and then mad at myself for feeling that way and grateful that I didn't have to write anything but could send an old block print of my coffee mug and overflowing ashtray.

I talked my brother Bart into coming with me for a weekend visit to Montreal, just so I could listen to people speaking French and pretend I was in Paris. The city was made of gray stone with fancy iron-work stairways going up ten or twelve feet to the front door, because of the deep winter snows, we figured, and there were small green parks and streets with cafés with tables set out on the sidewalk, and we had a great time. Two weeks later I rode a train back to Montreal, rented a room, and looked up a old man named Boisvert, a paper-maker I had known at the Museum School, and through him I met some other people who worked with handmade paper and among them a young woman named Denise. Denise invited me to a party where everyone talked politics, mostly about how to throw out the British and establish a country where everyone was French, and afterward she took me for a walk around the old quarter and then back to her room. She gave me her lighted cigarette to hold, then crossed her arms and grasped the hem of her jersey and started to pull it up. I said *Wait!* and told her I was only visiting Montreal, only for a couple of weeks. She had paused and now she smiled, saying "C'est bon cela," and pulled the jersey off. Denise had reddish gold hair and a wonderfully compact athletic body which she enjoyed, the same as she enjoyed making paper or arguing politics. I stayed in Montreal a few weeks and learned something more about paper-making, but when the cafés folded their umbrellas and pulled in their chairs I decided to head homeward. Denise came with me as far as the sidewalk outside the train station where we hugged and said goodbye, then she turned away and I went inside and that was the last I saw of her for many years. Every decade or so I find anew my old sketches of Denise, including a surprisingly vivid one I did with a ballpoint pen on a sheet of stiff cream-colored paper: Denise standing with her back to me, dressed but barefoot, combing her hair. I hope she's alive and well: she never minded if our love-making was imperfect, or if I was stupid about Quebec politics, or if I talked too much about Alba.

I spent the winter on Cape Ann, living at my aunt Gina's. This was after her affair with my cousin Nick and before she met the man she eventually married. Nick never guessed that we knew about him and Gina, but Gina had figured it out, Gina knew, and once when we were dancing at a jukebox she asked me, "What do they say about me?" I played dumb, but she said, "You know what I'm talking about." So I told her, "They say Nick had a crush on you and they wish you'd go get married to somebody." The music had stopped and Gina lit a cigarette, took a flake of tobacco from her tongue, saying, "They want me to marry a professor or a banker or someone and can you see me doing that?" and we both laughed. That winter I painted her café walls and fixed the wobbly chairs and tables, and I made a some big ink drawings with a brush, including a few of Gina and my cousin Arianne, and one large painting of the harbor from the café terrace. When I wasn't working I walked up and down the steep streets of Gloucester (which wasn't the pretty place it is now with those new brick walks and brass historical markers, but was a busy crowd of trawlers, draggers, screaming gulls, chopped ice, fish —the whole town smelled of fish) and every so often I'd ride the train to Boston to hook up with my friend Bill Boyle or Dave Katz or Peter Constantine or all three together.

By the time spring arrived we had made plans to head

north up the coast, working odd jobs and painting along the way, but Boyle got falling down drunk and broke his wrist, and Katz panicked at the prospect of living outside a city, so in the end it was just Costas and me. It wasn't so easy to find odd jobs and it turned out that whenever we did work three or four days we earned barely enough money to cover our expenses for the next two, so we quit working and paid our way up to Boothbay Harbor, the place where Robert Henri and his crew had made some good paintings in the Twenties and Thirties. We never did reach Monhegan Island, but Costas produced some good paintings, whereas I merely doodled in my sketchbook or sat on a huge rock and stared out to sea, like a stupid gull hoping to hatch something from the rock I was sitting on. We went broke in mid-July and decided to hitchhike down Route 1 toward Boston, which we did, catching one ride from Boothbay Harbor to Portland, and another from Portland to the Massachusetts line, and there we rented a sweltering room over a restaurant kitchen for the night. Costas went to sleep while I sat in a chair by the open window and smoked and brooded, for it had become clear to me that I had no life to go back to, that there was nothing left for me to do at my aunt Gina's café, and nothing for me at all in my old room at home, no woman I wanted and nothing I wanted to paint. I thought how I had painted so many canvases and had fucked so many woman and how it all added up to nothing. The next morning we went out to Route 1 together and I hung around talking with Costas until he caught a ride to Boston, then I walked back to the restaurant and talked the owner into hiring me to patch up the murals on the dining room walls.

The restaurant, Lorette's Farm, was an old rambling structure of joined buildings that stretched back from the road with each succeeding roof down lower than the one before, like an extended telescope. The dining room occupied the first floor front, and Mrs Lorette plus her daughter lived on the second floor, after which came the kitchen with my attic room, followed by the pantry, the dressing room for waitresses, and storage sheds and so on. The dining-room murals, which depicted workers along the Merrimack River, had been painted directly onto the finished plaster twenty years ago and had been washed down with soap and water every season thereafter, so the paint was now half scrubbed away and, to speak politely, they had never been beautiful, but they did reflect the civic esthetics of the 1930s, the same as those WPA murals in post offices around the country, and I was sorry years later when the place burned to the ground.

I worked on the murals only at night, after the dining room had closed, and then only for a few hours at a stretch, so that the paint odors wouldn't drive off customers, and during the day I sat by the window in my stifling room and read one of the books I found up there, Beauparlant's *History of Quebec*, or I lay naked on the cot and dozed, or tried to, for on bright days the room became an oven and I couldn't sleep until after the sun had gone down. My boss, Mrs Avril Lorette, was a strong woman with a handsome face seemingly drawn with black lithograph crayon and then redrawn and overdrawn, so that all the lines were bolder, the eyebrows and lashes thicker and the shading darker, even producing a duskiness above her upper lip. Her energetic daughter Nancy was seventeen, an earlier version of her mother, a lighter print, as the art critics say, with white highlights produced by the confectioners sugar she used on those pastries which she made each morning— "Before the busybody spies are up," she told me, laughing—a time when we could do what we wanted, so we did, morning upon morning, for we both had good healthy appetites. At ten each night Mrs Lorette would rap briskly on my door to wake me just when my room was getting cool enough to sleep in, and if I didn't promptly pull on my pants and go to the door she would come in and shake my shoulder, her hands scented with the blissfully cool odors of carrot greens, celery, fennel and apple. If I didn't open my eyes she would lightly scratch the nape of my neck, and if I still refused to open my eyes she'd pat my bare behind, singing "Up, up! Get yourself *up*," and she'd give it a sharp little whack. So one thing led to another in a chain of logical entailment, just as the old philosophers promised they would, and I wound up doing with Mrs Lorette what she expected me to do, the same as I did with Nancy.

By the end of August I was about finished with the mural and fatigued by what you might call my duties to the Lorettes, and I thought it would be best for me if I just slipped away without elaborate good-byes, so one morning I crammed my shirts, socks and underwear into my paintbox and quietly folded my easel. I ducked from my room through a small door which opened into the low attic over the pantry and I crept cautiously toward the bright square window at the end of the crawl-space over the attached shed. I was creeping along a rafter, dragging my easel and paintbox when unwittingly I set my knee on a rotted timber and plunged through the ceiling into the room below. I staggered around in a rain of crumbling plaster, splintered lath and two-hundred-year-old dust, and bumped into Alba. "*Renato!*" she cried.

"I thought you were in *Paris!*" I said.

"I got back a month ago and began working here last week. What are you doing?" she asked, brushing plaster bits from my shoulders.

"Murals. But right now I'm running away," I said, grappling with my easel and paintbox.

The Lorettes' voices came from an upstairs room, shouting at each other.

"You're running away from Mrs Lorette?"

"Her, too."

"From Nancy Lorette? From both?"

"Not my fault. It's complicated," I said.

"You mean you—" Alba had begun to laugh. "With both of them? I'll bet it's complicated."

"Got to get going," I said, briskly.

She gave me a quick smile. "You can take Jack's car."

"Who's Jack?"

"He is," Alba said, nodding toward a thick-necked athlete in a red-striped jersey who came stumbling through the doorway with a large, heavy sack on his shoulder. "Give him the keys, Jack."

We heard Mrs Lorette louder now, shouting in my room over the kitchen and kicking my bed to pieces. Jack slid the sack from his giant shoulder with a grunt, and tossed me the car keys. "The Chevy pickup," he said, wiping his neck with a handkerchief. "Don't let it idle too slow, it'll stall."

"Leave it across the river at the Union Garage," Alba told me, squeezing my arm. "Now go. Quick!"

Back in Boston I found a fair size place, a room with a view of the Charles River in slices between the other buildings. Some hours the river was gray and other hours it was yellowish or green and some times it was so blue you wanted to dunk your brush in it and slap it all over everything. I had been invited to participate in a group show in Cambridge and when I brought them my stuff I saw that the show was going to be good and that my work looked especially strong. I invited Alba to the opening and she came. I had never seen her dressed in style before and had never even thought of her that way, but here she was walking toward me in a suit — trim jacket, the blazing white of her throat and the stiff rise of her breasts, tight skirt — her hair in a thick glossy French twist, silver button earrings, flashy bracelets and high heels. It was a satisfying crowd and I met the other painters as well as the owner of a gallery in Boston and some brainy people from Cambridge. I introduced Alba to my father and mother and Bart, then afterward we five went to a Greek restaurant to celebrate and when dinner broke up they drove off, after everybody had hugged everybody, leaving Alba and me on the sidewalk.

I felt terrific. We walked along the river and talked of what we had been doing for the past nine years, walked until Alba's high-heel shoes hurt and she paused, took off her shoes, and we walked some more, then stood with our elbows on the guard rail above the silent, flickering black water and were still talking when the street lamps snuffed out, for by then the sky was milky blue and the scumble on the far side of the river became the uneven brick heap of Boston with the hill and the small gold dome of the State House, the thin tower of the Custom House (for it was still the old city of 1890), and the big chunk of the Hancock, light spilling between the low buildings and through the fog onto the motionless water. We just stood there looking at the silence and light, I don't know how long. "Do you ever think about that summer?" Alba asked.

"It was crazy. We were out of our minds," I said, still looking across the water.

"I was a kid. I thought it was supposed to be that way."

We were standing side by side at the guard rail and when our arms brushed I turned and found she was watching me, waiting. Her face was bare again the way it had been years ago and I could see all there was to see, one eye almost invisibly larger than the other, the dark sea-green irises flecked with uneven rays of lighter green and blue, the high contour of her cheek, the nakedness of her lips, and I got light-headed and kissed her mouth and had to grab the rail to keep from plunging. "I just want to paint, that's all I want to do now," I said.

"Anyway, I'm going to Paris—" she began.

"What!"

"—in two weeks. A formality, but I really want that doctorate."

I felt very strange, almost dizzy. We began to walk across the Mass Avenue bridge in the early morning light, the sky growing ever more spacious as we approached the middle of that long, flat span, all shadows evaporating from the air and the river brightening. My eyes weren't right and I couldn't figure out what was happening, except that the far end of the bridge seemed to be going farther and farther off, so when a cab came along I flagged it down and we rode the rest of the way to my place. As I opened the door to let her in I saw how stark the room was, but Alba said, "Oh, I *like* this."

She was looking at the low wall I had hammered together, just plywood and two-by-fours with my bed and books on this side, the other side all workspace. "The building's condemned, so the rent's low, is why I live here," I explained.

"What a terrific view," she said, walking to the windows that looked between the tenements and across the river to Cambridge. There was a dark streak on one of her legs where her stocking had a run in it from walking without shoes, the same as the mud on her leg the first day I saw her. I followed the stocking up to where it must be attached to her garter belt, searching for any shadow on her skirt which would show where a strap or clip pressed into her flesh. She had begun to walk slowly about, looking at the paintings that leaned against this chair, the table, that other chair, the stepladder, the paintings that stood this way and that way all around the room. She said, "I love being here. All the colors. And these are so much bigger than the ones at the exhibit. I —" and she broke off as I had put my hands inside the lapels of her jacket to wrench it open, so the silver button leapt off and hit the floor, ringing like a bell, and I yanked the jacket down her arms and pulled it off, and by then we were whispering so swiftly not even our guardian angels could have heard. I tore off my shirt, unbuckled my pants and lifted out just as she stepped from the fallen circle of her skirt. She started to unfasten a garter clip, saying, "Let me take this damned —" but I grabbed her away.

"Do you believe in God?" she asked afterward. We were naked on our hands and knees, looking under the bed for her missing button. I told her I hadn't made up my mind about that. She said, "I mean, is life just things bumping into other things and everything happening accidentally? Because if it is, then how did we meet and keep on meeting? If it's all just atoms banging into other atoms it doesn't make sense. But I feel it must make sense." All I knew was that I wanted to have her for the rest of my life. "There must be a meaning— ah!" she cried, holding up the button. She got to her feet and shook her head vigorously to untangle her hair, then began to pull a comb through it, which was a pleasure to watch, remembering how she used to rake her fingers through that mop to catch out the straw after we had laid in the field up back of her house. "I was only fifteen," she said, as if I had spoken.

"Fourteen, Ka-gi-gi, you were still fourteen."

"I should get dressed. And I should phone Susan and tell her where I am. Where do you keep your phone?"

"I missed a few payments and they shut it off."

I pulled on my pants, set a pot of coffee on the hot-plate, then broke open an English muffin and dropped it into the toaster for breakfast. Alba had put on her skirt and jacket and was gathering up her loose stockings and the garter belt and bra. "Home," she said, looking around, smiling. "Have I already said I like this place?" she asked. "I clean every week. It's clean junk," I assured her. We had another cup of coffee and a cigarette, then lay on the bed facing each other so I was able to look at her, look at her hair or her mouth or her eyes, which is one of the things I used to do with her years ago and which I had liked best, just lying with her and looking and talking or not talking, and I said, "Stay forever," and she began to speak as if she were running out of breath and at last she says, "Choose me," and I say, "I am, I do," and she shut her eyes and I kissed her shut eyes and her mouth and her trembling breasts, for her jacket had fallen open, and there was a *knock, knock* at the door and a *knock, knock, knock*. Alba sprang up, brushing her skirt smooth and clutching her jacket shut. "Pin, a safety pin, do you have a pin?" she whispered. I told her there were pins on the bureau, buckled my pants and trotted barefoot to the door. It was a man from last night at the gallery (straw-colored hair combed straight back, round face with circular eyeglasses), but I couldn't recall his name or anything else about him. "Gruenfeld," he said amiably. "We talked last night at the opening."

"Yes," I said.

"Good," he said. "Well, as you know, I—"

"God, yes! You have the gallery on Newbury Street. You said you liked the show. Now I remember."

"*Your* work. I liked *your* work. I tried to call first but the phone company claims it never heard of you and since you did say to come by any time and since I do like to make my visits on Mondays—" Then he turned and introduced me to the thin and rather bony woman who had been standing off at his side, and she shook my hand. "If we could just take a look around. Or perhaps there's a better time," he ventured.

"No, no, no! Come in, come in!"

I brought them in and there was Alba in her crisp suit and high heels, standing by the stepladder to sip her coffee, her unfastened hair shining in the sun. She carefully set the coffee cup on a step, smiled and came forward with her jacket neatly pinned shut so I could introduce her to Gruenfeld and the woman. I saw her bra and underpants trying to hide themselves under her rumpled breakfast napkin on one of the steps of the stepladder. "We'll just look around," Gruenfeld said cheerfully. Alba returned to her coffee and I sat on a stool and we watched Gruenfeld and the woman move slowly from canvas to canvas, his partner silent and Gruenfeld saying only *This is interesting* or *This is what I mean* or *Look at this* until twenty-five minutes had passed, after which he came over and took out a miniature notebook, wrote his gallery's address and phone number, tore out the page and gave it to me, saying I should make an appointment to have lunch with him and talk about my future, because he wanted to give me a show, then I walked them to the door where we shook hands and they left.

I turned around and said, "I'm a painter," for I had never known for sure, and Alba said, "I knew it all along."

She was hanging her jacket neatly over the back of a chair and her breasts shone in the sun, and now she unfastened her skirt and of course she had nothing on underneath. I threw off my clothes and pulled her down onto a warm blanket of sunshine so I could look even more, because her flesh had no shadows but only variations of light, light everywhere, shifting from milky white to cream to pale coffee to warm bread color, and that thick dark whorled mass of secret hair, uneven patches of color on her cheeks and her eyes glistening from the heat of her own flesh, her body so naked and incandescent that I must look again and again and again, filled with the power and exhilaration of seeing everything at once.

Alba went back to her place that afternoon and returned the next morning with a small suitcase and two boxes of books. I painted through fall and winter, though sometimes we fooled around, as when we smeared ourselves with paint and rolled us in big sheets of Japanese paper to print our own version of gyotaku, or when I cast a papier mâché bowl from Alba's rear, or painted the world's hemispheres on her breasts, or dunked my brainless prick in ink and drew on her back, but mostly I painted and painted better then ever, better than anyone else, had a successful show at Gruenfeld's gallery on Newbury Street and, when our building had to be demolished, we got married and went to France and there Alba picked up her doctorat (a fancy page of paper that they signed and tore from a book, like a check) and thence to Italy and Sicily and back to France, returning to the States in time to set up my first exhibit in New York. Oh, Alba, *this* Alba, *my* Alba.

PART TWO

The Summer of Renato's
70ᵗʰ Year,
in which there are
Unpredictable Complications,
One Exhibit,
&
Many Pregnancies

13

THAT WAS THEN, THIS IS NOW. SHE LIVES ON HER side of the river, I live on mine. Our kids have grown up and left home, the old cat has died and joined the dog, we've sold off the house and now we're living happily ever after, Alba and me, for I'm here in Boston with my own bed, three easels and five hundred paintings, while Alba is in Cambridge with everything else. We didn't plan it this way; we never had the leisure to plan anything in our lives. It just happened that when my friend Mike Bruno died I quit teaching and began to spend more time painting in my studio and it grew easy for me to sleep there because that way I'd be where I wanted to be when I woke up. Our children disapproved, said we were getting silly in our old age and complained that they didn't know where to send their letters home. They wanted us to stay put in the worn-out old house where they had grown up, us to keep watch over their forgotten school prizes and sports trophies while they explored the globe for adventures.

Skye, our daughter, who attended three different graduate schools and then dropped out to marry a nomadic anthropologist, likes to think of herself as a settled homebody who grows vegetables, bakes bread and raises children and, indeed, she has four children, but in the last decade they've trooped through seven different countries, haven't stayed at the same address two years in a row, and won't so long as her husband can find a grant or fellowship to keep them in rags someplace else. Brizio, our son, who has weighed dark matter at the Harvard astrophysics lab and untangled string theory at Stanford, this prince among intellectuals has disguised himself as a carpenter working for a solar house company and is living with a daft young woman who grows herbs for a living.

And Astrid, the comet in our planetary family, Astrid, who liked to call herself Galaxy, started out as a singer in a rock band, then married a guitarist but had the marriage annulled seven days later so as to take up fashion modeling, made a lot of money at modeling but quit to keep house for a widowed photographer, a sexy sexagenarian from whom she learned all sorts of things, even photography, and from whom she parted amicably to become a photographer herself, at which she was quite good, and later she became a movie publicist, moved in with a very young cinematographer and became a video director in advertising, then broke up with the boy cinematographer and now has her own business as a publicist-producer-director of low budget-documentaries. Those are the sedate children I've scandalized by moving into my studio.

When Mike Bruno pitched over and died he left a great empty room in my heart, actually a dozen messy rooms. That round, jovial man had been my best friend for thirty and more years. He had a sunny temperament dappled with melancholy, had huge appetites, a lavish mind, a dozen deep interests and a hundred flaws. He knew more about the history of art than anyone anywhere and could recall in detail every painting he had ever seen. He loved cookery and women and talk—God, how he loved to talk!—but above all he loved to look at paintings. I walked into the Newbury Street gallery where my first exhibit was still fresh on the walls and saw that restless soul looking at one of my paintings, shifting from foot to foot, opening and closing his fists, shaking his head, then he turned to me and began to talk about the work, remarking on this detail and that brush work and this passage and that color, sweeping his hand this way and that across the canvas as he lectured. He saw it all, he liked it. I told him I had painted it. "Good! Good! I'm Michael Bruno. Let's get lunch," he said, shaking my hand.

The last time I saw Mike he was propped up in his coffin, looking neither dead nor asleep but as if he were keeping his eyes firmly shut to reproach us for making so much noise. "No, he liked noise. He loved the sound of people having a good time," Finn insisted. "Then I wish we were having a good time," I told him. But I won't go on about Miles Michael Bruno or bring him up again.

14

THIS IS NOW AND I HAVEN'T HAD A ONE-MAN SHOW in a Newbury Street gallery in twenty-five years. The Strand Gallery opened on Newbury a year ago—blond oak floor, radiant lights, crap on the walls—and I thought I'd give it a try. I gave them twenty slides to look at, twenty slides from which you could have picked twenty superior to the dead stuff on their walls. The gallery never got back to me, so I was back to the gallery to collect my work. And here's youthful Mr Bell, smiling and pushing a lock of fine, light brown hair from his brow. "Ah, Mr Stillamare, good to see you again!" he said buoyantly. Bell was in his late thirties, a bright-eyed man with a freshly scrubbed look about him. "We've been slow and I apologize for that, but we really like your work. I wish we could take on more painters. Come into the office, come in, come in. Let me move those. Sit here. Let me move that, too. There. Now, how have you been?"

I had no idea what Bell was up to with this chummy chitchat, but I sat down and told him I'd been fine.

"Good. We like those slides. Very interesting work, very interesting."

Bell sat half on and half off the right front corner of his desk and swung his leg a bit to show we let no formalities come between us pals and also to show who was patron and who petitioner, and all the while he chatted amiably about the season and the weather and he wondered if you could sit at the cafés on Marlborough Street this early without freezing. His office was small, crammed with flat files, cabinet files and shelves of what looked like archive boxes, but everything was as nicely packed, latched and tucked away as in a yacht. The door beside his desk was open enough for me to get a narrow glimpse of a bigger office. I was about to ask him to give me back my slides when he stood up, saying, "I'm going to—adjust these blinds—dim these lights—turn on the projector. I want to review a few of these and have you tell me about them. Just tell me whatever you want to. All right? I'll ask questions from time to time. All right?"

He frowned briefly over a handwritten list on his desk, then began to project the paintings onto a patch of white wall across from us. We went through three huge Cape Cod landscapes, abstract in their flattened simplicity, two free renditions of a gold Filippo Berio olive oil can with a foreground of sliced tomatoes, two big scenes of couples sprawled on an open bed, another of a solitary seated male with his limp cock over his thigh, and five large canvases of women in the bath or shower. Bell had opened the window blinds and was instructing me on how hard times were for galleries when the door beside his desk swung open and here was Sonia Strand herself. "Sonia, this is Mr Stillamare."

"We like your work, Mr Stillamare," she announced, her voice a scratchy baritone.

I said thanks and we shook hands, her touch firm and startlingly warm. She looked to be in her very late forties, a tall woman with a wide bush of ruddy gold hair, blue crystal eyes and a dark red mouth.

"And I'm sure Peter has already told you we're carrying as many painters as we can—more than we can, I think—and our calendar is crowded as is." She went on that way for a while, then asked Peter would he please take her calls while she talked with Mr Stillamare. Then she shut the door and we stood in the middle of her office while she ran her hands up her temples and through those glittering bronze corkscrews of hair and looked around the room bewildered, as if she had forgotten what she was doing there. In fact, she did look out of place, this tall well-built woman not in a suit but in a heavy columnar dress with thick vertical stripes from top to bottom, as if she were a caryatid from some Greek temple. Her desk, actually a long glass table, was a cluttered patchwork of overlapping letters and notes and photographs, anchored here and there by glittering enameled boxes and a gold pocket watch, large and fancifully engraved. A sloppy buttress of unframed canvases leaned awkwardly against one wall, a chrome and black leather sofa sat against another, and a low table with a stainless steel coffee maker stood by the window. Her cloak, tossed over the arm of the sofa, looked to be lined with peacock feathers. "Say! Would you like a cup of coffee?" she asked, struck with the idea.

"Sure. Why not?" I said.

"Exactly!" She smiled. "Please call me Sonia and I'll call you Renato. Right?"

"Right!" It was her gallery and her party, after all.

So we stood at the window and drank from crummy paper cups while she told me that I had not been in many shows recently, but the ones I had been in were excellent, very well known and widely respected and, furthermore, it was apparent that my work had been evolving all that time. She toyed with a long silver chain and pendant that hung from her neck, saying, "I wish I could be more hopeful. The public is so strange these days. They flock to the openings, they look around and I know they like what they see or they wouldn't keep coming back. But they leave without buying."

She informed me for a while about the public, then settled herself on the shining folds of her cloak in the corner of the sofa and turned an open hand toward a nearby chair, a piece of Baroque bric-a-brac, suggesting that I should sit too, which I did. I guessed that she didn't have a cold but that her voice had a natural rasp to it.

"And yet there are buyers who would be interested in your work," she was saying. "I know them. It's all a matter of marketing. Painters don't like to hear that when they're young. But you understand."

She hesitated, for it was on the tip of her tongue to ask me how old I was exactly. I smiled and waited, wondering if she had a plan for this conversation or if we were going to talk in circles until she got bored and sent me out.

"You knew Cyrilly," she said.

I said Yes, I did.

"A wonderful woman."

I said Yes, she was.

"I met her when I was just a college student, but she was so kind. She really helped me. She seemed to know everybody in New York, every dealer and buyer."

I said Yes, she did.

"How did you happen to get associated with her?"

"I met her here in Boston. She was working with a man named Gruenfeld. A year or two later she opened her place in New York."

"Those were good years for the art business," she said.

We talked about Cyrilly, Sonia Strand telling me how tough Cyrilly could be when making a deal— "And yet she had that lovely light voice, so musical, not like mine," said Sonia—and how loyal Cyrilly had been to her painters. I said, "Yes, she was remarkably loyal—" and I was about to expand on the theme of loyalty to painters but was cut off. "I know," Sonia said, sighing. "That was a different era. The art world has changed a lot since then." I don't recall how much longer we talked or what we talked about, for I was getting impatient and didn't care if it showed. Sonia touched my arm and went to her desk, saying, "Just a minute. Don't get up." She left behind a light floral scent, at odds with everything else about her, and stood at her desk to look down for a long moment at one of the loose papers there, her hand absently holding the oblong silver pendant that hung almost to her waist. "You know," she said, without looking up. "I can't tell much from a photograph, I need to look at the painting itself. I like to look on Tuesdays." She turned to me. "What's a good day to visit you?"

"Next Tuesday."

"Next Tuesday it will be," she said crisply.

I told her how to get to my place and we shook hands, Sonia Strand giving me that firm warm grip while I looked directly into the blue crystal eyes, then I picked up my slides and headed back down Newbury, slanting over toward the Daily Grind.

15

THE DAILY GRIND IS HALF LEFT AND HALF RIGHT, which is to say that the counter is in the middle of the floor and you can turn left past one-hundred-pound sacks of green coffee beans and crates filled with tea, or you can go to the right, past a playpen set there first for the owners' kids and now for the toddlers of the hired help, and that side has a dozen little square tables, each painted a different color, clustered by the window. When I entered, Garland glanced up from the counter and said, "Hi, Ren," then she frowned and went back to her accounting problem, cross with the numbers for not coming out right. Garland is always about to fly apart and on a hectic day her eyes enlarge and her cheeks become a luminous pink while her fine hair flares out as if electrified and she's crazily beautiful, but not now.

I went to the men's room and had a long, merciful piss, all the while brooding on my sullen prostate and what might lie ahead for it and for me, wondering had anyone thought to write a poem on such a thing, as years ago I had written one about my upstanding young prick, then I shook off the last drops, washed up and went to a table by the window. Garland said, "You got mail," and left a couple of letters on the table as she went past. One envelope was from Scanlon and the other was just a folded sheet of lined notepaper sealed with a strip of tape, nicely fashioned by, it turned out, a former student who used to make frames for me. *Hi, Ren! We are just passing thru on our way home and can't stop, but we had hoped to find you here. Come visit us! Love, Daphne.* She had included a photo of herself, the angular gamin on the left, and Laura, a softly rounded rosy-cheeked lawyer, standing side-by-side in Daphne's pottery studio, each with an arm around the other's shoulders — in her Christmas card she had said they hoped to get married — and on the back of the photo she had written, *This is our family.* I liked Daphne. I opened Scanlon's envelope with the table knife and stuck the snapshot inside so as not to lose it.

One of the waiter kids came over, put down a cup of coffee, took my order and went off, the back of his gold shirt saying, *Property of Jay Gatsby.* I unfolded Scanlon's letter and settled down to enjoy it, knowing it was going to reveal his newest theory of painting, because Scanlon concocts a new theory every time he starts painting in a new direction, which he does every eighteen months in his endless search for what he calls the market. Ten years ago he had been on the way to becoming famous, but then the market shifted, his dealer got busted for hoarding cocaine, the gallery folded and Scanlon found it harder and harder to get a show. Scanlon says we all theorize and most of us don't know it, but Scanlon knows it and writes his theories in his letters and his notebooks, so if his paintings ever get famous his notebooks and letters will get famous, too. I couldn't theorize and paint at the same time, even when I was his age. The only good painter I ever knew who talked intelligently about his own paintings was Ben Shahn, about whom you hear nothing anymore, but he was a thoughtful man with an expressive black line, though his colors were more faded than I like, and he could really talk.

I was halfway through my sandwich when somebody came up and asked was I going to have a painting group this summer; I said no and went back to looking at the wild sketches Scanlon had included with his letter. Scanlon's sketches are always better than his finished paintings. Then I drank a second cup of coffee and watched the waitress (elongated torso with the slightly protuberant abdomen of a child) reaching and bending and ducking as she cleaned the empty tables; no abrupt squats or jagged pokes, but all fluent and harmonious, a pleasure to observe. Her swimsuit top revealed a tendril of tattoo on her shoulder, so I asked what it was and she said "A snake eating its own tail. It's a symbol of immortality, I think." She turned her back, pulled down the strap and looked over her shoulder at me, expectant. "Beautiful design. Great colors," I said, and she smiled with satisfaction and pulled up the strap, though in fact all tattoo colors are lousy.

I had half a cup more and sat there watching a kid in the playpen, but all the while thinking about a solo show in the Strand Gallery and about Sonia Strand coming next Tuesday to see more of my work and I thought I'd better tell Alba about this and ask her advice on how to manage it, because Alba is good at managing things, having practiced for years on me, then I went to the other side of the shop to see Gordon. "Don't ask me what I'm doing. I don't know what I'm doing," he said placidly.

Gordon Levy is forty-something years old, tall and thin, with a 1930s Art Deco face composed of a few smooth planes. I asked him what was wrong with the roaster, and he said nothing was wrong but he had decided to take it apart to clean it and he would never do that again. The only part of the machine still in place was the fancy front end, a solid piece of cast nickel scrollwork, which I suggested he put in the window as an art object. I held one of the curved metal plates around the barrel while Gordon screwed it back in place and we got to talking about the art market and the coffee market and tattoos. He said he'd met a woman who began with a single flower tattooed on her butt and every year she added another kind of flower. "When I got to know her she had an entire garden back there," he said. A young woman came up to us — a sharp face with a head of waxy black hair that stuck out in all directions — the same one who had come up to me a while ago when I was at lunch. "Listen, don't go to pieces," she said, a nasty edge to her voice. "But when I asked over at the college they said I could find you here. That's why I came over here."

"The answer is still no," I told her, amiably enough. "I don't teach anymore."

She stared at me, a line of mascara along her eyelashes, a silver rivet through the flange of her nose, some rings through her eyebrow. "That's not the point. You were my father's teacher. That's the only reason I even talked to you," she said, lifting her chin and compressing her lips now as if she were about to spit at me.

I started to ask who her father was but she had already turned and was striding to the door, leaving behind the after-image of her oily black leather jacket and chrome studs. The door crashed shut behind her and there was a moment of silence, then Gordon glanced up from the coffee roaster where he was still trying to adjust a metal hoop. "I didn't know you went for that type," he said.

"Can I use your phone?"

I phoned Alba, told her how things had gone at the Strand Gallery and said I would really like to talk to her about it, said I needed her advice about what to show Sonia Strand and how to present it (all of which was only the truth), and asked her about tomorrow. Alba said That's great news, but I'm going to the cooking class tomorrow and I won't be free until two o'clock. I asked her where should we meet at two. Well, she said, I can get over to the Daily Grind by two-thirty. That's where you're phoning from, isn't it? I said, "Yes, two-thirty tomorrow. Thanks, Alba."

16

WHEN I GOT BACK TO THE STUDIO I FOUND A postcard had arrived from my daughter Astrid, calling herself Galaxy again (*Am coming to Boston — will get in touch, have lunch together — love Galaxy*) which postcard I wedged into the door panel so every time I went out I'd see it and not forget, then I began to sort through my paintings to decide which ones to show Sonia Strand, but the idea of my work in her gallery intoxicated me so much that I couldn't sort anything from anything, so I quit and walked from the studio to the back room, back and forth I don't know how many times, then decided to tack the photo of Daphne and Laura onto the cork board but there wasn't any space, since I didn't want to take down any of the other snapshots or notes, so I tucked it into the frame and I taped Scanlon's sketches to the wall where I sometimes put my own stuff. Then I took out a big canvas and began slowly to prime it, a soothing routine, and I was still at it when a key grated in the lock and the door rattled open and here was Zoe, saying, "Hi, it's me." I said Hi, Zoe, and turned back to the canvas to keep the placid rhythm of painting the undercoat. I love Zoe and like everyone else I love she can get on my nerves by interrupting my work. She set a bag of groceries on the seat of a kitchen chair and came over to put her hand on the back of my neck, saying, "Feel that? I didn't wear gloves. It was so bright and sunny I didn't realize how cold it was. I'm freezing. — What do you think?" I told her summer wasn't here yet, and I went on painting.

"No, what do you think of this?" She stood beside me and ran her hands up through her hair, watching me.

"You got a haircut."

"Like it?"

It had been shaggy before and it was still shaggy, but shorter now, cropped in a way to make it look like a close fitting feather cap, but maybe I'm not describing it well because I didn't especially like it. "Very sleek. Aerodynamic," I said and went back to painting.

"I'll get vain if you keep flattering me this way. I discovered my hair is getting thin, Ren. I never conceived that would happen. It's not falling out, you know, it's just getting thinner, each hair is actually thinner than it used to be. I'm getting old."

I told her she was young and beautiful. Zoe was in her mid forties, actually rather late forties, late late forties, and had a firm body that she exercised relentlessly to keep trim. She also had pale gray-blue eyes that Alba had once called wolf's eyes, which I thought was an unkind remark but which Zoe took as a compliment. On the inside of her right wrist there was a birthmark, a raspberry stain like a splash of paint, which I had first seen when she was eighteen, and I'd told her it meant she was destined to be a painter and, in fact, she was now a graphic artist with her own studio, which is not the same thing as being a painter, but closer to it than when she was re-designing secondhand clothes or sewing what she called soft sculpture. Now I have to tell you something and it's no secret—Zoe is my daughter Astrid's mother.

"Astrid won't like it, probably won't," Zoe continued. "She's so critical of me."

"Astrid loves you."

"I know she loves me. I also know she's unreasonably critical of me," she said, walking away. "And she won't listen to anything I say."

"She sent a postcard inviting me to lunch. She didn't say when. It's on the door."

"She never says when till the last minute. She phoned me. She's inviting all of us to lunch—you, me, Alba," she said, glancing at the postcard.

We three hadn't had a meal together in months. I began turning the idea this way and that, trying to decide whether I liked it or not.

"Astrid likes us all together, you know," Zoe continued. "She always wants that. She's certainly not pleased with you for moving to this studio."

I ignored that last remark and continued to paint. I could hear Zoe taking things from the grocery bag, putting this and that on the shelf, and I heard the soft thud of the refrigerator door and the heavy clink of wine bottles. Zoe remarked that Astrid was calling herself Galaxy these days, as if she were still singing with the band or modeling again. A minute later she added that maybe it was good for Astrid's business, because it was different and distinctive. I went on painting. Then Zoe said she was worried because Astrid was so thin and needed to gain weight and was living too fast and maybe was taking pills to keep up the acceleration. I reminded her that Astrid was a vegetarian and took scrupulous care of her body and was fussy about what she put into it and wasn't the kind of kid who took pills. Zoe said she wished Astrid had more room in her life for the nonmaterial, the spiritual. Now Zoe was patrolling the edge of the studio, pausing at the big corkboard to study the photo of Daphne and Laura, then glancing across the other photos and notes, stepping carefully around the ink stone and paper on the floor, then moving past my grandchildren's crayon work to examine Scanlon's sketches. I told her she had been in motion ever since she came in and she should get herself a glass of wine.

"The only reason I'm here," Zoe said lightly. "The only reason I'm here is, well, I thought I'd stop in, see how you were getting along. That's all."

I said I was getting along fine and I told her about Sonia Strand wanting to see more of my work.

"Hey, Ren, that's great! Tell me more."

I gave up trying to paint. "Pour a couple of glasses of wine," I said. I figured if she wouldn't let me paint, and if she had come over to see how I was, we might as well drink and talk and let one thing lead to another, my bed being right here beside us.

Zoe filled two glasses and handed one to me, saying, "By the way, I have to be at a meeting in Cambridge by four."

"Then we should drink fast and act impulsively—if you're in the mood."

"Oh, I'm in the mood all right. But I have to get there early and meet with Derek ahead of time to plan things."

"Shit!" I said. I had hoped to avoid this, but I have to tell you that Zoe and the enterprising Derek Mallow had been playing footsie under the conference table for months; that's a fact. "Thanks, Zoe. Thanks for the *visit*. Goodbye!"

"Why are you mad at me?" she says in an injured tone, so I tell her, "You come up here with food and wine and now you tell me you can't stay! You come over to tell me you can't come over? I have better things to do, Zoe. I want to *work*," and by now her cheeks are pink and she cries, "This thing came up at the last minute. You're not being *fair*!" and I tell her loudly, "So I'm not being fair. I was working," and then she whips back, "It would help if you had a phone—"

"*Fuck the phone!* I'd never get any work done."

Zoe walked to the middle window and stood there looking out, her arms tightly folded and her shoulders hunched forward and, of course, she looked especially vulnerable since the haircut made the shape of her skull so clear and exposed the nape of her neck. I finished cleaning my brush and I hauled the canvas back to the wall. "Why is everything so damn difficult with you?" I asked, setting her wine glass on the window sill.

"I came over because I was lonely for you," she said, turning to me. We kissed, but when I put my arm around her it was like embracing one of my kitchen chairs. "Anyway, what makes you think it's me who's the difficult one?" she asked, and took a drink of wine.

We stood at the window and talked of one thing and another. Zoe said it had been so sunny today it was hard to believe it was still so cold, and we talked about Sonia Strand and Peter Bell, then Zoe poured herself another glassful and said Astrid was working too hard, chasing after glitz and glitter, and wouldn't listen to her mother anymore; I told her that Astrid was young and energized by her work, which was what I believed, and Zoe relaxed somewhat and refilled my glass.

"Which do you like more, food or sex?" she asked.

"The angels in heaven envy us for both," I told her. "We should have both."

"Be serious, Renato! It's a test of age, because young people choose sex and old people choose food." I laughed, and Zoe put her hand over my mouth and said, "How about tomorrow? I could come tomorrow afternoon and we could have both." Maybe it was the wine, but her face had the same warm light as when she was a teenage kid.

But I thought about my getting together with Alba tomorrow afternoon to talk about which paintings, and I didn't know when that would finish, so I put down my glass and told her, "I have to see Alba tomorrow."

"I thought you were seeing her on weekends. I thought you saw her last Sunday," Zoe said petulantly. I said right, but I had to see her again. Zoe looked at me. "I liked it better when you two were living together. At least I knew what was going on," she said flatly. We talked about food and not sex, and when she had finished her wine she give me a brisk kiss on the mouth and left.

17

FTER ZOE LEFT I TURNED TO MY INK-BRUSH WORK—
great sheets of delicious, handmade paper on which
I was trying to draw using a Japanese calligraphy brush—
and I had been going at it for I don't know how long when
there was a knock at the door. It was the same woman in the
greasy black leather jacket who had pestered me at the café,
her black bristle hair sticking up in clumps, thin silver rings
through her sooty eyebrow. "Hi," she said. I said Hi and we
looked at each other. "Can I come in?" I said No and started
to shut the door. "Hey, wait!" she cried angrily, shoving her
boot against the doorjamb. She withdrew her boot. "All right,
please! Please just wait a minute. Let me *explain*." I held the
door, waiting with my hand on the doorknob, and she said,
"I got in from San Francisco yesterday and I don't know anybody around here except you." I told her she didn't know me
either. "I'm broke. I maxed out my credit card to get to Boston," she said. I asked her had she tried Travelers Aid, told her
they could take care of her better than I could. "I was hoping
you could help me out," she said.

"You mean money," I said.

"No. I just need a place for tonight and then—" I had tak-
en my hand from the doorknob and started to wave her off,
no more than a gesture, but she flinched and threw up an arm
to shield her head.

"Hey, calm down," I told her. "Who are you, anyway?"

Her cheeks had reddened slightly, but she gave no other
sign that she had thought I was going to punch her. "My
name's Avalon. We don't know each other but you knew my
father. You and my father were friends."

"So you say."

"I have proof. Look," she said. She slipped a hand into her pants pocket and pulled out a beat-up wallet, flipped through her little album of cards and photos until she found what she wanted, then held it out to me. "Here's a picture of him when you knew him," she said. It was a black-and-white photograph of a young man with dark, rather long hair, cramming a suitcase under the front hood of a VW bug. The photo had been taken just as he turned to the camera and started to say something. The face was familiar, but maybe because the big hair looked so much like the late sixties that it reminded me of people I had known back then. "And here's one of him and you. —I know it's real, because that's the front of a stage I went and looked at today," she added. It was another black-and-white snapshot: me and that other guy clowning around, leaning back to back against each other, while behind us was the Charles River and a quarter circle of the open-air Hatch Shell where the Boston Pops plays concerts in the summer. "See. That's him and that's you, right? That's you and my father."

The photo or the smell of her leather jacket or something else about her began to stir some uneasy memory. "What's your name?" I asked.

"Avalon. Avalon Flood." In addition to the rings through her eyebrow and the rivet in the delicate bell of her of her nose, she wore a row of little silver rings through the rim of one ear and what looked like a miniature bolt through the lobe of the other one. "Flood," she repeated.

It had begun to come back to me. "I remember your father," I told her.

"He's dead. Can I come in?" Her gaze darted over my shoulder, this way and that. She left the door open behind her and came in a couple of steps and paused, looking around. "I guess you spend a lot of time painting," she said.

"I'm a painter."

"I know you're a painter! Sometimes I say stupid things."

She shifted from foot to foot, shot a glance into the shadows of the other room, but stayed where she was. "Married?"

"Yes."

"Where's your wife?"

I told her my wife lived across the river in Cambridge, but Avalon seemed not to listen, her gaze flicking from this to that, around the room. She had a lean, sharp face with quick eyes, a good throat, and the rim of her jersey undergarment was clean. "Do you have a bathroom?" she asked. I said yes and she stepped back out the door and returned with a big lumpy backpack which she dropped to the floor, and at her other side stood this kid, a boy about seven or eight, maybe nine years old—who knows?—holding a big toy airplane. "This is Kim," she informed me. Kim had a round Asian face and steady, velvet-black eyes which regarded me with passive curiosity

"Hello, Kim. —Where did he come from?" I asked her.

"He's mine. I'm his mother."

"Great. Got any more out there?"

"No. Where's the bathroom?"

Later, while I was preparing the pasta, I asked Avalon about her father, Brendan Flood. "He was a computer programmer," she said. "He used to draw pictures for me when I was a kid, and he told me about the art school and about you, but he wasn't a painter." I remarked that when I knew her father he had been programming computers, yes, and doing a lot of other things as well and, I added, she might want to know that he was also a little cracked, not falling apart crazy, but cracked, and I had liked him for that, too. She said she could believe he was a little cracked, all right, because that would explain how come he married Sandra ("An airhead.") who, when Avalon was ten, drove away in their convertible and never returned, and it might explain why he later married Linda ("A bitch.") Anyway, when Avalon was fourteen her father died of melanoma cancer ("Too much sunshine. In the end he got burned to a crisp and that was the end of my dad.") so Avalon was sent to live with Linda's mother in Sacramento ("Because Linda didn't want me. She wanted to play around and she didn't want me there to watch.") but Linda's mother ("The bitch's mother.") didn't want her either and a year later Avalon was sent to live with Linda's unmarried younger sister ("An asshole.") in San Francisco. After a year there, Avalon moved in with a classmate ("Not too bright but not a slut, either.") and completed her high school courses in Sunnyvale. "I also took courses at San Francisco State," she said. She went on a while, but I wasn't much listening to her, thinking instead about Brendan Flood, whose whole life had come and gone.

After we had finished eating but were still at the table, she said, "I have two photo albums. That's all I have from when he was alive. Linda took everything else and sold what she didn't want. No one wanted the photographs, so that's what I inherited."

"Where'd you get Kim?"

She said nothing but looked at Kim who was at her side, warming up his airplane, wheeling it slowly into position with a soft, powerful hum. "He's very well behaved, isn't he?" she said, caressing his back as he taxied slowly down the table. "He's half Japanese, that's why," she explained.

"Is that why? Where's his father?"

"In Japan, I suppose."

"You don't know?"

"As soon as Kim was born I took one look and knew who his father was, but by then he was gone. I suppose he went back to Japan. He was a student at Stanford, from Osaka."

"Kim is a Korean name," I told her. "The Japanese and the Koreans hate each other. Who named him Kim?"

"I named him after his father. Kimura. That was his last name. I couldn't recall his first name. It was something like —oh, I don't know—anyway, all I could remember was

Kimura. So he's Kim. I think it's a good name for a boy, don't you? I'm teaching him about Japanese things so he will appreciate his Japanese background. Like, I'm teaching him how to use chopsticks. And he's learning Japanese. I got a teach-yourself book and taught him numbers in Japanese. —Kim. Kim, come over here." The pilot had been heading toward my fresh ink-on-paper work, but now he banked slowly and made a wide turn and began the long descent toward our table. His mother said, "I want you to count something. Please." She pulled him against her side. "See these things on the table? Just these. Can you count them?"

Kim kept a grip on his airplane. "There's five," he said quietly. "What's so great about that?"

"I want you to count each one in Japanese," his mother told him. "Like in one, two, three—only in Japanese."

He pointed at each of the dishes and wine glasses, this time saying, "Ichi. Ni. San. Shi. Go. Roku."

"There! You see?" Avalon had turned to me in triumph. "Isn't he a smart kid?"

I said yup, a wonderful kid, let me show you where you two can sleep. I took Avalon and her good-tempered bastard to the other room, which is where I stored my old paintings and everything else I couldn't cram into our expensive cement tomb in Cambridge, and I dragged a mattress edgewise from behind a wall of big canvasses. "This is great, isn't it, Kim? This will be fun. And now," she added, turning to me, "I want to give him a bath because we spent last night at a shelter and only God knows what low-class germs live there. Do you have a towel? Maybe two towels, actually." I got her two towels, and after she had given the kid a good soak and rubbed him dry she wrapped him in the other towel and seated herself on the floor of my studio, letting him fall asleep with his head in her lap. "Why did you come East?" I asked her. "Why Boston?"

"San Francisco isn't a good place to raise a child. It's all very advanced and enlightened and it's a freak show."

"So you just packed up and came to Boston."

"That's right," she said, caressing Kim's head, running her slow fingers complacently through his black bristle hair in rhythm with his breathing.

"And you looked me up because I knew your father."

"Actually, I looked you up because you knew my mother."

"Not me. I didn't know her. No."

"My father said you knew about her. He told you about her. He told —"

"Nope," I said, cutting her off.

"He told me so."

"What did he tell you?"

"My mother was an angel, right?"

18

I KNEW BRENDAN FLOOD AND I KNEW ABOUT AVALON'S mother, because when it was over Brendan told me about her. Whenever he spoke about her he said she was an angel, and I have no doubt she was — either that or she was crazy and Brendan was stoned. According to Avalon, her mother and Brendan met in August — which is absolutely true — an August so hot that asphalt melted in the streets and seven of the trees along the river burst into flame. The air was boiling in his apartment, so Brendan had propped open the skylight and was lying naked on his back on the bare floor, his hands clasped behind his head, trying to keep cool. He was staring up at the square of blue sky as if from the bottom of the sea when a body as naked as his own floated ten feet above the skylight, thrashing and clawing and choking — then it stopped thrashing and sank very gently head-first with the legs floating out behind, a swimmer whose lungs had filled with water, and came to rest with a white cheek flat against the skylight, the mouth wide open and the eyes like blue quartz. Brendan lay there trying to puzzle out what had happened, then he pulled up a chair and stood on it, reached out through the open skylight to grapple a leg and hauled the body down feet-first into his arms, himself crashing sideways onto the floor under the sudden weight. He got up and— What can I say? This was a bare-assed young woman, maybe eighteen, with a wingspread of over twelve feet.

A bitter stink of burnt feathers hung in the air and, in fact, Brendan noticed that the trailing vanes on both wings were singed away, revealing a sooty membrane underneath, and her right arm was seared. He rolled her onto her back. Her wide eyes were as sightless as two pieces of turquoise, as if she had drowned in air. He was wondering was she drunk or stoned or in a narcoleptic fit when she stumbled to her feet, knocking him aside. She glared at the skylight and began to howl —a freezing sound that started as a single icy note, solitary at first but soon joined by others all pitched the same and all in different timbres until it seemed a whole orchestra was shivering the room, cracking the windows, exploding bottles, glasses, light bulbs. Brendan had clamped his hands over his ears, had run as far as he could and continued to bang his head against the wall until the desolate cry ended. "Who are you?" he asked, gasping for breath.

She turned her stone eyes toward him and spoke, or tried to, but all that came out was a kind of mangled music.

"Stop!" he cried, ducking his head and clapping his hands to his ears again. "Stop!"

But she went on until there was nothing but shards of sound, then she shrugged and said something like *Oh, shit*, tripped over the mattress on the floor and plunged into a deep sleep. Brendan wiped the sweat from his eyes and watched to see if she would stir, then he righted the chair under the skylight, stood on it and pulled himself shakily onto the roof with the hope of spying some explanation. There was only the commonplace desert of tar and gravel. He dropped back into his room, chained the door and wedged the chair under the doorknob. He was trembling from exhaustion when he returned to look at her—one long white wing lay folded across her rump and the other spread open like a busted fan across the mattress and onto the floor. He crept slowly from one side of the mattress to the other and watched the light shimmer this way and that on the feathers as he moved, feeling ashamed of himself when he paused at the glimpse of gold hairs at her crotch. He had always understood that there was no difference of sex between angels, that angels were not male or female but pure spirits. He told me he didn't know what to think, much less what to do, and it got to be so quiet you could hear the faucet drip. So Brendan retrieved his little tin box of joints from the window ledge and sat on the floor with his back to the wall, struck a match and began to smoke, keeping his dazed eyes on her all the while.

She slept for two days and two nights, or maybe it was three days and nights, or maybe only that one day and night —Brendan lost track because he fell asleep himself. When he woke up she was sitting cross-legged on the mattress, looking at him with eyes as clear as a summer sky. "You need a shave," she told him, for her voice had cleared too.

"I've been busy," he said, startled.

She was looking around at the bare white walls and scuffed wood floor, at the banged-up guitar case and the old record player and the short row of records and books on the floor against the wall. "Yeah? Doing what?" she asked, skeptically.

"Thinking about things, meditating." He had gotten to his feet and had begun to search hurriedly for his underwear or his pants or any scrap of cloth to hide himself.

"You ought to eat more. You look like a fucking bird cage on stilts. What's your name?"

"Brendan Flood," he said. He hadn't found his underwear

but quickly thrust a leg into his blue jeans anyway. "I've been on a fast. I've been meditating and fasting," he explained. "Who—"

"Meditating and fasting? Holy shit!" She laughed. "Who pays the rent here?" She sounded a lot like Avalon when she talked.

"Me. I work nights as a programmer. Listen—" he began.

"So what else have you been doing? Hash? Acid? Come on, Brendan. Don't look so surprised. I know you've been smoking grass. The air is full of it."

"Listen, who are you?"

"I'm an escapee, Brendan. Just like you. You can trust me. Jill," she added as an afterthought.

"That's your name?"

"They named me Morning Glory," she said sarcastically. "But you can call me Jill, yes."

"How did you get here?"

"Well, you've got a chair jammed against the door, Brendan. And I didn't scale the walls. I came in over the roof. Remember?"

He groaned and rubbed the heels of his hands against his closed eyes. "What day is today?" he asked, not opening his eyes.

"How would I know?"

He looked at those wings which stood like snowdrifts behind her shoulders. "Do those come off?" he asked.

"Are you being funny? This is me," she said, glancing down at her breasts, cupping and lifting them. "As fucking naked as I get."

Her flesh was the color of the dawn horizon, so beautiful it frightened him, but he gathered his courage and looked at her—her face, the hollow of her throat, her breasts and the honey-colored hair of her crotch. Yet at the first surge of desire he felt a chilly counter current, a fear that his lust was a monstrous sacrilege that would bring the wrath of God down on his head like a hammer. He escaped to the bathroom to piss and discovered a long gold hair stuck to the damp wall tile. He filled the washbowl with cold water and doused his privates, thinking to put out the fire and clean himself at the same time, but it was his brain that was ablaze and just when he was dunking his head it came to him that the creature in the next room might not be an angel at all, might be some delusion fabricated by Satan, whereupon his legs gave way and he pitched forward into the faucet and came up choking. He wondered if he were going crazy.

He went back to the room and found her seated cross-legged on the mattress reading one of his books, *The Poetical Works of William Blake*, which was where he kept his cigarette papers. She looked up and began reciting "And when the stars threw down their spears and water'd heaven with their tears —" but saw that Brendan was already aroused, up and rising. "Ah, you devil," she murmured, tossing aside the book to grasp his shaft. "Did he who made the lamb make thee?"

Brendan was doomed to remember their lovemaking for the rest of his life. It began simply enough when he threw himself to the mattress and pulled her onto her back, hoping to get a hand on her breast and a knee between her thighs, but before he could make his next move he felt her finger-nails pierce his rump and felt his cock being seized as in an oiled fist and he slid in deeper and higher until he couldn't tell whether he was fainting or screaming with pleasure. He had staggered to his feet and was carrying her upright, her legs around him like a vise, stumbling now against the chair and then the table and now crashing against the wall and again the table, carrying her at last as if she were miraculously weightless or as if she were actually carrying him, as if he were on his back, hooped in her arms and legs, her wings beating slowly but just enough to keep them afloat above the mattress and table and chairs. And when he came it was a long, long rush in which his body gave itself completely away, such a long rush that he could feel the marrow being drawn sweetly through his spine from his distant fingers and toes, and at the end of it every one of his bones was hollow and his skull completely empty.

Later they lay side by side on the sweat-soaked mattress and Brendan, believing he had been turned inside out and the secret lining of his life exposed, told her all about his student days at Cal Tech where he learned Fortran and Cobol and other machine languages of lethal boredom, followed by his years on the road as a Zen guitarist with Zodiac, which had nearly driven him crazy, and how for these past three months he had fasted and prayed, waiting for God to give him a message or vision or signal of some sort. When he was finished he looked at Jill and she said, "I'm hungry. Are you hungry? I know I am. I'm starved." Of course, there was no food in the place. So Brendan pulled on his clothes and hunted up a pair of jeans and a T-shirt for Jill, but she refused to wear them because, she explained, she couldn't go out. "Going out gives me an anxiety attack," she said. "I get panicky and throw up or pee in my pants if I go out." So Brendan went out and came back with three hamburgers and some sliced pickles. He sat across from her at his wobbly table, bit into his hamburger, looked at her shining breasts and watched her eat. She tore through her food— "Are you going to finish that?" she asked him, glancing at his plate—and when she had downed the last half of his hamburger she wiped her mouth with the back of her hand and said she wanted to go up on the roof to take a look around. He asked her didn't she want to wear something, anything, to cover up, and so on. "For Christ sake, Brendan, this is 1967! The last dress I owned was made of colored paper." But she pulled on a pair of his shorts and Brendan set his chair under the skylight, gave her a boost and pulled himself up behind her.

Remember, this was Boston's Back Bay where the roofs are flat and the brownstones are built shoulder to shoulder with no space between them, so you can walk from roof to roof to roof for a quarter of a mile before coming to a cross street. Brendan watched her looking around and realized she might have come from just a few roofs away and nowhere more exotic. She had shaded her eyes with her hand and was gazing across the pipe vents, TV aerials, skylights and chimneys to the soft horizon. "What city is this?" she asked him.

"What do you mean, what city! This is Boston! Don't you even know what city you're in?"

She whirled on him, saying, "You're so smart and you don't even know what day it is! I never said I was smart. I never went to college. So fuck off!"

Brendan flushed. "It's the twelfth. Or the thirteenth. I stayed up all night to watch the meteor shower on the eleventh. So it must be Saturday. I think."

"What difference does it make what city it is, anyway?" she muttered, sullen.

So they dropped back into Brendan's place where he stepped out of his blue jeans and she peeled off her shorts and they knelt face to face on the mattress and began to make love again, and it would have been even better than before except that Brendan had begun to doubt that anything could be so good or that he could be so fortunate or that Jill (or Morning Glory or whatever her name was) could be what she appeared to be.

Three nights a week Brendan crossed the river to Cambridge where he worked as a computer programmer, but other than that, these two slept at night and made love by day, all day, every day. They ate of course. Jill still refused to go down to the street, saying she had a bad case of agoraphobia and dreaded open space, so Brendan went off for groceries and came back with take-out hamburgers and pizzas and Chinese, plus pasta to cook up right there. Brendan never gained a pound; in fact, he lost a few. "Are you trying to starve yourself to death?" Jill asked him.

"Food dirties the windows of perception," he told her.

"Because, do you know what they do to people who try to

kill themselves but fuck up and don't do it right? They strap them down and do things to make them regret their mistakes. Believe me," she said.

When he asked her how come she knew about such things she said, "I'm an escapee. Remember?" which was what she usually said whenever he asked her about herself.

But mostly they made love. There were days when they clowned around, as when they lathered themselves in whipped cream and licked it from each other's flesh, and hours of heavy sensuality when he lingered and she opened to him with the languor of a flower and, to be sure, there were moments when he rushed her like the whippet that he was.

According to Avalon, Jill's feathers had begun to show color and in November she announced that she was pregnant. Now Brendan noticed that whenever they made love the points at the trailing edge of her wings glowed translucent pink and each successive time they joined the color reached deeper into the feathers, like dye soaking into fabric, until the wings themselves took on a pale rose cast, a shade which deepened each day and, in fact, the hue at the tip of each feather began to alter from red to maculate gold in the way of a spotted trout, and from that to a grassy emerald to an iridescent sapphire such as you see in peacock feathers, thence to a purple so luminous it tinted the room. Her eyes changed, too. Some days they were so clear that when he looked into them he saw sky, clouds, stars, albino doves. Other days they solidified into black mirrors and she would turn her blind face to the skylight and scream, then hurtle from one end of the room to the other, dashing herself ruthlessly against the walls until she dropped, the pulse beating furiously in her neck, her soundless mouth stretched open and her wide eyes like agates. When she'd come to, she'd shiver in his arms and though her teeth were chattering she'd grin and say something like, "I graduated from Boston Psychopathic with a degree in paranoia. What do you think? Am I a fallen angel or what?" He would pull her across his lap and hold her head to his shallow chest, rocking her until she drifted to a peaceful slumber, his brain spinning in confusion.

Brendan had never wanted a telephone in his place and now he couldn't afford one, so he called from a public booth at the nearby health-food store, searching for a gynecologist or obstetrician or plain medical doctor who would make a house visit, but of course there wasn't one to be found. He did come across a midwife's card on the bulletin board there, so he phoned her and, since she lived only a few blocks away, she said she'd come around to examine Jill the next day. But the next day when Jill found out who was at the door she barricaded herself in the bathroom and refused to come out till the midwife had gone. Jill informed Brendan that she didn't need a doctor or midwife. "What do they know? We can do this ourselves. You're smart. There are books on this," she said. He broke into a sweat, but bit his tongue so as to say nothing and went out and came back with five books on childbirth.

"No. Not these," she told him, exasperated. "There's this French doctor who helps women give birth under water. Get the one by him."

"You'll drown!" Brendan cried, remembering her face as he had first seen it pressed against the skylight almost twelve months ago.

"Not the woman, asshole! The baby. The baby gets born under water in a tub. Get that one."

He didn't go looking for the book but it wouldn't have made any difference if he had, because several years were to go by before women gave birth in tubs of warm water at Dr. Odent's clinic in Pithivier, France. When Brendan awoke on August 11 Jill was flat on her back in labor beside him, her fingers deep in the mattress ticking, her hair stuck like gold leaf on her damp forehead and cheeks. He pulled on his jeans and jammed his feet into his sneakers and stumbled down the stairway, his loose laces whipping and snapping at each step, and ran to the health-food store where he phoned the midwife. Seven minutes later the midwife's car turned onto Brendan's street and began to nose hesitantly along the row of parked cars, looking for a place to stop, but Brendan pulled her from the wheel and hustled her up the stairway and into his flat. As the midwife later testified, Jill was seated naked on the wood chair under the skylight, the baby wrapped in a bloody dish towel on her lap. "Don't come any closer!" she cried, jumping up. She scrambled awkwardly onto the chair seat and stood wavering there as if under the endless impact of a waterfall, the swaddled infant now crying in her arms. "Brendan, take the baby. It's a girl, like me. —You stay back, lady!" she shouted at the midwife. Brendan received the baby from her. "We crazies are the only true rebels against God," she said, reaching toward the open rim of the skylight. Then this Jill, or Morning Glory or whatever her name was, pulled herself out to the roof and jumped off, finishing her long dive from the battlements of heaven.

19

LATE THE NEXT MORNING I HIKED OVER TO COPLEY College where I used to teach; I was hunting for anybody who knew anything about Sonia Strand and her gallery. By the way, if you're ever in the neighborhood take a look at the sculptured wall behind the reception desk. You can still make out road signs embedded in it, along with a guitar, peace symbols, a mailbox, wooden window frames, tambourines, multipaned glass doors, mirrors, transistor radios, cast human torsos (breasts, pudenda and bums), plus groups of big mismatched letters spelling out LOVE, up, down and sideways. I began to teach at Copley the same September the wall went up, a lively wall saturated with the happy playschool colors of the late 1960s and pierced with glass window panes through which you could spy naked children and women with long shinning hair and sunny breasts. The school was just getting started; we teachers were young, the students even younger, and we fooled around in ways which your more enlightened, progressive and prudish generation now forbids. As for the wall, the sex police purified our vision by covering that beautiful artifact—the best work in the building—with a coat of dead white paint and that's the way it's been ever since.

It felt strange to be back there, seeing all those students in the hall and no familiar faces. Then I bumped into Nils Petersen with a big poster under his arm. "Hey, man. It's been a long time. Good to see you!" he said, slapping my hand. "Are you going to be around later? I have to teach up in the lab in five minutes. Come along."

I like Nils. He's thin and wears his gray hair in a short pony tail, but on him it looks all right. On our way upstairs he raved about all the colors he was generating on his new computer. Years ago artists like Nils used to compose their work by hand, using pencils and rulers, and they separated colors by hand. The way you separated a color was by hiding all the others under a translucent ruby red sheet, because the camera was loaded with ortho film which couldn't see through red; of course, that meant you had to cut a separate ruby for each color—that's where the skill began. There used to be a special swivel knife made by the Ulano company and if you wanted to see a master at work you could watch Nils cutting a ruby with that knife. He had a meticulous dexterity that made me dizzy, and I still have a couple of things he designed, not the printed product but the master pages composed of layer upon layer of sweetly cut ruby sheets. Now the graphics room is called a media lab and Nils does everything on a computer.

We stopped outside the media lab where Nils tacked the poster on the bulletin board—*Pixels: An Exhibition of Com-*

puter Art. I asked was he going to exhibit any computer art in the show. He said yes, so I said I'd go see it, and I meant it. Frankly, computer art is shit without the smell.

I asked him what he knew about the Strand Gallery.

"They have good cheese and expensive wine at their receptions," he said. "Why?"

I told him I was thinking of showing them some slides.

"Sonia Strand makes the decisions. She has a couple of people over there with her, but she's the one who does the deciding. That's what I hear. —Are you going to be around later?"

I said no, but I'd see him at the show for sure, or before then, so Nils went in to teach and I went off to the faculty lounge. The lounge hadn't changed—a leftover space with two scruffy bentwood seats and a busted armchair with tufts of cotton coming out the corners. The window sill held a coffee pot, a stack of styrofoam cups and a cigar box with coins scattered in it. I had turned to leave when a thirtyish woman in a bulky black bathrobe came in, Azarig Tarpinian behind her. He saw me and his face brightened, saying, "Well, well, well. Look who's here." The model seated herself in the armchair and opened her magazine. Azarig turned on the electric heater and asked her if she wanted a cup of coffee—she didn't—then he came over to the window, saying, "Hey, it's good to see you. We've made great progress since you've been gone. Now we're giving a course in the theory of painting. Not practice, *theory.*" He laughed. Azarig is a large, comfortable looking man. We stood there talking while he made a cup of coffee. I said I had just bumped into Nils and he's deep into computer art.

"He's good at it, according to critics and people who claim to know," Azarig said.

"It's art without finger prints."

"You haven't changed," he said.

"My favorite old artist is the one who covered his hand with red pigment and pressed it against the wall in a cave in

Chauvet. That was thirty thousand years ago. But I know how he felt just then. He felt like us. This is my hand. Look. This is me."

Azarig meditated over his cup of coffee, then glanced up and said, "You know about Hammerman?"

"He retired to the Cape. What should I know?"

"He had to go back to the hospital. They performed an orchiectomy. That's the fancy name for castration." Azarig turned away and looked out the window.

"It sounds barbaric," I said.

He shrugged. "They say it slows the spread of the cancer from the prostate. It's a treatment."

We stood side by side at the window, looking down at the street: the slow and uneven stream of cars, the pigeons descending, the people walking along in the bright sun, all as if nobody ever died. There was a rustle of paper as the model turned a page in the magazine she was reading. I asked Azarig how he himself was doing these days.

"I take something for blood pressure, something else for cholesterol," he said. "And you?"

"I'm all right. My prostate numbers aren't good," I admitted. "I'm supposed to get it checked again. The doctor hasn't found anything so far. You never know."

We agreed that God could have done a better job with the pump and the plumbing and, as a matter of fact, agreed that even Azarig or I could have done a better job, and then I asked what had he been working on, and his voice picked up as he told me about some figures he had done in wax and so on and so forth, and I asked him what he knew about the Strand Gallery.

He laughed. "Sonia Strand? She's interesting, like a big painted statue."

"I meant the gallery."

"Her husband was a dealer in gemstones down in New York. Her last husband, anyway. Precious and semi-precious stones, but not diamonds. After he died she moved up here and opened the gallery. You like her?"

"I don't know yet."

"The family came over right after the war. Her father was an art dealer. Viennese."

The model had put aside her magazine and was looking our way, trying to catch Azarig's eye, and when he saw her he glanced at his watch and put down his styrofoam cup. "It's show time," he said. Then he walked the model up the hall to life class and I headed downstairs where I bumped into Eloise Carol, author of "The Male Gaze as Rape," who believes that male artists assault their canvases, attempting to objectify and dominate whatever they paint, whereas women use their brushes to caress and nurture their subjects. We shook hands and I went out, happy to leave the old place, buy some paints, eat lunch and see Alba.

20

ALBA ENJOYS TELLING ME WHAT TO DO AND HOW to behave, so when I asked what she thought I should show to Strand she didn't hesitate. "Show everything from the past three years," she told me. "Keep everything else in the back room."

"You mean, *hide* the other stuff?" I said.

"That's *not* what I said! But if Strand liked those nudes, that means she likes big canvasses and lots of color, so put those up front. And when Strand comes to look, you should—" but I broke in to say "I've done a lot of work in the past three years and I can't put it all up front."

"Put the best up front, and when Strand—" she began, but I told her "All of it is good."

"I know all of it is good, Ren, but not all of it is best."

As I said, Alba likes to run things and if you don't watch out she'll run your life, but I figured she was probably right about the paintings. I looked at her, but she said nothing, merely waited, satisfied. I asked if she knew anything about Strand's confederate, Peter Bell, but she didn't, so we went back to re-arranging the pieces of gossip we had picked up about Sonia Strand. Alba asked me did I remember Leo Conti still had his gallery, and I said yes, I remembered him and had heard he wasn't doing so well. "And he remembers you," Alba said. "I think he'd like to see your work. In fact, I know he would. In fact, he told me so," she added, pleased and hopeful. I asked didn't she remember where his gallery was, and Alba said, "East Cambridge," and I said Not exactly the center of the art world, and she said, "East Cambridge has some interesting parts."

"A small old factory building is interesting?" I asked.

"If it has a gallery in it."

"Yeah, well," I said.

"I think it's worth looking into." I thought it was dismal, but I supposed Alba was trying to be helpful so I bit my tongue and didn't say anything. Besides, she looked fresh and attractive, which was a change, for she had put on a new sweater, soft and tight, and had swept her hair into a glossy French roll, all of this for me, or for the cooking class she had attended earlier today, which I doubted. Now she began to talk about Astrid, saying that she had phoned last night and we were all going to have lunch together. "She plans to come by your studio around noon, or maybe at one or two o'clock, but she couldn't say what day, exactly. Everything is up in the air," Alba added.

"Everything is always up in the air with Astrid. She's calling herself Galaxy again. I wish she'd settle down, get her feet on the ground."

"She sounded fine on the phone. She sounded happy and energetic," Alba said.

"She needs to focus her energies more. She zigs and zags and is all over the place, running after glitter. Maybe you could speak to her about that."

"Me? She has a mother. Why me?"

"Because she will listen to you, because you're not her mother."

"Renato, she's fine. She's a splendid young woman. She's doing well in New York. If you want, I'll remind her that when she was a year old she renounced Satan and all his allurements and empty promises. As her godmother I can do that."

One of the coffee kids, the Gauguin female with black eyes and cinnamon flesh, appeared at our table bearing a tray loaded with pastries; we didn't want any, so she drifted back to the counter. Alba was telling me about some country property she had looked at yesterday, a big farmhouse with outbuildings, which is what we had always talked about buying, only this one turned out to be on a corner between two roaring highways so she crossed it off the list and now the list had nothing on it. "But be honest, Renato. Are you still interested in our buying a place in the country?"

"Of course I'm interested. What do you mean?"

"You'd give up your studio here in Boston?" she asked.

"I'd have a studio in the country—in a barn, in an outbuilding."

"What about your famous privacy you're always talking about? And you do know what I mean," she added.

"I'd have all the privacy I'd need in the country."

"Damn it, Renato! I'm not going to shut my eyes if you go out to your studio with some fuckable, some, some—"

I cut in to hush her, saying, "Nothing has ever gone on in my studio that you didn't know about! More or less. And—."

"Oh, spare me!" she cries, looking around, exasperated at finding nothing to hurl at my head. "You want us to live in the country and you'll have your studio there, too?"

"Yes. *I* want it. *You* want it. —That's what you want, isn't it?"

"Well, I'm not so sure. I'm beginning to like the way we're living right now," she says complacently.

I came to a stop, not knowing what to think or which way to go. "Is that what this is really about?"

Alba turned away to look out the window, content to leave the conversation as it was, so that I could puzzle over it and worry about her meaning, that being one of her little stratagems, though I didn't fall for it. It was a bright day, chill and windy; we watched a man without a coat trot past, one hand holding a briefcase, the other hand clutching his lapels together at his throat. Here in the café, where it was pleasantly warm, the sun lay slantwise down Alba's arm and across our table and the air was fragrant with freshly roasted coffee beans. "Have you seen Zoe recently?" she asked.

"She stopped by the studio on her way to a meeting in Cambridge," I said, for I had learned how to tell the truth and get away with it. "She didn't stay long. She had to get there early, ahead of time, to prepare something."

"What's she up to these days?"

"We talked about Astrid, mostly. —Do you remember Brendan Flood?"

"Anything else?"

"Nothing much. —Listen, do you remember Brendan Flood?"

"Are you trying to distract me? Yes, I remember Flood. That was ages ago. Is he back in town?"

"No. He's dead but his daughter is here."

"Oh. That's a shock. Well. How's his little girl?"

"She's not so little anymore and she has a child of her own, a little boy." I told Alba about Avalon and Kim and suggested that Alba might like to help them out, or at least help me get them off my hands, but no. "Why should I always be the one who takes care of the strays you bring home?" she asked.

I told her it was her nature to do so, that she had a generous heart and that, furthermore, I hadn't brought Avalon and her kid home but, I repeated, Avalon had knocked on my door and when I opened it she had thrust the kid inside. By then Garland had come from behind the counter, pulled a chair to our table and sat down with a sigh. Her face had a delicate pink flush with a glaze of fine perspiration and she plucked at her blouse to bring the cool air to her flesh. "Why do you put up with him?" she asked Alba. "I don't. Not any more," Alba told her. Then they began to discuss pastry dough, how to make it fine and flaky, and I took off.

21

WHEN I GOT BACK TO THE STUDIO AVALON WAS standing bent over the table with a newspaper nailed flat under her palms while she studied the help-wanted ads, and without lifting her head she said Hi, and kept her frown on the small print, making a great display of concentration. Kim was lying on my bed, humming, his dirty bare feet propped against the wall and his eyes glazed with boredom. I had bought five little wood homunculi, each shaped like a bowling pin the size of my thumb, and these I dumped on the blanket beside his head. "Passengers," I told him. "They want to fly to anyplace you can think of." Avalon looked over her shoulder at me and at Kim, who had swung his feet down and was sitting up now. "I'm getting a job," she announced.

I said that was welcome news because—I reminded her —she couldn't stay here. I asked what jobs she had held in California, and she said Lots, and I said I had already guessed she had lots of jobs, probably lots and lots of jobs, and I asked her what was her last job. "I make silver jewelry, rings and chains and bracelets and things like that. I've got some in my backpack. I designed them. I'm a designer, you could say. —Don't look at me that way! I used to work as a designer in a shop on Fillmore. In San Francisco. I designed tattoos." Kim had trotted into the back room and was now piloting his airplane back to my bed where the bored passengers lay in a heap, waiting. "Kim, what do you say to Renato? What do you say when somebody gives you a gift?" his mother asked. Kim looked at me: "Do you want them back?" he ventured. I told him no, he could keep them. "Honey, what do you say?" his mother prompted. "Thank you," he announced, resuming his flight plan.

I took a roll of masking tape from the caddy and got down on my hands and knees to lay out a border on the floor, and Avalon said, "I used to work in a New Age shop selling crystals, herbal soaps, mind-body books, massage oil, things like that, and that's where I sold my jewelry. I've got some in my pack I can show you," she added. I asked what else she had done for work, and she said, "After I quit college I got on a crew putting down asphalt driveways in Orange County. That was my first full-time job. I developed a good body that way and afterwards I worked in a health and fitness club and they used me as a model in their advertisements, so I got into that, into modeling, and then into acting, in a couple of plays, intellectual ones, but that's a stupid life and it doesn't pay as much as waitressing, which is the other thing you do when you're an actor, you waitress even when you get a role. And I was a weather announcer on a TV station in the Valley. —What are you doing? What are you taping the floor for?"

I told her I was laying out a border and that I wanted her and her kid to stay on *that* side of it and not to cross over to my side, and when she looked blank at me I said, "I'm going to be moving a lot of canvases back and forth and I don't want you or Kim to touch anything. Understand? A gallery owner is coming up here next week to look at some paintings." Well, she said, you needn't be so grumpy about it. "Now you tell

Kim," I said. She told Kim not to cross the taped line on the floor, not even where it zigzagged, not to cross it or Renato would go crazy. "Understand?" she asked him. Kim nodded yes and stared across the taped line, freshly curious about my work table, his black eyes like spots of wet ink.

I asked Avalon what kind of job she was going to go looking for, and she said she was looking for a job that paid well; I asked what was she good at. "I'm good with animals, for one thing. I worked for this old veterinarian and I was good at it, only she retired and I had to get another job. I learned a lot at the vet's and then I went to work as a lawyer's assistant, but all I learned on that job was I didn't want to be a lawyer. And I'm good at managing a shop. One place I managed was a photo shop in a mall, one of those places where you go and dress up in a costume and get your picture taken. I ran the shop right up to when I had Kim, then I didn't work for three months and when I went back there they wouldn't hire me again, because I insisted on part-time, so I could look after him." I asked did she ever think of learning something so she could get a decent job. "You mean like learn Russian, or the atomic table, or something? I already know a lot of things." I told her I was sure she knew a lot of things. "I don't know why you're so sarcastic. I do know things. I know five different kinds of massage. I know how to make rag paper. I know the Dewey Decimal system. So what?"

I turned away and began to clean the room, gathered up the big sheets of paper I'd been working on, stowed my ink dish and ink bar, and swept the floor. I fried rice and peppers for dinner that night, and afterwards Avalon cleared the table and washed the dishes and dried them and put them away, and that was all right by me.

Early the next morning I pulled canvases from the stack that leaned against the studio wall and I propped them up here and there, all around the room, so I could decide what to show Sonia Strand. Kim had come out and was sitting cross-legged on the floor, on his side of the taped line, watching me. A while later his mother came out in her jeans and undershirt and made him breakfast, then she sat at the table with a purposeful blank face, drinking a mug of black coffee and staring over his head and out the window. I said good morning. "I would have said good morning but I didn't want to bother you," she replied. I couldn't tell if she were being pious or sarcastic. I asked what did she plan to do for the rest of the day, because, I told her, I was going to be sorting through my work and I needed room to move around in and quiet to think in. "I'm going out to look for a job," she announced. I went back to my canvases and some time later I saw she was in a black sweater and had put on black eyeshadow and deathly pale lipstick. I ignored her and continued working, but soon enough I felt her from across the room in her black leather jacket with the chrome studs, just standing there, shifting from foot to foot, waiting, tense.

"Yes, damn it, yes," I told her over my shoulder. "I'll take care of him. Go!" She whispered a couple of words to Kim, kissed him and ducked out the door. I dragged some canvases from the back room to the studio and stood them against the others and kept shuffling them around until I noticed that Kim had flopped onto my bed and was lying on his back with his head over the edge, his face upside down, watching me. "Let's take a walk," I told him.

We left the plane and its passengers at the studio and hiked down to the river, which this morning was a dark metallic blue with a million tiny dents flashing and glinting on its surface, for a chill breeze was sweeping up from the harbor, and there on the grassy bank we discussed the changing shape of the clouds that scudded overhead ("They're made of fog," he informed me. "That's why they change shape."), and watched a solitary oarsman in a shell pulling up stream. I remarked that the figure in the shell seemed to be sitting on the water, like a waterbug, but Kim said he didn't know what a waterbug was, so I told him that if I moved to the country I'd invite him out and I'd show him some waterbugs. I said that I didn't really know him and asked him to tell me something about himself. "You know my mother and she can tell you," he said, walking off to pick up a stone. I said I'd much rather hear from him; so we discussed his favorite number, which was two, and trolley cars, which he also liked, and a TV show he used to watch called Doctor Who; so, between skipping stones on the river and talking on these and other topics, we passed a couple of hours, then went to a cafeteria on Mass Avenue for a bowl of soup and on to the studio.

Avalon returned late in the afternoon and was clearly discouraged, so I didn't ask if she had found work but suggested that her search might go better if she took some of that jewelry off her face, to which she retorted that I sounded old, and I told her yes I was old and I'd rather sound old than stupid. "Anyway," she said, "one shop I went to said they wanted to look at my designs, my rings and bracelets, so I'm going to show them next week." I asked her who was going to look after Kim if she ever found a job and had to go to work, and she said she would enroll him in school, and I said, "Which school? You're not going to be living *here* and you don't know where you'll be living, so how do you know which school?" I'll figure something out, she mutters to herself, and anyway the school year is practically over, and it's almost summer and—. "No it isn't," I tell her. "And that kid ought to be in school."

"Oh, for Christ sake leave me alone!" she cries and pulls Kim into the other room. Avalon didn't come out until an hour or more had passed; she had been wearing the black turtleneck jersey all day, but came out in a frayed black sweatshirt with the sleeves cut off. She saw I was frying some flounder, so she set the table for three and we sat down to dinner. She had gotten over her sulk and now talked easily, even drank a second glass of wine while telling me about Santa Cruz where she had hung out for a time. Her sharp face with those bits of glittering metal was about as beautiful as an ax blade, but her biceps were admirably firm and despite her head of black hair her forearms had a fine brownish-gold down.

Early the next morning as I was going out the door Avalon said, "You know that café where you were talking to the manager or the owner or somebody like that when I came in?"

"What about it?"

"You could tell them that you know me and that you know I'm honest and that I can waitress. I'll do it. And that way you'll get me and Kim out of here."

It sounded good to me, so on my way back from the river I went around to the Daily Grind and asked Gordon did he remember the woman in the black motorcycle jacket with chrome studs, the one who was pestering me a couple of days ago, had rings in her eyebrow and so on. "Sure," he said. "She was in here yesterday, asking for a job. Said you'd give her a good recommendation. I told her to come back next week." When I got back to the studio I told Avalon that I'd throw her and her kid out if she ever again used my name without asking me first. Her face went blank and she pulled Kim into the back room so fast he tripped and got dragged the last yard.

I sat myself on a stool in the middle of the floor and looked at the paintings set all around the room and I attempted to decide which ones to show to Strand, but since bawling out Avalon my brain had stuck tight as a piece of jammed machinery and I couldn't get it to think. I made a pot of coffee, which routine is always soothing, and poured myself a cup and just as I had seated myself again on the stool Avalon appeared in fresh black eye shadow and that ghastly pale lipstick, clutching a small rucksack in one hand and tugging Kim with the other as she slammed out the door. After they had gone, the studio began little by little to fill up with silence, and sunlight settled slowly on the edges and surfaces of things and sank into the paint so the colors resonated, and I was able to make choices.

Later that afternoon, when I dragged one of the canvases from the studio to its storage place in the back room, I stumbled over Avalon's backpack which lay on the floor by the mattress. The backpack was a huge lumpy green nylon thing, the size of a small trunk, with a padded harness, lots of straps and buckles and a multitude of pouches, zippers, loops, mesh pockets and, sure, an open space where the rucksack had been attached. She had been in Boston only a few days, but she was quick and I figured that by now she knew where to go to lay out the little square of black velvet on which she displayed her tawdry silver bracelets and cheap wire rings, and I could see her sitting on a stone step in Copley Square or maybe standing against a wall on Marlborough Street, that bright shifty look in her eyes and the scrap of black velvet with her glittering junk down on the pavement between her boots.

I was at the sink washing dishes when Avalon and Kim came in, the kid scooting past—"*Watch out I have to go the bathroom!*" Avalon was tired and her face being made up like a corpse didn't improve her looks. "Sell much?" I asked cheerfully. She shrugged. "Get arrested for not having a vendor's license?" I asked with the same cheer. "No, I did not get arrested," she said. She went to the back and when Kim came out of the bathroom I asked did he wash his hands, and he said he forgot and ducked back into the bathroom. Avalon had thrown herself face down on her mattress, still in her black leather jacket. "I made soup. It's in the pot on the stove," I told her. At first she didn't stir, then she slowly rolled over and wearily lifted her arm and said, "Pull," so I pulled her to her feet and she said, "Thanks," as she went to the kitchen. After they had the soup, Avalon gave Kim a bath, then read him a story from one of his tattered books and put him to bed. I was writing a letter to my daughter Skye. "Seeing as how you don't have a TV or anything, do you have any magazines?" Avalon asked me. I showed her the stack of *Art New England* and she looked through a few issues, then she sighed and said she guessed she was too tired to read, so she took a shower and went to bed.

I spent Sunday with Alba in her expensive concrete shoe-box. The place is all window at one end and there we ate a nice brunch that included a crepe fancy, which she had learned to make in her French cooking class, and while we ate I talked in circles about which paintings I definitely wanted or maybe did not want to show Strand, and whether I was displaying too many or too few, and so on and so forth. As I said, Alba has good sense about these things and, furthermore, she likes to give instructions, so by the time we had a last cup of coffee she had told me which paintings she thought would go best. After brunch we pushed on through the *Globe* and the *Times*, dozed in the sun by the window, hiked to the Square and back again, then she made a light dinner and I washed the dishes. Now, the day having gone well, I asked did she want a brandy and, after turning my offer this way and that to inspect it, she decided she was going to take a long bath and I should bring the brandy to her in the bedroom when she called, so I waited and lit a few candles ("Please, Ren, the fewer, the better.") and we made love like old gods, which is to say slowly, luxuriously, majestically. ("You smile, Alba, but that's the way I'll remember it.")

When I got back to the studio around midnight every light in the place was ablaze. Avalon lay asleep on her side, her cheek on her palm, her body curled around a checkerboard drawn in chalk on the floorboards, and her son lay sleeping above her on my bed in his pajamas, his dangling foot almost touching her head. I picked up Kim and carried him to the back room and laid him on the mattress, then I went back for his mother. She wore no makeup and in sleep her profile had a neat, chiseled edge, her closed eyelashes like a single black brush stroke. I said, "Hey, Avalon," and waited, then said it again, but she didn't stir so I jabbed her butt with the toe of my shoe and she opened her eyes, then turned her head and looked up at me. "I put Kim on your bed," I told her. She scrambled to her feet, glanced around in a daze, then stumbled to the back room.

22

NEXT MORNING I SHUFFLED THE CANVASES, SO the ones Alba thought would do well were displayed better, and I took down Scanlon's drawings and put up some of my own, then I went out to phone Sam Geist, an old painter I knew. Geist used to get into town once in a while, but he was ninety-one or ninety-two now and didn't go out and, as I hadn't seen him for months and was feeling energetic and expansive, I phoned him. I got his wife, Rita, who said I hope you're coming over for a visit this time. He needs to talk to somebody.

I had expected that. I drove out to Geist's and Rita let me in, a thin woman in her eighties with a sharp face that had darkened but otherwise not changed much over the years, as if it had been hacked from wood. "This way," she said, admitting me to the overheated interior. "Sam," she cried. "Renato's here. He's brought pastry, the kind you like! —He dozes off," she confided to me. "Go in."

The room was as neat as a display in a furniture store window, except for the uneven jumble of framed photographs crowded onto a small table. Sam was wide awake, seated forward on the edge of his chair, watching me, his hands folded atop the gray aluminum cane that stood between his knees. His face had dwindled since I last saw him, but his eyes were glistening brightly, his white hair standing up in long tufts like soapsuds or a dandelion gone to seed and half blown away. "Come over here, Ren." His voice had a rustling whispery sound and his iron-cold hand startled me when I grasped it. "Rita, get the poor man a chair!" he croaked. They bickered over which chair I should sit in, then we all agreed to go down the hall to the kitchen. Rita stood in front of Sam and took his hands— "Are you holding? Hold on, Sam. Are you holding?"—pulled him waveringly upright and held him under his arms until he had braced himself with his cane. "All right," he said. "I'm all right! You're in the way, Rita!"We made a slow passage to the kitchen, a bare white room with an old-fashioned stamped tin ceiling, each plate and cup and bowl in its proper place on a shelf, a fresh white oil cloth on the table. Sam lowered himself unsteadily into the chair I held for him at the table, then Rita set out the pastries and began to prepare the coffee. "What's going on in your life?" Sam asked me. I began to tell him how I was trying to get Sonia Strand interested in my paintings, but he broke in to tell me about Newbury Street galleries ("Thieves!") and about some paintings he had seen in New York a few years ago ("Junk!") and about an article he had recently read in *Art News* ("Crap!") Rita brought the coffee to the table and sat down, asking how was Alba, so we talked about Alba and then Sam asked about each of my children in turn and by name. "He's showing off his memory," Rita said. "He's gotten vain about his memory."

"You remember Russo?" he asked me.

"Yes, I remember Russo." I had known Russo for decades and he had introduced me to Sam.

"I was thinking about him the other day. You know he wanted to get to be ninety. Because then he was going to have a big retrospective show. He thought if he got to be ninety he could convince some gallery to give him a retrospective. He died at eighty-nine." He hesitated, as if he had lost the thread of his story. "I don't know if that's comic or tragic," he said at last.

I asked him how old he was, himself.

"All that Communist crap," he said, his voice rasping. "If Russo hadn't spent all those years working for the Commies he could have had twice as much time to paint. You know, he didn't begin painting until he was fifty. He got out of jail is when he began to paint. When he was underground he used to spend a lot of time hiding in museums. Before that he thought he was a sculptor. I remember that huge concrete sculpture he made. He was twenty and thought he was Michelangelo. They put it on display in Grand Central Station. Then he joined the Communists. What a waste."

I said I had always liked Mike's work, most of it.

"He was a good painter," Sam said soberly, meditating on it. "He painted every day. Even to the end, he painted."

I remarked it was nice that the gallery at U Mass had one of his big canvases.

"But those political paintings, those aren't his best, those social statements. You remember whenever he talked about painting he got lyrical and talked about soul and spirit and the human heart. All that Marxist materialist shit would go out the window when he talked about painting."

I said yes. "I remember once—"

"I'd tell him, you're no goddamn *Communist*. You're a *Romantic*! His best paintings were those big peaceful ones, those huge soft colors." His hands had begun to tremble and his eyes glistened even more brightly.

I said I agreed.

"We talked a lot, you know," Sam told me. "We didn't agree but we talked. No one talks any more. There's no one to talk to." One of his eyes overflowed a drop, but he didn't notice it.

"Sam, take Renato to your studio so he can see what you've been doing." Rita stood up, removing her cup from the table.

"Everyone's dead," he barked. Later his voice resumed its usual strained whisper, a sound like rustling paper or dried leaves. "You remember that room where Russo used to paint? It was so small he nailed a mirror to the wall in back of him and when he was painting he'd take a hand mirror and look in it so he could see the mirror behind him and that way he could see what his work looked like at twenty feet." He began to laugh.

"He knows all that," Rita told him. "Show him your new works, honey." She began clearing the table.

"I got to pee," Sam told me. "Do you have that problem yet?"

Sam shuffled off to pee and when he returned we went outside and crossed slowly into his studio, a refinished garage in back of the house. It was the dead of winter in there. Bleak light from the overhead windows illuminated the cold stillness — the hardened dabs of paint on the table top, the row of old, crumpled paint tubes, the jar of dusty brushes, the paintings stacked deep against the walls. I held Sam's arm as he settled himself onto a piano stool in the middle of the room, then I switched on the electric heater. "Take a look at those," he told me, nodding toward a stack of painting. "Move them out. Go ahead. You won't break anything." I had seen them before, but I followed his instructions and pulled out the ones he wanted me to look at and I talked about those, telling him how much I liked the way he had shifted this perspective or had treated that patch of color, and so on and so forth, while he remained perched on the piano stool in silence, his hands at rest on the top of his aluminum cane, his eyes liquid bright, watching me.

Geist had painted the New England landscape for more than seventy years, smearing his paint onto the canvas in thick, energetic layers, simplifying the earth's ravines and hills and stony outcrops to elemental shapes, depicting the occasional farm house or barn as flimsy as a strawberry box and the new highway no more substantial than a ribbon laid across a rock. He was a good painter and for a while had been known as the Grant Wood of New England, a witless comparison that he detested. He liked the work of George Bellows and John Sloan, and painted in that tradition, but for the last several decades no critics had taken his painting seriously and his achievement had been forgotten. Just before we left the studio Sam led me to the work table and there he opened a portfolio of ink sketches I hadn't seen before — dried weed stalks, leafless trees and meticulous studies of bare, thin, twiggy tree branches which interlaced and overlapped and crisscrossed, seeming to reveal in their tangle a scrawled message or semaphore which remained never quite decipherable. I liked it all. "This is good, very good," I told him. Sam nodded in sober agreement, then he closed the portfolio and leaned heavily on my arm and we left.

23

*T*HE VISIT WITH SAM DEPRESSED ME ALL THE WAY back to Boston, so instead of climbing upstairs to the studio I walked over to the cheap end of Newbury Street and into the stream of mostly young people, hoping it would do me some good. It didn't do me any good at all. I sat down among the empty chairs outside a café. It was sad to see Sam enfeebled and though I know it didn't pain me the way it pained him, still it gave me a lingering ache. He was fortunate to have a sturdy wife and two married daughters, plus a granddaughter who visited him once in a while. And for sure his five-inch obituary would appear in *The Boston Globe*, recounting his success in the thirties and forties, and listing which of his paintings were still in the so-called permanent collections of New England museums.

A waiter came out and asked what I'd like to order, but it was chill outside so I went in and got an espresso. Let me add that Sam Geist was in that generation of painters who came of age during the Thirties and Forties and saw their works turned into old-fashioned junk after the war. Geist always said it was émigré intellectuals who derided American painters as parochial and promoted instead "crap that could have been painted in a cellar in any country on the globe." He was thinking of Action painters and Abstract Expressionists and maybe he was right. No matter the history, Geist was forgotten because nobody big chose him to be remembered. Some painters can't afford a pot to piss in while others get rich selling their shit and it all depends on which one the patron chooses. Sam had been rather well known in New England and now he was watching his reputation getting erased bit by bit, which is rotten, but that's what happens if you outlive your patrons. Painters fight against invisibility and how long you live is how long the fight goes on. A year or two before Mike Russo died, he and his wife put together all their nickels and dimes to buy their first house and rebuild the attic into a studio, and in the pain of his final months the old revolutionary still dragged himself up the narrow stairway to paint because, he told me, "The object of art is to revolt against death."

As for me, I wasn't getting any younger sitting at this café, so I finally climbed up to my studio. I cut a wedge of cheese, took a handful of olives and walked up and down, reviewing the work I was going to show Sonia Strand, and after thinking about this for a while I went to the back room and dragged out a big bright painting (horizontal nude female across bottom foreground, shutters in middle open to black iron balcony, greenery and blue sky across upper background) which looked like a poster, *Travel To Southern France This Summer*, but might be the only thing she liked. I tucked the bogus thing in among the others, then I lay down for a nap.

I woke up hungry, ate the stale heel from a loaf of scali and decided to make pasta with tomato sauce for supper. I was tossing this and that into the sauce when little Kim comes through the door, announcing that he's going to school tomorrow, and a moment later Avalon comes in, smelling richly of coffee. She drops her black leather jacket on one of the hooks by the door and while one hand still clings to the hook she reaches down with the other and yanks off her boots, *thump, thump*. I asked how her day had gone. "I roasted coffee all day. I mean, I roasted coffee all day after dragging those goddamn sacks of coffee beans from the storeroom. You know how much those things weigh?" She was wearing a sodden T-shirt (DAILY GRIND), stained with sweat and coffee oil. "Look at this," she says, pulling from the jacket pocket a train of wadded white cloth which she shakes magically into a blouse. "I went in wearing this. I thought I was going to waitress. It's filthy!" I told her to take a shower. "Those sacks weigh two hundred pounds, some of them," she informs me, and she goes on to say that Garland— "What's wrong with that woman's nerves?"— told her to enroll Kim in school and to do it tomorrow morning or to not come back to work. Then Avalon pulls the sweatshirt over her head and walks to the back room, using the shirt to mop under her arms as she goes. I told Kim we were going to have pasta with putanesca sauce tonight. "I don't know if I like putanesca sauce," he said. I told him I certainly hoped he would like it and, furthermore, I said, I was going to show him three different kinds of pasta and he could choose which shape he liked best and we'd eat it for dinner. "Well. I guess you'd better let me see them," he said, very businesslike. Kim learned the difference between fusilli, conchigle, and rigatoni, pronouncing the Italian beautifully when he told his mother about pasta shapes at dinner, after which she brought out her paperback *Teach Yourself Japanese* and went over a lesson with him.

24

SONIA STRAND HAD SAID THAT SHE WOULD ARRIVE at ten in the morning. My studio is the only door at the top of the stairs, but after Avalon and Kim had gone out I wrote my name on a big white rectangle of paperboard and tacked it to the outside of the door, then I left the door open a ways and took a shower, put on a fresh shirt, flung open the windows, made a pot of coffee, slammed the windows shut, and drank a mug of coffee while reading *Teach Yourself Japanese*. A little before ten I heard somebody coming briskly up the stairs and I went to the door just as Sonia Strand appeared—wide bush of ruddy gold hair, crystal blue eyes and that dark red mouth not out of breath—we exchanged hellos as she shook my hand and stepped inside. She was alone and I wondered whether that was a good or a bad sign, since most gallery owners appreciate a hireling or other sycophant with whom they can compare notes afterward. I took her cloak, the one with a lining that shimmered like peacock feathers, and asked would she like a mug of coffee, but she gave a large wave of her hand as to brush the offer away and said, "No. I'll get to work right now."

I retreated to the stove and poured another swallow of coffee into my mug while she turned her attention to the paintings, moving herself back and forth a bit in front of the canvas as if to get it in focus. She stood with her fist on her hip and her other hand ever so gently, almost invisibly, slapping a small black notebook against her leg. She was all business but not in a business suit, attired instead in another long columnar dress, this one sleeveless, with a checkered panel of stiff cloth across her bosom, each big square divided diagonally, half black and half white, reminiscent of a Weiner Werkstatte design or the score card for a bowling match.

"These paintings, it's always interesting to see them in their true size," Sonia said a bit later, sounding as if she had a chest cold. "You can tell a lot by looking at a slide, but not everything."

I assented.

"And I like your brushwork, too. That's another thing that never shows up properly in a slide." Now I remembered that the somewhat hoarse baritone was her natural voice.

In ten minutes she had examined most of the paintings whose photos I had brought to the gallery and presently she began to look at the others. I walked over to the canvases and asked did she want me to bring this or that one forward. She waved her hand and said, "You show me." I began shifting the canvases around, letting her look as long as she wanted, of course, before sliding a fresh one to the front. She said nothing but looked with complete steadiness at the work, one hand holding the little notebook, the other hand on her hip or toying with the flat, heart-shaped pendant of silver that hung from a thin chain almost to her waist.

"I wonder, can you take that one out and set it against the wall over there?" she asked.

It was the one that looked like a travel poster; I stood it against the wall.

"No, no," she said. "Turn it so it faces the wall. It's really not any—. I mean, it doesn't—."

I turned it, face to the wall.

"That's better, thank you."

She continued to look at the canvases for a few more minutes, and she asked what name or descriptive phrase I used for this, that, and the other one, which she then jotted in her notebook. She turned to me and smiled broadly. "These are wonderful," she said. "I really like them. I'm impressed by your work. Bold design. Rich colors. I'm impressed. Yes."

There was a space of silence.

"But what?" I asked her.

"No but. There's no but. I admire your work."

"Thank you."

"I noticed some drawings," she said, turning to look at the half-dozen I had taped to the far wall and forgotten.

"Yes."

She strolled over to look at the drawings, one in pencil and one in black crayon, the rest done with a black felt-tipped pen. "You like Klimt or Schiele?" she asked at last. She was looking at the nudes.

"Some of their work, yes."

She turned to me and smiled. "Ever been to Vienna?"

"Not yet."

She came and sat in a kitchen chair and looked around slowly at the studio, taking it in for the first time, and now her gaze lighted on me and lingered, as if I were someone new and interesting. She smiled. "I'd like to have you at the gallery, but I don't know if I can," she said. "Our calendar is filled, unfortunately. But I want to have you. I do want to have you. It's a matter of scheduling. I can't give you anything right now, but I'll look at our calendar and see what's possible. I'll tell you what our plans are and where we might do something. If you'll let me," she added.

"Of course I'll let you," I told her.

"Good! I'm glad you're so professional. Some painters seem not to know how a gallery works. I'm glad you do. You understand the constraints we have to live with."

Now Sonia smiled and tilted her head back, thrusting her hands into that broad mass of reddish gold hair as if it were so tightly packed it hurt her and needed to be loosened, her gesture so open and informal that I took it to mean she felt the difficult part of our meeting was over. She let her hands drop onto her thighs—*slap!*—bringing her flesh to my mind. Her gaze raked across my throat and chest, then returned to my eyes. She seemed to be waiting for me to speak, but I watched only to attend to her whims and didn't want to risk saying the wrong thing, and I wondered if I should ask did she want a mug of coffee now, and in the end all I did was smile at her. She said she supposed that we must have been to some of the same openings and she wondered why we hadn't bumped into each other before. I told her I didn't go to many openings. "Well," she said, "I'm going to send you an invitation to our next opening and I hope you can come."

"Of course I'll come." I went to the stove and refilled my mug with coffee and, as I had my back to her, I spread open my shirt below my throat to show some chest hair, for she seemed to be interested in that. "Can I bring you a cup of coffee?" I asked over my shoulder.

"No, thanks. I have to get back to the gallery now."

I sat in a chair at a polite distance opposite her. She asked did I photograph my work myself, or did I use a professional photographer; I told her I had shot most of them myself and my photographer friend, Michiko, had done the others.

"I could put you in with another painter," Sonia said a moment later. "That's one way of getting you onto the calendar. But I'm afraid your work would overpower hers. You should have a show of your own."

"That would be great."

She had encircled her wrist with her other hand, and now she was idly stroking her arm, arousing the reddish blond hairs. "One of the shows we did last year was devoted entirely to drawings. I wish I had seen your work. Those nudes would have done very well. They're really not nudes," she added, reflecting on them. "They're actually naked men and women. Rather the way Klimt and Schiele drew them."

"That's one way of looking at them," I said, always agreeable.

"It's Klimt who made his models undress only part way—or is it Schiele I'm thinking of?" Her thumb continued slowly to massage the succulent white flesh on the inside of her elbow, stroking a blue vein.

"It doesn't matter. I know what you mean," I assured her.

"They weren't nudes in the classical sense," she said. "They were women who had taken most of their clothes off. They were naked and they knew it and the drawings showed they knew it."

I realized morosely that she wouldn't be interested in seventy-year-old me, but this is how she behaved with the up-and-coming young pricks so eager to get into her gallery, and it had become a habit with her.

"Your drawings are rather like that. Would you agree?" she asked.

I laughed. "Sure! Why not?"

She laughed too. "Exactly. Why not!"

We talked a bit longer and when she started to get to her feet I sprang up, pulled my chair out of the way.

"Thank you for letting me see your work," she said, gathering her cloak over her arm.

"Thank you for coming," I said.

"I'll get back to you in, say—" she broke off. "Well, it will be a few weeks before I can sort things out. But I'll be in touch. Soon."

While we walked down the stairway we talked about Vienna, Viennese cafés, and espresso machines. At the downstairs door we shook hands firmly, then she stepped out into the sun and I trotted back upstairs, happy. I began to haul canvases to the back room, but quit and ran over to the Daily Grind to phone Alba and tell her about Sonia Strand's visit. I told her how Strand had swept in and what she had been wearing and the way she had looked at the paintings and what she had said about getting a place on her calendar and what we had talked about and so forth. That's wonderful! Alba said, and I said, "I think so, I hope so," and Alba said That's terrific, Ren, that's wonderful. I told her which paintings I had put out and we talked back and forth about the Strand Gallery. Before we said goodbye, she told me Astrid had phoned this morning. She's coming to Boston the day after tomorrow, Alba said, and we'll come by the studio to pick you up at one-thirty. All of us, OK? she asked, and I said, "Great. See you then."

25

I DON'T KNOW HOW YOU CAN CONFUSE DRAWINGS BY Gustave Klimt with drawings by Egon Schiele. Schiele's line jerks and cuts like a knife being dragged through flesh —his own, I suspect—whereas Klimt has a fluid, caressing stroke. Schiele made a lot of interesting sketches of young girls, but wasn't careful and eventually got himself a couple of weeks in jail. All I know is, if you let them hang around your studio and do whatever they're forbidden to do at home, like reading a book or eating French fries or whatever, after a while they'll relax and sprawl this way and that and now you've got yourself a spicy little twelve-year-old model, plus a chance at prison time. Klimt was an ass man and said he knew some women whose fannies were more beautiful than their faces, which I believe, and he drew a joke caricature of himself, his head on a body which is all and only a woman's grand rear end. Not my passion, though I can still recall the glossy touch of a certain fresh rump and the kiss I gave her sweet blond asshole. Schiele was born twenty-eight years after Klimt, and twenty-eight years later they both died of influenza in Vienna. People talk about how tormented Schiele was, but to my mind there was more wrong with Klimt, since he never married but fucked all over the place and left fourteen bastard kids to take care of themselves, though maybe that was because he sprouted in claustrophobic hot-house Vienna and not out-of-doors Paris.

I would have relished talking with Mike Bruno about all this, about Sonia Strand and about Klimt and Schiele and Vienna in 1918 and everything else, but poor Michael was dead and there was no one above ground to talk with, certainly no one who would enjoy observations on the buttery privates of twelve-year-old girls or the smooth behinds of their mothers. Alba claims she understands this furnace in my head, and maybe she does, for she used to stoke it herself every other day and throw cold water on it between times. The company of men was what I wanted, so the day after Strand's visit I crossed over to Cambridge to have coffee with a couple of friends. The afternoon was rainy and gusty, and it was pleasant to sit by the café window with these guys (Kadish, McCormac, Winthrop) to watch it rain and to talk of this and that, but I never got around to telling them about Sonia Strand or my hopes to get a show in her gallery, much less how tired the brainless thing was getting. On the way back to Boston I felt so solitary—or maybe you could say I was just lonely for Mike Bruno—anyway, I felt better when Avalon and Kim came in the door.

26

NOW I HAVE TO SAY A FEW THINGS ABOUT ASTRID'S childhood, since she's about to arrive, which means I have to say something about Alba and me and Zoe, for our marriage hasn't been as neat and symmetrical as yours may be and our family is smaller, or larger, than it seems. We first met Zoe in 1968 when she was, let's say, seventeen. Back then my shows were getting good reviews and Alba, more beautiful than ever, was discovering how very much she enjoyed motherhood as long as she could also get out in the world, so out we went, making our way together like a pair of avid explorers. One night at a party Alba came up behind me, saying, "This is Zoe from Maine who's come to Boston to seek her fortune." Beside her was this mini-dress kid with flushed look of an excited child and ironed hair that hung past her shoulders like beaten gold. We shook hands and she said, "Your wife is wonderful, I've been pouring my heart out to her." We took her home with us, lighted the kindling in the fireplace, pulled the sofa cushions onto the floor, smoked a couple of joints and lay in front of the fire to stare at the flames and talk, or not talk but just sprawl together and, sure enough, one amiable caress led to another.

I won't go into details, not even the ones I remember. It turned out that Zoe had done threesomes before, but it was the first time for me and Alba, and it never could have happened—forget my happy dreams and gross appetites— never would have happened except that Alba had become giddy over Zoe and wanted to show off for her, wanted to demonstrate the beauty and power she had recently become sure of, wanted to impress Zoe in exactly that way. Alba will shrug and deny it, say that we were all stoned that night and that she was no more in charge than I was and that, after all, Zoe was the one who had done it before; but no matter what we did in the dark heat of the fire, each of us like a hesitant bather sinking cautiously into a scalding tub, no matter how we turned or paired or rolled in that floating world, I saw Alba putting on the show with Zoe as our conspiratorial voyeur. Afterward we tucked sleepy Zoe under a blanket on the sofa and crept upstairs to bed to be in our proper place for the children, come Sunday morning.

We kept in touch. We had Zoe out to the house for a Sunday brunch, bumped into her at an anti-war rally that spring, and she came with us to a faculty exhibit and a few parties during the summer. And, yes, the three of us played around together more than once, but that fall she met a young man and moved with him to distant Seattle and we assumed we wouldn't see her again. Yet a month later we received a letter from her, beginning *Dear Alba + Renato (or can I say Ren)*, which told about life beside Puget Sound, so Alba began to exchange letters with her and once in a while I sent her a note or, more often, a sketch with a line or two on the back, so

Zoe and I exchanged letters, too, which is how it came about that she had two correspondences, one with Alba and one with me. She had been in Seattle about six months when she wrote us that she had discovered she was pregnant; she felt fine, she said, but she wasn't going to marry the young man, a tidy roommate and traveling companion whom she liked but didn't love and who was already on his way to British Columbia. She'd begun reading a book about religion and decided that she was a deist, because she believed God had created the world but abandoned it and that's why it was such a mess.

Zoe went to nest with her mother in the old house in Penobscot, Maine, the same house her father had fled the day Zoe was born, which exit her mother blamed on Zoe, and after Zoe's baby arrived Zoe moved to Boston and invited us to her place. Her apartment wasn't much more than a closet with a skylight and little Astrid was asleep, bedded in a yellow plastic laundry basket in the corner. Zoe poured three mugs of instant coffee and we sat on rickety chairs around the foot-locker she used for a table. "Astrid's almost eleven months old, actually. Not three months," Zoe told us with a fleeting smile. I was puzzled, that's all. Zoe was kneeling by the basket and now she folded the blanket away from the baby's head, as if to show us that she was, in fact, almost eleven months old. I was about to say, "Time flies," but everything fell to a strange silence and slowness. Zoe drew the sleeping baby ever so gently from the yellow laundry basket and seated herself on a wood kitchen chair, cradling the baby in its blanket. She glanced at me and at Alba, then lowered her head to the baby and her face glowed, as if the baby were a lighted candle. Alba had not moved. "She was born in Seattle," Zoe told us, looking up. "I should—I would have said something, told you, but I. You both. I'm sorry. I didn't know what to do." Alba didn't move but asked Zoe what she was telling us, and Zoe confesses she was already three months pregnant and knew it when she left for Seattle, then Alba slowly asks Zoe does she need to tell us anything else, and Zoe says no, nothing else, and at last every-thing comes to a stop and I ask Zoe, "Am I the baby's father?" and Zoe looks at me and says yes. Alba's lips were pale, her face white. "What do we do now?" Alba asked.

None of us knew what to do. Alba and I drove home in silence and later that night as we were undressing for bed she turned to me and spoke for the first time. "I have only one question," she said. She was naked, with her arms across her breasts and her hands tucked into her armpits as if she were chill. "Did you ever get together with Zoe when I wasn't there?" she asked. Her face had turned to stone. I said, "No," which was the truth. She looked at me, then she dropped her hands and turned to get into bed and I said, "I'm Astrid's father and that means—" but she cut me off, saying, "I know what that means."

We told the kids. Fabrizio was two years old and didn't care one way or the other about this trivial infant, whereas Skye was six and happy to have a baby sister, accepting as an-other grown-up oddity that her sister had me for a father and Zoe for a mother—though she did privately question Alba about it and some days later questioned Zoe about it, too, before being satisfied that this genealogy was known and un-derstood all around. We got our parents together: my mother clapped her hand to her forehead and burst into Italian, say-ing I already had a good wife and now I was ruining every-thing, then my father twice cleared his throat as if to speak but said nothing, while Alba's mother looked alternately an-gry and bewildered.

On days when I wasn't there, Alba had Zoe and the baby come to our house, for Alba can be wonderfully generous, devi-ous and calculating, all at the same time, though she can't tell you which is which. I don't know what went on in her mind, nor do I know how Zoe felt about Alba, how much was friend-ship or gratitude and how much was strategy. As for Alba and me, we slept on opposite sides of the bed for a few weeks and when, later, we did make love it was stark as knives. Then one Sunday—I don't know how deeply she planned this or if she simply had a whim—Alba had Zoe and the baby Astrid come to Sunday breakfast with all of us, so my whole family was together for the first time. And that night, for reasons I don't understand, I was aroused mindlessly, as if by Alba in heat, and I caught her in the bedroom and didn't quite get to the bed but took her to the floor, which pleased her just fine.

Now, as everyone tells me, Alba is a beautiful and easygoing woman, but let's be clear about this, Alba likes to manage people and she was managing the three of us so well there were moments I suspected she was enjoying herself more than she let on. She informed me one night that they had agreed Astrid would be baptized in May, that Alba would be godmother and that I should ask Mike Bruno or somebody to be godfather. After the baptismal party little Astrid stayed mostly with us, with our kids, while her mother took courses at Mass Art every morning and waitressed the rest of the day, spending her nights in a sleeping bag at a friend's place in Boston or, on weekends, in our fold-out bed. Zoe took Astrid and decamped to Boulder for a while, returned to Boston, left for Los Angeles (we had Astrid each summer), came back to Boston, moved to Taos (now we had Astrid during the school year) and settled in Boston, during which fifteen or twenty years she had two marriages, two divorces and one miscarriage. Amid all her coming and going I had grown fond of her, and I told her so. "And I, of you," she said.

Alba believes that if you're a romantic you love only one person because the one you love is so radiant and blinding you can't even see the rest of the world, but if you're not a romantic and not blind you can be in love with two or three at once. "It happens," she says with a shrug. Zoe doesn't think so. "No, no, it's the other way around," says Zoe. "It's the romantic who tries to love more than one at a time, but it's all make-believe. Because in this world, in my world anyway, we're selfish and vain and jealous. We want to be loved and we don't want to share."

27

WHEN I OPENED THE DOOR TO ASTRID'S SHARP knock-knock she gave me a tight hug, saying, "Hi, dad, let's go," and pulled me by the hand, the same as when she was seven, clattering breakneck down the stairs and out to the sidewalk where Zoe and Alba stood waiting beside a big yellow taxi. "Now we're all together," she declared. Astrid is a good-looking young woman and that's a fact: her hair was drawn back as tight and glossy as a chestnut fresh from the tree, her face angular and windswept, a streak of color on each cheek—our accelerated daughter. I gave her another hug, throwing my arm around her back and pressing her sharp shoulder blades to feel if she had enough flesh on her (she didn't), taking in the breezy scent she used. "Let me look at you," I said, backing off. Zoe said She's as beautiful as ever, and Alba said She's stylish too, and all the while I was thinking she's skinny as a stick. "Let's go," Astrid said, holding open the door to the big yellow cab.

As we rattled toward the restaurant Zoe prompted her to continue telling about the conference she had gone to this morning, so Astrid told us how well it had gone and who she was going to meet this afternoon, but before she could say very much we had arrived at the eatery, a glassy high-speed place with a continuous row of bars—salad bar, fruit bar, juice bar, bread bar, and so on—followed by a long dining bar, which meant you entered at this end, chose your food, ate it further along, and went out the other end. "Is this place designed like my digestive tract, or have I've got a terrible imagination?" Zoe asked. The women discussed Astrid's black velvet jacket and her white silk blouse, and it gave me an odd pinch in the heart to see how more aged Zoe and Alba looked now that Astrid was here. When I got the chance I asked my daughter about her current film project, and she told us about it and told us a lot more about trying to raise money to finance it, and went on about a young man, whom she had met last week, who owned *TrendSetters* or some other trash magazine and he knew people who had money to invest in movies. Later Astrid told us about a great party where she had met Abdi, the celebrated hair dresser— "And, mother, let me repeat that I do like the way you've cut your hair," she said—and Cindi Ross, the high-fashion model, and Ricardo Carlos, the same Carlos who had invented a new dance step last year. While Astrid was talking about the party, Zoe and Alba had glanced sideways at each other, then Zoe composed herself and said she knew the party must have been exciting but that, frankly, those people sounded, well, flashy and emp-ty. Astrid replied that no, actually, Cindi was a hard worker; then she smiled and slid her hands slowly across the table to grasp her mother's hands. "Don't worry about me. I can take care of myself," she confided.

We left the dining bar and as I was going out the door be-side Astrid I asked her, "How's life?" and she said, "You mean how's my private life, right?" and I said, "Right," and she said, "By the way, dad, speaking of private lives, how much longer do you plan to camp out at your studio?" I told her I wasn't camping out, I was living there so maybe I could do some real work before I died, and she said don't be so morbid; then Alba spoke up behind us, telling her that we were still look-ing for country property. "Yeah, well, I've heard that before," Astrid said, pausing so Alba and Zoe could join us. Alba and I insisted we were telling her the truth. "I hope so. And so does everyone else. Especially your children," Astrid said. In the taxi Alba asked had she heard anything from Brizio or Skye, and she said yes, she had gotten a long letter from Skye describing an expedition Skye and Eric had taken up some mountain in Indonesia, and yes, she and Brizio talked on the phone about once a month to catch up on things, and no, she didn't know if Brizio was planning to return to physics or to continue building solar houses, but she did know he enjoyed working outdoors.

When we got to Copley Square, we three got out of the cab so Astrid could drive downtown to her conference, then Astrid got out too, to say goodbye to us, we thought, but instead she stood by the open door, squinting in the sun, and she said, "Oh, by the way, you remember Harry?" She meant the randy old photographer she had lived with a few years ago, a widower decades her senior; we said yes, we remembered. "You remember I went to his funeral?" And we said, yes, we remembered that, too. "Yeah. Well. Anyway, you remember how I met his son at the funeral—actually, we had met before but we got reacquainted at the funeral—and how we had dinner together a month later?" No, we hadn't remembered that. "Yes, you do," she insisted. "His name is Wes and I'm sure I told you. Anyway, we had dinner, you know, and then we had dinner again a couple of days later, and so on."

She stood on the sidewalk with one hand atop the open door of the taxi, the other hand shading her eyes from the sun, and she smiled at us, waiting.

"And so on?" I said.

"And so we've kept seeing each other," she concluded, smiling. Alba said, "Oh, you mean—" and Zoe said, "You like him," and Astrid said, "Yup. I really like him and he really likes me." I asked did Wes know that Astrid had lived with his father, and she said, "Of course he does. I'm the one who convinced Harry to make up with him. When I moved in they hadn't spoken to each other for over a year." Zoe asked what his name was. "Wes, mother, Wes. It's short for Weston. And this—Wes and me—this is different." She smiled briefly, her sober gaze shifting from Zoe to me to Zoe. "I thought

I should tell you." She tossed her head and raked a thin hand through her hair, then she laughed, her face becoming luminous. "That's wonderful," Zoe told her, and I said, "Yes. Great. That's great, Astrid."

"He's just right," Astrid told me. "You'll like him." Then she gave her mother an impulsive hug and kiss, gave me and Alba a kiss, squeezed my hand and ducked into the cab, waving goodbye, her phone already in her other hand as the cab shoved off. Zoe had taken a step into the street to watch the cab disappear into traffic and when she came back she asked if Astrid had ever told me about Wes or Weston or whatever his name was, and I said no, but I admitted that I had never been able to keep track of her friends, not even when she was in high school. Alba said she hadn't heard about Wes before today, but that Astrid certainly looked happy about him. Zoe and I discussed Weston for a while, then Zoe said, "Astrid always knows what she's doing when it comes to men, even when she's doing the wrong thing, and she wouldn't say this one was different from the others if he wasn't, so, well, anyway—" She broke off and looked to me for help. "He's different from the others and that's a good thing," I said. Alba suggested that we wait and see. We debated a little longer but in the end we all agreed to wait and see, because Astrid wasn't a kid anymore but a smart young woman and, besides, there wasn't anything else we could do.

28

GOD CREATED ADAM AND EVE AFTER WORKING FOR five and a half days on everything else, because he wanted spectators to his achievement, needed at least a couple of people to say, "Oh, wow! That's *great!*" because above all else God is an artist, creator of heaven and earth and all things, as the Catechism says, and creators want others to enjoy and appreciate their works and would like themselves to be admired for their handiwork. It's a long and lonely trek to that place where you paint not for viewers who never come, but simply because you can, because you're good at it, and because there's pleasure in making the vision visible. It's a place you go to when there's no place else to go. God wouldn't have liked it there and neither do I.

Now, these days the prospect of my show at a good Newbury Street gallery energized me so much I would walk up and down, jittery in front of the canvass, trying to calm down enough to paint. There were mornings I felt in me the powerful legs—hindquarters I could say—of my great, great grandfather, the Cavallù who was man from the waist up and stallion from the waist down, but that's a story for another day and, besides, I'm his great, great grandson only by adoption. Every morning I'd trot a mile or two beside the Charles, then scramble up the stairs two at a time to my studio, eat breakfast and begin painting and keep painting until I was about to drop, at which time I'd stretch myself out on the floor to rest.

Once I fell asleep there and woke up with Avalon crouched over me, her ear to my chest and her fingers searching for my carotid artery while Kim stood in the doorway, his eyes big as saucers. "Christ! I thought you were dead!" she cried angrily. "Not yet," I told her. I got up and stumbled around and began to prepare dinner. Avalon watched me and when I fumbled a pan into the sink she said, "Hey, I'll cook," but I said, "No, thanks," and waved her off because, frankly, Avalon didn't know how to cook. Whenever she prepared dinner it turned into a bowl of noodles or a soggy mix of chopped vegetables and rice and, no, I didn't believe her when she said it was because Kim needed more practice with chopsticks. I was buying the food and she was paying for half of it; she made breakfast, I cooked dinner. But that evening we began to work the stove together and every evening after that I tried to teach her some Mediterranean dishes. "First of all, olive oil," I told her, holding up a bottle from Tuscany.

"Extra virgin," she says, reading the label. "You're either a virgin or not, so what kind of crap is an *extra* virgin?"

I asked her did she know what virgin olive oil was. "Pure," she says. "No," I informed her. "Pure is the grade below virgin. You get extra virgin by pressing unbruised olives. Virgin is more acid than extra virgin and—"

"Wait, wait! Let me guess. The less virgin you are, the more *acid* you are," she says, laughing at her own witticism.

"The important thing is taste," I told her, undeflected. "Extra virgin is like wine. It has a taste and a color from the soil where it grows. —Are you listening?" And so forth every evening.

Actually, Avalon listened more carefully than I guessed and caught on faster than I expected. "She's a worker," Gordon told me at the Daily Grind. "Doesn't talk much. Doesn't smile much, either. But she works," he said. I watched her drag a huge burlap sack of coffee beans across the floor toward the roaster. She was in her Army camouflage pants, baggy things mottled with green and khaki and black, and a white swim-top, her bare arms and shoulders glistening with sweat. "Everything stops when her kid comes in, so she can look at his school work and tell him what a great one he is. But she gets the job done," he told me. "Did you see her jewelry we've got by the cash register? She asked if she could sell it there and we said yes."

"Of course I've seen it. She wears a lot of it on her face."

"If you don't like her, why do you let her live at your place?"

"I didn't say I didn't like her. I just don't like her in my studio."

Which is why I visited Michiko Shimada. She sometimes rented out part of her place and, frankly, I was hoping to move Avalon and her kid out of my studio to anywhere else. I liked Michiko. She had come to this country from Osaka about a ten years ago with her camera and not much more, had worked at odd jobs (waitress, artist's model, teacher of Japanese) and had established herself as a photographer. I don't think I'd heard her say five words in a row about abstractions such as politics or esthetic theory, but she brought a deep engagement to anything she looked at and was herself worth looking at, her body a stylized rendition of a body, the long mass of her hair a single brush stoke of black ink, the breasts and buttocks indicated by pale shadows, and that face a smooth bronze sheet on which were inscribed her lips, nose and eyes.

Now she opened the door to her studio and we exchanged Konnichi wa. She smiled broadly, a brilliant oblong smile, and said something that I didn't understand. I said Foku de tabemasho—let's eat with forks—meaning I'd used up all my Japanese. She made tea, we looked at her photos, talked about this and that, and I discovered Renato wasn't going to say anything about Avalon and Kim because, after all, he liked Machiko and didn't want to mess up her studio, her work and her life. As I was leaving, I invited her to dinner at my place and told her I had somebody she might like to meet. "Yes, thank you. And who is this somebody you want me to meet?" she asked. "Two somebody's," I told her. "A small boy and his mother." I don't know when I had begun to think that maybe she could hire Avalon as an assistant.

•

One afternoon I was working when Zoe turned up to say Hi, and I said Hi, and went back to take a couple more swipes at the canvas, and she said Well, do you? and I said What? and she said I've already asked you twice—do you want to take a break now or do you want me to leave? and I said Yeah, and added maybe another brush stoke, and she said Yes to which? and I said Yeah, I need a break now. So Zoe turned to make coffee and I began to clean up and I was surveying the canvas when Zoe said, "What did you do with the coffee canister? And where did you put the grinder? Where is everything?" and that's when I knew I had better tell her about Avalon and Kim.

So I brought out the fancy Italian mugs Zoe had given me and set our chairs by the window, and there we drank coffee and took biscotti from a plate on the window sill while I waited for a good moment to tell her about Kim and his mother. Zoe said she was through for the day because nobody would call with a job late on a Friday afternoon and, anyway, she added, a nasty pain had developed again in her upper back, just at the edge of her wing bone, and she couldn't work anymore, even if she wanted to, and she didn't want to — only then did it break through my skull that Zoe had come here to yield herself to whatever comfort I might offer.

Now, one way to undo Zoe is to undo her knotted muscles. So I unrolled the frayed old futon while Zoe stepped out of her shoes, hung her jacket and blouse on a chair. She stretched herself face down on the futon, resting her cheek on her arm. "Do with me what you will," she said into the crook of her elbow. I unfastened her bra and began to massage her back, first smoothing the bra lines, then sliding my thumbs up into her trapezius and finally rolling the small muscle that edges her wing bones, that last causing her to groan with pleasure and to close her eyes. Later she turned her head to rest her cheek on the back of her hand, murmuring, "I've been meaning to ask, what's this taped line on the floor for?" That's when I told her about Kim and Avalon. Zoe didn't say a word. I massaged a bit longer, then slapped her clothed rump and dismounted. "The girl sounds like a tramp," Zoe said sharply. She sprang up and began to fasten her bra, keeping her back to me. I put my hand gently to the nape of her neck but she jumped away. "This is a bad time of the month for me, so fuck off," she said. She stepped into her shoes and strode to the back room, took a look around, returned. "I don't know how Alba stands you," she said, buttoning her blouse.

"Come on, Zoe."

"I'm tired and I'm annoyed. Hope you get along with the little boy," she added, snatching up her jacket. "Bye."

I got along well with the little boy. Kim was a good kid, if you had to have a kid living in your studio. I had given him a ream of cheap paper and a box of colored markers and after dinner, after he had finished his homework, he would stay seated at the kitchen table, drawing energetically and talking about what he was drawing, which was never trucks or dinosaurs, but diagrams, maps and floor plans. He drew the layout of his schoolroom for me, an elaborate plan which showed the location of the teacher's desk, his own desk, his friend Kevin's desk, the art supply closet, the big maps (these were shown in detail), the fish, the flower box, The Flag of the United States of America, and for his mother he drew an equally detailed plan view of the Daily Grind with the cash register, coffee roaster, coffee bags and café tables properly arrayed and labeled.

I had to go to Gloucester to rescue three paintings which had been languishing in the ratty back room of a gallery since last fall, so I drove up on a Saturday and brought Kim and his mother along to give them a change of scene. After I had stashed the paintings in the wagon, I drove up and down Gloucester hill, showed them Our Lady of Good Voyage with a fishing boat in the crook of her strong arm like it was baby Jesus (a wood statue I love) showed them where Gina used to have her café, then down to the harbor to walk out on the wharves, and over to the Fitz Hugh Lane house ("The only painter who could paint silence," I tried to tell Avalon) and to a shop so she could buy an absolutely necessary picture postcard of the harbor. After lunch we walked along a deserted stretch of Good Harbor beach, Kim racing up and down the hard sand while his mother searched for sea shells, then home to the studio just as a gusty rain blew in from the Northeast. The steep little town isn't the way it used to be when I was growing up, when the harbor was busy with

fishing boats and seas were crowded with cod, but I could see
Kim and Avalon liked it and had a great time.

•

As planned, Michiko Shimada came to dinner. I introduced
Kim, who shook her hand in a grownup way, saying politely,
"Hello, I'm pleased to meet you." And a moment later Avalon
came from the back room, barefoot and in black velvet shorts
belted with a chromium dog chain, a black elastic jersey top
(very tight) and around her neck a black leather dog collar
with pointed chrome studs. "Yay! Mom's all dressed up!" Kim
exclaimed, delighted. I forgot to mention the pale lipstick and
the thick black eyeliner. I introduced Michiko and Avalon
to each other. Michiko smiled and said, "It's a pleasure to
meet you," but Avalon had already turned away, saying, "Yeah,
I'll get the wine." Kim went back to drawing his Metro map
while we three stood at the window, wine glass in hand, and
discussed the weather or, to be precise, Michiko and I discussed the weather while Avalon remained silent, as if ab-
sorbed in listening to us, her sharp gaze slicing back and forth
from Michiko to me and back again. We sat down to dinner,
the chrom neck studs and facial rings glittering in the candle
light, and as soon as everyone's plate had been filled Avalon
pointed her knife at Michiko, saying, "You're wondering what
I'm doing here." She lowered the knife, her face seeming to
push slightly forward toward Michiko. "I fit in fine here. No
matter what anybody thinks, even if they think they're old
friends with Renato."

I stiffened in my chair, hoping not to slap Avalon's face,
and Michiko, her lips parted, hesitated to speak.

Kim announced, "I can name all the stops on the Red Line
and the Green Line." He looked around the table, cheerful
and expectant.

"That's *great!*" I told him, slapping the table top. "Let's
hear them. Right now."

"Only the main line, not the branches," he said. Then he recited all the stops from Alewife to Braintree on the Red and from Lechmere to Riverside on the Green. Avalon watched her son avidly, her hand hovering an inch above the table, ready to caress his head the moment he finished.

"An intelligent young man," Michiko said.

"He knows Japanese," Avalon told her. "Please, Kim, count in Japanese."

At his mother's prompting Kim rattled off the numbers and the dozen or so words and phrases that made up his Japanese vocabulary. "Ah, good, very good," Michiko told him, smiling. "Yoku dekimashita ne! Yoku dekimashita," she said. Now Avalon smiled, told Michiko a little about Kim, swapped anecdotes with her about San Francisco, told her about her job with a photographer, drank down a third glass of wine, relaxed. The dinner went well and long after Kim had said, Can I be excused? and gone off to fall asleep over his maps, we sat there talking into the night. Our Avalon had become quite talkative, annoyingly so. She asked Michiko had she ever heard of sel gris or fleur de sel. No, Michiko hadn't. "Renato is teaching me about salt. He lectured me about olive oil and about vinegar, now it's salt. Sel is French for salt."

"Oh, *sel*, yes!" Michiko said. "I was taught some French in school."

"He's teaching me how to cook Mediterranean because, like, we're a family."

I looked at Avalon, hoping my stare would shut her up or at least slow her down.

"We're not fucking or anything like that," Avalon said.

"*For Christ sake, Avalon!*" I said.

"I have to think about my reputation. I don't want people to get the wrong idea."

"I know Renato for a long time. I won't get the wrong idea." Michiko smiled. "Not to worry, Avalon."

Afterward, after Michiko had left and we were at the sink,

Avalon asked was Michiko as nice as she seemed. "Yes, I said. "She is. She's very nice."

"Are you fucking her?"

I stopped and looked at her. "What's *wrong* with you?"

"There's nothing wrong with me," says Avalon.

"Yes, there is. You dress like a whore and you're rude and you're insulting. And since you're so concerned with your reputation, which is laughable, you should move out."

Avalon's face went blank. She lifted her chin, then carefully hung the dish towel on the rack and went to bed without another word.

They didn't move out. Kim went to school, Avalon went to work. The prospect of my having a show on Newbury Street had energized me, so scores of new paintings blossomed in my head, and not only paintings but also drawings, tile designs, wood sculpture, a type-face and lines for a poem on my prostate. I'd get up early, trot by the river which would still be asleep and gray as glass, then back to the studio to paint, which I was doing better than anyone.

29

YOU CAN DRAW BY PISSING ON SNOW OR BY USING a computer, but pissing on snow is better because your art will express your humanity and mean something to anyone who sees it, so I would not have gone to the opening of *Pixels: An Exhibit of Computer Art* except that my friend Nils Petersen had some work in it and had asked me to come. Alba and I arrived to a thin crowd of mostly young people who knew one another and didn't want to talk with anyone old, so we passed invisibly among them to view the computer prints and to look at the screens' endlessly repeating images. After the tour we made small talk with Nils and his wife

Hanna, during which I told Nils his work was the best in the show and I praised his multitudinous colors, which pleased him, I hope, then Alba and I visited the wine-and-cheese table which displayed not only wine and cheese but also platters of cold cut meats, gorgeous hillocks of sliced fruit, and a handsome young woman pouring white wine into a row of flimsy plastic glasses. More people arrived, including some from Copley College, and we had a pleasant chat with Azarig and his wife Anna, then later we bumped into Marc, a friend whose poetry I can't decipher, and his wife Simone, a performance artist, but forgivable because of her verve and knock-out good looks. Zoe arrived, greeted Alba with a great hug and me with a hasty hug followed by a quick turn away to dramatize her annoyance with me.

Later Alba and I talked with Sebastian Gabriel, accompanied as usual by his young daughter Kate, a gangly girl with braids and an eager smile, braces on her teeth. Sebastian is one of the finest papermakers in New England (he made the paper I used for my Genesis series) but thin, disorganized and failing at business since his wife walked out on him. I asked Kate if I could bring her a ginger ale and she said yes, then followed me to the soft-drinks. We conversed, agreeing that the animated computer designs were kind of dull but that it was interesting to meet all these artists. Katie sipped her ginger ale and told me, "My father makes beautiful papers, you know, but computers can't print on my father's paper. I don't know what we're going to do. He says we'll get by, but I worry about him. He's impractical, you know." I told her that great artists would junk computers and work by hand in order to use her father's beautiful paper, and I asked what she had been reading recently, for I knew she was an avid reader, and she told me about a five-volume story by Lloyd Alexander, the same epic my daughter Skye had loved, so we talked about that brave tale or, rather, she talked while I listened and smiled and nodded, remembering Skye when she was that age.

I took another stroll around the gallery and discovered that most of the artists in the show used to design book jackets or advertisements, not that I deprecate the work of graphic artists; indeed, from my father I learned to admire particularly the work of Eric Gill, the British craftsman who designed the famous Gill sans serif typeface and who also cut clean and supple wood engravings, a religious man who took to wearing monks' robes, though I was disappointed to learn that he fucked not only his daughters but his dog, too. A while later Azarig and a witless cyberhead named Roth and I got into a discussion about the giclée reproduction method where prints are stored in digital form and then squirted onto paper by a computerized urinary machine. Azarig remarked that storing a print in digital form saved a lot of space and Roth began to rhapsodize about the technology of digital printers and about this great computer artist and that great video artist, and so on and so forth, and eventually he got around to asking had I made any use of these exciting new print processes. "Look," I told him. "Printing means scratching something up, smearing it with paint, then pressing it onto paper with your hands or your feet. It takes a certain skill. What you're talking about is machined crap." After which surly declaration I hunted around for Alba and finally spied her seated languidly and somewhat fatigued in a corner with Zoe who was talking and laughing, flashing her hands about as if she were juggling invisible balls in a private entertainment for the two of them, a typical Zoe maneuver when she's sore at me

I ended up at the wine table and while the young woman was pouring bogus Chablis into my plastic glass I asked her what she did in real life. "I'm an environmental scientist," she said, handing me the drink. "During the day I take the temperature of Boston Harbor but it doesn't pay much, so I do this one night a week. What about you? What are you in real life?" she asked. So we talked about personal identity and true life and after a while I began to think how our Brizio, living in disguise as a builder of solar houses, might like this comely scientist, for I certainly did, when a skinny young lout came up and said, "Mr Stillamare, I'm Frank Vanderzee. I admire your work and I was wondering if you were going to have a show where I could see more of it."

"You want to talk to me or to Winona here?" I asked him.

He had a good-natured smile. "You, actually."

"I've seen you someplace."

"Drinking coffee at the Daily Grind," he said.

"Yes, and you're a painter. —You need to eat more."

He smiled again. "If you could visit my place some time I'd like to show you what I've been doing."

He looked like a nice guy, but I had no wish, none at all, to see his work or anyone else's. I would have returned to my ontological chat with Winona but she had moved to the other end of the table, so I was stuck talking with this Vanderzee (chest hair boiling from the V of his shirt) and eventually I said I'd drop around to his place one of these days.

Later I was talking with Sebastian when Alba came up to tell me she wasn't feeling well—she was going home and did I want a ride back to my studio or did I want to stay here and find my own way home. I asked was it a headache or an upset stomach or what, and she said it felt like being seasick with a high fever and now all she wanted was to go to bed. I walked with her to her car—it had rained, the air was sweet and the sidewalk smelled of washed stone—told her I'd phone in the morning, then she drove off to Cambridge while I returned to the gallery, for though I dislike going to these gathering I also dislike leaving them, and there I had another hour of company before I made a midnight walk back to my studio, a pleasant walk on clean, drying streets, but also melancholy, because it reminded me of the homeward walks we used to take when we were young and the city was new.

The next morning I drove over to Alba's concrete dovecote, knocked on the door and waited, then let myself in. She

looked dead in bed, propped up by two pillows with her eyes
sunk shut and her arms just two peeled sticks on the blanket,
her face as still and white as an old fashioned mortuary photograph. "Hey, Alba!" I croaked, shaking the bed, frightened.
Her eyes opened, passive and uninterested. "I'll call the doctor," I told her. She shook her head no, whispered that she
had thrown up during the night but felt better now, just tired,
then she closed her eyes. Her forehead was hot and sweaty.
I phoned the doctor and made an appointment for the following afternoon, which was the soonest I could get, then I
drove back to the studio, left a note for Avalon, stuffed some
clothes into an overnight bag and drove back to Alba's. The
doctor listened to her chest, diagnosed pneumonia, cheerfully
wrote out a prescription which he said was for a new, powerful medicine. Sometimes I watched Alba while she slept
and knew my life would be over if she ever died. During the
day I caught up on my reading, at night I rolled myself in a
blanket on the bedroom floor and went to sleep; after seven
days Alba's fever abated and I drove back to the studio, made
a note that Alba should have a chest x-ray and I should have
my annual physical, then dove into painting again.

30

OF COURSE, THE PAINTING DIDN'T ALWAYS GO WELL.
There were times when I suspected I'd done my best
work years ago and, as I hadn't been able to make a name for
myself back then, I felt it was useless to go on now and, in
fact, there were days when I didn't paint at all, or painted badly and made such a mess there was nothing to do but punch
my stupid fist through the canvas and kick the stretcher to
bits. A couple of decades ago I had done a series depicting
a group of three people—some showed a woman and two

men, others displayed two women and a man—where one figure was clothed and at least one other was unclothed, a psychological arrangement that critics said was derived from Giorgione by way of Manet, which was agreeable to me and profitable too, though in fact they were inspired by something else, and now in one of my lousy canvases I was trying to assemble a group of older figures, some of them unclothed, but the thing was no good.

Avalon and Kim were distracting me. There's the tent Kim made from an easel and a blanket, a teepee that stood in the studio for a week while he and his friend Anwar played at being Navahos, and here on the counter are a dozen of Avalon's bite-size buttons for me to swallow and choke on, and her blouse with a threaded needle through the cuff and, for all I know, three other invisible needles scattered where I slice my bread, and there's her underpants and bra hanging from the shower-head and, wedged between two of her cologne bottles, this sheaf of old papers, *my* sheaf of old papers, the reading list hand-written and annotated by my uncle Zitti. "What are you so grumpy about? It's only a book list, for Christ sake. I was only looking at it. I wasn't going to erase anything," she complained. *"Don't pry into my things!"* I told her, which was hopeless, since the back room where she and Kim slept was where I stored most everything. And here's Kim again, cross-legged in front of my father's open tool chest, a row of stone chisels on the floor arranged according to size; I explained the use of each one as I retrieved it, then I padlocked the chest. And here's Avalon, saying, "Why don't you talk to me? You're always writing letters. Every night, scribble, scribble, scribble." You might try it yourself, I say, shoving a sheet of stationery across the table at her. "Oh, sure. Who would I write to?" All right, so she had no one to write to. And when I needed to take a break, needed to go out to converse or go brood by myself, I couldn't enjoy the Daily Grind because Avalon would be there, trying to get the espresso machine to detonate, hauling sacks of beans or tending the roaster, her face glistening with sweat and her jersey—*my* jersey!—sagging dark and damp between her breasts and under her arms.

One night I got in late and there was Avalon, propped against my pillow on my bed, one of my old sketchbook-journals open on her lap, for at one time I had thought all artists kept notebooks and I had tried to keep one. I asked what the hell she was doing. "Kim's asleep and I didn't want to wake him with a light, so I'm reading out here," she explained, setting her wine glass on the floor.

"No, damnit!" I said, slamming the journal shut and yanking it from her. "Why are you reading this?"

"I was just looking at—" she began.

"Don't snoop!" I told her.

"I wasn't snooping, I just hap—"

"Does the word privacy mean anything to you?"

"You know, Ren, you'd be a lot nicer if you'd just loosen—"

"And you should ask before wearing my clothes!"

Avalon jumped up, grabbed her sweater at the neck and though I told her *Keep it, keep it, you can keep that one!* she was already pulling it over her head and threw it at me.

One night I was at the kitchen table writing a letter to my brother Bart when Avalon sat down across from me with a couple of books, but I went on scribbling and didn't look up. "Want to see my pictures?" she said briskly. I finished my sentence and gnawed on my pen awhile, trying to grapple the next clump of words, but Avalon stayed waiting so finally I gave up and looked at her. She had two small photo albums, the kind that hold one snapshot per page. "I know you're paranoid about being interrupted but it's getting late and I thought you'd like to look at my pictures." She was sitting up straight and businesslike with a hand flat on each album. Abruptly she dragged her chair around to my side—"Move over a bit," she said—slid my letter away and laid a shiny pink album in front of me. "I have lots of photos and you'll recognize my dad right away, of course," she told me, flipping open the cover. There were a few black-and-white photos of Avalon's father, Brendan Flood (puzzled smile, bushy hair), holding squinty toddler Avalon in his arms, then some color snapshots of Avalon standing alone on a brown lawn which looked like it had the mange, though the colors were so faded I couldn't see for sure, then pages of brighter color pics of Avalon and her father and the empty silhouette of another person who had been carefully scissored out, a neat decoupage which left not even a sliver of Sandra, the airhead, or Linda, the bitch.

Avalon said a few words about each photo — "That's me at the beach," or "That's us at the redwood forest," or "That's me again." — which explained nothing, and though I tried to focus on the dumb images I grew increasingly aware of Avalon sitting close against my side, her bare arm grazing mine each time she turned a page. We must have finished the pink album, for she closed it and placed in front of me the glazed lilac one. These photos were the same as the earlier ones except that little Avalon (blondish hair, by the way) was getting thinner, taller and more awkward, and she was making friends — "That's me and Jenny," or "That's Diego's band," or "That's Charlotte and me and Valerie," or "That's me in Diego's car." — page after page after page. Then she turned the last page, closed the glazed lilac cover and turned to me. I had never seen her so close before, the wire rings along the rim of her tender ear, the miniature rivet that pierced the delicate flair of her nose, the loops of wire through her eyebrow, and her eyes — the blue iris with smoky black specks which, for a moment, gave me the weird sense of being at the bottom of a deep well, staring up at the sky. She was looking at me in a needful, pleading way which I'd never seen her use before, as if now I were supposed to say something or do something, and I wondered if she expected me to kiss her for showing me the photo albums. I didn't move and she said, "How come you never introduce me to your wife or that Zoe person?"

"You're not going to be here that long," I told her. She stared blankly at me a moment, then swept up her albums and went to the back room. I finished the letter to my brother, then washed and went to bed, but didn't get to sleep right away and instead I thought about Avalon back there on the mattress, curled around Kim, and thought how strange she was and I wondered what misalignment of the stars had brought it about that she was here, what cosmic machinery had busted and left her and her bastard kid living in my studio. I knew Avalon was desirable in her way, though you wouldn't have seen it, and Alba came to mind and I thought how luxurious our love-making had become and later it was Zoe I was thinking about, which should have confused me, but by then I was drifting and so drifted to sleep.

One night I came home from Zoe's and saw that Avalon had stuck something big as a pasta bowl flat against the studio wall. "What's *that?*" I ask her. She says it's an air purifier. "What are you talking about? And who are you to nail anything to my wall?"

"It's an air purifier. It takes the poisons out of the air, because the—" she begins.

"What poisons? Are you out of your little mind?"

"The poisons are toxins that come from your paints. This place smells of paint and you've lived here too long to notice. Paint has toxins that—"

"I know about paint. I've been painting all my life. I'm a goddamned professor of paint."

"I read in—"

"Don't injure your mind with reading." I pull the *Artists' Air Sponge* from the wall and begin loosening the stump that stays behind.

"Kim is a growing boy. If he breathes toxins—"

"He won't breathe toxins."

"He sleeps in a room with a hundred big paintings stacked

against the wall. I keep the windows open as much as I can in there, but it gets cold at—hey! What are you doing? That's mine!" she cries and snatches the *Artists' Air Sponge* from the big trash can.

Winthrop has no sense of smell and says it's the turpentine that did it to him, but I suspect it's the same ailments as have already turned his nerves into a tangle of sparks and dead wires, because my nose is still all right. There was a time when I did use lacquer paints and, in fact, I was crazy about them because I could float one delicious color on top of another, but the lacquers tainted the air and twice Alba found me knocked out on the floor and had to drag me by my armpits from the studio, so after the second time she said, "No more lacquers!" and that was the end of that.

On one of those days when things were going badly I threw my brush across the room and hunted up Winthrop to have lunch with. When I got back to the studio Avalon was in the middle of the floor, scooping up her scattered photo collection. "How come you're home at this hour?" I asked her. She had scrambled to her feet. "The coffee roaster. Gordon's fixing it. He said I could take the rest of the day off. It broke down again," she said, her cheeks glowing, her eyes darting this way and that. I saw the old blanket chest at the foot of my bed was open, so I knew the photos were my snapshots of Alba—half dressed, costumed or naked—and the loose envelopes on my bed were my letters. "Get out," I told her. Avalon held the photos out to me and they went flying when I grabbed her wrist. "I showed you *mine!*" she cried, jamming her heels against the floorboards. I had already turned away and was dragging her to the open door. "You can't do this, Ren!" I swung her hard and shoved, but she whirled— "You can't do this, you shit!"—and whacked my face hard, stinging. I began to pry her fingers from the doorjamb when abruptly she let go, trying to clutch at me while I beat back her furious hands, then she ducked down and grabbed my leg. "Get out of here and get out of my life," I croaked. I wrenched her thumb backward so her hand sprang open and I kicked her away and slammed the door, locked it. I was panting. I walked up and down the studio, trying to catch my breath, then got down on the floor and began to pick up the photographs. Avalon had begun to beat on the door, crying, *You can't do this, Ren. This isn't you!* but I went on gathering the photos. I sorted the envelopes by the postmarks and put everything back with the other stuff in the chest, though my head felt like it was going to explode. Avalon stopped pounding on the door and now in the silence she said, *If you don't open this door I'll kick it in.* I went to the kitchen sink and turned on both taps, my hands still trembling. *It's a flimsy door, Ren, and I'll kick it to pieces. You bastard! You fucking bastard! You*—I dunked my head in the sink and kept it there, the water shooting down on my skull, filling the bowl, overflowing, pouring down my legs. I came up for air and turned off the taps and the studio was silent.

I threw myself face down on my bunk and after a while my insides ceased trembling. I wondered if Avalon was still outside the door but then remembered she would have to go to the Daily Grind to meet Kim when he came from school, so I got up and looked at the clock over the stove and saw she must have gone by now. Her keys were on the counter at the end by the door where she always tossed them (tiny chain with a glassy tag: photo of Avalon on one side, her son on the other) but not her wallet, which meant it was still in her pocket, since she never carried a purse like other women.

I went to the back room to look around. A couple of weeks ago she had enlisted me to help drag the bookcase away from the wall, so it became a low wall itself and made a room within the room, an alcove for the mattress. The mattress was made up neatly on the floor, a bed without legs, and lying along side it was my old sleeping bag where Kim nestled down each night, though he often crawled into his mother's bed before dawn. Some of Kim's strange maps were tacked to the wall. Avalon had furtively removed half a dozen books in a row from my bookcase and laid them flat atop others to clear a space for her grooming tools (emery boards, lipsticks, clippers, crayons), and she'd done the same on other shelves, making spaces for Kim's toys and for her own treasures, hers being a chipped clam shell she had found during our walk on Good Harbor beach, an ugly photo postcard of Gloucester Harbor she had bought the same day, the cork from a bottle of Asti Spumanti we had drunk one night when I thought my painting was going especially well, plus other such prizes, including a brush I had thrown someplace and a mug that said *The Daily Grind* which she had probably stolen. I hauled Avalon's huge backpack to a standing position, grappled it up and lugged it through the studio and set it outside, leaning against the wall, then I took a wine carton and tossed in Kim's loose jerseys and pants and socks, also swept his toys and his mother's sundries into it, and set it out beside the backpack.

I locked the door and drove off in my wagon, not wanting to be near when Avalon came back to fetch her stuff. I don't know where I headed, but when I discovered I'd crossed the river and was in Cambridge I swung off the avenue and navigated the back streets to Zocco's place. Zocco wasn't in. I swung around and headed to Harvard Square, parked in an over-priced garage and walked to the Café Paradiso. No one I knew was there. I ordered a cappuccino and a cannolo and was satisfied to sit outside by myself, looking at the street and the crowds streaming past, and later I took out my pad and wrote a few pages to my son Fabrizio. When I returned to my studio the backpack and the box were gone; the pair of pants and the two jerseys I had bought for Kim lay scrambled on the floor by the wall, but at least she had taken all the toys. I figured if Avalon had her head screwed on right she had gone to the Daily Grind and asked Garland to take her in and Garland, being Garland, had said yes.

I felt good, relieved, free. For dinner I boiled rice and

stuffed it into a pair of pepper halves, poured tomato sauce over the rice, ate up and washed it all down with Chianti from the bottle, belching as contentedly as I wanted, then I wrote a couple more pages to Fabrizio, after which I painted well and farted happily till midnight and went to bed. When I woke up it was still dark and I lay there wondering why I had awakened. I got up and went to the bathroom to piss, but for a long time there was only the clamping pain and no pee, then it dribbled for a while and left no relief but only a blurred ache. It came to mind about cancer in the prostate, the way it reaches into you down there and spreads, a horridly familiar thought which I tried to shake off, then I wiped the spattered rim of the john bowl with a fistful of paper, flushed it away and washed up. Instead of going to my bed I turned the other way and stood for a minute looking into the back room where the light from the hall illuminated a triangular piece of Avalon's mattress. I got back to my bed but I couldn't go back to sleep, even though my mind was calm and empty.

I thought about lying alone, as I was, in this black room with my blind canvases, and Alba across the river asleep in our big bed in that concrete mausoleum, thought about this being a stupid way to live, and about Zoe amid her down pillows on the thin hard mattress she said was good for her back, and I thought about my paintings and were they any good and could I make myself known before dying, and I thought about Skye and Astrid and Brizio, about their busy lives and their plans. I suppose I wasn't actually thinking deeply about these people but only picturing them for my own solace, knowing that they cared about me, for if they didn't care, then everything I had done would be gone and I would be nothing, just another old man with pee on his pants. It was a while before I got to sleep.

The philosopher Montaigne, perhaps Italian as uncle Zitti believed, says that your inner self is a place of contradictions and that to live well you have to learn to live with your inconsistencies, and he's right. Now, this next morning, I picked up Avalon's key chain with my studio keys on it, stuck them in my pocket and went around to the Daily Grind. Inside the air was thick with the smell of roasting coffee beans. Garland was wiping the marble counter top and when she saw me she stopped and stood there watching me as I walked around the sacks of beans and on to the back of the store where Avalon was tending the coffee roaster. The gas jets shimmered like sapphires and there was a sound like gravelly surf as the beans slid endlessly inside the rotating drum. Avalon seated herself back against the stone window ledge, one boot on the floor and the other on a rung of the coffee roaster, her narrow eyes darting here and there beyond me. I thought to tell her that she never had a right to turn up at my door and I had no damn reason to take her in. I fished out her studio keys and started to give them to her when her hand slashed past, snatching them from my fingers and shoving them into her pocket. She settled back more comfortably on the window ledge, her gaze shifting around the room. "Thanks," she said, looking at me at last. "You're welcome," I said.

31

ONE DAY AVALON CAME HOME AFTER WORK AND said Zoe had left a phone message for me at the Daily Grind, which message was that Astrid is getting married and please phone me. "What does she want *me* to do?" I wondered out loud. "Sounds like she wants you to phone her," said Avalon. The next morning I went to the Daily Grind and phoned Zoe who said, We've got to talk about this, so you bring the wine, I'll the make the dinner. I told Avalon I was going to have dinner at Zoe's. "She talks to me like I'm bizarre or something," muttered Avalon, scooping up a bucket of coffee beans. "Maybe because you gave her your life history when all she asked for was a cup of coffee," I suggested. "Only because she came in here to spy on me and I gave her what she wanted," Avalon said, pouring the beans into the coffee roaster.

Zoe's studio-office is front and back on the right, and the rest of the old house is her home. That evening I knocked on her bright blue door (Blue Door Graphics) and she greeted me with, "Astrid barely knows the man and wants to marry him instantly. She said late spring or summer, remember, but yesterday she phoned to say she she's thinking of getting married right now." I followed her to the kitchen and began to adjust the corkscrew, her elaborate gadget of gears and levers, all the while speculating about Astrid. "Well, what do you think?" Zoe asked me.

"I don't know. Maybe she's pregnant. We should think about that."

"She'd tell us if she were pregnant," Zoe said, quite firm. "Wouldn't she?" she added, searching my eyes for the answer.

"I hope so. I think so. Sure." I went back to working on the cork.

"She's always told us when she was in trouble," Zoe continued.

"Yes, but getting pregnant isn't the same as getting into trouble, not when you're planning to marry the man."

"Maybe she only thinks she might be pregnant and is getting us ready, just in case."

"She might do that," I conceded. "Probably would. She's prudent that way, after the fact."

"Alba thinks Astrid has known this man longer than we know about."

"She's probably right about that. —Ah! Open at last."

"Fill our glasses. I'm starved." By the time we had finished dinner and washed up we had decided to recommend to Astrid, whom we must remember to call Galaxy, that she should

live with Weston a while before marrying him and, furthermore, she should keep the key to her current apartment just
in case living at Weston's didn't work. By fitting together the
loose jigsaw facts we had of Galaxy's life since she left home,
interlocking them with the meager handful of tidbits she had
given us about Wes, we were able to compose that stretch
when she was living with Wes's father, Harry, whom we had
met a couple of times (bald head, bright eyes, springy step)
and by prompting each other's memory we were able to figure
when she could have met Harry's son and when, after Harry
died (hang-glider, downdraft) she must have begun to see
more and much more of Wes.

The dinner and the wine and our long, agreeable talking
together had warmed my heart and I knew that Zoe felt the
same warmth, because sharing our complaints and worries
about Astrid always aroused her tender feelings and, in fact,
any deeply intimate conversation opened her to amorous sug-
gestions. So, being in the mood as I was, after I had dried the
last dish I looked around the kitchen, thinking to prolong
my stay and thereby let one word lead to another, though a
single glance showed me there wasn't anything more I could
do except say good-night and go back to the studio. "Oh, have
another glass of wine. I'm going to have another glass," Zoe
said, rescuing me.

I threw my jacket back on the hook and we took the bottle
to the living room where Zoe slipped off her shoes and settled
into a pillowed corner of the sofa, stretching her legs across
my lap so I could massage her feet, which massage was always
melting bliss to her. I held her heel in the palm of one hand
and with the other I began to work on her toes, after which I
sank my thumb into the long muscle of her arch, causing her
to sigh with pleasure and to sink further into her corner, and
so on till I wrapped my hand around her sharp ankle, holding
it snug till the marrow of her bones went warm. Zoe stood up
and reached under her skirt to tug her pantyhose off, rolling

the misty material down her legs into a storm cloud which she swept away with a bare white foot, then she seated herself in her corner of the sofa again, the smoothing down of her skirt leaving a warm perfume to fade in the air like the after-image of her swan-white thighs. That's fancy language and I use it to show I was old but aroused and the wine had gone to my head. She slid her legs across my lap again so I could massage her calf muscles, and for a while she sipped her wine in silence while I worked on her hard, silken flesh. "I'm alone now, really alone," she told me.

"What are you talking about?"

She tilted her head back and drained the glass with one swallow. "Astrid marries Weston. What happens to me?"

"Astrid has been on her own for years and you're still her mother. Nothing's going to change that."

"But this is different. She's getting married and it's going to make a difference. I'm going to be right back where I was thirty years ago," she said, setting her empty glass on the floor.

"It's *not* the same as thirty years ago."

"No. Thirty years ago I had hope, I had a future."

"Christ! You're still *young*, Zoe. The one who's old here is *me*, not you. The day will come when you're my age and you'll wonder what you were talking about."

"You have a family."

"Yes, and you're part of it."

"You have no idea how hollow that sounds," she said, abruptly swinging her legs from my lap. She poured the last of the wine into her glass, drank it down and then seated herself on the floor with her back pressed against my knees. "Anyway, I don't want to be part of somebody else's family any more. I want to be the center of my own," she said, bowing her head, her hair so short, the shaved nape of her long neck so naked and vulnerable. I plowed my hand through her hair, trying to recall the thick shining weight of it when she was a young Renoir, then I began to massage her right shoulder

which was always stiff and sore because of the way her be-
loved computer mouse monopolized her right hand.

"I want to get out and meet people, new people," she said.

"Has anyone stopped you?"

"No. But you undermine my confidence so I don't leave."

"You left and got married twice. And that's not counting
the other times you left."

"I married two times, period. That not so much. Or so
many or whichever's the right way to say it."

"And I don't know what you mean by undermine. I've sup-
ported you in everything you've ever done. When have I ever
undermined you? What have I ever done to undermine you or
stop you or hinder you or whatever it is you're talking about?"

I went to the kitchen, grabbed another bottle of wine,
rammed in the corkscrew and wrenched out the cork, poured
myself a glass. I was at the sink, staring through my reflec-
tion in the black window and thinking glumly how I should
go back to my studio, when Zoe came in behind me, saying, "I
used to have friends in San Francisco and Taos. I haven't been
to San Francisco for five years and I can't even remember the
last time I was in Taos." She reached past me to put her glass in
the sink, taking care not to brush my arm with hers. "Are you
coming upstairs or not?" she asked brusquely, not moving away.

I looked at her. Her hairstyle, that cruel scissoring which
left only a close fitting cap of feathered hair over her skull,
made her appear more fragile than she was, made her eyes
seem larger, too. She looked at me and waited, her pale irises
all depth and need one moment, but hard as opals the next.

"After I finish this glass," I said, sullen.

When I got upstairs Zoe was in her soft dark robe and as
I entered she turned off the bedroom light, leaving on only
the small lamp in the corner, its illumination as dusky as the
perfume that now hung in the air, a rutting scent she knew
I liked. I tore off my shoes and socks and had just tossed my
shirt on the chair when she said, "I've been thinking."

"This isn't the time or place—" I began

"I want to say something," she insisted.

"Is that what we came up her for? For a damn lecture?"

She had seated herself on the edge of the bed with her hands in her lap. "You undermine me by saying you love me."

"Fine!"

"Because if you love me why should I go looking for somebody else to love me when maybe there's nobody out there who will."

"Fine. I won't say it anymore." I shucked off my pants.

"You say you love me and so—"

"You damn well know it," I said impatiently.

"So I've come to depend on it."

"You can depend on it." I tossed my underpants on the heap and was naked.

"Yes, up to a point."

"Have I ever let you down?"

"You know *exactly* and *precisely* what I mean!" She sprang up, flung her robe onto the chair—or tried to, for it billowed and fell short—and now we were both naked.

"You've known from day one—" I began, exasperated.

"Love everybody, love nobody! Who do you love, Ren? Or have you lost the list?"

"We've been here before, Zoe. This road leads nowhere."

"We've never been anywhere else!" she cried.

"You want me to forget about you? Is that it? What do you want? What exactly and precisely do you want?"

"*I want to be loved most!* I want to go somewhere where I'm loved most! Is that so vain? Is that so impossible?"

After her words, in that silence, I reached toward her but she slapped my hand away. "Am I supposed to go back to my studio now?" I asked.

"I didn't say that!"

"You want me to stay?"

"You want to leave? You expect me to drive over to your

place at this hour?" She flung open the bed and stood there looking at me, her arms tense at her sides, waiting.

"Great. This is just great."

There are times I've wished *this* Renato were not *that* Renato. What can I tell you? We lay together in the frail light of the corner lamp, as wary as animals in an eclipse, and yet it gave me comfort to comfort her, to run my old hand gently through her hair, no matter her hair was short and thin, so she would know I knew who she truly was and knew she was desirable, and in a while she pressed her cheek to mine so we couldn't see each other but had to signal through our bodies and make conversation that way, one word leading to another. At breakfast she said, "You know this doesn't change a thing," and I said, "I hope you're right, I wouldn't want you to change," and she stopped with the toast half way to her mouth and she said flatly, "You're a bastard, Renato," and I said, "Yes, maybe. I was found on a doorstep."

32

I HADN'T HEARD A WORD FROM SONIA STRAND, SO I decided to go around to her gallery to show her I wasn't so old as to be forgetful or dead, and to ask when she was going to put me on her exhibition calendar. I pulled open the heavy glass door and here comes Sonia herself in gleaming trousers of crushed brown velvet and a blouse which looked to be sewn from a Renaissance flag, reaching out to shake my hand, saying, "Mr Stillamare! Renato, so good to see you." Her hand was soothingly warm and as she smiled her eyes wrinkled at the corners, her gaze lingering on me as if we were close friends who through some shared misfortune hadn't been able to see each other for months. "Come," she said. "I just finished a note to you and, since you're here, we'll save the postage—" She led me to her office, snatched up a stack of square white envelopes and plucked out the one with my name on it. "An invitation to our next reception. Please come. There are people I want you to meet and they'll be here. And I want them to meet you. You'll come?"

"Of course." I don't know anything more tedious than somebody else's gallery reception.

"And now—" We were standing in the middle of her office and Sonia put her hands on her hips and glanced around with a slight frown, as if searching for something. She wasn't quite so tall as I had remembered, but stood straight and tall enough to be imposing. The large glass table she used for a desk was blanketed with a quilt of overlapping letters, note cards, loose photo-slides and other such trash, all held in place by those fancy little enameled boxes she kept as paper-weights. She opened the door to Peter Bell's cubiculum, said a few words to him, then pressed the door shut. "Say!" she said, turning to me. "Do you have time for an espresso?"

"Sure."

She smiled. "But not in a paper cup, right? The last time you were here I scandalized you with paper cups, I could see that, so I went out and purchased these little beauties, thin as egg shells. And in just a minute we'll have coffee." Sonia had gone to the espresso machine by the window and began to load it, her back to me.

"The reason I came by—" I began.

"I hope you came by to ask about your exhibit," she said, glancing over her shoulder.

"Exactly."

She finished with the machine and turned to me. "As you know, I've already written out a calendar for the year. And we're completely booked. You know that, too. But I don't want to wait until next year, I want to exhibit you this year— if that's all right with you," she added.

"That's all right with me."

"Wonderful! Now that means I'll have to write you in on top of somebody else. It will be a two-artist show. I'll try to choose somebody who won't be completely overpowered by your work. That won't be easy." She smiled. "But I can do it."

"And when would that be?" I insisted.

"This fall. Fall's best," she said crisply.

"Good," I said as crisply as she.

Sonia attended to the sleek little coffee machine while I took a couple of restless, irritable turns around her office, bumping into her Baroque side chair and nearly putting my boot through a painting that leaned against a tall file cabinet.

"Renato." There was a note of gentle rebuke in Sonia's voice; she opened her arm toward the chrome and leather sofa. "Make yourself comfortable. Please."

I stayed standing. "I don't paint miniatures. You've seen my work."

"Yes, I've seen your work, and yes, you don't paint miniatures. What are you getting at?"

"How much wall space do I have if there's another painter here?"

"Don't worry about wall space," she said. "You do the painting, I'll provide the gallery. Now enjoy your espresso. Please."

Sonia handed me a cup of coffee, sipped her own and by way of conversation she asked had I seen the big show at the Fine Arts last fall (I had and I said so), and what had I thought of it (I had thought it was crowded and said so), and how about Zircon who was finally breaking onto the national scene at fifty-five (I'd piss on him if I could, but I kept mum about it), thus we stood in the middle of her office and made amiable gossip about nothing much and carried on our private calculations. What I knew for sure was that I had advanced toward an exhibition date, but had been maneuvered away from having the gallery to myself and now would have to share the space. So all the while we chatted I watched her eyes, those blue crystals, and listened to the pitch and timbre of her voice, which always sounded as if she had just awakened and I was the first person she spoke to, and I waited for her next move or for the chance to make a move of my own. "Actually," she said, "I'd love to put some of your drawings on exhibit, too."

"Why is that?" I asked, thinking how drawings sell for less than paintings and we'd both make less money.

She set her cup slowly and very gently on the desk. "Because your drawings are extraordinary. The ones I saw in your studio, those figures who look, oh, not like nudes at all, but like naked people, people who have taken off their clothes. In a sense, most nudes are still clothed. The conventional ways of portraying bare bodies are so—so high-minded, so sanctimonious, so non-sexual, that when we look at them we don't see nakedness at all."

"You're right about that."

"Thank you, Renato." She smiled slightly.

"But I don't want to use up wall space on drawings," I told her, my voice edgier than I intended.

"Think about it."

I laughed. "I'll certainly think about it."

"Be careful you don't crush that little cup in your fist."

"What?"

"Let me take your cup."

"Oh! Sorry."

Sonia set my egg-cup beside hers on her desk and continued across the room to open wide the door to the gallery and I followed her out. The stuff hanging on the walls— balanced designs, harmonious colors, meticulous brushwork, rigor mortis—gave me a headache and I wanted to leave, but I figured I'd better ask when were we going to talk about prices, percentages, and how many paintings. I began to say, "When are we going to—" but Sonia was sliding both hands into that wide bush of copper colored hair, shutting her eyes for a second. "You know," she said, opening her gaze onto mine. "We should discuss details—" I started to say I agreed, but Sonia hadn't finished talking. "In a week or so. As soon as I have time to sit down and write a letter. I'm *un*-believably busy right now, so there may be a delay, but don't take it amiss. Busy is good," she added, smiling.

Peter Bell walked up with a handful of mail and a letter knife with fancy enameled handle. "Good to see you, Mr Stillamare."

"Good to see you, Mr Bell."

"The weather is warmer. The cafés are setting out tables," he said, smiling.

"Must be spring," I said.

We shook hands and he trotted away to his kennel. Sonia had opened one of the letters and glanced inside, saying, "I'll need two-thirds of the selling price."

I didn't realize she was speaking to me until she glanced up from the letter. "Agreed?" she asked.

"You'll take two-thirds?" I said.

"Not always, but this time. Yes."

"This time, yes," I said.

Then we shook hands and I left.

•

I phoned Alba and told her, "I've just finished talking with Sonia Strand about my exhibit and it's a disaster."

What are you talking about? Alba asked me. What happened?

"She doesn't want my work, she's taking sixty-six percent, she wants a handful of drawings, she's trying to get rid of me."

Is she giving you a show or not?

"No. Or yes, if I share the gallery with one of her farts."

What did she say, exactly?

"That I'm lower than whale shit."

Where are you calling from?

"Copley Square. Why?"

Why don't you go to the Daily Grind and —

"I don't goddamn want another goddamn cup of coffee!"

Or go see Winthrop or Zocco or Hay. Or I'll come around if you want.

"How about a long lunch?" I asked her.

I can't have a long lunch, I've got that cooking class. But tomorrow's good. Or do you need me to come in right now?

"No, I'm all right. Tomorrow where?"

Alba suggested Thoreau's Garden over in Cambridge and that was fine with me.

"Thanks, Alba. Sorry to bother you."

No bother. It's part of the marriage vows, she said.

•

I hiked to the Daily Grind because I couldn't figure what else to do and along the way I thought about going around to see Win or Zocco or D'Arcangelo, but I didn't know how much I wanted to tell them, because first I wanted to think some more about Strand and what she was proposing and what she meant and what I should do next, though I knew Zocco and the others would be sympathetic and so on and, on third thought, maybe I should talk about it to clear my head, or maybe write to Scanlon who was sure to offer advice, but in the end I decided not to tell anybody anything. I never had to think even twice about what I told Mike Bruno. When I got to the Daily Grind it was low tide (three tables, the rest empty) with Garland at the counter bent over a work schedule, scowling, scrubbing away with an eraser as if she were working on a botched crossword puzzle. I asked was Gordon around; she sighed into the page and said he'd taken the day off. Avalon was in back by the coffee roaster, folding empty burlap sacks and tossing them onto a pile that had mounted to her knees. She saw me watching her, wiped her forehead with the back of her filthy hand, saying, "What are you doing here at this hour? Why aren't you painting?" I told her I'd stopped by to see if I had any phone calls. "You look lost," she said. I asked Garland could I use the phone and without glancing up she handed it to me. I punched in Zoe's number and was informed by her machine that no one at Blue Door Graphics was available to take my call right now but please leave a message at the tone, so I hung up. I headed home to the studio, but I didn't feel like painting so as I trudged along I took detours and while I was browsing through a store window I decided to go in and buy Kim a compass, because he liked to draw maps and if he had a compass we could survey the neighborhood and draw some good ones. The place was stocked with boisterous outdoor gear — hiking boots, collapsible stoves, yellow pop-up tents, a rack of glittering canoes — and over to one side were a couple of neglected compasses at the end of a row of gadgets that could tell you your location based on signals from satellites nailed to the sky. I bought a compass, the real kind that works with a magnetized needle, and went to the studio.

That night, after we had finished cleaning the dishes and pans and after Kim had gone off with his compass, I sat at the table and wondered what to do. I tried telling myself that Sonia had not cancelled my show but only reduced it, which was true, but I didn't get any lift from that, none at all. After a while I remembered I had been meaning to write a letter to my brother about our mother and how to get her from his place to Massachusetts but I didn't feel like writing a letter to anybody about anything. Avalon said something and then went to take a shower and I sat there feeling tired. I was gazing mindlessly at the canvases stacked against the wall and at the big one braced against the easel, but all I saw was the broad area of canvas and stroke upon stroke of paint, and all I felt was how tired I was, as if my energy had been seeping away, ebbing away for months, and I had not noticed and now I couldn't move. I thought how I could die right then and the thought of dying meant nothing to me, meant only the end of this stupid struggle, a struggle so stupid I couldn't make out what it was for, or maybe I was too tired to see. I sat there a long spell, but if I had more thoughts I can't recollect them, because all I remember is me reading a book at the table when Avalon sat down opposite me. "You've been morose all day," she announced. Go away, I said. She went away, but after she had put Kim to bed she came back. "That's the same page you were reading half an hour ago, you're not making much progress," she said. When I looked up at her she handed me a glass of wine. "You need company," she said. I gave up and closed the book, whatever it was. "Why don't you ask me one of those cooking riddles?" she suggested. I don't know what you're talking about, I said. "Like the other night when you said, you know, a hungry man goes to the kitchen and all he can find is a piece of bread and a bottle of olive oil and some-thing, I forget—but you know what I mean. Remember?" Oh, that, I said. "Well?" she said. I couldn't figure out what she was up to, but at last I said, "All right. A hungry man goes to the kitchen and all he can find is a stale loaf of bread, just the heel of the bread, stale, and a can of peeled tomatoes, and an onion. What does he do for dinner?"

"He puts the peeled tomatoes in a pot. Adds water." She hesitated. "Cuts up the onion and puts it in with the peeled tomatoes. That makes a kind of soup. He heats up the soup. And."

"And?"

"Drinks the soup and eats the stale bread?"

"No. He puts the stale bread *into* the simmering soup. It softens the bread, the bread soaks up the soup. It's delicious." I picked up the book.

"Ask me another."

"Why?"

She clamped her hands on mine to stop my opening the book. "Come on, Ren. A woman, a woman this time, goes into the kitchen and all she finds is —"

Her hands were not so big as mine, but blissfully warm,

her fingers strong and smooth, and my flesh under hers looked like old leather gloves. I shied away from my hands, looked over to the kitchen counter and I tried to come up with a puzzle for her. "Some sugar, one fresh egg and a bottle of Marsala," I said at last.

"What's Marsala?"

"Sweet wine."

"She cooks the egg and drinks the Marsala!"

"You would."

"And you?"

"Drop the egg yolk in a pot, add a little sugar and beat it to a thick creamy yellow, add a spoonful of Marsala and whip it to a froth."

"Then what?"

"Then eat it."

"Raw? Eat the egg raw?"

"You can heat it if you want. You hold it in the air over the heat—just like this, see, so it doesn't cook—and add the wine and whip it up."

"Ren, it's still raw and it sounds gross."

"On the contrary, it's marvelous."

"Oh, sure. Show me. Let me see you eat a raw egg."

Avalon kept nagging until at last I got an egg and some sugar and began to whip up a zabaione, but I didn't have any Marsala so I threw in vanilla extract instead. I ate about half and then lifted the spoon to her mouth. She drew her head back. "I bet it tastes like when somebody comes in your mouth."

"You'll like it almost as much. That's sperm, this is egg. Taste it."

While I held the spoon, Avalon stuck her tongue cautiously into the zabaione, then took it into her mouth and swallowed. I finished that spoonful, then scooped another and held it out to her, and so the spoon went back and forth between us until the zabaione was gone, after which I refilled my glass with wine while Avalon asked in three different ways what had gone wrong today that made me so moody. I took a drink and passed the glass to her and told her nothing had gone wrong that couldn't be fixed by shoving a bomb up the ass of every gallery owner in Boston, and Avalon smiled, tossed her head back, drank down the rest of the glass and informed me that an artist's life is a hard life, as she well knew, being a silversmith herself, though she admits that her jewelry at the Daily Grind is actually selling, piece by piece, then she hands me the glass and asks what kind of writer is Alba, and I say she's a known essayist, an occasional restaurant reviewer, a sometime book reviewer, a now-and-then translator of French poets, a part-time curator of artists' books, a scribbler of pornography which she calls erotica and a former art critic who never lifted a finger to help her husband's career, and Avalon says that she herself never wanted to get married but now, seeing how Alba and I live, she thinks maybe she should get married because living apart that way she'd have somebody to write letters to, though she doubts she'd write as many letters as I do, even if she had a dozen kids. So the glass traveled back and forth between us until the bottle, over which we said good-night, was empty and she went to her room; as for me, grateful she had taken me out of my black mood, I dropped into bed and lay there feeling tender-hearted toward her, but quickly fell to sleep and, except for rising once to pee, slept as forgetfully as an old log rotting in a field.

33

THE NEXT DAY I DROVE ACROSS THE RIVER TO Cambridge to have lunch with Alba at Thoreau's Garden though, frankly, I liked Thoreau's better when all it had was paper plates and a menu of bean sprouts and raw carrots, none of this fakery with rusted farm tools hanging on the wall. "That's because you're getting old and grumpy. Start eating, you'll feel better," Alba told me. While we were devouring a Greek salad I told her about my visit with Sonia Strand, made a vigorous re-enactment with every word and nuance mimicked from the original scene, so I was surprised when Alba calmly replied, "That doesn't sound so bad."

"Doesn't sound so bad? I'm going to end up with nothing! *No percentage, no wall space, no show!*"

"She didn't say no—let me finish, Ren—she didn't say no exhibit. She did put you on the calendar, which is what you went to see her about. You don't know what's going on at the gallery. I'm sure she has her own agenda and I'm sure we don't know it. She may have certain buyers in mind for drawings, your kind of drawings. She's asked for your work and she's not going to ask for work unless she thinks she can sell it, so she must think she can sell you. For all you know, she may be trying to get rid of that other painter, the one she's putting you in with."

Alba didn't say anything more, so I went back to my bowl and picked away at the greenery, thinking about what she had just said, all of which I supposed was more or less true but at the same time it didn't feel satisfying, and after a decent pause Alba asked how was my salad and I said fine and asked how's hers, and hers was fine too. "We don't know her agenda," I said. "But we know it has to do with money. That's what the dealers are dealing in, money. There's painting and there's, there's—"

"Marketing and money," said Alba.

"I didn't think I'd end up this way. I would never have started if I had known I was going to end this way."

"It's not ended. You're not ended," she said calmly.

It meant the world to me when Alba said things like that, which is one of the reasons I married her, though I didn't know it at the time. "You don't think so?" I said.

"I don't think so. I'm sure you're going to go on painting."

"I'm tired. It's getting easier and easier not to paint. Days go by."

"I thought you were working. You were, weren't you? A while ago you were painting more than ever."

"I'm painting, but nothing's happening. I mean, I have this energy—it's good, it's good energy—but I can't connect, I can't connect it to— I've got some good ideas, some good pictures. I've laid them out, a few of them. They're good. I know what's good. But it's easy to put the brush down. It's easy to walk away from the canvas. It's never been that way before."

"It's been that way before," she said.

"Not like this."

"That's what you always say. —Listen," she said, reaching for her purse, a deep leather sack the size of a horse's feed bag. "Before I forget, we got a letter from Skye. They've really enjoyed Sydney—strange to think of it getting to be winter down there—but they're ready to come back to the States. Wait a sec. It's here someplace. Here. But read it later, Renato, not now. She says they should arrive here by late summer. That's the important part. The other parts are interesting too, of course. —Heard anything new from Astrid? I mean Galaxy, anything from Galaxy?"

"No. And I don't know if that's good or bad."

"Zoe seems more relaxed, as relaxed as she ever gets, anyway."

A Greek salad not only makes a good lunch but also provides a pleasurable distraction, because you can pursue this or that small sharp taste or swerve onto a wholly different one or, if you want, seek out a new texture or a fresh color, and then you're happily swabbing the inside of the bowl with a slice of coarse bread and feeling the vinegar on your tongue, but I was all the while thinking of the Strand gallery and the paintings on those walls and the paintings in the galleries up and down Newbury Street. "What I do," I was telling Alba, "I do better than anyone—I'll say it to you, I won't say it to anyone else—I do it better than anyone. I'm not saying I'm the only one who can paint, but I can paint. But what's the use of doing it when nobody is going to look? Nobody's looked at my work for the past thirty years. I've been developing and moving ahead and now I'm where I want to be, but I'm all alone here, because no dealers or buyers or lookers came along with me. Now if anybody happens to see my work it looks odd to them, because they haven't been watching it get this way for the past two or three decades. So why should I fucking paint?"

"I'm not saying you have to paint. But you certainly do it better than other painters. And there's people who do like your work," she added.

"Where?" I said, looking around.

"Have you thought about Conti's gallery right here in Cambridge?"

"Is that still standing? I thought they had knocked it down so they could sell the bricks."

"It's still there."

"I heard Leo Conti was flat broke."

"He's getting there. But Conti thinks of himself as a benefactor to the public, so he keeps the gallery open."

"He had a nice accounting business, too bad he sold it."

"He sold it so he could be a patron of the arts. If he goes broke now, he goes broke satisfied that he was more than just an accountant."

"I don't want to show there."

"How about Mimi's Café?"

"Me?"

"For that series on paper. The Genesis series. They're finished aren't they?"

"They're finished but they're not going to hang in Mimi's Café."

We concluded with a cup of coffee and didn't say much, Alba taking an interest in the stamped tin ceiling while I studied the floor boards, or we looked past each other to watch the other patrons. "Why don't you come around to the studio and look at the paintings and tell me what you think?" I asked her.

Alba put down her coffee mug and looked at me in a friendly, good-natured way as if I'd just said the stupidest thing she'd ever heard. "No, Renato."

"I'm not going to bed with her."

"I admire your restraint."

"No one's there during the day except me. Anyway, you might like Avalon, despite what you've heard from Zoe."

She shrugged. "What's the point, Ren?"

"I could use your help. I need your help," I said. "I need you."

"Sure."

"My muse."

"I cannot believe you're this hard up," she said.

"You could stop by early in the afternoon, whip up an omelet for us. Make your cooking teacher proud. What's the chef's name?"

"Michelle," she said.

"Famous?"

"Famous in France," she said.

34

I DECIDED NOT TO PAINT FOR A FEW DAYS SO AS NOT to spoil the stuff I was working on, because if I kept at it while I was feeling this low I'd just piss on everything and turn it to mud, so at the hour when I would have been walking up and down in front of a canvas, I stood at the kitchen counter and emptied the old glass Mason jar of all those slips of paper on which I'd written chores that needed to be done. I sorted the scraps (*fix CHAIR, See Urologist, buy 2 Tires, shower curtain, Make appt w/ urologist, socks et cetera, Umbrella, Urologist prostate exam*) and threw out the one in Avalon's jagged handwriting (*Get us a real toaster that doesn't burn my fingers every damn morning.*) I repaired the kitchen chair, then crammed the remaining notes into my pocket and got myself out the door. It was a balmy day, so I cranked down the car window and chugged along, trying to enjoy the weather despite my gloom. I bought the socks et cetera and shower curtain, then drove out to Tire World to get two new tires put on, then to a phone booth to make an appointment with my dentist, because I had a tooth which had recently grown sensitive to hot or cold, and I bought an umbrella. I got back to the studio by mid-afternoon and found in the mail a biggish envelope from Scanlon, which envelope I decided to open later as a treat. I ate lunch and then lay on the floor, a book under my head and my hands folded on my stomach, still glum but too tired to care. After the nap I got up and pissed and dribbled, which reminded me again to make an appointment with the urologist to get ye olde prostate poked, then I drove over to Cambridge to the Café Paradiso to read Scanlon's letter and to see if Winthrop or Cormac or Hay or anyone would show up.

Scanlon had stuffed his square manila envelope with a thick letter, a handful photos, some drawings, a couple of slides, and a big glossy chromatic brochure of his show in Toronto that had just closed. He said he had rediscovered my studio address and had now written it into his Notebook —if you knew Scanlon you'd know it was an honor to be in his famous Notebook which, I figured, must be up around volume seventy-five. He wrote in detail about the show and mentioned a new strategy, which he'd tell me about later, for recapturing the position he had held in the art world a decade ago, and about how little he was getting for his paintings nowadays, and how the only honest way to make a movie about Gauguin's life would be to make a movie about five other painters who lived back then and leave Gauguin out of it, and how Elaine deKooning went around and fucked Rosenberg and Hess and Egan, and those guys were so happyfied they went out and told the world Elaine's husband was the greatest painter since Picasso, and Scanlon's question to me was this: would we have heard of Bill deKooning if Elaine had been a lousy lay? As I said, it was a thick letter, and at the end he wrote that he was coming through Boston on his way to Maine and he hoped I'd be free to have dinner or lunch or some other meal with him.

I sat by the window in the Paradiso, sipping the cappuccino and holding Scanlon's slides up to the light, one after the other. As usual, he had re-invented the way he painted and these canvases were completely different from the ones he'd last showed me and, frankly, though I usually like the way Scanlon paints, I'd like it even more if he evolved and deepened instead of zigzagging all over the place, chasing sales. Anyway, it would be good to see him again, to get acquainted with what was going on in New York, and I could tell him about my latest meeting with Sonia Strand and ask what he thought about the deal. I looked at the drawings and spent a long while with the fancy catalog that had accompanied his exhibit and, after I had finished a canollo, I ordered another cup of coffee. The waitress was plain and crabby, no pleasure to talk to, and the customers were a dull and depressing troop. I slid Scanlon's brochure back into the envelope and wondered how long I was going to go on trying to make a name for myself: I felt bone tired of the struggle. It was strange to have every art dealer in twenty-some years tell me that no one would want my work, and still to go on painting and to grow more certain my work was good, sure to last. I was amazed to be so convinced, seeing as half a lifetime ago I had exhibited in better galleries, gotten bigger notices and sold at higher prices. I knew my work was alive and lasting, the same as I knew my career was a miserable limping thing, and I sat there in the Paradiso and thought this is a little like dying, this long failure, this dwindling away to nothing, and like some dying man who can't believe he's dying, I still think my work is good and must survive. I heard a bark, realized I had laughed out loud at myself, and to cover that little eccentricity I coughed and cleared my throat, then got up and paid and left.

•

That week I cleaned house. In the studio I pulled and shoved everything into the middle of the room, then sponged down the walls and scrubbed the floor. I was pushing everything back against the walls when Avalon came in from work, Kim in tow. "How soon till you clean the storage room where you sentenced Kim and me to go sleep?" she asked. I told her I'd get my paintings out of there tomorrow and she could clean the room herself. "Hear that?" she said to Kim. "You got a lot of papers and stuff to pick up." The next day I lugged half a dozen boxes of gear and most of my paintings from the back room, careful not to disturb Avalon's precious trash, and when she got back from the Daily Grind she began cleaning. I was at the stove when I heard her singing — a low, warm voice — the first time ever. I strolled down to the back room to see if the voice was coming from Avalon herself or only from one of her electronic gadgets. It was Avalon who turned and stopped open-mouthed and the singing stopped with her, like a light going out. Kim was on his hands and knees on a map of Boston, playing with the compass I had given him. "Get a sponge. Join in the fun," Avalon told me. I announced I was going to make dinner and was wondering when she wanted to eat. "Anytime soon," she said, then she bent to dunk the sponge into the bucket and turned back to the window, but didn't sing anymore, which I regretted.

Next day while we were cleaning the kitchen Avalon said,

"As long as you're so hysterical about improving everything around here, why don't you get a little tub for the bathroom?" I calmly pointed out that the bathroom had a shower and there wasn't enough space for a tub, but she said, "A person might prefer a tub, even a little wooden one, to soak in, with nice bath soaps, bubble-bath soaps." I told her I couldn't think of anyone who would want to slop around in a bubble bath. "You yourself might be just that person," she said. "You could soak in the tub and read your Melville and Ovid there, instead of reading them on the can." I asked her what the hell she knew about my reading habits. "Only whatever book I find on the sink when I go in there in the morning. And if Ovid is such a classy poet as you say he is, why do you read him in the crapper, isn't that a sacrilege or something?" I stopped scrubbing the grill and looked at her and was about to shout in her ear that Ovid was a *classic* poet, not *classy*, but she continued to say, "And I notice the book you use for a pillow on the floor has a book mark that hasn't moved for a month." It was a book on theoretical physics, just the right thickness. "I'm trying to learn what my son is doing," I said. "Or what he's not doing, since he abandoned physics and transformed himself into a carpenter."

"Why do we keep this weird-looking thing?" she asked. I told her It's a plate and well-bred people put their food on it when they're eating. "I know it's a fucking plate, but what's the design with the ugly face and three legs for?" But she wasn't interested and before I could tell her about Medusa, she had wandered over to the cork board and now was looking at the photos and postcards. She told me it was too bad the way I had jumbled everything – snapshots, letters, glossy Polaroids, old photographs. She studied a couple of the brownish-gray photos in cardboard frames. "Your ancestors don't look comfortable," she told me. I told her I didn't have ancestors. "I come from a long line of orphans and foundlings," I said. She asked what did I mean. I told her how I was adopted. "Who are these?" she asked. I told her it was my father and his kid sister, Vivianna. "She must have hated being dressed up like that," she said.

Then she was at the wall calendar, saying, "Why don't we get rid of these?" and she began fingering the papers I had pinned to the calendar. "They're always out of date," she added. Avalon had already unfastened the clothespin and now a flock of invitations circled around her, avoiding her wild grasp as they fluttered to the floor. "Listen while I explain again what the word privacy means," I told her.

She was right about the invitations being out of date, all but two of them, one from Finn and the other from Sonia Strand. Finn invited me to all his East Coast openings to demonstrate that he wasn't the sort of person who dumps unsuccessful friends when he becomes famous, and I accepted his invitations to show I wasn't mean-spirited about his good fortune or ashamed of myself. We had never been especially close, but I had liked Finn even though his work method drove me crazy. He would earnestly sketch and erase, sketch and erase for weeks until he had something presentable, then he'd draw a grid on it, transfer it to a canvas and work at it for several more weeks, then he'd call in friends and ask what they thought of it, then he'd scrape and repaint till any quirks were smoothed out, leaving it all as light and airy as a slice of white bread. The invitation from Sonia Strand was for the gallery's exhibit, *Transgressing the Boundaries of Desire: The Art of Judi Flowers*. According to the invitation, Judi Flowers broke through the decorum traditionally imposed on woman artists and portrayed the female body in a series of subversive sado-masochistic poses. When I drew women that way it had been called pornographic, but Judi Flowers controversial work was a compelling critique of patriarchal something, I never learned what, because I threw out her invitation with Finn's and everything else.

•

After three days of housecleaning I took another half day to go through my file cabinet, throwing out this and that until I had only one alphabetized drawerfull (Automobile to Medicare to Social Security), then I slammed that drawer shut and drove over to Cambridge to get a cup of coffee and see if anyone was around. Tom Hay was sitting in the Paradiso with his chin on his chest, half reading a magazine propped against his cup, and when he saw me he brightened and sat up with a smile, a delicate looking man but true as a compass needle. He asked what I'd been doing and I told him I'd been straightening up my papers— "So I can drop dead now and everything will be in order, no problems for my wife and children. How have you been, Tom?" We talked about his children, his writing, his lower back, his publisher, his wife's blood circulation, my teeth, my prostate, my painting, my children. He asked had I seen Winthrop recently and I said no, not recently. "He's got some kind of neuropathic something," Tom said. "Oh, that. Yeah. But no tremor. Not yet anyway. He just moves a little cautiously, I notice. He's begun a new series of paintings. Good stuff," I said.

"Yeah, he's good. Frankly, I don't see any difference between his work and what's getting all the money and attention in New York. And you're good, too," he added. "How come you're not famous?"

"I don't know. You've written half a dozen books, why aren't you famous?"

"That's a total mystery to me, Ren. Maybe I'm not the right religion or ethnicity or class or sex—I mean gender, whatever they call it nowadays." Then he talked about critics and postmodernism and what he called the French Disease, by which he meant some weird French critical theory, and told me about a scholar in New York who wrote articles about nonexistent books to show that advanced criticism was independent of actual authors or their texts. Later he got onto politics and was discoursing about those assholes in Congress when

Karl Kadish came in and we pulled up another chair. Karl was wearing an old-fashioned vanilla straw hat and a puckered cotton jacket, white with blue pencil stripes, and tucked under his arm he carried a foreign journal printed on flimsy airmail paper. "I see by your jacket it's summer," Tom said.

"Someone has to keep track of these things," Karl said soberly, setting his hat gently on a nearby chair.

"When Karl takes off his necktie I'll know it's July," Tom told me. We asked about Karl's wife and children (his daughter married to a rabbi, his son to a Lutheran pastor) and what he, Karl, had been doing, which led to gossip about in-fighting at Harvard and thence to Indian tribes of New England and about the Red Sox and Updike's old essay on Ted Williams' last day at bat, about the old Celtics team with Larry Bird and Robert Parish and Kevin McHale and what a front line that had been. Tom was always contrary about sports, especially Boston teams, and he bad-mouthed Bird and Parish, so it wasn't as much fun as it could have been, but still it was good to talk. We were onto politics again and those assholes in Congress when Lou Zocco and Cormac McCormac came in together, shaggy Cormac's big torso and short legs giving him the appearance of a bear walking on its hind legs. Tom Hay waved them over but stayed only long enough to exchange hellos before he had to leave. Cormac was in a white shirt with the sleeves rolled up and big blotches of sweat under his arms, ebullient because yesterday he had gotten some pieces back from a new foundry and they looked good. He turned to me and said, "Hey, Renato, I bumped into your wife last week and she's looking great since you left her. More beautiful than ever."

"What are you talking about? I didn't leave her, I didn't leave anybody."

"Yes you did," he said jovially. "And now you're living in your studio with this young woman, wears black leather undies and brings you espresso in bed."

"Who told you that?" I asked him.

"I read it in the newspaper. Or maybe I heard it on the radio. I forget which."

"You split?" Zocco asked me, genuinely concerned.

"God, no. I'm spending a lot of time at the studio, is all. I'm living there, more or less."

"He goes home on weekends for a good meal," Cormac told him.

"Maybe it's not his fault," Karl suggested. "Maybe Alba threw him out and only lets him back in on weekends."

"Ah, women," Cormac said.

"Refresh my memory," I told him. "How many wives have you had?"

"Oh, them," Cormac said. "I'm a flawed man. I had hoped for something better in you."

"Where did you happened to see Alba?" I asked.

"At a fancy grocery store in the North End, sells gourmet vegetables, exotic meats, expensive edibles."

"And she told you we had split?"

"Of course not. She's too loyal for that. But she did look great—beautiful, glowing—so I deduced you had left."

"No, you ran into Zoe," I said flatly. "And she talked, told you some nonsense about me."

"That, too. Day before yesterday."

I asked Zocco where he'd been that I hadn't seen him for some weeks and he said he and his wife had been in France, so the conversation got onto the French and French cuisine, Kadish saying the French prepare a meal like lovers who expect you to admire their technique, whereas the Italians want you to enjoy it. "And the British hope you'll get it over with quickly and feel better afterward," Cormac added. Then we had another cup of coffee and talked about life on other planets orbiting other stars, and about women, the persistence of desire and did some old men have bull's balls or just an old habit, talked about Zocco's sailboat and Kadish's plans to retire and what Cormac should do about his beard, which, he claimed, was thicker on the right than on the left. Now if I was captured by love-starved Amazons and taken to their tropical island with only my paints and brushes, as often happened in my boyhood, I could be happy, but I'd miss most the company of men like these.

35

ORMAC WAS ONLY FOOLING AROUND, PLAYING for laughs. But I suppose if you had never seen Avalon and if you heard I was living with this woman, this athletic woman half my age, I suppose it would sound like I must be having a great time plowing her, this old bastard painter making a final surge heavenward before falling down, down, down to his jealous grave. Actually, I've never fucked all over the place. I've been loyal to Alba and to Zoe and haven't bedded other women, or so few as to be none when looked at in perspective, and aside from some accidental tumbles on the studio floor I've lived like a eunuch. As for these stories about Renato Stillamare — young Renato lolling about the studio with a couple of ripe, melon-breasted women, old Renato chasing around his easel after a firm little fanny, creased like a peach — these comic concoctions come from Michael Bruno who loved to tell stories. I'll say only this about Mike. One night he didn't answer our knock at his door (we'd come to celebrate Nixon's impeachment), so I went in, heard him lecturing on Dante, followed his voice up the stairs and found him sitting in bed with naked Pam on one side and naked Clarissa on the other, himself in the middle wearing only his eyeglasses, a huge volume of the *Inferno* open in his lap, and a platter of cold chicken at hand. The startled trio looked all agog at us, then Mike waves his glasses and says, "Join us!"

But spoilsport Alba only laughs and says, "Next time, when there's more men."

The other one to tell lies about me is Alba herself. I don't mean when we've had a fight and she's still sore at me the next day and says serenely to our guests, "Oh, Renato would fuck a snake if he knew a way to hold it down. —Right, Ren?" I mean when Alba tells stories and doesn't finish, I mean the way she tosses out a remark or starts to say this or that and then breaks off, as if there's a thing she could say or stories she could tell about what a bastard I am, tales she won't tell because she's a loyal wife. Maybe she does this to dupe the world into believing I'm a beast and not an old man with a swollen prostate who gets aroused only to pee, a great priapic beast, and how with nothing more than her bitchy look and the crack of her whip she can control this wild hairy thing—not tame him, for he's not tamable, can't be housebroken—but managed, managed only by Alba. Or maybe she does it purely to help old me think better of myself, better a beast than a toothless, clawless, mangy, moth-eaten mongrel lapping water in his cage, which I am.

Frankly, Alba's good at cooking up spicy stories, knows how to serve them hot and how to tell me what I like to hear, goading me to join her in the telling. You can call them sexual fantasies or you can call them plain lies—no matter—she began these playful fictions years ago when our kids were safely in school and we could steal an hour to meet at the studio (the sun blazing in the window, our clothes in a heap in the corner) and she continues, when she feels like it, even now in the bedroom (a lighted candle on the bureau far away.) Not always, but sometimes as we embrace she whispers endearments, such honey-soft words that even my name sounds sweet in her mouth, calling me her god from the sea, her dark lover, her bull, yes, and her stallion, yes, yes, each whispered word more licentious than the one before, holding me in her warm cupped palm or raking me with her nails while telling me what this handsome, this hard, this silky sweet beast wants, needs, must have. She makes a drama about us and not only us but whoever else she guesses I fancy, arranges the props and directs us actors, and her breath is so warm on my ear when she whispers, "Would you like to do that? Would you do that to me?" for she knows what we would do if we dared, and her whispers are an incantation that transforms us so we are no longer acting but doing what we must because of who we have become. Alba says that in the final moments of our love-making, in those moments when the universe crushes together, she comes to know her fiction is truer than facts and that we are as she says we are whether it happens that way or not.

But it's a fact I had never touched Avalon and if Cormac had met her once he'd have figured I hadn't. Avalon's eyes were shifty and her expression too sharp, wary and predatory for anyone to think of her as an easy lay; furthermore, Cormac preferred his women to have what he calls rondeur, which is a foppish French word meaning roundness or, as they say in heaven where the angels speak Italian, rotondo, whereas Avalon was lean, angular. Then there's the off-putting silverware tacked to her face, plus her black-leather-and-chrome-spike collars, wristbands and belts, not to mention the clothing from some Army depot, dreary khaki which she had recently begun to enliven with blouses of velvet or lace or vinyl from a Déjà Vu boutique, one of those second-hand shops that are up one flight of piss-smelling stairs or down four damp steps from the street. Cormac wouldn't have gone for her; nobody would have gone for her.

As for me, I had thought of using Avalon as a model and I was thinking of it again. I was looking at the shaggy hair and the ax-blade face, the smooth notch in that nicely defined collar bone, the precise workmanship of her feet, her strong legs, the deep tense hollows of her arm pits, and that navel with a little silver ring at the lip, winking — taken all together, she made me want to paint, made me want to paint all sorts of things and not just herself alone. She didn't show off, didn't flaunt her body or display so much as a breast or butt, never mind anything else down there. On the other hand, she wasn't coy; a couple of times she burst into the bathroom to snatch her panties or bra from the rack when I was in the shower, and I once broke in on her own steaming Niagara, shouting at her, "Get out I need to pee!" and she shouts back, "You pee in the shower? You should learn to pee in the crapper! Try it!" and as I couldn't hold it in any longer I peed. But mostly she stayed out of my way.

Sometimes I wondered why I never thought to give her cheek a caress at the breakfast table or to pat her neat end when she went by, but I didn't. She was learning how to cook and how to keep house, and she had always been scrupulous about keeping herself and her kid clean. She loved her son and it had never entered her head to leave him on a snowy doorstep when he was two or three days old.

36

I WAS BORN WITH TEETH OF CHALK BUT MY YOUNG dentist, son of the gentle philosopher-dentist who used to work on my teeth, is a buoyant and energetic man who believes he can resolve any tooth problem. He peered at my aching molar and at x-rays, then cheerfully told me that the tooth needed root-canal work and a crown. I asked him how his father was and was his mother still sewing quilts, then I sank into the chair and let him stuff a rubber sheet down my mouth and grind away the silver amalgam anciently packed in the tooth. He bored deep into the nerve canals, took more x-rays, and crammed the hollowed chambers with gutta-percha, inserted a post, leveled off the tooth and took an impression of it, made a temporary cap, then told me to come back in two weeks to fit the permanent crown to the stump. Afterward, craving solace, I drove around to Alba's and she made tea for me to sip while the anesthetic wore off, and later she comforted me with dinner—fish, massaged with butter, sprinkled with oregano, fried in a pan, showered with lemon juice, garnished with watercress, washed down with white wine—after which I fell tranquilly asleep, made love when we awoke the next morning, then returned to my studio.

Alba's cooking had changed. It had always been satisfying, for she could give me whatever I wanted, but over the past few months her cookery had become fancier—or not fancier, but foreign and more sensuous—or maybe nothing had changed and I was just taking a greater interest in food because, as Zoe said, when you get older you get less interested in sex and more interested in food. Michiko laughed at all this and said, "Alba cooks wonderful dinners and now she's learned some new recipes from her cooking teacher, I think." Michiko, no clothes on, was kneeling at the low table where she had set the ink stone (suzuri) and ink bar (sumi), and now she loaded the brush (fude) and poised it vertically over the paper, her own image sliding left and right in the camera's view finder as I tried to fit everything inside the frame, from the coppery nape of her neck to the black point of the brush. I snapped the shutter, the camera clicked and whirred and fell silent. Michiko had swept a broad vertical line down the middle of the paper, ending her stroke with a deft push that left a neat feathered tail in its wake. "Remember," she murmured, not turning her head. "That's my camera and my film and I get to develop the pictures and throw away the ones I don't like." She paused, frowning slightly at her calligraphy.

"Just keep going," I told her. "This is good. Just keep going. It's good."

She suspended the freshly loaded brush above the paper again, studying her next move. "This isn't the way to do it," she whispered. "My teacher would be ashamed of me, to see this

—this mess I am making." But she kept writing and I kept shooting. I went for the smooth concentration of her face, the shallow contours of her torso and the delicately spare design of her arm, wrist, fingers, those slender pale petal fingernails, and simultaneously the thick inky brushpoint and sweeping black strokes, the kanji on the paper being so like her precise body, that body being a kanji itself. When I had finished the roll of film, Michiko laid the brush aside and modestly drew her pants across her lap. I gathered up the scattered sheets of paper and turned away so she could get into her clothes. I studied her brushwork: "I recognize moon," I said, not turning around.

"Haiku by Basho," she told me. "I'm dressed for public now. —I still don't understand what you want to photograph for. Or what you're looking for."

I turned around. "Neither do I. But I'm sure there's a meaning in it someplace, a sign, something to read. Like that harpooner from New Bedford with tattoos all over his body."

Michiko smiled. "Are we going to lunch now? There's a noodle shop I want to try." So I took her to lunch at the noodle shop, then she went on her way and I went to my studio to not paint.

The harpooner was tattooed with hieroglyphics which explained the meaning of life, or so he said, but the man couldn't decipher them and neither could anyone else. Now Michiko's body was marvelously smooth and blank, but it incarnated the same sort of undecipherable text. "Man, I don't know what you're talking about," Scanlon told me, laughing. We were standing side by side in my studio, looking at canvases. "You mean you want people to *read* your paintings?" he asked.

"*No, no, no!*" I said.

"What then?"

"All I'm saying is that the body is different, truly different, from anything else you can paint. All I'm trying to do is paint it so it says—. What it says."

"Great," he said flatly. Scanlon is a short, large-shouldered man, with bright eyes, a small hooked nose and a thatch of mottled brown hair sweeping back from the top of his balding head, as if he were standing in a strong wind. He folded his arms across his chest and surveyed the final canvas that leaned against the deep stack by the wall. "Have I seen everything? You got anything else around here to show me? I like this big stuff. You get a bargain when you buy a Stillamare. —Anything new in the back room?" he asked.

"The only new thing back there is Avalon's knapsack."

"Avalon's the woman you wrote me about, the one with the kid and no rent money. I remember. My memory is still pretty good. Did I remember to tell you I sold almost every painting in my Toronto show?"

"Twice already. But that's all right. It's good news. You can tell me again if you want."

"I'm not convinced yet, that's why I keep saying it. I still can't believe it. —I'm starved. Let's go out to lunch and you can tell me what you think of those photos I sent you."

We walked toward Copley Square, Scanlon discoursing on the international air of Toronto while I mutely wondered if I could have a sell-out show anywhere on the planet, then we came to an overpriced French bistro that Scanlon decided was right for us, and as soon as we had our napkins in our laps he said, "You haven't told me how things worked out for you at the new gallery, the one you wrote me about, the Strand, I think it was. What happened there?"

"I'm getting to that. I wanted to show you the paintings first," I said, uncomfortably aware that I was stalling.

"Good paintings. But my opinion doesn't count. What did the gallery have to say about them?"

"Your opinion counts a lot."

"Sure, sure. But what did the Strand woman say?" he asked again.

"She said a lot of different things. I'm still negotiating."

I hesitated, wanting to talk about it and at the same time so embarrassed at my failure that I wanted to shut up. "Sonia Strand wants to give me only half the wall space, wants to cram me in with some other painter."

"Oh?"

"And she wants sixty-six percent of whatever I get," I confessed.

He frowned, bit his lip. "Tough tit to suck on."

"Exactly."

"Let's get some food in our bellies before we discuss this," he said, briskly looking around for a waiter. So we ate and talked some about the camping trip he and his wife were planning, and even more about Toronto and the photos he had sent me of his exhibit there. I preferred the work he was doing a few years ago, but didn't want to hurt his feelings by saying so and, anyway, he had devised a fine theory that showed how his recent paintings were at the front of a radical movement in contemporary art, and since his theory pleased him as much as his paintings, we conversed about the theory. Then we began talking about Sonia Strand. "Find out what she likes and give it to her," he says, quite off hand.

"She doesn't know what she likes. Galleries don't know what they like. All they know is what they think they can't sell," I say. "Because galleries don't go broke by turning down painters, they go broke by taking on painters they can't sell. So they learn right away what they can't sell. After that, they want to be astonished. Astonish me and if it's something I can sell, I'll take it."

"She's looked at your work, right? She's told you which ones she liked, right?" Then he leans forward a bit and drops his voice to confide to me. "Give her more of what she likes. —It works in bed, too" he adds briefly.

"Wonderful. When do I get to paint what I want, the way I want?"

"You've been doing that all your life," he says.

"No. I've been teaching in a second-rate art school all my life. I did what I had to do to make a living. I have two wives and three kids, remember? Now I'm old and I don't want to die pretending to be somebody else just to get into a gallery."

He puts down his coffee cup so hard it rings and he looks at me. "You think that's what I'm doing?" he asks abruptly.

"What?"

"You think I'm bogus because I'm finally able to sell again?"

"Of course not! Hell, I wasn't even —"

"Because nobody bought my other stuff. I know you liked those things, but I couldn't show anyplace except college galleries. Those paintings died a quiet death." He jerks his head aside, annoyed. "They were a waste of my time."

"How can you say that? They were good paintings, terrific paintings. You found a way to go. You've got to stay with it, go farther and farther, then it will develop and change naturally. Let the buyers catch up later. That's the only way to go."

"Yeah. Well. That's you, Ren. Not me. I'm interested in selling."

"You think I'm not?" I had to laugh.

"You know Magnussen's in Manhattan?"

I told him I didn't know spit about the art scene in the city any more, and that was the truth.

"It's a good gallery. New but good. I sent him the big brochure from the Toronto show, the same as I sent you, and he asked to see my new paintings. I had a couple like the ones in the show, so I sent him slides of those."

I said Hey, that's great, told him it was terrific news, hoping I spoke with warmth and energy because, actually, I felt suddenly fatigued by his good news and ashamed of myself for feeling that way.

"Well, maybe he'll like my work or maybe he won't," he said with a philosophical sigh. "You never know."

I agreed you never know.

"I haven't had a good gallery for a decade," he said soberly.

I said yes, and oh, and well, and sank into thoughts of my own career.

Later, out of doors on the sidewalk, we agreed we should get together more often, and that a lunch in Boston or New York wasn't enough, and I congratulated him again on the Toronto show and the bid from the Manhattan gallery, then we said Take care and See you soon, turned and went our different ways. I walked down to the river and trudged upstream to the Fens and over to the Museum and then to my building, which isn't a terribly long trek as I'm in good shape for an old man, yet by the time I had climbed the stairway to the studio it felt like I should have died some while ago.

37

I GOT A BRIEF LETTER FROM LAUREL BRUNO, MIKE'S widow. It was just a hasty note, she said, because she had dreamed she was in the airport at Phoenix and Mike was there, too, and the dream was so vivid she wanted to tell me now and not wait until her next letter. She was so happy to see Mike, all the dreariness dropped away and she asked him What are you doing here? because even in the dream she knew he had died, so there must be some explanation. And Mike said I came to wish you bon voyage and to tell you not to worry, enjoy the trip. When she woke up she felt only a tinge of sadness, but when she was setting the table for breakfast she burst into tears and couldn't stop crying for a long time. She supposed the airport was in her dream because she was planning to fly to San Francisco to visit friends. Laurel wrote about her job and what she called the *ascetic* scenery of Arizona which, she added, she was still not used to. I read the note a few more times, then put it in the box where I keep things about Mike, just slid it in under the lid, so as not to look at the photos and letters inside.

The only time Mike returned to visit me was outside the Back Bay café where we used to meet sometimes. The air was amazingly bright and I said Let's get a table with an umbrella, and he said I can't stay long, but the sun's great, isn't it? I was heartsick because it was clear he didn't feel how much I missed him, but he was in good spirits, quite his round old self, and when I opened the menu it had a column of paintings the size of postage stamps. That was two years after he died and I haven't seen him since.

38

I BEGAN TO PAINT AGAIN AND IT HAPPENED THIS way. On Saturday morning Sonia Strand appeared at my door accompanied by two muscular louts who, I assumed, carried her sedan chair, but it turned out they had come along to manhandle one of my big paintings— "That one, the one with all the yellow," Sonia said—downstairs and out to Sonia's van, because she had a whimsical rich couple coming to her gallery, a couple who enjoyed previewing and sometimes actually buying canvases before they went on display. "And I think they might appreciate this one," Sonia told me over her shoulder as she— "Bye!"—drove off.

By the time I got back upstairs Avalon had escaped from the back room and was standing at the middle window, looking down into the street where the van had been parked. "Who was *that* bitch?" she asked without turning around. I told her the bitch was Sonia Strand who owned the Strand Gallery and maybe the bitch could sell the painting.

"That was one of my favorites," Avalon said crisply. "One of your best."

"One of my best? You've lived here all this time and haven't said ten words about my paintings and now you're a god-damned art critic?"

She turned and looked at me. "What are *you* so grumpy about?"

"You want a list?"

"Listen, I don't like Kim and me being shut in the back room every time there's a knock on the door." Her voice had turned annoyingly sharp.

"Quit complaining, Avalon, this was the only time and I already said I was sorry!"

"You. Did. Not."

"All right, goddamn it, I'm sorry!"

She stepped up to me and spoke in a harsh whisper. "You said you wanted to take Kim out to make maps, so do it." She bobbed her head once toward the back room to indicate where Kim was. "He's going over to Anwar's this afternoon and he's going to spend the night there. So if you're going to take him out, take him now."

I took Kim out. My plan was to search for a North West Passage to the Charles River, so we took our bearings outside the front door of the apartment building and headed toward the Fens, thence to the Museum and onward to the river. While we were tracking from the back of the Museum to the river he told me I had forgotten to shave. I told him I was giving my face a vacation this week. "There's no vacation for faces," he said. I told him, "Hey, are you counting steps or not? You're supposed to be counting." That kept him quiet until we reached the street corner. "How many steps?" I asked, flipping open my sketchbook. "The same as the last bunch, I guess," he said vaguely. "We're going to get lost if you don't do your part. Which way do we go now?" I asked him. He turned the compass on his palm, watching the needle veer and tremble. "Three-hundred and forty-five degrees," he said at last. When we reached the river bank we sat on a busted bench by the water and drew a map of our route based on his compass readings, and I asked did he think we'd be able to find our way back now. "I don't need a map to do *that*," he informed me. I told him that wasn't the point. "Your face is going to be white if you don't shave it," he said, cautiously touching my jaw. I stayed very still and squinted across the river, letting him rub my cheek as long as he wanted. "Wow, it feels weird and scratchy!" he said, taking his hand away.

"Listen, we were going to figure out how wide the river is without going across it. We were going to use a little geometry. Remember?"

"You were going to, but I'm bored now," he told me.

So our morning together didn't turn out quite as I had hoped, but at least we produced a map, and when we returned to the studio Avalon had prepared us lunch, which was grated raw carrots, diced tomatoes, chopped cucumbers, sliced green peppers and shredded lettuce, all of this wrapped cold in a flavorless tortilla. According to one of Avalon's holistic theories of food, vegetables should be kept near freezing, then scrubbed in cold water and eaten chill; that way they would invigorate the mind and raise us to a higher plane of consciousness. I unwrapped my tortilla, painted the inside with umber Dijon mustard, tossed in a handful of feta cheese and pickled olives and rolled it up again. Avalon was wearing my bathrobe, her hair turbaned in a towel. "I took a shower and I didn't want to get dressed till I finished lunch," she explained. "Because after I take Kim to Anwar's I'm going to Jenny's wedding. Remember?"

"Now I do," I said. Jenny was one of the waitresses at the Daily Grind.

"You've never seen me in a dress,"

"You showed it to me when you bought it. It's black."

"I showed it to you. That's not the same as seeing me in it."

"Mom looks funny in a dress," Kim volunteered.

"I'll bet she does."

"You two, a lot you know about dresses. It's a killer dress and I look great in it."

As it turned out, she didn't look bad. The dress was black, sleeveless, very short and very tight, held up with what they call spaghetti strings—two thin straps, thinner than my shoelaces—which left bare her shoulders, the hollow of her throat, the strong division of her breasts. Actually, she looked good, even in the black fishnet stockings. "What do you think?" she asked me, standing taller in new high-heels. "Am I a killer or not?"

"Mom, you're not a killer," Kim informed her.

Her hair had lengthened since I'd known her and no longer stood like a tar brush but—now black at the tip and pale at the root—it fell thickly every which way, tucked behind her ears and over the nape of her neck, making a tawny foil for the cruel silver rings and rivets in her ears, eyebrows and nose.

"You look fine, Avalon. Very Killer. Remember not to outshine the bride."

I drove them to Anwar's place where Kim jumped out and ran off without a good-bye wave, then I took Avalon to the Daily Grind where she joined two other waitresses, all three sharing a taxi to the wedding. I drove back to the studio, checked the mailbox and found a postcard from Sebastian Gabriel—you met him with his daughter at the *Pixels* exhibit—saying he had finished making the paper I had asked for and would I come to his place to take it away, please. I clothespinned Sebastian's postcard to the margin of the calendar to remind me to drive over to his place next week. After that I wrote a letter to my brother Bart about our mother's money, which we were managing, then wrote a note to mother, though it was impossible to know how much of my bland weekly gossip she actually retained, her nowadays being only a distraction, a confusing jumble of flimsy scenes through which she could see vivid dramas from thirty, fifty or seventy years past and, according to my brother, she was beginning to misremember or even forget those events, too.

I started out the door to mail the letters but remembered I wanted to take the dirty laundry out too, and as I was pulling the lumpy laundry bag from the back closet I saw my bathrobe was sprawled across Avalon's bed in a warm, cozy embrace of her pillow. I took the foolish thing away. On the floor at her bedside she had a thick paperback novel, beneath which lay *The Craftsman Entrepreneur: How to Sell Your Handiwork*, and under that was *Teach Yourself Japanese*. Avalon had taken over another shelf in the bookcase, stuffing my books sideways on top of each other to make room for a row of chrome-spiked, black leather chokers and bracelets (I tried on a few, none fit), a couple of covered cardboard boxes (jerseys, skimpy underpants) and a glassy jar of *Nuage D'amour* bath beads as a bookend for my copy of Montaigne's essays. She had a bottle of cologne which smelled rather like my after-shave, but she had no perfume. (Avalon had a way of lifting her head and flaring her nostrils to pursue an unfamiliar scent, and although she got used to wisps of Alba's perfume on me she never did accept Zoe's and would rub her eyes until they were red and blow her nose, claiming that she was allergic to something in the air.) She had used colored markers, the ones I gave Kim, to draw art nouveau flowers on a cardboard box where, I discovered, she kept each school paper her son had brought home, plus her journal (fake green leather, fake gold corners) which—please note!—I didn't open. I don't know how long I stood there, entranced by her things, the trinket details of her life that I couldn't look at when she was around, but at last I woke up and headed out to mail letters and take the dirty clothes to the laundromat.

I stopped at the laundromat, a lonely space with a desolate aisle of washers and dryers, plus a solitary woman folding towels, stayed only long enough to toss the clothes into a washer and then headed over to the Daily Grind. I sat in the sun by the window with coffee and a muffin while at a nearby table a little boy and his mother were discussing the possible outcome of a fight between Tyrannosaurus Rex and a plane equipped with rockets, the kid kneeling up on his chair and talking vigorously, one hand attacking the other; his mother listened attentively, then smiled, captured one of his hands, and began arguing a point. The kid sat back, one leg tucked under him, the foot sticking out beneath his bare thigh. I sank my chin on my chest, scribbled him onto my paper napkin, crumpled the napkin into my pocket and put the cap back on my pen. His father had come in and sat down beside him, one hand lightly on the nape of his son's neck, and now plowed gently up under the shaggy thick soft black hair. I looked out the window and was unreasonably happy.

I phoned Alba with the prospect of being with her for dinner and bedtime and Sunday brunch, but got only her recorded voice telling me she couldn't come to the phone just then but to please leave a —. I hung up, half remembering that she had told me she was going away this weekend, told me something about going with a woman friend to look at country property in Maine, or maybe she had said it was to a restaurant which had an especially fine cuisine or a clever chef or something like that. I phoned Zoe but got only her recorded voice and hung up. I went back to Edward Hopper's Laundromat, pulled the damp clothes from the washer and tossed them into the dryer, then went outside and sat on a bench to watch the people walking past until the clothes dried. When I got to the studio I looked into the bathroom with the thought of cleaning it, but it was quite clean (one tightly curled pubic hair, burnt gold, on the wall of the shower), so I wrestled the big unfinished canvases around till they faced me and I looked at them and they were good and I was back painting.

39

I PAINTED STEADILY AND WHEN THE OLD BONES and sockets began to ache I walked up and down, then I made a pot of coffee, filled a mug and went back to painting. I don't know how long I painted. I went to refill my mug and found the coffee pot was empty, so I turned to the refrigerator to get something to eat. Avalon had a gallery of Kim's art posted on the refrigerator door, including his old sketch of me with brushes stuck every which way in each gigantic hand and a brush sideways between my teeth, and I had to laugh because here I was with a brush and an empty coffee mug in my left paw and three brushes in my right and I felt good. Maybe Scanlon is right when he says if you paint you have a theory of painting, whether or not you know it, and maybe he's right when he says you paint to exhibit, because nobody ever painted just to have something to hide, but I know for sure I paint because I'm good at it. I opened the refrigerator door and ate a chunk of Romano, washed it down with three swallows of cold wine, grabbed a handful of olives, then went back to the canvas and when the light began to weaken I turned on the flood lamps and kept painting.

I don't know when Avalon came in, but I heard the water running in the bathroom and later I felt her standing behind and a little to my right, watching me try to work, then she came around to my left so close I could smell her ninety-nine-cent cologne, then back to the right, so I said, "Sit down and tell me about the wedding," simply to keep her out of the way. She was happy and went on prattling for I don't know how long, but after a while she said, "You're not listening," and I said Yes, I am, and she said, "What did I say?" and I turned around to look at her and tried to recall. She was still in the black micro dress and fishnet stockings, her arms folded, waiting. I told her Your make-up has come off. "Very observant, Ren. That's good in a painter. I washed it off an hour ago." I decided to give up and began to clean my brushes.

"Tell me about the painting," she says.

"What do you mean?"

"Tell me about the painting, the one you're working on."

"There's nothing to tell. It's a painting, not an event, despite what some moronic critics have said. You don't tell about it, you look at it."

"Try," she says. "Please. —Pretty please with goddamn sugar on it," she adds.

I went over to the canvas. "These figures, there's geometry and color and there's psychology. Now, the geometry, the depth as well as the flat surface, the way the bodies are arranged, makes the psychology, composes the psychology and— Never mind. See this? This is good, this whole passage in here, all through here. Good, very good. Nobody else can do this the way I do. Nobody." I paused to look at what I had done, where I had gone, and then began to look at what I had to do next and began to see how to go about it, which is one of the secret pleasures of the work. Then Avalon broke in on me. "That's it? That's all you're going to tell me?" she says.

"Are you hungry?"

"No, but you are," she says briskly. "I'll make something for you. I'll make zabaione."

"You?"

"You said you liked the way I made it a couple of nights ago. You melted my heart." She laughed.

"I'm not hungry. I changed my mind."

But she was already at the kitchen counter.

"I'm going to take a shower and go to bed. Goodnight," I told her. I pulled off my socks, tossed my shirt on the bed and went into the bathroom, had a great long, satisfying piss, stepped into the steamy blind shower and, as sometimes hap-

EUGENE MIRABELLI

pens when the work is going well, saw the next passage and luxuriated in that streaming knowledge and even knew the brush strokes, toweled myself dry and started out to the studio with my pants slung over my arm—"Hey, there," Avalon says—stepped back to take our bathrobe, *my* bathrobe, from the hook. "I thought you'd gone to bed," I told her, wrapping up.

"I told you I was making zabaione," she says, going to the counter. "I put it in mugs, one for me and one for you. Taste it," she says, handing me a mug full of creamy whipped zabaione, a muted yellow cloud with a dark shadow to it. "Here's a spoon. Taste it."

It didn't taste bad. "What did you spike it with?"

"Rum," she says, lifting her mug to tap it against mine.

"Very original, Avalon."

"It's an art. Nobody else can beat egg yolks the way I do," she says, smiling at me.

I laughed and touched the side of her face, meaning only —I don't know what I meant, except to be friendly, but she was looking at me in such a way that I caressed her cheek and pushed up into her hair, hair so soft and thick it startled me and my hand jumped back. She looked at me for the space of a heartbeat, then stepped up close, watching me and waiting, so I stroked her hair again and yet again, cautiously so as not to frighten her off. "I like it here," she says quietly. "It's safe. I feel safe."

"Good. That's good." I stroked her hair.

"I'll move out, Kim and me, we'll move out as soon as school is over, you know."

"I know."

"I, Kim and me, appreciate every—"

"Let's sit down," I told her, going to a chair at the table.

Avalon sat down across from me, saying, "I'm saving a lot of money this way and I appreciate all the—"

"Finish your zabaione. And tell me about the wedding."

But instead she shoots me a glance over her mug and slouches down in her chair and placidly says, "I'm not talking to you."

"I'll listen this time."

So Avalon told me about the wedding, which was performed out of doors with everyone standing in a circle around Jenny and Mark which, Avalon said, was really good because, frankly, churches give her the creeps, not that she has anything against Jesus, though Jesus never stayed up the night with a sick child, certainly not his own sick child— "The wedding, Avalon, the wedding." —and about the reception with the long tables under the trees, and how everyone from the Daily Grind sat together and had a great time and there was dancing and on and on she went. I did try to listen, but in a while all I was doing was looking at her and seeing not the hard pins and rivets and rings but only her clean face and self, which I had never seen before, and all I wanted just then was to watch her and even after her voice had stopped I went on watching and "What?" she says abruptly, "What did I say wrong?"

"I like you, Avalon."

"Are you trying to get me into your bed?"

"I wouldn't even dream of it."

She looked sharply at me. "Why not?"

"I'm too old."

She thought about it. "That wouldn't stop you if you wanted to. You're not *that* old."

"I'm much older than you."

"Everybody thinks I'm leeching off you or they think you're fucking me, or both."

"What do we care what everybody thinks?"

She gave me a sudden smile and these little lights danced in her eyes. "*We* don't care," she announces, smiling, and I wanted to caress her face again, wanted to put my old gorilla hand through her hair. But instead I got up and went to the sink to wash out my mug and a moment later she comes up, puts her mug under the running water and begins to wash it. I guessed she'd go off to bed now and I tried to think what to say to keep her here; I wanted to stay up all night and I cleared my throat to speak, but nothing came out, and in the magnifying moment I saw the tense stretch of her dress, saw the smooth warm texture of her skin and the subliminal blue veins as if I were only an inch away. Avalon had dried her mug and now she set it upside down on the drain board, saying, "I was sort of surprised to find you here. How come you're not across the river with your wife?"

"Alba's away for the weekend. And I'm back to painting, so it's all for the best," I told her.

"Where'd she go?"

"I don't know."

"You're a pair, you two. What about the other one?"

"Can't you say Alba or Zoe? And Zoe's not *the other one.* She's Zoe. She's Astrid's mother and she's been a mother since she was seventeen or eighteen. She hasn't had an easy life and I thought you would have some feeling for that." I had tried to say something to keep her here beside me, but all I had done was bawl her out.

Avalon shrugged and half turned away. "If you weren't home when I came in I'd have put on some music. That's what I do when you're not around. The weekends you're away we get real loud. The big space in here makes it sound like, grand. You ought to try it, Ren. Get some rhythm in those old bones."

"I know what it sounds like in here. I used to do that." It came out defensive even in my own ears, but I didn't know what else to say. "You know the crate full of records back there? My player broke and they don't make players for those records any more, that's all. I used to have a great hi-fi. I played a lot of music."

Avalon laughed at me. "Hi-fi. Yeah, I bet you had a great

hi-fi. Those old 78s are so godawful stiff they're like dishes, like platters. They're like old-fashioned crockery. They're antiques."

I kept her there, kept her there talking, though to be truthful it was me carrying on both sides of the idiotic conversation while Avalon was busy massaging her thigh or stretching this arm behind her head, then that arm, then pressing her hand hard into the small of her back and with the other hand squeezing the bare nape of her neck and the long muscle that slants to her shoulder. She was some package in that tense micro-dress, despite the chromium trash nailed to her face, and I wanted to caress her cheek again or close my fists on the warm satin flesh of her arms, sink my teeth in the succulent scruff of her neck. In a moment she was going away to bed and I started to touch her hair, but she watched me so I dropped my hand.

"That's all right," she says, matter-of-factly. "I like it when you do that."

"You're all right."

"But I don't know why you're so stingy with me," she says. "Everyone else gets a piece of you. I notice when you meet people in the street you open your arms so wide you smack me in the face. And at the Daily Grind you give everybody a touch or a pat on the shoulder. You put your arm around Michiko and kiss her. You give Garland a squeeze. The other day I saw you pick up one of the kids in the playpen and toss her in the air till she hiccupped, she was laughing so hard. But you won't even touch me with your little finger."

"That's not true, Avalon."

"Yes it is."

"It's because I don't want to start down that road."

"What the hell road are you talking about?"

"There's no fool like an old fool. I know it. I know it and I know me. I'll be damned if I—I'm going to bed."

"If you what, Ren?"

"I'm going to bed. It's past my natural bedtime."

"Let's stay up all night," she says.

"I'm going to bed."

So Avalon abruptly vanished to the back room and I turned off the rack of lights above the canvases and then the other lights, one by one, and crawled into bed. A short while later the dim light from down the hall went out and Avalon was in her bed, too. I lay here with no thought in my hollow head, only a desire to lie in the dark and be filled with the dark and be blotted out, but after a while my eyes adapted and the windows grew luminous, revealing the slanted stack of stretcher frames, the big easel, the kitchen chairs, and what looked like a string of glittering pearls forgotten on the floor beneath the table. I rolled over and faced the wall. I didn't want to think about the canvas I had been working on because then I wouldn't get to sleep, but if I didn't think about my work I'd think about Avalon and a minute later I'd be galloping down the hall to make a joke of myself, an old buffoon who still hadn't learned how to rein in the horse he was born on. I don't know how long I tossed back and forth between those tangled sheets, don't know if it was twenty minutes or an hour, not being able to rest my thoughts on any one thing except should I stay here or should I go there, thinking I'd be a fool to try it with Avalon and then thinking I'd be a bigger fool to stay here, then back again. At last I threw aside the bedcovers, stumbled to my feet and pardoned Alba for her crazy flirtations, her lunch-and-coffee men friends, pardoned her passing fancies with this aging poet and that young athlete, pardoned the little sins she told me about and the bigger ones she didn't, pardoned her for doing whatever I was about to do. I turned to the hall and here was Avalon, saying quietly, "I heard you get up and I thought I'd meet you half way." We stood there so close we almost touched and I felt, or maybe I only heard, her ragged breath, then she pulled her T-shirt up over her head, her elbow brushing my cheek and the warm smell of her skin filling my head, tossed the pale cloth into the dark and now she was as naked as I was. I held my gut tense, vain even in these shadows, but Avalon was already stepping past me to lift the bedclothes and get into my bed and I got in beside her.

How much do you want to know? We settled against each other awkwardly, our shocked flesh receiving volt upon volt until our bodies found alignment, front to front on our sides. "I'm clean, no problems," she says quietly. "Me too," I tell her. "You know I never fucked around—not in the last few years, anyway," she says. "Me neither," I tell her, kissing not the cruel rings in her eyebrow but the pierced flesh there, kissed her cheek, her ear, whatever she offered as she pressed her face this way and that against my mouth. Her hand glided from my shoulder to my hip to my flank with a caution so gentle it startled, just as the softness of her glittering shaggy hair had startled; she had a vigorous embrace and such tenderly inquisitive fingers as to doom a young man to her touch, and I was grateful to be old.

"I knew I would make it.—Oh, you sweet man, you lasted like nobody else," she says afterward, breathless and sweaty and happy, as if she had just won the Boston marathon. I told her Lasting is the only new thing an old man has, and rolled onto my back, exhausted, and let her rest half on me, the bed being so narrow, and after I got my wind back I got up naked and starving and looked into the white glare of the refrigerator. I took out a bottle of wine and the big end of a thick pizza we had made yesterday (a school of anchovies deep inside it, the whole topped with green peppers, gold onion rings and delicate pink leaves of prosciutto), then shut the door on the light. "I can do anything in the dark except eat," says Avalon, "so do you want the electricity or the oil lamp or those beeswax candles you're always telling me never to use?" I lit the oil lamp and Avalon put her plate ("The one with the ugly face on it," she says) on the near side of the table, where Kim usually sat, her knees bumping mine in a friendly way. The pizza was dense with flavors and the wine felt clean going down and the lamplight made Avalon's flesh as gold as a ripened pear, such as you would want to bite into, and "What are you scowling at me for?" she says. I'm not scowling, I tell her. "Yes you are," she insists, sinking her teeth into the pizza. It's the look I get when I'm hungry, I tell her. "If we run out of food you can eat me," she says and then she begins to laugh at her witticism, holding her hand over her mouth, swallowing, then laughing, coughing and laughing. "Be careful, you'll fall out of that chair," I tell her.

"Oh, God," she says, wiping her eyes, gasping. "I feel good." And she sinks back in her chair and sighs happily and looks at me and says, "Tell me again about my mother."

"I've told you about your mother twice a week. How many times do you want to hear the same story?"

"All right, tell me about my father when you and him hung out together." I was about to tell her You've heard all that, too, but seeing how happy she was I relented and said All right, then I refilled my glass and took a drink and wiped my mouth meditatively on the back of my hand, all the while trying to recollect poor Brendan Flood. I began by saying how the great thing about Flood was he did so many things, how he programmed computers, which in those days were huge monsters big enough to fill a room, how he wrote poetry, how he painted—no development there, but I didn't say that— and played the guitar and had his own band, how he liked to recite whole pages of Thoreau or William Blake or Allen Ginsberg because, like them, Flood was an angel-headed hipster burning to connect to the starry dynamo, and I told her about the urban commune he tried to organize and the peace march he led into a riot with the police, and how at a rally on the State House steps he ended his poem by tearing open his shirt to display LOVE in red lipstick on his chest, told her these and fifty other things, knowing I had forgotten hundreds more and regretting it. "What did he tell you about my mother and me?" she says.

"Have some more wine."

"But I like that story."

"No."

"Aren't you interested in your mother?" she asks me.

"You mean the one who left me on the doorstep or the real one?"

"Your birth mother," she says.

"No, not at all."

"Don't you want to find out why it happened that way?"

"I've never been curious about that. And there's nothing left to find out at this date. It's all gone."

"She must have had a reason for doing what she did and you should find out," she says. I told Avalon I wasn't interested, which was true, and that I was happy with the way things had turned out, which was also true, but Avalon went on anyway. "You should find out. Because maybe she wanted you to find out and to understand," she says.

I drained my glass. "If she wanted me to know something she should have left a note."

"I give up," Avalon says, letting her hands drop to her bare thighs with a loud slap. "And I have to go pee," she says, getting up.

Avalon went off to the john and in my head one thought led to another, so when she came back I asked her, "How many rings do you have down there?"

"Two," she says

"Don't they get in the way?"

"They didn't stop *you*, did they?"

I thought about it. "I felt them."

"You're supposed to."

Avalon drank her glass, tilting her head way back to get the last of it, and I don't know why it was such a pleasure to see her that way — her arm up, the tight pectoral and lifted breast and the underside of her jaw, her throat working beautifully. I supposed it would be impolite to ask why she had pierced those tender labial petals, but I asked anyway. "Why did you put them there?"

"Fun and games," she says, setting down her empty glass. "I was going through a phase, you'd say. Back then I used to have rings in my nipples, too, gold hoops, but I took them out when I got pregnant. You can breast feed a baby even if you have rings in your nipples, and I've seen it. But I didn't want to." She rattled on about piercing in San Francisco but maybe she saw I was heavy-lidded because she wound up with, "We're out of wine and I'm going to bed. What about you?"

When I came back from the john I blew out the lamp and got in beside Avalon, she lying hard against the wall, and told her If I roll over I'll crush you. "I'm not crushable, so you can relax," she says, her breath on my arm. I stretched out on my back and folded my hands behind my head, thinking to lie steady as a king carved on a tomb, fearful if I relaxed anywhere my old guts would rumble or I'd fart or I'd leak, as had begun to happen these past few years. I stared at the foggy ceiling or across the room at the tall gray window oblongs and in a while Avalon sank against my side and I wondered how she could make herself so weightless whereas my own bones felt so heavy, and then I noticed her breathing had slowed and deepened, for she was asleep and easy in her sleep, and I relaxed somewhat and thought how strange it was to be lying here with Avalon, as if the machinery of the heavens had slipped a gear, and I cautiously put my arm around her, and I felt better that way, and while trying to think of young men who would be fit to marry her I wandered off to sleep.

I woke up stiff. The air was pale in the studio and colors were just beginning to show when I lifted the blanket and slowly rumpled it down to look at more Avalon as she lay asleep on her stomach, her face to the wall. She had strongly defined scapulae and a long spine and — *lo and behold!* — two large symmetrical wings tattooed in white ink spread out and down to clasp the neat round of her buttocks. It wasn't a bad design in its own rapturous and vulgar way and I don't know how long I lay propped on my elbow, studying it, wondering what comic constellation of motives made her get tattooed in such elaborate feathery detail but in an ink so bland it was almost invisible. Then she awoke and my dawning prick bestirred itself, or maybe it was the other way around — no matter — for when Avalon slid her flesh warmly against mine and began to turn in welcome I closed my hand on the nape of her neck and took her from behind, kept her from seeing this old man's avid gargoyle face in the bright morning air.

40

MEDUSA'S ECSTATIC FACE (THOSE SHOCKED EYES, that gasping mouth) was on a plate that Avalon grabbed from the kitchen shelf only when she wasn't looking, because it was so ugly. I can't recall when my mother first showed me the cheap blue kerchief imprinted with the map of Sicily which had been wrapped around infant me on the doorstep, but from the beginning I was fascinated by the strange face in the center of the map above the word SICILIA — a face crowned with something curled or twisted, and from the head grew three muscular legs chasing each other around, so there were two legs spread near the bottom and one at the top. At first I took it for the head of Christ crowned with thorns. "No, that's Medusa," my mother told me.

I asked why Medusa was so angry. "Because her hair has turned to snakes, see, those are snakes," she said. "She was a beautiful woman and very proud of her long hair, very vain, but her hair was changed to snakes and now she's so mad that one look from her can turn you to stone." I believed it because my mother herself had flown at me with her black hair twisted every which way, her face white with rage and her eyes big, swatting at me as I dove under my bed or jumped out the door. "Perseus cut off her head and that's her head," she told me. She began to turn the edge of the kerchief and I cried, "*Wait! I want to look some more!*" but she was already folding it away, laying it deep in her cedar hope chest. "Benvenuto Cellini made a statue of Perseus with the head of Medusa, a bronze statue, which he cast all in one piece. He was a great artist, that Cellini."

My mother enjoyed telling me stories about Cellini, but I was more interested in Medusa. I came across the three-legged figure on a book cover at Veronica's house, on a cracked plate at Nick's, fashioned into a trinket on my aunt Gina's wrist, and drawn on every map of Sicily. Medusa was one of three Mediterranean sea spirits, the mortal one but also the most beautiful, so beautiful that the old sea-god Poseidon went mad for her, surged from the waves, and with sea water streaming from his beard and flanks— "He *ravaged* her on the floor in the temple of Athena," Veronica informed me—*ravished* her on the floor in the temple of Athena, whereupon Athena, that bitch so envious of Medusa's powerful beauty, turned Medusa's long black hair to snakes.

I asked why there were three legs that way, as if they were joined at the hip in back of Medusa's head. "Because there's three corners to Sicily," my father told me, hunched over the slate he was inscribing. "That's called the trinacria, that design. It stands for Sicily. Those three legs with the head of Medusa in the middle." I asked whose legs they were, which caused him to laugh and straighten up. "Those are nobody's legs. Go ask your uncle Zitti" he said, sweeping his leathery hand across the slate to brush away the grains. "That's the sort of thing he'd know."

Trinacria was an ancient name for Sicily. "Derived from the Latin," Zitti told me. "Which is derived from the Greek,

trinakrios, which means triangle—we used to call you Trinacria when you were little, but your mother put a stop to
it—and the Greeks called the three-leg symbol a tryskelion,
which means three legs." But no one could tell me whose
legs they were. Years later when Alba and I were hitch-hiking
through southern Italy we came to a museum displaying ar-
tifacts from nearby Pompeii, and among the rotted ax blades
and block planes stood a small naked bronze man, grimacing
as he staggered along with an ancient erection as big as either
of his legs. "Now *that's* an accomplishment!" Alba said. The
poor guy, corroded and grayish with age, had been support-
ing this burden for two thousand years, and when I saw him
I knew those were his three legs running around Medusa's
head. "But in every trinacria *I've* ever seen, each leg is just a
leg," Alba insisted. I informed her she had to see these things
as symbols. "If we're looking for symbols," she says, laughing,
"Medusa's head isn't a woman's head with snakes at the top
and a gaping mouth, it's her big hairy down-there."

Metamorphoses such as happened to Medusa happen often in Sicily, for it's a place where gods and goddesses, animals, women, men, spirits, and angels have taken each other
by love or by force and made beautiful monstrosities since
the beginning of time. Demeter, warm goddess of corn and
grain, used to stroll the plains of Sicily and it was there in
a field by the town of Enna—it's true, you can visit it—
Hades stalked Demeter's slender daughter Persephone,
clamped his cold hand over her mouth and dragged her underground, after which her grief-crazed mother refused to
bless the harvest, so crops withered and nothing grew until
Hades agreed to release Persephone, though only for half the
year, for which six months Demeter allowed fields to bear
again. The first to take Demeter was Poseidon, that same
Poseidon who later ravished Medusa. But Poseidon in his
youth didn't live in the sea; no, in his youth he was the shining god of horses. Demeter fell in love with Poseidon, fasci-

nated by his rippling power and gentleness, and she walked beside him in the fields, caressed the dark hair that trailed over the nape of his neck like a storm cloud, and led him to her bed where they mounted each other this way and that for one whole year. From their union came the horse, Arion, and a daughter whose name can never be said, and the blood of Poseidon flowed in the veins of my great great grandfather Cavallù, who was born with the hindquarters of a horse. The only reason I'm confessing these things is so you'll know what's in Sicilian blood and how come I'm this three-legged man, corroded and grayish with age.

41

I GOT OUT OF BED AND SURVEYED LAST NIGHT'S WORK to see if it looked as good in the morning—it did—and I must have picked up a brush because I was painting when Avalon brought me a cup of coffee, saying, "God, don't you ever quit?" Not when the work is going well and it was going well till twenty minutes later when she said, "We have to go get Kim," so I dunked the brush and we drove off to get Kim. When we got there, Anwar's mother had invited Kim to stay through lunch, which was all right with Avalon, so we headed back to the studio and Avalon said, "I'm all dressed up, so why don't we get Sunday brunch at a nice place." In her eyes she was all dressed up, wearing her belly-button jersey top, the black one with silver threads in it, and her black velvet shorts with the chromium dog-chain belt. I stalled, told her I'd have to shave first. "You look fine, very distinguished, very mature. Let's go," she said. So we dined on over-priced waffles at Aujourd'hui, very mature me in shaggy white stubble and happy Avalon in black velvet shorts displaying a warm crescent moon of bare flesh beneath each rear hem.

Actually, nothing much changed in the way we lived—
each morning Avalon went off to the Daily Grind to roast
coffee and sell espresso makers, while I trotted up and down
the river, returned to the studio and painted; she still slept
with Kim at her side, I had my bunk to myself. But early one
misty afternoon here she was back in the studio, saying, "All
right, I thought it over and bought some film, so let's get going." I loaded my camera, took about twenty shots of her in
the silvery light while she pulled off her jersey, shucked her
jeans, unhooked her bra and stepped out of her flimsy underpants, then took a hundred more right here or over there or
just fooling around (she grabbed the camera, snapped a few
of me) and ended with seven different shots of her standing in the middle of the bare floor with her hands clasped
behind her head. I put aside the camera which, thinking of
all the snapshots it had inside, purred happily as it rewound
the last reel of film. I brought Avalon a handful of bra and
underpants and with my other hand gave her lovable rump
a pat—or tried to—actually, she cried "Ha!" and hopped
sideways so I missed, then she waltzed around the easel and
when I lunged after her she jumped past me, circled the table
and dove behind the stack of big canvases that slanted against
the wall, her tail gleaming for a moment as she scooted down
the little tunnel at the bottom of the stack. We are made to
the image and likeness of God, as the Catechism says and
as I know when I'm painting well, and every now and then
God just plays around, makes a fool of himself or herself or
themselves.

"Now tell me about this painting," Avalon says one day,
pulling up her jeans and buckling her belt.

"I thought we went over that."

"No, this other one. I have a problem with this."

"But I don't and I painted it."

"I don't want to be critical, but I—"

"Excellent decision!"

"How come some of them took off their clothes? I understand nudes, but this—"

"Do you like it?"

"I don't think it's a good idea to have kids that age in the same picture with adults when some of them are naked."

"Listen, do you like it or not?"

"I feel the way you do when something I make for dinner turns out weird and you eat it anyway," she says.

"Try the landscapes and still lifes."

I said earlier that nothing much had changed, but maybe I should have said the change was subtle and, now that I think of it, sometimes the change wasn't so subtle; like, one evening I was at the table writing a letter to Brizio when Avalon sat down and announces, "I forgot to tell you—I did you a favor—I made an appointment for you to see your doctor."

"You did *what*?"

"Because, Renato, every time I pick up the list of things we need to buy, like milk or cereal, there's always those little scraps of paper saying, *Make appointment to see doctor*, or *Make appointment to get poked*, or *Make appointment to get finger up ass*, so I copied down the phone number and phoned from work and they had a cancellation and I said you'd take it. I thought you'd be pleased. Next Tuesday at ten," she adds.

"Goddamnit, Avalon, mind your own business and leave me alone!"

"I wrote it on the calendar. You're welcome."

Kim had memorized his multiplication tables long ago, but he didn't have a single poem in his head, his teachers believing that poetry would take up too much space and that if he ever needed a poem he could look one up in a book, so we began to recite some lines each night after dinner. We had gotten to that place in Paul Revere's ride where there's *a hurry of hoofs in a village street, a shape in the moonlight, a bulk in the dark*, and Kim was having difficulty memorizing the next couple of lines which, frankly, aren't very memorable, but at last he got them and finished the lesson with *That was all! And yet, through the gloom and the light, the fate of a nation was riding that night!* Great stuff.

Kim dashed off and his mother said to me, "I read that poem you wrote about apple tarts." I asked her what she was talking about. "In the cook book, the one that's falling apart, I was looking through all those loose pieces of paper with recipes and one of them was a poem in your handwriting. It begins, like, *For apple tarts, my best advice is cut the apples up in slices,* and something like, *add cinnamon or other spices,* and I forget the rest, but I thought it was pretty good." I went to get the cook book. "Does the recipe work?" she asked.

"Of course it works, if you read the whole thing," I told her. Frankly, I was overly pleased with the little jingle, so I shuffled through the scraps of folded stationery and found it. "See — *lightly flour a rolling pin and roll your dough out flat and thin to fold those spicy apples in* — and so on and so forth." It seemed good at the time.

"Very clever, Ren."

I unfolded each square of stiff old paper (wine stains on the margin, herb leaves in the crease) and read the recipe, then turned it over and read the names scribbled on the back. Alba had written the recipe and our dinner friends had signed it, and we had kept the notes as souvenirs. Now I laid the open papers on the table and recalled as best I could each gathering, some in this studio, but the joyful spirits would not come when I called.

"What's wrong?" Avalon asked.

"Nothing. We had good times."

"You don't look it."

"They're gone," I told her.

"There'll be other times, other dinners."

"Too many of the people are gone."

"You have lots of friends left," she said, getting up from the table. "You're always having coffee with somebody at the

Grind or else you're over in Cambridge with those guys or at somebody's studio and you're always writing letters to some friend." She had come back with the wine bottle and two water glasses and now she filled the glasses and handed me one. "Tell me about Alba."

I drank down half the glass. "I love Alba and would die without her."

"Oh, for sure," she says airily, dismissively. "But that's not what I asked."

"What's there to tell? Alba is big-hearted, good-natured, intelligent, and every year a little more bossy and prudish."

"She looks beautiful in the pictures," says Avalon.

"Those are old. She doesn't look that way anymore."

"Don't be a pig," she tells me.

"Alba's a beautiful, warm, thoughtful woman who keeps a dagger wrapped in her hair in case she needs something to shove in your heart."

"How come you're not living with her? I mean, why did you leave now, after all those years?"

"I haven't left, I'm just living here in my studio. Maybe I'm not living with her because I want to paint. Maybe I'm tired of being managed. Or maybe I don't like living with a person who writes gallery reviews for the *New England Newsletter*, celebrating assholes. My first mistake was teaching her how to look at a painting. Now she thinks she's a critic. I love Alba but she's a complex subject, too fucking complex to talk about, and I wasn't kidding when I said I'd be lost without her." I drank the rest and set the glass hard on the table with a bang and looked at Avalon who was still watching me. "Satisfied?" I asked her.

"No. But tell me about Zooey."

"Not Zooey. *Zoe*. Her name is *Zoe*. Is that so hard to say?" I drank another half a glass. "Zoe comes and Zoe goes. When she's single, she can't stand being single. When she's married, she can't stand marriage. She's broken out of two marriages

and wants to try it a third time. She did try celibacy one year
—bought some ugly dresses at the Salvation Army store,
wore no makeup or jewelry, went off on a spiritual retreat run
by monks and ended up in bed with the abbot. She's full of
contradictions that make her interesting to men, except the
ones she marries. I think the only person she trusts and loves
completely is her daughter. Zoe needs a home, that's all. Or
maybe not. She's a difficult woman, very difficult, too difficult
to talk about."

"If you want to sit here drinking all by yourself just say so."

"No, no, no. When I'm drinking or eating I like company.
—My idea of heaven is all my friends at a big table where
every one's talking and enjoying a meal that goes on forever."

"Because you're Italian," she says.

"Sicilian. There's a difference. And the reason I like friends
around my table is because I was born at dinner, at a long
table with my grandfather at one end and my grandmother at
the other and lots of people on both sides. Did I ever tell you
I was born at a dinner table?"

"Yes, and I still think you ought to find out why it happened."

"I'm going to bed."

"Do I get a goodnight kiss or what?"

After that kiss and a bit more she went to her bed and I
went to mine, where I stretched out in sweet tiredness, folded
my hands behind my head, and listened to the rain patter on
the window. I thought about my work and knew I was getting
to where I had always wanted to go and, in fact, I was so close
I could see the way there, could see it clear. I knew I wasn't
going to get there because *there* keeps edging off the horizon,
but that didn't bother me. I was grateful to have lived so long
and to have learned this much. What I mean is, I had finally
learned how to paint. I wanted to phone Alba tomorrow to
tell her all about it. I wanted to show her the new work, the
way I used to, so afterward we could eat and she could tell me

what she thought about the canvases, which ones she liked and what she thought was strong or lame in each one, but even while I was thinking it I knew she wouldn't come, not to the studio, not so long as Avalon had a key to the place. And the more I thought about all this, the longer I envisioned it from Alba's slant, the more I wished I was a different me and not this same old man with one hand on a brush and his other in a bush. Despite all her foxy cleverness, Alba couldn't see through walls, couldn't see that I was going to my chaste bed like a monk each night, couldn't know I was living like a misfortunate castrato, more or less like a castrato, comparatively so. All she could figure, with Zoe's inventive help, was that I kept some skanky girl in the back room so I'd have a body to fuck whenever I began another canvas—though they both knew me better than that. Anyhow, all this was going to change. We knew, Avalon and I, that she was moving out with Kim after he finished the school term, though when I thought to calculate how soon that would be I discovered I didn't know the school's closing date. I wondered if the schools in Cambridge were better than in Boston and wondered if Alba would help find a place for them over there, but then remembered how high rents were in Cambridge and thought how Avalon needed to get a better job and thought about Kim, a good kid—had felt myself floating off to sleep, but beached to wakefulness again—and mused how strange that reading a recipe and a scrawl of long-ago names could wring my heart like it was a soaked dishrag. I thought of the big dinners we used to have in the studio, everyone bringing a platter of food or a bottle of wine, the bowl we made from a cast of Alba's peach fanny, when we were young and the future was radiant around us like an aura, and I thought it would be good to have a big dinner again and if Alba could find us a place in the country we could set the table outside in the shade of a big tree and began to think who we would invite and was adding names to the list when I floated off to sleep.

42

*I*N DR. CADOC'S OFFICE I PEED INTO A FUNNEL-SHAPED beer glass, then dropped my pants and, still standing, seized the top of the examination table in a hard embrace while the doctor, his hand in a tight translucent glove, pressed a lubricated finger to my anal ring and pushed strangely inward and continued to push ever and ever more deeply inward (my teeth clenched) to feel through the flesh of the rectal wall my faithful prostate gland hidden on the other side, then his finger turned in a slow relentless sweep (my mouth gasping open) and made one last push which forced — *expressed* was his medical term — a few drops of seminal fluid onto a glass slide which his other hand held beneath the drooping head of my abject penis; there was nothing unusual afloat in my urine or seminal fluid — "Everything looks clear. All you need is a blood test," he said, letting me out on parole.

43

*O*NE NIGHT AVALON SAYS, "I SHOWED YOU MY PHOTO albums and told you about me, and I'm not prying, Renato, because I know you get hysterical about your privacy, but why won't you tell me about you?" and I said, "What do you want to know? I'll tell you everything," and she said, "I know you're not curious about your birth mother—."

"Right."

"—Which I don't understand. So tell me about the one who adopted you."

I told her about my mother, Bianca, and how she had four

sisters and four brothers and all of them were dead now except for two sisters, told how her father had come here from Sicily with nothing but an English dictionary in his pocket and how he worked hard and got himself a wife and a big house in Lexington and a villa in Palermo and nine children. "His name was Pacifico Cavallù and he's the one who found me on the doorstep. Everybody was sitting at the table in the dining room and there comes this knock at the big front door. Three knocks, like this," and here I hit the wall with my fist the way it had been done every time I heard the story. KNOCK KNOCK KNOCK. "There were thirteen people at the table that night. My grandfather got up with his napkin still tucked in his vest and went to the door and it was snowing and there I was. That was seventy years ago."

"And you still don't want to find out who your mother was who left you there, right?"

"I know enough. I know when the baby was born she went to leave it at the church, the parish house, but she made a mistake and left it at the wrong place. Because my grandfather's house was on this side of the church and the priests lived on that other side. She got pregnant by accident and left me at the wrong door by mistake, that's who she was."

"First of all, she didn't get pregnant by herself. And Second, maybe she didn't—"

"I'm grateful she didn't leave me in the snow and I'm grateful she got the wrong house."

"Let it go, Ren. Tell me about your father."

So I told her about my father, Fidèle, who was called Fred, and how he was an artist and master craftsman, a stone cutter, because his mother and father had died in the influenza epidemic of 1918, both mother and father on the same broiling August day, and how his father's last words to him were *Salvaguarde tua sorella*—Protect your sister—and how the day after the funeral my father wrote a letter to the Wentworth Institute to withdraw from the engineering classes he had been attending, after which he went downstairs to his father's shop and wrote to the dozen or so customers who had unfinished job orders, assuring them that he would complete his father's work. He cut and re-cut stones and set and re-set tile from seven in the morning till seven at night, six days a week, until he had learned how to do it right and had finished each order, and in the summer of 1927 he was the man who set the tile and raised the carved stone lintel over the door to Pacifico Cavallù's store on Prince Street. One of the Cavallù daughters brought him a glass of water and as he tossed back his head and was drinking it down she looked at the working of his throat and at his chest where the damp shirt clung, and when he handed her back the glass she said, "My name is Bianca, what's yours?"

"I like that Bianca," Avalon said. "But you told me once you came from a family of orphans and foundlings. So where are the orphans and foundlings?"

"My father's parents died when he was nineteen and his sister was fourteen. They were orphans. He had to take care of her and she was a wild one. Even at fourteen. That's why his father said to protect her."

"Who was the foundling?"

"My father's father."

"Where was he found?"

44

ON THE ROAD FROM PALERMO TO VUCCARINA THERE used to be a tavern run by a man and a woman, and they had a girl in the kitchen named Serafina. One hot afternoon (August 15, 1893) Serafina was plucking a chicken when a young man appeared out of nowhere and asked for a drink of water. "Water," he said hoarsely. She looked up to see him standing there—slender as a willow wand, with sunburned cheeks and pained, glittering eyes. "If you would be so kind," he added with a wan smile. Then he fell on his face in a faint. Serafina snatched the bucket of water from the sink, dropped to her knees and began to wash his face. "Oh, God," she murmured, loosening his collar with one hand and pressing the cool damp cloth to his forehead. "You're beautiful, beautiful, beautiful. Please wake up. Please." When he came to, the only thing the young man saw was Serafina, her wide sea-green eyes and her gold hair. He looked at her a moment, then shut his eyes and shook his head and opened them again.

"Don't move," she told him crisply. "I'll get you something to eat."

"No," he croaked. "Only water. I'm fasting."

"You're starving to death," she told him, dunking a cup in the bucket. "Drink this. There's food in the pantry that nobody else knows about. I'll go get it," she said, springing up.

The young man drank down the cup of water, then climbed waveringly to his feet and hauled the bucket to one of the long tables and seated himself there. The tavern door and both windows were open and he stared out at the dusty white yard, wondering where he was. The sun was beating down like a hammer and it seemed he could hear it going bam-*bam*, bam-*bam*, bam-*bam* in his head. Serafina came back carrying a platter with a chunk of provolone, a big handful olives and a string of dried figs.

"Eat up," she told him with a broad smile. "The boss and his bitch are asleep upstairs."

"You don't understand," he said with a parched voice. "I'm fasting. I'm waiting for a sign from God, a vision."

"Oh? How long have you been waiting?"

"Nine days. No. Yes. I think. Well—" He looked embarrassed. "I can't remember."

"What's your name then?" she asked, smiling at his confusion.

"Fidèle," he said. "At least I can remember that."

"I'm Serafina," she told him. Then she tore one of the figs from the string with her teeth. "You're not from around here."

"I was brought up in Palermo at the Orphanage of Saint Jerome and now I'm a student at the seminary next door to the orphanage."

"So you're running away?" Her sea-green eyes shone with delight. "I'd like to do that."

"Oh, no," Fidèle said, startled. "I came out here to pray and fast and wait for a sign from God, a call to the priesthood."

"What a waste," she said without thinking. "I mean, why do you need a sign from God? Doesn't the abbot take care of all that?"

"Because I don't feel fit to be a priest!" he cried. "Because I'm tormented by terrible visions. Because despite all my prayers—even in the middle of my prayers—something breaks into my head and distracts me. I thought if I left the city and came out to this simple, this bare, this, this—" He fumbled for the right word.

"To this God-forsaken wilderness of dry dirt and stones. Yes, go on," she prompted, sinking her strong white teeth into another fig.

"I thought if I came out here and prayed and fasted and mortified my flesh, purifying myself, then God would give me a vision, a blessed light to let me know for certain that I was clean enough and strong enough to serve Christ at the altar. But instead the distractions have been growing worse. I try to pray and it's as if someone were singing in my head, singing not words but single notes, weightless shimmering notes that hang in the air like flakes of gold. A beautiful voice, a woman's voice." He closed his eyes and wiped the sweat from his eyelids with his palms. "She's a contralto," he added shakily.

"Are you getting enough sleep?"

"When I sleep I have nightmares." He swung his fists down on the table so hard—*crash!*—that the bucket jumped, quite startled. "Last night I dreamed of angels plunging from heaven like meteors, their wings in flames, the air sizzling. And today it feels as if my head is on fire," his voice cracked and his hands shook.

Serafina closed her hands over his and looked into his glittering eyes. "You should rest here in the shade and eat more," she told him.

Fidèle snatched back his hands. "Some days I don't even know who I am!" he sobbed. Then he lifted the bucket as high as he could and emptied it on his head.

Serafina cried Hey! and turned round to fetch a towel, but when she turned back he had already pulled off his shirt and was using it to mop his head and neck.

"I've never told these things to anyone," he murmured, clearly puzzled.

Serafina saw how his bones were beautiful and strong, the flesh of his stomach as tight as a drum, and suddenly she wanted to pull his head against her breasts, to feel his fiery cheeks and parched mouth. "You look like a bird cage," she said tenderly.

"But I feel much better. It's amazing." He smiled and looked around. "My head is clear for the first time in days. I'm ready now. I'm *ready*. All I need is a quiet place to pray." He smiled again, as if seeing her for the first time. "How old are you?"

"Eighteen. Almost eighteen. Practically eighteen. What's wrong?"

"I'm so happy—" He broke off, not knowing what he wanted to say.

"Listen. Let's get out of here. I've got some money hidden upstairs. I'll go get it."

"Money? All I need is a place to pray. They have rooms upstairs?"

In fact, the stairs had groaned and shuddered because somebody heavy was coming down. Now in strolled the boss, Mazza, a large barrel-shaped man tucking his shirt into his pants, buttoning his fly, scowling. "What's the fuss about? What's going on here?" he demanded, looking from one to the other.

"This gentleman wants a room," Serafina said.

"This gentleman without his shirt? And is that his little prayer book on the floor? He looks like a runaway priest to me. I can smell a priest even in my sleep."

"He wants a room," Serafina repeated.

"By the day or by the hour?" Mazza asked, unfolding a soiled apron.

"Until tomorrow morning," Fidèle said, picking up his prayer book and looking at it as if he had forgotten how to read.

"Up the stairs and down the hall, the room at the end. If you want the girl, you pay extra," Mazza told him.

"What?"

"He was making a bad joke," Serafina said, her cheeks reddening. "Let me show you the room."

"I'll take the money now," Mazza said evenly.

So Fidèle paid and followed Serafina up the narrow stairs and down the hall to the little whitewashed room. It had a bed over here, a table with an oil lamp over there, and in between was an open window with a brilliant blue square of sky. At that moment Fidèle was so happy that he wanted to break out singing, but when he turned to tell Serafina about it she was gone. He shut the door behind him, took off his shoes and sat on the covers with a pillow between his head and the wall. His body felt wonderfully light and at the same time it seemed to have a compressed power deep inside, as if he were about to spring up from the bed and fly off, soaring to extravagant heights in great circular sweeps and turns and rolls and volutes. In fact, he felt too giddy to pray, so he simply waited for the vision to appear. His eyelids grew heavy and then heavier and soon he was asleep.

Only God knows how long Fidèle slept. When he opened

his eyes the room was dark and the open window was crowded with stars. Sweet air embraced him like an arm (smooth and soft and warm) and there came a tender ripping sound, as if his soul were being torn open. He groped for the oil lamp, struck a match and touched it to the wick, then something soared over him or through him, knocking him to the floor at the foot of the bed. Now the room was drenched with golden light and she stood just inside the window, her airy white garments floating down into silence while a luminous golden cloud hung about her head and flakes of gold lingered in the air like shimmering music. She had a scissors in one hand and a sheaf of paper money in the other. Fidèle shut his eyes, shook his head, opened his eyes again.

"I am an angel of God," she whispered.

"An *angel?*"

"Shhh." She put her finger across her lips to show he should lower his voice. "Yes. Angels are pure spirits, without bodies, having understanding and free will," she explained.

"Oh." Now Fidèle had spent a year at the seminary, but he wasn't a fool and he knew this was Serafina herself in her nightdress. "I see."

"Angels were created to adore and enjoy God in heaven," she added, just as in the Catechism.

"I know. But what are you doing in my room?"

"Angels were also created to assist before the throne of God and—and they have often been sent as messengers from God to man, and are also appointed our guardians," she recited. "I'm here to give you a message," she said.

"And what might that be?"

"There is a certain young woman who works here like a slave in the kitchen, and waits on table and cleans the rooms. Not to mention being forced to do other filthy things."

Little by little the flakes of gold floating in the air had settled to the floor, as if they were chicken feathers cut loose from a pillow and gilded by lamplight.

"Serafina?"

"Yes, that's her name. And when you wake in the morning she'll be gone, but don't believe any lies about her, because anything she took belonged to her and she earned it and didn't steal it."

"Is that why you cut open the pillow? To get at the money?"

"And if you ever see her again, take her away with you to Palermo."

Fidèle knew he would never be a priest, for the sight of her breasts through the gauze of her dress was beautiful to him, and when he looked into her eyes his heart felt as if it were being squeezed in his chest, and he thought how wonderful it must be to have a mother and father in the flesh, how fortunate to have a wife and child.

"Any other messages?" he asked her.

"You should stop fasting and eat more." The she blew into the chimney of the oil lamp and vanished, leaving him alone in the darkened room.

Fidèle's eyes gradually grew accustomed to the dark. The stars crowded back into the window, then one by one they faded and the sky began to lighten. He heard boots going down the stairs and up the stairs, doors being wrenched open and slammed shut, heard Mazza cry, "Where's the damned girl! Where's the goddamned girl!"

That afternoon (August 16, 1893) Fidèle was walking back along the dusty road from Vuccarina to Palermo. His shirt was stuffed with oranges, his pockets with provolone, prosciutto, raisins and figs. This is amazing, he thought. Here I've been eating all morning and I'm still famished. The roasted brown grass, the baked cactuses, the rocks cooking in the sun, everything—even the yellow sky heavy with sand blown over from Africa—everything looked beautiful to him. If the world were an egg I'd swallow it in a gulp, he thought. Little by little he was able to make out somebody standing on a huge boulder way ahead of him where the road forked, one road to Palermo and the other to Mondello. He prayed it was Serafina and in a while he could see that it was. When he reached the foot of the boulder he stopped and looked up at her, but Serafina was gazing steadily out the road to Mondello. "Ciao, Serafina!" he called up to her. She turned and looked down at him and smiled. "Ciao, Fidèle," she said, her voice as refreshing as a drink of cool water. She was dressed in a white dress, rather like a First Communion dress but without a head shawl, and she had a bundle of clothes under her arm and a framed photograph with a glass cover.

"Where are you going?" he asked.

"They say there's a beautiful beach at Mondello. I've always wanted to see the sea."

"Come with me to Palermo," he said.

"Whatever for?"

"I want to say good-bye to the gardener at the Seminary. He is like a father to me. And they have a beautiful harbor at Palermo with ships that sail all over the globe. Come with me."

Serafina climbed down from the boulder and joined Fidèle.

"Who is in the photograph?" he asked.

"This is my mother," she said.

If you had been there Serafina would have shown you the photograph, because it was the only thing she had of her mother and she was very proud of it. And you could have heard them talk as they walked down the road to Palermo, their voices getting smaller in the distance, Serafina saying, "Yes. She was from Venice. And I have her eyes and hair. And I like water. That's because she was from Venice where the streets are made of water."

45

A LETTER FROM THE STRAND GALLERY ARRIVED, saying, *Dear Renato: The large painting which you have on loan to our gallery has failed to find a buyer, I'm sorry to say, despite its obvious merit. As you know, I had hoped to place your work in our exhibit schedule, but current and future commitments make that impossible and, regrettably, we will not be able to show your work at the Strand Gallery. Sincerely, Sonia Strand.* I looked at the letter a few more times to see if I had missed a merciful phrase or word, but it had only two sentences and I hadn't missed a thing. Sonia had a large signature, a sweeping S followed by a vigorous zigzag flourish.

I made a cup of coffee but then, feeling so tired, I sat down at the table and stayed there a long time looking across the room at my canvases and I saw down a long perspective how all of my life converged toward this solitary room filled with these stretched canvases, saw that my years added up to this broken wall of worthless painting. After a while I got up from the table but something happened—the chair tumbled over backwards and I fell forward, grabbed the edge of the sliding table but crashed to the floor anyway. I climbed to my feet and pulled myself up straight, focusing on my father and how he worked at his craft and took pride in his good work and how he faced the world calmly though he never got the recognition he deserved. Keeping him in mind, I walked over to the kitchen counter, started the heat under the kettle, took down a bag of Italian Roast and carefully made a cup of coffee using a paper filter and the ceramic coffee funnel which had been given to me by Brizio, who might still need my help in life; when the coffee was finished, I added a splash of whole milk and took the mug of coffee with me while I walked up and down to look at the paintings. It was hard to think and, being exhausted, I sat down at the table and was resting there when Kim came in happy to show me his school papers, a big stack of papers, and then Avalon kept saying something. "Well, do you?" she insisted. I asked her What. "Do you want me to warm up your coffee? You've got two mugs of coffee on the table and they're both cold," she said. I told her no, and she went away but came back later with Sonia's letter and said, "What's this about?"

"Don't read my mail, Avalon. How many times have I told —"

"I already read it. What does the bitch mean she won't be able to show your work?"

"The bitch means she won't show my work."

Avalon read the letter again, frowning and chewing her lip. "Well," she said, tossing the letter onto the table. "There's lots of other galleries."

"No. I've been to the other galleries. At one time or another I've been to every gallery in New England. No one wants to show me. My work is over. I'm finished."

Avalon studied me a moment, then started to open her mouth to say something but changed her mind, took the coffee mugs from the table and emptied them gently into the sink. We worked side-by-side at the counter making dinner, talking about nothing much or, to be exact, Avalon chattered while I kept thinking about the Strand Gallery and at last I said, "I'm going to go get my painting back," and I left.

I drove in and when I got close to the Strand I began to look for an empty stretch of curb but didn't find one and so went down Newbury past the gallery, maneuvering around a couple of stalled cars and onto a side street, turning up one block and down the next until I found a place to park. The evening air was dead still, as if waiting for something, and suffocatingly warm so that by the time I had hiked back to Newbury I was sweating. At the Strand Gallery half a dozen people were outside on the stone steps, chatting and laughing, drink in hand, happy in the light streaming through the Strand's open door. I crossed the street away from the gallery, tugging the damp shirt from my chest and pumping it like a bellows to cool me down. I looked at the reception crowd inside the big window, the women with bare shoulders, the men in jackets. A woman's laugh floated up from the cluster of people on the steps. I crossed over to the gallery and went in, the place alive with light and the noise of people talking. I pushed toward the back, passed the artist on display (elegant jacket, torn blue-jeans with paint smears) and was wedging my way around the wine-and-fruit table to Sonia's office when Peter Bell caught up with me. "I'm here for my painting," I told him. "Yes, of course," he said, popping in ahead of me, extending an arm to clear the way. He closed the office door behind us, caught his breath and said, "Our men aren't here tonight. Maybe it would be easier to pick it up tomorrow. What do you think? It's a big painting and it really takes two to manage it properly, two or three. I think you should come back tomorrow. It's best for the painting. What do you think?" The canvas leaned along a side wall, a gilded rococo chair at the end of it.

"I'll take it right now." I mopped my face with my sleeve.

He went reluctantly to the far corner of the room and unlocked a metal clad door, saying, "It's going to be difficult. You have to negotiate down the stairs to the ground level out back. As you can—" But I had pulled the painting away from the wall, got in back of it, reached as wide as I could on the long crosspiece of the stretcher, then grabbed a hold and started toward the door to the showroom. "I'll go out the front. Just open the goddamn door," I told him.

"No, no, no, you don't want to do that! Mr Stillamare, please, oh—"

I leaned the painting back against the wall, pulled open the showroom door, grabbed the stretcher crosspiece, and lifted.

"Please—" he cried.

I swung around little by little to line up the forward vertical edge of the stretcher frame with the open doorway and now slowly started forward as Bell scuttled sideways ahead of me, grabbed the upright edge with both hands and helped to steer it through the doorway. "Slow, slow, slow," he said, muting his voice. "The table is out here, the credenza with food—."

Sonia Strand took me in with a glance, turning aside and spreading her arms to gently brush back the guests who were beginning to look this way, still chatting. My arms stretched along the crosspiece, my cheek pressed to the back side of the canvas and I, not being able to see much, followed Sonia, her garment of shimmering beads blue and green and violet, as she began to make a corridor through the crowd toward the open front door, rain falling through the doorlight. My stretched arms weakened and then trembled and the bottom of the frame banged on the floor. "Bell! Get on this side!" I croaked. I tried to lift the stretcher, but my arms shook and lowered it to the floor again. I waited a moment, then grabbed the crosspiece and lifted. I took a step, somebody crying *Watch out for the food!* as I fell into the canvas, tripping over the bottom of the frame and toppling all onto the edge of the table, smashing and dragging so I sprawled on the canvas under a cascading tower of plates, tumbling fruits and cheeses, a big green bottle still spinning slowly on its side, dribbling a stream of pale wine—I scrambled to my feet in the silence, grabbed the edge of the painting and hauled it face down across the floor, tilted it up on edge and dragged it out the door and down the steps, the rainy gusts snapping it this way and that like a sail until I came to a cross street where I turned the corner and leaned it, face out, against a brick wall.

I stood there, my head throbbing, while people hurried past hunched against the blowing rain, and a kid bare to the

waist sailed by on a skateboard, his black hair a mass of thick
ringlets, his coffee skin glistening. I jogged one block over
and two blocks down, sat in the car with my head against the
wheel, panting, then drove back to the canvas and parked half
on the sidewalk, got out and swung the back of the canvas
against the car, then shoved it up onto the roof and roped it
there. I drove home and slid the canvas down from the car
roof—discovered the stretcher was busted at one end—and
dragged it through the apartment house door. I climbed up
to the studio and Avalon came down with me to hold the
trailing edge of the frame while I pulled it up the stairs. She
didn't say anything while we were hauling it up, but as soon as
we got inside the studio she said, "Take off your clothes and
take a shower or you'll get a chill and die." I gave her my shirt,
then I got a dish towel and blotted the face of the canvas,
got two more and worked on the back around the stretcher
while Avalon, hands on hips, watched me and when I was
through she said, "Take a hot shower, *please*." I pulled off my
clothes and got into a hot shower. I don't know how long I
was there but Avalon reached in and turned off the water,
then she grabbed my wrists, pulled me to my feet and gave
me a towel. I put on a pair of pants and a sweater, and we sat
side by side on the floor by my bunk and drank cheap white
wine in silence for a while, then Avalon put her arm through
mine and, for no reason at all, confessed about her shabby and
unfortunate life in San Francisco until I went to bed.

46

*M*IMI'S CAFÉ HAS EXHIBIT SPACE ON THE TOP FLOOR.
The roof is all skylight and there's a big square hole
in the middle of the exhibit space so that light can shine
down to the swank dining tables on the second floor and to

the bar below that. I'd been to the Café gallery before, but only because some of my students had shows there. This day I brought one of my big Genesis pages and photographs of the others in the same series. The gallery manager, Ms Finch, looked at my handiwork and was shuffling through the photos when she said, "I don't see how I could show these." She looked up and handed the photos back to me. "The people who come to Mimi's are younger and they wouldn't go for work like this. I think they'd be put off." She smiled firmly. "I'm sorry to have taken up your time. I know you must be as busy as I am." Then she shook my hand, said goodbye and walked away.

That night I lay dead in my bunk but awake, as if I were a ghost haunting my own studio, and I wondered what would become of these paintings when I was gone, whether they would live in light or die too, because it's impossible to sell the left-behind canvases of a dead man who never was famous, never sold much, and whose reputation fell apart in his middle age, and my Alba—who never helped me get a gallery, never helped me find a dealer, never helped me sell a canvas—this Alba won't begin to nurture my work and reputation when I'm pushing up daisies. I've turned the pages of *ArtNews* and *Art in America* and caught myself witlessly looking for my name in the announcement of an exhibit or in a gallery review, because it's hard to believe my name can't be there one time or another, can't be there ever, and that in this living world I'm invisible: Alba no longer believes in my work, no longer believes in me, and this is what it feels like to be dead.

Next morning I woke up late with a headache, but I had a good long piss, washed my face and trimmed the beard—titanium white, it looked like. I checked the big painting (*Berkshire Fields*, painted when the artist was only 61) and, although the stretcher was fractured at one end, it had survived the rain and had dried well, the canvas tightening somewhat. After breakfast I went for a slow, useless walk along the Charles, then came back to the studio and was making a mug of coffee when Kim came in the door and said somebody had phoned me at the Daily Grind. I asked him what he was doing home from school at this hour, and he said, "School's out. Yesterday was the last day. Don't you remember?" and I told him I had forgotten but, yes, now I remembered. When we got to the café Avalon told me, "Your doctor called and he wants you to call him back. Here's the number." So I phoned the doctor and his secretary said, "Oh, yes, Mr Stillamare, the blood test numbers came back from the lab and they're in the range where we look for cancer, so Dr. Cadoc would like to see you for a biopsy."

47

ALBA DROVE ME TO THE UROLOGIST'S OFFICE WHERE I introduced her to Dr. Cadoc who, I realize, I've not described before, a gentle stoop-shouldered man with bright eyes and a whimsical smile. Maybe you know that to get biopsy samples from the prostate gland they insert a firm cylindrical probe up into the rectum, like a .38 caliber handgun up your butt. I hadn't any need to think about it before. "This device does two things — it makes an ultrasound scan and takes tissue samples," Dr. Cadoc said, showing me the probe. I told him it looked too damn big. "I'll tell you each time before we take a sample. You'll hear a click and feel a tap inside, like a little hammer, but don't be alarmed." That's when the hollow needle stabs through the rectal wall to take a bite from my prostate, I said. "Yes, but you won't feel it. And don't be alarmed if you discover blood in your urine later today. Of course, there's some discomfort from the probe. It's uncomfortable. But the procedure sounds worse than it actually is," he said. "—And this is Jane. She'll be manipulating the probe and I'll be here watching the scan and choosing the sites to sample." Jane was a beefy plain-faced woman with grayish hair which had been cut so it resembled an iron helmet. "Take off your shoes and trousers and underpants," she told me, yanking a long sheet of waxy paper onto the examination table. "Then get up here and lie on your side facing the wall. I hope you're not some nervous Nellie," she muttered.

Afterward, in the car, Alba asked me how I felt and I said I don't know, I feel OK, I think I'd like a cup of coffee. We sat side by side at a little round table in the sun, drinking our coffee and viewing the people and the cars, as if I were still part of the ordinary afternoon. A couple of bronze guys in shorts dropped their bicycle helmets on a nearby table and stood there talking, one of them unfastening his sport gloves and the other one mopping a handkerchief on his neck and throat; and beyond the bicyclists three girls were chattering, the blonde constantly sweeping up a hank of hair, holding it, letting it go, then sweeping it up again, while here in front of us a college kid had pulled his bare foot into his lap to examine the underside of his heel. "Everybody's so young and so healthy," I said.

Alba looked around. "That man over there is about twenty years older than you are," she said.

"He looks out of place."

"Well, you don't look out of place," she told me. "And I like your white beard."

I sat there and thought about going back to the studio, but I didn't want to paint or to think about painting and I didn't even want to go to the studio. Alba broke in on me, saying, "You can stay at home, you know. Why don't you stay at home?" and I said All right. Late that night we had a glass of wine and as I had been thinking of the kids most of the day I said, "They're far enough along. They'll make out all right," and Alba said, Yes, they'll be fine, and I said, "I wish Brizio would settle down, get started on something serious. He's better than what he's doing. He could use some help," and Alba said, Brizio will do fine. I said, "They're good. They're as good as anybody. That's one thing we did right."

"We did a lot of things right," she said.

That night my piss came out looking cloudy and the next morning I found I had dribbled blood onto the bed sheets. Later I phoned Tom Hay who seven years ago had told me over a café table that he had just learned he had a cancerous prostate. Now we went out to a bistro for lunch and I told him what was going on, saying, "This is only a biopsy and I'm coming apart."

"Man," he said. "I think you're doing fine."

The next day Cormac phoned me, which meant Hay had told him, so we all met for coffee at the Paradiso, sat outside under an umbrella, shaggy Cormac saying, "So, Ren, how are you doing?" I told him I was getting bored with my morbid thoughts about death, impotence and incontinence. He searched me a moment, then shifted his bulk in his chair as if to change the subject. "You look good with that beard," he said. So we began to talk politics or art or sports or something, and though I wasn't paying attention it was better than being in solitary confinement in my skull.

The next morning when I got up to piss, nothing came. Not a drop. I washed and shaved and tried to piss again, because the need was getting painful, but all that happened was a hard dry cramp deep inside. Alba drove me to the hospital emergency room and by the time we got there the pain had grown so it seemed there was only this heavy ballooning agony down low and nothing else in the world. After twenty minutes the triage nurse admitted me from the waiting room to one of the examination rooms, and by then I was sweaty and shaking somewhat but just able to unbuckle my belt and tear down my pants while Alba rushed some paper towels onto the floor because the pain, like an enormous slowly clenching hand, now squeezed out all my crap - "Oh, God! Oh, shit!" I cried.

Somebody cleaned up the mess and somebody else came with a clipboard and asked us questions and told me to get onto the bed; ten minutes later a lanky guy appeared with a file folder, shook my hand and introduced himself as doctor somebody and asked me if I was Renato Stillamare. I said, "Yes, but I don't know for how long." He said not to worry, he would insert a catheter and I'd feel fine. I said Tycho Brahe died this way. "Tycho Brahe? I knew he had a silver nose, but I didn't know about the urinary blockage." A young woman appeared and handed the doctor a kit containing the catheter and bag. "This is Maria. Now I'm going to put some ointment on the tip of your penis, make it numb," he told me. I said Yes, do it. "It will feel chilly, cool," he added. I agreed it felt chilly. "I'm ready to insert the catheter," he said to Maria.

"*I'm not!* Let me grab a hold of something," I said and grabbed the steel bed frame. Alba had come over.

"Just a steady -" he said and shoved it in like a knife to a scabbard while my body arched up from the bed and I shouted, "*Ow! Damn!*" A moment later he asked, "How are you feeling?"

"Better than a couple of minutes ago," I said.

"I should think so," he said, ducking down to adjust the catheter and bag. He reappeared, file folder in hand. "Think about surgery," he said.

"I'm no good at surgery."

He smiled. "Dr. Cadoc can take care of that for you. He's a good surgeon. I'll send him a report. —Sorry to meet under these circumstances, Mr Stillamare."

About an hour later we left the emergency room; Alba drove and I slumped cautiously in the passenger seat with a catheter up my old prick, a water-filled balloon banging around inside my bladder and a plastic bag strapped to my leg. A day or so later Dr. Cadoc phoned and said that the biopsy had found no cancer.

Dr. Cadoc, my age, had retired from surgery, so it was performed by one of his young associates, a brisk fifty-year old. He had explained how many pieces of equipment they were going to insert up through the urethra, *my* urethra. Now it was the morning to do it. "What are you so worried about?" he asked me.

"Death and other side effects," I said.

"You won't die unless you get hit by a truck after this is over," he said.

"Incontinence."

"We've been over that. Very unlikely."

"Impotence."

"We've been over that, too. Also very unlikely."

"Retrograde ejaculation doesn't sound like fun."

"Is he always this way?" the anesthesiologist asked him.

"He's an artist, a painter."

"When does that stuff they gave me take effect? I'm not feeling happyfied," I told them.

"I'd say it took effect some while ago," the surgeon said.

The anesthesiologist asked me to roll onto my side so he could give me the spinal. I rolled onto my side.

"Maybe you've done this a thousand times," I said to the surgeon. "But it's new to me."

"No, I haven't done this before," he said. "But I've always wanted to try."

48

THREE DAYS LATER I WAS BACK AT ALBA'S, BUT before I left the hospital I was instructed not to lift anything heavier than ten pounds and not to try sex or anything similarly pleasurable, but to drink lots of water. When I pissed it felt like I had a flamethrower down there. I was tired, mostly. I lazed around the apartment and wrote letters to the children and napped. Lou Zocco came around one day and asked how it was ("I'm peeing bloody urine, looks like Chianti," I told him.) and Tom Hay came by a couple of days later ("It's the color of Calabrian Rosé. I'm waiting for the Bianco.") and they each took me out for a coffee, but mostly I stayed with Alba and read whatever she had lying about the apartment, not even reading but just looking, and Zoe came over for dinner, bringing a sweet desert each evening.

Threadbare Sebastian Gabriel, the paper-maker, came by and since I was getting my appetite back we went to lunch at a bistro in the Square. "I brought the load of paper to your studio," he said. "Your Avalon let me in."

"She's not mine," I told him.

"Anyway, she let me in and I left it stacked on the floor, but you should put in on a table or pallet. —Your new work looks great," he added. "All those new canvases, fantastic. Getting ready for a show?"

I wondered how much Avalon had told him about the Strand Gallery mess; from his skittering gaze I figured she'd told him enough to make him unsure as how to talk to me. "I'm always ready for a show. —Now tell me about that bright daughter of yours, tell me about Kate," I said, to change the subject.

"Caitlin's trying to teach me accounting." His face lit up, as it did whenever he talked about her. "She's organizing my business into folders with different colored labels on them. She loves doing that kind of stuff." He talked about his daughter, and then about his ex-wife who was already a mid-level executive at a Manhattan brokerage firm, and about his paper-making business which he felt was taking in more money this year, even if he didn't know how much or how keep track of it, talked about what he called the yin and yang of the paper-making business, and about his favorite deep thinker, Carl Jung (alas), and about how he was going to rearrange his workshop according to the rules of Feng Shui, which I took to be some kind of screwball Chinese geometry, and how his daughter had found some great things for him to wear at a second-hand shop called Déjà Vu All Over Again, and about an eighteen-speed bicycle he had bought to save wear and tear on his car. As we parted he was quite cheerful, saying, "I'll bring a pallet to your studio and get the paper off the floor. And you get well. My father had one of those operations a year ago and he's fine now, pissing like a horse." I didn't see a lot of Sebastian and had forgotten what an amiable good guy he was, despite his head being stuffed with straw.

49

I WAS GETTING RESTLESS AT ALBA'S PLACE. SHE WAS working at her desk, a nineteenth-century escritoire with a computer, and I asked her, "Know what this apartment is like?"

"Ummmm," she says, undeflected from the computer screen.

"Alba, know what this apartment is like?"

"In a sec," she says.

"Alba."

She turned to me. "Yes, Ren, it's like a concrete box with windows, it's like a concrete rabbit warren, it's like a concrete dovecote or a row of concrete pigeon holes or a concrete mausoleum, or it's like a concrete columbarium and we're the funeral urns inside it—I especially liked that one. Did I forget something?"

"I'm bored."

"We could drive out to look at that country property I was telling you about. It's a nice day for a car trip. Want to do that?"

Alba snatched a couple of roadmaps from one of the desk's little drawers and drove us deep into the country to the real estate office where we met the property agent, a dignified old man, who led us to the farm. The sky had changed from blue to the color of old zinc. The house was a narrow two-story box, chalky white clapboard, vacant since last fall, and we walked up the stairway and through the empty rooms and down the back stairs as if exploring a gigantic dried-out sea-shell. It was pleasant to come out to the soft pattering rain and we set off on a footpath, picking our way between two rows of decrepit apple trees that the agent called an orchard, and came to the barn.

The broad sliding door at the front had long since dropped from the rail and jammed in the ground, unmovable, but there was enough space between the door and the frame for us go in edgewise. It had a surprisingly good interior volume, the soft gray light falling from a row of small windows set high in the long side walls and from the large open square in the distant back wall. From the dark interior you could look through the open square to the outside scene. There was a hushed drumming of rain on the roof. I walked to the far end, waiting for the familiar scent of feed and manure which I hadn't smelled for a long time, but there was no odor. There was a cantilever beam overhead sticking outside with a big rusted pulley at the end and rain was blowing in the open frame. The land slanted down and away from the back of the barn, so from where I stood there was a ten-foot drop to the black soggy ground, then the dark green field spread out and rolled downhill for a while before it leveled off against a hazy green grove of trees that marked the end of the property. It felt good, standing there.

On the drive back we discussed the property, but we reached no conclusion except that it had been pleasant to stand in the barn and look at the green horizon under the misty rain. Now the rain had stopped, the sun came out and broad wisps of steam floated up from the black road. When we got back to the apartment I was tired again—I never understood why such minor surgery made me that tired—so while Alba went back to her desk I stretched out on her cushy sofa and drifted off. When I woke up the place was as hot as a pottery kiln. I found Alba in the bedroom where she had stripped the blankets from the bed and was lying on the sheet, naked and asleep against a pillow like one of those second-rate nudes by Carl Frieske (American, 1874-1939), one of his sleepy full-breasted, satin-bellied woman laid out so your only thought is to get your knees in there and fuck your way to glory.

I went to the kitchen and while I was making a glass of iced tea Alba woke up and said, "If you're making something cool make one for me too." I poured a glass for Alba and took it to the bedroom just as she was reaching for her dress. "You look good without clothes," I told her. "I wish I were up to it."

"I'm sure you will be," says Alba, lifting her arms to let the dress fall over her head and unfurl downward. "Give yourself time."

"I began to slow down a couple of years ago, you know, even before this."

"I hadn't noticed," she says.

"Which is another reason I'll love you forever."

"I hope so. Zipper," she says, turning her back so I can zip it.

"But it's true, I have less urge than I used to."

"You have plenty of urge."

"I'm down to where I have about as much craving as a woman."

"Are you trying to be clever? I'm not amused."

That evening Alba concocted a dinner which was mostly asparagus, a new recipe from France.

"I have the urge to paint," I said. "That's a start."

"Then you should paint."

"All I need is a place to exhibit."

"I've told you about Leo Conti."

I thought about that a while. "You say he likes my work?"

"What he's seen of it in galleries. That was a few years ago," she added.

"I could show him some new things."

"You should."

I drank down the last of my wine. "I wish you'd look at my new work," I said.

Alba made a display of searching for the lemon slices but didn't say anything.

"Why don't you come over to the studio?" I suggested.

"Yes. That would be delightful. For you, at least."

I poured myself a bit more wine. "I don't like the way we're living. —You and me, I mean."

She smiled, fleetingly. "Who else would you mean?"

I drained my glass again.

"And which one of us moved out?" she asks.

"I haven't moved out. I'm trying to work. I'm trying to work and I'm trying to make my life into something."

"So am I," she says, showing about as much emotion as the Queen on a playing card.

Alba and I have never completely understood each other, which I believe is a good thing, and on that occasion I understood her even less than usual. But I was healing well, due partly to nature and mostly to Alba, and I was restless to get back to my paints and canvases. The next morning I packed up my stuff—there wasn't much—looked around to see if there was anything of mine in the apartment I wanted to take back with me, asked Alba if I could borrow a book I had just noticed on her desk, *Cinéma en France* or some damn thing, and while I was at it I scooped up one of her road maps and a couple of sheets of information from the real estate agent about country properties. Then I crossed the river to Boston and my studio.

50

I OPENED THE DOOR TO MY STUDIO AND THE PAINT-
ings lighted up the place. The handmade paper from Sebastian lay in a neat stack on a pallet he had brought, and on
my bunk there was a big white envelope from Michiko, in
which envelope I found the hundred or so photos I'd shot
of Avalon. In the back room Avalon's mattress was made up
with Kim's sleeping bag on one side and a few books on the
other – a thick volume by Carl Jung, plus a big flat paperback
called *Mehndi and Bindi* and her old *Craftsman Entrepreneur*.
On the bookshelf with the lipsticks and chrome-studded
leather straps she had added two stolen photos of foolish old
Renato, one with his big blurred hand grabbing toward the
camera and another with him saying something, his arms
wide open.

I went back to the studio to look at the paintings again
and the more I looked the more I was amazed that I'd ever
doubted them; they were better than anything I'd ever done
and looking at a couple of unfinished canvases made me hungry. Avalon had put a few tomatoes in a bowl on the kitchen
counter, as I had asked her a hundred times to do — though I
hadn't asked for the small box of menstrual gear — and there
was half a loaf of scali in a paper bag, so I sawed off a chunk
of bread, sliced the tomatoes, grabbed a handful of olives and
carried everything on a plate while I walked up and down in
front of the unfinished paintings, because it was a pleasure to
eat and to see what to do next. It felt good to be at work on
a canvass, and even though I quickly got tired and had to sit
down, I was able to paint again later while sitting in a kitchen
chair, and I was still painting when Avalon came in.

"You're here," she says, coming across the room and smiling broadly, this strange-looking young woman—for she did look strange after not seeing her for a while—her shaggy hair dyed purplish rose and brassy yellow, silvery rings piercing her face, this Avalon, my Avalon. I stood up and she hugged me not in the old grab-ass way but with such gentleness, as if I were an invalid, while I sucked up coffee dust, her cheap cologne and her secret Avalon smell.

"Did you notice I didn't touch a thing?" she says proudly. "Everything's just the way you left it. Sebastian brought that paper for you and Michiko brought a bunch of those photos you took of me. And your mail is on the kitchen counter—see?—right here beside the Mason jar, and a list of phone calls you got at the café. I haven't touched anything of yours or moved a thing. I kept it like a goddamned museum in here. All I did was, I swapped around some pots and glasses in the kitchen cabinet and I put that ugly Medusa dish out of the way under the counter. I put all your winter sweaters in the bottom drawer—don't look at me that way! And I happened to see those photos and took out one snapshot of you for my wallet, but that's all. Three, I mean three, three photos. And I bought some film and for our camera, I mean your camera, and took some pictures of Kim. —What's that?"

"It's an old bamboo fishing rod."

"I know it's a fishing rod, Ren."

I told her it was for Kim. "Oh," she says, thoroughly pleased. "And what's in the little box?" she asks, and I told her it was a gyroscope for Kim in case he didn't like the fishing rod. "He's out with the Rodriguez kids, skateboarding," she says "You go back to painting. I'm going to take a shower."

That evening Avalon cooked pasta putanesca, which she enjoyed calling whore's pasta, and afterward we walked down beside the river, me carrying the rod and Kim energetically kicking a stone zigzag ahead of us. When we got back to the studio he banished the rod to the back room and spent the rest of the evening lying on the floor, the gyroscope forgotten on the kitchen table, while he read and re-read an advertising pamphlet about skateboards.

I was tired again, so I lay on my bed and looked at my accumulated mail, threw away the Charrette catalog, threw out the glossy announcements inviting me to a dozen different gallery receptions and tore to small pieces a request for the pleasure of my company at the New England Arts Awards Ceremony where I could witness the growing fame of other painters. I put aside the letter thanking me for my annual contribution to the Robert Wren Foundation (Rob had died years ago, had a crush on Alba one summer and would come Sunday mornings with his griddle and batter to make flapjacks for her.) I kept the wedding invitation from my former student, Arthur Chan, and the hand-bound notebook by Dave Koppleman, who had come to me terrified from electro-convulsive therapy, and the thank-you poem from anxious Emily Bright who used to throw up before class. I saved the letter from my Fabrizio for last, as a desert, but it turned out to be only a brief note which said he was coming to visit us, not saying when, and P.S. he was bringing Heather with him. I read it a few times to see if there was something between the lines — the couple had been living together for two years and had seemed content to go on that way forever — then I gave up.

After Avalon put Kim to bed I took the big white packet of photos, dumped them on the table and began to sort through them. These weren't carefully controlled prints, just standard stuff, but all I wanted was the image or the logos of the body and these were good enough, especially some photos toward the end when Avalon was just standing relaxed and looking directly at the camera. I had covered the table top with prints and was working there, so Avalon took herself, plus her book and digital music box, to sprawl on my bunk. "Earphones, and I'll play it so low you won't even hear it," she assured me. I sorted and resorted the photos till I had what I wanted and by then Avalon had padded barefoot to the back room and returned to say that Kim was fast asleep. She sat down at the table and told me, "This is a great book. It's all about mehndi and bindi. Which, I dare say, you don't know anything about. Mehndi is the art of henna tattoos, an ancient art, like in India, and bindi is the same thing only with jewels, jewels on your face and body."

"You're right, Avalon, I don't know anything about it."

"See?" Avalon slid the book around so I could look at it. "Here. Let me show you some pictures. Move over." She sprang up, came around and sat on the edge of my chair, sliding her arm under mine to lay her hand on the page. "Look," she says, very businesslike. "This is mehndi, all this design on the woman's hands and her face. All those dots. See?" The flesh on Avalon's cheek and collar bone had a humid gloss, but because she had taken a shower there wasn't any odor of coffee or cologne and I wasn't close enough to pick up her scent. "Not on me, Ren. On the woman in the picture." She smiled. "I know what you're thinking about. You want to know if I've found an apartment. You want to know how soon I can move out. Right?"

"No."

"Liar, liar, pants on fire."

I laughed. "I wasn't thinking that at all."

"You'll be pleased to know I've been looking at apartment rentals."

"I'm pleased."

"I thought it was expensive in San Francisco, but it's worse in Boston, it's insane. People are crazy around here. Where do the assholes get the money to pay those rents?"

"They save by not buying my paintings."

"I looked at one rental so small you couldn't keep a canary in it. Then I found some cheap places in the paper, but when I looked on Kim's map they were way out in Natick or Saugus or someplace named just as weird. I've been thinking of Somerville. What do you think?"

"Somerville used to be cheap," I said. "I'll ask Sebastian. He lives out there."

"I was talking to Garland at the Daily Grind and she said Somerville was a good place. So I've been thinking of Somerville."

I was listening but not very well because, frankly, I was ready to go to sleep. I hadn't stood up painting at Alba's and hadn't taken a walk along the river after dinner at Alba's, so I guess it was natural to be more tired here at the studio with Avalon. I don't recall what else Avalon said about rentals or what we talked about. I finished my wine, rinsed out the glass and washed up for bed. Avalon was waiting by my bunk. "Good-night kiss," she says, embracing me gently, as if I might break. Then she went to her bedroom and I to slid under my covers. The bunk felt narrow after sleeping in our bed at Alba's and I missed the warm touch of her body, but before I could think about anything beyond that I was asleep.

51

I WAS STRETCHED OUT ON MY BACK, LOOKING AT THE book about French cinema—the book I had scooped up from Alba's desk—when Avalon came over, lay down on the margin of the bed and began to pester me with questions about my surgery. I told her to think of it as an old clogged pipe; an expensive plumber had cleaned out the pipe. I went back to the book. She wanted to know how much of the prostate was left. I told her I had a lot of prostate to begin with and there was a lot left, then I went back to the book and Avalon kept turning this way and that to get comfortable. Then she was quiet for a while until she said, "Who does this hot love note belong to?"

I asked her what love note.

"This one. Listen to this," she said. She began to read from a sheet of blue-tinted stationery. "*One eats this delicious flower before it has climaxed, and if it has been prepared in a certain way, kept at a loving simmer for just so long, then—.*"

"Where did you get that?" I asked her.

"It was here on the floor by the bed. Let me read you some more. *The delicious petals make no resistance but fall open, hot and humid-.*"

I snatched the stationery sheet from her fingers. "It says artichoke right at the top. It's a recipe for artichoke—."

Avalon grabbed it back. "Oh, sure," she said. "Let me read you—Let—Ouch! Ren! Do you want to hear the rest of this? Calm down. Remember your age."

I dropped the open book over my face.

"Where was I?" Avalon said. "Ah, here! —*The delicate petals make no resistance but fall open, hot and humid beneath one's fingertips, yielding, desiring to be eaten. Now the erotic feast begins—.*"

"Let me see that," I said.

She held the little blue sheet tight between both fists, but turned so I could read.

"It says *exotic*," I said. "*Exotic* feast, *not* erotic."

Avalon turned the paper back and continued to read. "*One bites down tenderly, most tenderly, and while holding the soft petal between one's teeth, slowly —.*" She had a low, rippling laugh. "Oh, oh, oh. I better stop before this excites you and hurts your, your surgery," she said.

I gave up trying to read and closed the book about French cinema. "Go away," I said.

"You sound like a travel agency," she said. She rolled onto her stomach and propped herself up on her elbows and looked at me. "We're going to be friends forever. Right?"

"Right. Now I want to get ready for bed."

"We'll still see each other after I move. Right?"

"Right."

"Somerville isn't the other end of the world," she said.

"Right. And I'm really tired."

"Just because a person— Why don't you please put your arm around me and tell me —"

I put my sleepy arms around her and drank the delicious warm smell of her skin.

"I would like us to be like blood relatives who had to put up with each other, no matter what happened," she said.

"I love you, Avalon, and it's past my bed time."

Avalon went away to her bed. Although I was tired I didn't drift off to sleep but floated between sleeping and waking, my eyes growing accustomed to the dark so the stretchers, the chairs and the table, loomed out of the shadows. I didn't want to think about my paintings because I knew no gallery would show them, knew I hadn't become famous in my time and my time was up. Avalon was looking to move out and I was almost finished with the canvases and maybe Alba was right and Conti would exhibit my work and Alba and I would live in a house in the country and our friends would come to dinner. I don't know how long I lay there tired but not sleeping and yet not thinking, an old man with withered privates in a narrow bed without his wife. At last I got up and padded over to the sink to get a glass of water, and while I was drinking I heard Avalon stir—*bam*—we bumped into each other. "I have to tell you something," she whispers. We were both naked, the imprint of her warm flesh still vibrating along my nerves where we had collided. "I have to tell you," she whispers again.

"All right, tell me."

"I'm moving to Somerville to be near Sebastian, because I love him and he loves me and probably we'll live together, but we decided I should get a place of my own for a while before moving in with him until —"

"Sebastian? My friend Sebastian?"

"He came with his daughter to bring you his hand-made paper."

"Jesus! What happened?"

"Nothing happened. We just talked," she says.

"You just *talked?* You just *talked* and decided to go live together? Christ! What kind of a conversation was it!"

"Please, Ren."

"You and Sebastian. Horrible!"

"Please, Ren."

I sat down on the edge of my bed, exhausted. "You and Sebastian. Jesus fucking Christ!"

"You promised—"

"I'm going to bed."

"You said—"

"I'm going to sleep, Avalon."

She stood there waiting, but I didn't say a word to her, so she went away and I rolled back under the bed sheet.

I got up late the next morning, the buffoon in a comic opera, the foolish old basso profundo who guards the door while his beautiful young ward, the soprano for whom he lusts, climbs out the window with the hero, an up-and-coming tenor. The deserted look of the studio told me Avalon had gone to her job at the Daily Grind, taking Kim with her. I showered and was looking around for my underwear when the door flew open and here's Avalon. "Why aren't you at work?" I asked her, stepping into my shorts.

"Because I told them I had to have a talk with you," she says. "Garland knows how difficult you can be, so she said okay, get it over with."

I pulled up my pants, buckled my belt. "Have you notified the newspapers?"

"I want to tell you what happened when Sebastian came and I—"

"I don't need to hear this. You can go back to work."

"I'm going to tell you and you're going to listen," she says.

I ignored her by looking around for my shirt.

"I opened the door and Sebastian was standing there with

his daughter," she says. "Only I didn't know it was him and his daughter. He looked—well, you know how he looks—and he said, I'm Sebastian and this is my daughter Kate, and he touched his Kate's hair just so gently on top, just stroked it down like—"

"And that did it. Suddenly you knew you wanted to go live with him," I said, ducking and grabbing her wrist as she began swatting at my face.

"You're a real bastard!" she spits out, wrenching inside my fist.

I let go of her. "Sebastian's all right. He's a good guy. Go live with him. Go, go."

"*Don't try to get rid of me!*" she shouts.

"I'm not trying to get rid of you."

"Yes you are. Because you're a selfish, vain old man. You want me out of your studio but you don't want me living with anybody else. Your feelings are hurt and you want to punish me by throwing me out of your life and turning your back on me. You can't do that! We're friends for ever. You said so yourself. *For ever.*"

"I'm going for a walk by the river."

"You can't do this. I'm special to you. *You care for me!*" she cries.

"I'm going out."

Avalon dove at the door, shot the bolt and whirled around to face me. "What can I do to heal your fucking pride! I'll do whatever you want!" she sobs.

She was out of breath and her eyes glistened and my guardian angel, disgusted with me, drove a spear into my heart. I faltered. She waited, watching me.

"Come on," I said at last in a voice that sounded strange to my own ears. I put an arm around her shoulders. "I'll walk you back. I'll never abandon you. You can tell me about Sebastian while we walk. Let's go."

Along the way Avalon told me in detail about Sebastian's

visits to the café and the slow walks back to my studio and how Sebastian or, more precisely, Sebastian and his daughter Kate, had captivated her. "Like, picture this girl in braids and this tall man standing beside her, behind her but watching over her," Avalon said. They had discovered certain signs in their lives that showed they were destined to meet. Like, for example, when Sebastian was a boy his family had moved here to Boston exactly the same month that Avalon was born here, and years later young Sebastian had driven across the country to San Francisco and walked the same streets as Avalon, who was only fifteen at the time, as if he was searching for her. And for six months Avalon worked in the shop of a paper-maker named Shozo Takeda—"I told you about that job and how come I knew how to make rag paper," she said. "And don't look at me that way, Renato, because I know I told you because I remember you didn't believe me."—which was destiny preparing her to understand Sebastian's craft. And destiny prepared Sebastian to understand Avalon's life by having him take care of his daughter by himself and bring her up by himself, so he understood how hard it is being a single parent, working and bringing up a kid at the same time. Kate's mother was a total delinquent, like that bitch Linda who fucked up Avalon's life when Avalon was a girl. "Did you know Sebastian's wife didn't want the baby?" she asked me. "She wouldn't have had it except she was such a brainy bitch she got past the third month before she even knew she was pregnant and that's when Sebastian married her, because he wanted the baby." All that was destiny and mystical, but you could see how their lives fit together in practical ways, too, because Sebastian couldn't learn the business side of his craft and was always going broke, but Avalon had money sense and for weeks before she had even met him she had been reading a book about the craftsman entrepreneur— "How do you explain *that!*"—and she could keep Sebastian's accounts for him and help him with new business ideas and, well, she had

thrown away her birth control pills. So my Avalon and the
gangly paper-maker had fallen in love.

"I should think you'd like him," she says. "He's like you,
only younger."

I laughed briefly. "Lucky for you, he's not like me at all."

"What do you mean?"

"You two were meant for each other," I said.

"You mean it?" She had stopped in the doorway of the
café, turning to search my face. "Yes. You do mean it," she
says, relieved.

Garland had glanced up from behind the counter, her
hands on her hips, ready to swat at me if I got close enough,
but I was already gutted and boned so I took a table by the
window and one of the kids brought me breakfast.

52

THE NOTE ON BLUE STATIONERY THAT AVALON HAD
read to me the other night was a recipe for steamed artichokes. I figured it must have fallen from between the pages
of the French cinema book I had taken from Alba's desk. The
recipe wasn't in Alba's handwriting and I thought maybe Alba
had borrowed the book with the folded paper in it, but Alba
had scribbled here and there in the book's margins, so it was
her book. Then I found four more blue stationery sheets behind the blanket chest where I had first dumped the book. All
the recipes were in the same bold handwriting—artichoke,
puff pastry, and an elaborate dinner that extended across both
sides of two blue pages, all written in a fancy, sneaky style
that made them sound like they were about something other
than food.

53

*L*ITTLE BLACK THOUGHTS WERE CIRCLING INSIDE
my skull like Van Gogh crows and I wondered what
somebody else would make of those recipes, but Mike Bruno
wasn't around anymore and Cormac or Zocco would enjoy
this too much to be helpful, so I went to the Daily Grind and
showed them to Gordon who frowned and then laughed and
then shrugged and handed them back, saying, "Beats me." I
drove over to Zoe's studio, Blue Door Graphics. She was busy
with a pair of clients, so I went upstairs and poured a cup of
coffee from her breakfast pot, heated it in the microwave and
took it to the sitting room, a place I've always liked—a large
bay window overlooking the leafy back street, comfortable
chairs and, yes, one of my painting (great slabs of clean color)
stored on the wall, plus a gouache I did of Astrid when she
was twelve.

Zoe arranges her books chronologically, according to
when she acquired them. She says this way it's easy to find
whichever book she's looking for because she can always remember when she first read it and, she says, the rows of book
titles make her diary. You start at the top bookshelf on the
left (Dr. Benjamin Spock's *Baby and Child Care*, paperbound,
the cover bandaged together by adhesive tape) and go down
the bookcase, then to the top of the neighboring one and
so on around the room through new age paperbacks, plus
a little white album of wedding photos, a shelf of business
books, past a pamphlet on divorce, then poetry and novels,
plus a leatherette folder with a second marriage certificate
and a solitary wedding photo, and eventually to a pamphlet
from Planned Parenthood on safe and legal abortion, then
a row of feminist manuals, past the journals of Anaïs Nin

and a big biography of Georgia O'Keefe and up to the present at a volume with the bookmark still in it (*The History of God* by Karen Armstrong, clothbound.) I was looking at the snapshots we'd taken of Astrid's graduation from Hampshire when Zoe came up the stairs.

"I'll take you to lunch," I said.

"You know the way to a woman's heart. Tell me how you are."

"Fine. I'm fine. Is that a sunburn?"

"Forgot my sunblocker. Want to walk? If you feel up to it, there's a place within walking distance, you know."

We walked slowly to CHEAP EATS and sat outdoors and while waiting for our eats I gave Zoe one of the recipes to read. I watched some kids playing basketball, then Zoe finished reading and looked up. "It's a recipe for puff pastry. What's so remarkable about that?" she said, handing it back to me. I asked her wasn't there something else there. "Only that it's over written," she says. "Maybe over ripe."

"Don't you think there's a hidden meaning where it talks about the dough expanding and lifting, growing five or ten times bigger than it was? And then this line— *Glorious to see, light in the hand, heaven in the mouth.*"

Zoe looked blank, then she laughed. "Oh, how shy-making. What else do you have there?"

"Nothing."

"Let's see," she says, plucking the stationery sheets from my hand. "Artichokes," she says, reading. A short while later she looks up, saying, "This other is a menu for a light dinner, very light, just an appetizer, an extraordinary appetizer. Not like that nonsense about puff pastry or those, those steamy artichokes. This is romantic. Very romantic."

"What are you talking about?

"The wine is listed. And even the candles. It's beautiful, I *love* this. And I like the description—it's flowery but forgivable—of preparing the melon and wrapping each piece in a strip of prosciutto, arranging them, sprinkling the black pepper, adding the lemon wedges. This is a preface, a foreword, a—"

"What do you mean?"

"And the dessert, the peach Melba with raspberry sauce. Sure, yes, this is a romantic dinner, a wonderful romantic dinner," she says, finally looking up.

"Meaning?"

"You eat this first, dummy, because it's light and not filling. It stimulates the appetite. It enlivens all your senses. It creates a thirst and hunger, but not the kind that can be satisfied by more food or wine." She smiled and handed the pages back to me. "These are valentines, Ren. Each recipe in this menu is a love letter. The little dinner is just a beginning, it unwraps you. Or unzips or unbuttons. —Where did you get these?"

"Never mind."

"Not that athletic Californienne you're living with," she says.

"Can't you say Avalon?"

"Yes, that's the one."

Our cheap eats had arrived. While we were eating, I asked Zoe what she had been up to.

"Over the weekend I went to Newport and watched a sailboat race," she said. "Many races, actually."

Her big bland stupid friend Derek Mallow owned a sailboat and he liked races and this was Zoe's way of telling me she had finally gone off with him. I wasn't surprised or, to be precise, I shouldn't have been surprised if I had been paying attention, but I had preferred not to think about any of it.

"The weather was beautiful, sunny with a light breeze," Zoe continued. "We stayed through Monday and didn't come back until the next morning. We were in this extraordinary bed-and-breakfast, an old inn that dates back to the eighteenth century. The sun was glorious, but we pulled down the shades and spent most of the last day testing the bed, a huge four-poster."

"Don't tell me the details."

"You wouldn't think it to look at him, but he's insatiable. He's also somewhat rough," she said smugly. "I was shocked."

"Zoe."

"You'd never guess what he —."

"For Christ's sake, Zoe, keep your secrets to yourself. I'm not your hairdresser."

"I had a good time."

"Splendid."

"I need a good fuck every now and then," she said.

We didn't talk for a while but ate our sandwiches and watched the kids scramble back and forth across the abandoned parking lot, shouting. There's nothing to say about this Derek Mallow — whom I had hoped to omit — beyond his being a big, soft, boneless guy with his own consulting business, an ex-wife, two children in college, a sportscar that sounded like it was farting and a sailboat — and that's the whole man in a sentence. "You think I'm making a mistake," Zoe said flatly, shading her eyes with her hand as she followed the basketball players.

"Hell, Zoe, you know him a lot better than I do."

"You think I'm wasting my time again?" she asked, the fine lines at the corner of her eye deepening as she squinted at the hoop and its torn net.

"How would I know?"

The kids quit playing and ebbed to the shade where they had stashed some bottles of water.

"I suppose I shouldn't even be talking to you about this," she said, turning to me.

"I suppose not."

"Did you just laugh at me?"

"At you? No."

After lunch we headed back to her studio, passing the basketball players who were fooling around now, squirting water at each other, dodging, spitting, whooping.

"Now tell me where you got that romantic menu," Zoe said.

"At Alba's. But it's not her handwriting."

"Maybe they're written by that chef she was taking lessons from."

"Michelle?"

"Yes. —He's going back to France. I think he's already gone."

"Who's going back to France?"

"Michelle, the chef. Michelle Reverdy. You met him," she says. "—Ren, are you coming?"

"Michelle? Michelle? *I thought Michelle was a woman!*"

"It's a French name, after all. Can be male or female," says Zoe. "Anyway you met him. —Hey, are we walking together or not?"

"I never met him. The *chef*? Oh, God. The *chef!*"

"I thought you met him when Alba began taking lessons," said Zoe. "Those are probably his recipes. That's probably his menu. Alba really liked those classes," she added.

I groaned. "I know. I know she did."

"Frankly, I think she was a little intimidated at first. I mean, she was afraid she was going to be intimidated. But Michelle isn't one of those tyrannical French chefs who makes you feel stupid and clumsy in your own kitchen. Quite the contrary. He has a nice way about him."

"You met him?"

"She took me to the class once, to show him off, I think. And afterward we had coffee with him. Late fifties, maybe older, vigorous, full of energy, overflowing with it," she said brightly.

"You think he was likeable?"

"Definitely, but I don't think *you* would have liked him."

"Why not?"

"He believes cooking is an art, like composing music or writing or painting. He talks about it that way."

I told her she was right, that I wouldn't have liked him, that we would have argued and it was best I'd never met the man, though Zoe insisted I had.

54

THAT AFTERNOON I DROVE ACROSS THE RIVER TO Alba's to ask what was going on between her and the fancy French chef. She came to the door, pen in hand and reading glasses peering from her hair. "Renato. What are you doing here?"

"I found these recipes in your book, the one I borrowed, the one called *French Cinema* or something like that. So, here they are." I had begun to feel dizzy or sick to my stomach.

"Oh, you shouldn't have driven over here for that," she said, taking the folded blue sheets. "They're only—they're not that important." She walked into the apartment, letting her voice trail over her shoulder as she placed the notes on the small desk. "Want something to drink? Cinzano, diet Coke, wine, coffee? I was about to make a fresh pot. You know what we have." She continued into the kitchen. "What will it be?"

I cleared my throat, said coffee would be fine.

"How are you feeling these days?"

I told her I felt fine, not as good as new, but at least I was able to piss.

Alba turned on the water and began to fill the pot. "Did the boy like your grandfather's fishing pole?" she asked, her back to me.

"It belonged to one of my uncles. And the boy's name is Kim, you know." My voice had come out sharper than I had expected. "He and his mother are moving out, moving to Somerville."

Alba put the pot aside and twisted opened the coffee jar.

"That should give you more room in your studio," she remarked, tightening the prissy wrinkle lines at the corners of her mouth.

"She'll be getting together with Sebastian. They're in love, the real thing, Avalon and Sebastian."

Alba refused to look my way. "Sebastian's a good man," she said at last, carefully spooning coffee into the pot. "I wonder how Caitlin will take it. She still so young and —."

"Caitlin will take it just fine," I cut in. "She likes Avalon — why not? — and Avalon likes her. Who wrote the recipes?" I was out of breath.

She looked up at me. "What recipes?"

"The recipes I brought you just now. The recipes on blue stationery."

She turned away and reached for the coffee mugs, saying, "Those were written by Michelle, the chef I took cooking lessons from."

"What did you and the chef do besides cook? You and this chef, when you were alone together, what —."

She whirled around to look at me, the color leaving her face. "You have some nerve, asking me a question like that! Good God! You're incredible, unbelievable."

"So, what did you and this chef do?"

"*Who are you to ask me questions! Who do you think you are?*"

"I take it you did more than plan meals together —."

"*Fuck off!* You can take it any goddamn way you goddamn please." Her cheeks, white as paper a moment ago, were flushed now. "It's *my* life, what's left of it. I do what pleases *me!*"

"What does that mean?"

"It means I'm not going to answer your prying, domineering, selfish questions. *So don't ask!*"

I felt like telling her how ugly her face was when she was angry. "Is it finished between you and him?" I asked.

She plunged her trembling hands among the coffee mugs,

knocking them left and right, snatched one and hurled it at me but wild, the pieces exploding from the fridge to ricochet off the cabinets and go skitter scatter across the floor. "You shit!" she cries, her eyes flashing. "You bastard!"

"I'm not fucking Avalon."

"You mean you've *stopped* fucking her is what you mean! You mean you've stopped because you're still bleeding down there."

"She's in love with Sebastian."

"I don't give a rat's ass who she fucks. That's your problem."

"She's moving out. She's going to be living with him."

"Don't waste my time. Go away," she said, her body stiffening.

"I suppose Michelle's gone back to wherever he came from."

"Go! You, go," she cries, waving her hand, brushing me away with a shooing gesture. "Get out!"

"Has he gone or not?"

"Fuck you, Renato! Fuck, fuck, fuck."

"Is he gone?"

"Don't you raise your hand at me!"

"I have never in my life—."

"Yes, he's gone, you poor bastard, yes. —Now get out of here."

"No. This is my—."

"Just go," she cries, her eyes brimming. "You make me sick. I don't want to see you!"

"Alba."

"I don't like you," she sobs.

My stomach lurched, my insides loose and weightless, as if I had stepped off a height and was falling and falling, endlessly.

"Don't say that. For God's sake, Alba—."

She was drying her eyes with the heels of her hands. "I don't—."

"Alba, shut up!"

"I don't like you anymore."

I put my hands over my ears, turned and left and turned again, stumbling at the door. "I'll see you tomorrow."

"I don't want to see you." She pushed the door shut, closing me out.

As I drove from Alba's I had to throw up, so I pulled over, opened the door and I must have fallen out, because I was on my hands and knees, vomiting on the curbstone and cars were going by. Afterward I was on a bench by the river, still on the Cambridge side, looking at the water. The world looked as if nothing had happened. Cars and trucks moved across the bridge and sped silently on the far side of the river. I was empty as a sack turned inside out. At the boat house on the far shore a young guy had lowered a racing shell into the water and was pulling away from the ramp, heading zigzag to the middle of the river, where he aligned his craft and then sliced downstream, farther and farther away, his oars glinting rhythmically.

55

*T*HE NEXT DAY I TRIED TO PAINT BUT FELT LOWER than whale shit and could barely stand up and thought to lie down, but instead I wandered into Avalon's room and looked at her colored jerseys, neatly folded and stacked, and the things on the bookcase shelf—her black leather dog collar, her silver rings and chains—but I just looked and didn't pry into anything. She still had those stupid photos of me propped up against the books. I drifted back into the studio and studied the snapshots on the cork board, mostly the photos of Brizio, Astrid and Skye, then I sat down on the floor and stretched out on my back with my hands folded on my belt and let everything go blank. I don't know how long I had been lying there, waiting to die, when Kim came in the door and announced he was hungry and wanted to eat. After a while I asked him what he wanted to eat and he said a grilled cheese sandwich, so I hauled myself upright and made a grilled cheese sandwich and set the plate on the table with a glass of milk, then I laid myself down on the floor again. Kim ate, idly swinging his legs so one of his shoes rhythmically banged a table leg—bump and bump and bump and bump and bump and bump and bump. I closed my eyes. "Jamal is homey," he announced, accenting his words to sound like Jamal. I kept my eyes shut and a little later Kim said, "I ax Jamal could he teach me on his skate board. Can't nobody skate the way Jamal do." And still later he added, "He be going to the car wash wit Jeff tomorrow." I got to my feet and when our little wise-guy had finished the last of his milk I told him I had to do errands. I drove us to the Daily Grind where he was happy to stay and help Gordon roast coffee beans while I crossed the river to Alba's.

Alba opened the door, but kept her and on the doorknob, ready to shut it in my face. "What do you want?" she said. I didn't know what to say and for a moment we just stood there while I hunted for words. Then Alba turned and walked back into the apartment, leaving the door open and I followed her. In the kitchen she didn't say anything, so I said, "Want a glass of Cinzano?" She shrugged and said she didn't care. I said, "White or red?" She shrugged listlessly and sat at the kitchen table, turning away from me to look out the window. I said, Let's try white poured over ice cubes." I took out the white but there wasn't much left. "There's only enough for one glass, so we'll have to have red.," I told her. I got the ice cubes and prepared the drinks and sat across from her. Alba was still gazing out the window and she looked old, really old. I searched the lines in her face, wondering how many I had put there, and I felt rotten. I looked out the window and sipped the Cinzano. The vermouth had a satisfyingly bitter taste.

56

MORNINGS I WOKE UP EXHAUSTED. I DON'T KNOW which day I went to the Daily Grind and phoned Cormac McCormac, asked him if he wanted a visitor, and he said Yes. I lugged my gloomy self into my car and headed out to his place, which is one-third of the way to rural nowhere — the land out there going to seed — turned off the pike and went over hill and down dale, passing through a forgotten town where the movie palace had a blank sign and the church was boarded up, then into a lonely village center (Jake's Auto Body Repair, Best Wash, Tina's Lunch) and out a meandering road between a half mile of cornfield and a stony hillside with cows and a rusted bus, past an abandoned railway station and on to Cormac's place. I bumped along the ruts toward his barn to park beside one of his cairns and spied his broad white shirt in the black square of the barn doorway. He came out and halted, squinting in the sun and turning his shaggy head this way and that, like a bear from a cave, then the screen door at the house slapped shut and Karen McCormac was on her way down the path to me. We stood there talking, half way between the house and the barn. "Want to have lunch and then look around, or want to look around first?" Cormac asked me, scratching his bearded cheek.

"Let's look around," I said.

Actually it wasn't a barn but a big work-shed that he had built a dozen years ago to replace the old barn that had been his original studio; inside he had a steel I-beam frame with a block-and-tackle hanging from it and a long bench with sculpting tools — not just mauls and chisels and rasps and sanders, but power saws, acetylene tools, riveting guns and other heavy junk. He showed me what he had been working on, particularly some metal castings which I liked, and a big bronze thing, shaped like a spinnaker, which had been commissioned by a software entrepreneur to decorate corporate headquarters. After a while, I had to sit down to take a rest; like I said to Cormac, it's surprising how a little surgery can take so much out of you. Later, while we were touring the vegetable garden, Karen called to us, saying she was hungry and why didn't we come to the house for lunch now.

Karen McCormac is a good-natured woman, a retired schoolteacher who wears her hair in braids and has a torso that is, as she says, flat as a pine plank. She had set the table on the back porch, so we ate overlooking the vegetable garden and, beyond that, the field with some of Cormac's stone pieces, and after lunch Cormac and I stayed on the porch with a few cold bottles of ale. It was good to tilt our chairs back and sit with our heels on the railing and drink and not talk, just enjoying the restful quiet while the sun shone and not much happened. The sky was brushed in very lightly with a particularly limpid blue and there was a row of painterly white clouds about a quarter way up from the horizon. "I'm glad I invited myself here," I said at last. "I like the view. And I like what you've done with the clouds. You handled the perspective just right, too, not so deep and not completely flattened out either. But it's those heaps of white clouds that impress me most."

"Yeah, the clouds were difficult. But I'm not a painter. Maybe you could have done better."

"I thought I might get a show at the Strand Gallery, but it didn't work out."

"Oh." Cormac was squinting at the horizon and he didn't move or say anything more for a while. "Yeah, I know what that's like. That can make you feel dead, real dead, as in dead dead. —And yet?" he said, turning his face toward me.

"I'm still alive."

He turned back to the horizon. "Yeah, being alive is good,"

he said. "Being alive beats all. —How's the plumbing repair? Everything working all right?" I told him I hadn't had a
chance to try everything yet, but so far, so good.

We sat there and drank and didn't talk much, exchanged
some gossip about galleries is all, and when he asked had I
seen any interesting shows recently I had to tell him no, said
I used to rely on Alba to tell me about interesting works but,
since she quit reviewing galleries and began to review French
bistros, I've fallen behind. "Alba's doing restaurant reviews?"
he asked me. I said No, said she had taken a course in French
cooking and got infatuated with it, that's all. When he asked
about Zoe I said, "She's seeing a lot of some soft boneless rich
guy named Mallow whose great ambition is to win a sailboat
race at Newport." Cormac smiled at the horizon and said, "I
know you're just trying to be nice, but I can tell you don't like
the man." And I had to agree, I didn't.

Later he asked where I was living now and I told him, "I'm
back in my studio. I'll stay there until I finish up this batch
of paintings. They're not going to Newbury Street but they'll
go someplace. I hope." Cormac said he was sure of it, said my
paintings were destined to find a gallery, said the problem was
that most galleries were run by timid assholes. Then he asked
what happens when you do finish these paintings, meaning,
would I stay in my studio or go back to living in that concrete
tomb with Alba. I told him we want to buy a place in the
country. "I don't want to live without her," I said. "In fact, I
can't live without her. The only reason I'm at my studio is to
paint." Cormac glanced at me and then gazed out at the field
and the horizon and I knew he didn't believe me. "Sometimes
Alba's hard to live with," I added. He thought about that a
while and then said matter-of-factly, "They all are, sooner or
later, one way or the other." But I felt I had been unfair. "Of
course, Alba puts up with a lot," I emended.

He laughed and said, "She puts up with you, you mean."

"Mostly she puts up with me. But she's not perfect. She

has lapses. Don't be deceived. There are times when she turns into her other self and recites all my sins, which she's carefully memorized, so she can go out and do something nasty, which she's been thinking of and longing for, some act of revenge."

"Whatever that might be," says Cormac. But I said only Yes, whatever that might be, and I left it at that. Later he asked about that woman in the studio, and I said Avalon's fine. I was about to tell him she's moving out, when he said, "I can barely manage one woman. How do you juggle three? Bigamy is difficult enough, I should think. But trigamy, or whatever it's called—."

"It's called trigonometry," I said.

"How do you do it, Ren?"

"I don't do it. You have it backward. They do it. And anyway, Avalon's moving out. She's moving in with Sebastian."

"Gabriel? Sebastian Gabriel?" I was gratified to see Cormac as surprised as I had been. "It's a match made in heaven," I said.

Later we got onto wise-ass art critics, Cormac telling me a story about Greenberg and how Greenberg ruined some of David Smith's sculptures, a story I think he'd told me before. Cormac had met Greenberg years ago. "The guy was a great fucker. That was a different epoch when I was married to number two and she was crazy about that whole freaky New York crowd. She had a friend on the Bennington faculty who taught literature, so we'd drive up there and Rachel would try to meet the artists who taught there or who hung out in the hills around there. I think she married me so she could meet these sculptors and painters and if she got lucky she'd get laid by someone important. I figured that out later. I still haven't figured out why I married her—or number one or number three, for that matter." So we were back to talking about women and Cormac said he was thinking of doing some figurative pieces because then he'd be able to say he needed a model. "That would be fun, a young woman with breasts up here like apples. —Though I'm beginning to wonder if I'd be able to do it," he muttered. I told him I was sure he'd be able to do figurative pieces. "No," he said. "Do the woman, the actual woman—fuck her, I mean. I can still do it in my imagination, but I'm beginning to wonder if I could do it with an actual stranger, not Karen." I told him I was sure he'd be able to do it with a stranger, too.

"But I don't know and I'm afraid to find out. I've become a dutiful husband from fear of impotence." He gave a short laugh.

"Are you serious?"

"Maybe." He studiously poured the last of a bottle into his glass. "I don't know."

Later he said he'd been thinking about Maillol being seventy-three when he got this Dina Vierny to pose for him, she being fifteen at the time. "And she had all that firmness and roundness and balance and lightness—man, she was juicy!" He laughed with pleasure, as if he were actually remembering her himself. "Then the old man died and she spent the rest of her life building him a museum, a chateau, a whole chateau devoted to him. Now she's so old and so fat she won't let anyone take her picture. And in a while she'll be as dead as Maillol," he added.

Cormac carefully lowered his empty glass to the floor, sighed, folded his big paws on his belly. There was just the sunny air over the field, a spacious quiet and the occasional buzz of a bee and the whir of grasshoppers. Cormac asked me did I ever think about death. I said Yes, too often.

"I don't understand death at all," he said. "What's it for? What's the point? I still haven't figured it out." I told him the catechism said it had something to do with Original Sin. He said, "I thought Original Sin was when Adam and Eve had their first fuck. It was so much fun they thought it must be forbidden. That's why they got fig leaves to hide their privates and pretend to God they didn't know about fucking. That's what I thought."

I said No, said they had been fucking all along like animals and they didn't know what they were doing, but after they ate from the Tree of Knowledge of Good and Evil they woke up to what they were doing and decided it was evil, so they got the fig leaves.

"There's nothing more innocent than plain fucking," Cormac said. "Why did they think it was evil? Who put that thought into their heads? God gave them free will but when they used it God got so sore he invented death, and I still don't understand it."

I thought about that for a while. "I haven't figured out living," I told him. "I always thought I'd examine my life when I got older and had more time. I had an uncle who told me the unexamined life wasn't worth living. I think he was right, but now I'm older and I've got less time than before. The last time I had a clear view I was beginning to paint and was about to get married. I could see the way ahead, the way to go, but that was the last time. I don't know what happened next. I tried to live right, but it was all I could do just to get by. It's the same with painting. I can't paint and think about it at the same time, so I just paint."

That's the way the afternoon went. We weren't twin brothers, Cormac and me, but we'd known each other a long while and I liked him; I liked the way he did his job, happy to do it right and happy to make a living at it—yet ready to drop whatever he was doing and just sit and talk, or not talk, if that's what you needed. He was overweight and he peed a lot, I guess from diabetes, but I never heard him complain about it.

57

I DON'T KNOW EXACTLY WHEN I BEGAN TO PAINT AGAIN. Alba and I weren't all right, not at all, but we were right enough to go to Bread Alone together for cinnamon rolls or to the Mondello for an espresso. So I was painting again and feeling good about that, good enough to go to the Daily Grind when I needed a break, and there I bumped into the skinny guy I'd met at the Pixels exhibit, Vanderzee.

We exchanged hellos and because I felt guilty about not having gone to look at his work I told him I'd get over to his studio someday soon. While we were talking, Avalon saw me and came over but before she could bawl me out I told her, "He's skateboarding with Amal because Amal has two skateboards. Mrs Gupta is at her window keeping her eye on them, so don't worry."

The next day I drove to South Boston, looking for Vanderzee's place, and ended up outside a grocery store displaying signboards written in what I guess was Vietnamese. I found a parking space and walked to his address, a dirty brick structure that had been a factory seventy-five or hundred years ago. I hadn't phoned to tell him I was coming because, frankly, I was hoping he wouldn't be in and I'd leave a note to show my good intentions and get off without having to take a guided tour of his work. I knocked on his door, but before I could scribble my note the door opened and here was Vanderzee.

"Oh! This is great! Come on in," he said, pulling me along and turning to happily announce, "Hey! It's Stillamare. Renato Stillamare's here." The place had bare brick walls and big windows; a bunch of mismatched furniture sat in the sun to the left, a crowd of paintings stood to the right. "Gail," he said, calling to an elegant cinnamon woman with high

cheekbones and large gold hoops in her ears, a child cling-
ing to her orange dress. "This is Renato Stillamare." Gail and
I shook hands, her ivory bracelets clicking, and she said she
was glad I had come by. "You're the one who paints nudes like
landscapes and landscapes like nudes. Right?" Vanderzee had
scooped up the child and was steering me toward a young
man in a white suit whose name I didn't catch, only that he
was a magician. We shook hands. "I'd like to stay but I'm
about to disappear," the magician said cheerfully. He strolled
out the door accompanied by a pale woman, a pre-Raphaelite
redhead in a translucent paisley dress, leaving us at a long
plank table cluttered with crockery and the scraps of a meal.
I apologized for arriving unannounced, told Vanderzee I was
sorry I hadn't phoned ahead, but I'd been driving through
the neighborhood and thought I'd knock on his door with
the hope of finding him in. "And I'm glad you did," he said,
setting the little kid down on his feet. "We had a late lunch
and would never have stopped talking. Want anything?" he
asked, reaching toward the beer bottles on the table. But I was
distracted by the wild splashes of color on the canvases in the
background. "Or let me show you some paintings," he said.

I had already walked over to the stack of very large stretchers that were leaning against a pair of posts. "Yes," I said.
"Show me." Vanderzee lifted the first canvass, stepped sideways several paces and leaned it against a studio easel, then
came back to my side to view it. I knew he was good from
the first glance. "Great," I said and told him what I liked. He
pulled out a dozen big stretchers one at a time, letting them
stack against each other at the easel. Some were stronger than
others, but none of them was a mess and when he occasion-
ally failed it was because of boldness or misapplied energy; he
was good and he was going to get better.

He took up the last canvas, lifted it gently sideways to lean
against the others, unwittingly exposing behind it a busted
sofa where a woman lay curled around the baby in her arms.

She blinked and squinted in the sudden light, raising her head to look at us. "Oh! You remember Winona," Vanderzee told me. And, yes, it was the flaxen-haired woman who had been pouring wine at the Pixels exhibit. Winona sat up and buttoned her blouse, still cradling the baby. "Can I get you something to eat or drink?" she asked. "I've been napping. I think it was the beer," she added. Winona and Gail cleared a patch of table and Vanderzee stoked a leaky espresso machine while I give him the names of some New York galleries I thought would welcome his work, and I would have helped him more if I could. I stayed there the rest of the afternoon, for Vanderzee was congenial and I enjoyed the distraction of his company and his women, but on the slow drive home I returned to myself who was melancholy, lonely and old.

58

I HAVE NO THEORIES ABOUT WOMEN. IN MY TWENTIES I read a deep book about female psychology, hoping it would help get them into my bed, but that never worked, so I gave up on theories. I couldn't theorize about Alba and live with her at the same time, so she remains as much a mystery to me as I do to myself, inexplicable and contrary—Alba, that is—all of which is to say that when I asked Alba would she come to the studio on Sunday for brunch with me and Sebastian Gabriel and his daughter Caitlin and Kim and, sure, Kim's mother, she said, "Yes."

I doubt that Alba herself knows for sure what goes on in her opaque heart. She may have wanted to get a look at Avalon because Zoe had gone to the Daily Grind more than once to watch Avalon and to chat her up and then—I'm certain—had reported to Alba that the skanky bitch wore rings in her face and she, Zoe, didn't know who to feel more sorry for, Renato or Avalon. And Alba may have wanted to see Avalon right now and not later, not at some other place but here in the studio, so as to get a better sense of what was going on between me and Avalon. Or maybe she decided to come merely to display her power. That would be easy enough because Alba has such a long history in this studio that if she walked in tomorrow the walls would recognize her voice, the chairs would welcome her and every little thing—dishes, cups and even the spoons in the drawer—would proclaim loyalty to her, our Alba.

The brunch was Avalon's idea. I went along with it to show her what an open-hearted man I was and to show Sebastian that Avalon and I were merely friends, buddies, pals, and if I had ever given her a second thought or, silly old man, ever kissed her on the cheek, it was purely paternal and not something weird like, say, fucking her frontward and backward on that narrow bunk over there.

Now as soon as Alba surprised me with her "Yes," I began to think of the four of us and what kind of quartet we would make, each of us singing from a different page. I tried to see Alba coming in on Renato as he was setting the breakfast table with young, barefoot Avalon—that stopped the action right there. I rearranged the scene and had Sebastian and his daughter enter first, then Alba enters and is greeted by the happy couple, Sebastian and Avalon. The next morning I went to the Daily Grind and phoned Sebastian, told him the brunch would begin at ten, then I phoned Alba and told her to come to the studio at ten-thirty, for brunch would not begin until sometime after that, maybe at eleven.

As it happened, they both arrived at the same time, their chat and laughter floating up the stairway ahead of them, at which sound Avalon came running from the back room, flung open the door and eagerly stepped out—"Hi!"—into Alba who had started to step in—*wham!*—clutched each other to keep from falling, then awkwardly disentangled, Avalon backing into Sebastian with a brief laugh while Alba slipped sideways into the studio with a carved smile. That took care of the introductions.

Alba was in a summer dress she knew I liked, one with a long slit up the side, though this morning the slit ran only a hand's breadth above her knee. Avalon wasn't wearing those black velvet shorts that let a crescent moon of flesh hang beneath each rear hem, no; for I'd told her that Sebastian, after his divorce and accompanied by his daughter, liked a softer, more womanly woman — which was probably true — so Avalon had visited the Next-To-New shop and the Déjà Vu All Over Again boutique and was now wearing a filmy dress with sleeves of curtain lace, plus turkey feather earrings. As for Sebastian, apparently he had stolen his clothes from a scarecrow and left the poor thing naked in a corn field. I had lugged two saw horses, a couple of wood chairs and a plank tabletop from the back room, so we had more space than we needed and that was probably a good thing.

At first the conversation was stiff, but innocent Sebastian had discovered that he liked to talk, now that his wife wasn't around to correct him, and Avalon always had something to say, so Alba and I had only to add a few words now and again to keep them going. We heard about Sebastian's ten-speed bicycle and about windmills that could generate enough electricity to free us from dependence on foreign oil. I learned about undyed, unbleached cotton, and a lot about chi, which is a natural vital energy flowing through ghostly channels or meridians on the non-physical or, as they say, subtle body, and I listened while Avalon and Sebastian unfolded secrets about the seven chakras, which are places on the subtle body where the energy gathers, or flows to, or from or through. Caitlin said she didn't believe in chakras or meridians or *chi*, especially since she had seen the diagrams and thought them ugly, but she did like Tarot cards, not for telling fortunes, which she told us was a scam, but because the cards were beautiful and she and her friend Noel had invented a game where they played the Tarot cards and made up fabulous stories about the images on them. Young Caitlin was especially pretty, I thought, as she had unbraided her hair that morning and brushed it smooth, so it hung half-way down her back, glossy as a chestnut just hatched from its shell. Avalon, on the contrary, had somehow dyed the roots of her own hair a russet brass.

After the brunch, Avalon and Sebastian went off with the kids to amble along the river while Alba and I washed the dishes. While I was cleaning the waffle iron Alba walked to the doorway of the back room and stood there a few moments, looking where Avalon and Kim slept. She came back and wiped a bowl, set it on the shelf. "Kim has a nice new basketball," she remarked, breaking her silence. I said Yes, but I learned he's not much interested in basketball. Alba dried the last of the tin ware, laid it in the drawer and drifted away. "Are these photos of Avalon?" she asked. I turned and found her at the cork board, looking at some snapshots. I told her there were no photos of Avalon there. "Who is it then?" she asked. I went over to look. There was the same old jumble of overlapping photos — Brizio, uncle Zitti, Galaxy, father, mother, Skye, my lost aunt Vivianna, Alba, and a dozen other relatives — and slid in among them were old snapshots of Avalon that she had taken from her albums. Yes, I said, that's Avalon. I went back to the sink, squeezed out the wash rag and hung it up. I said, "I think the brunch went well." Alba didn't answer. She had gone to the window and was looking out. "There's some Asti left in the bottle," I told her. "Want a glass?"

"I'll be leaving," she said, not turning around.

I poured the last of the Asti into a glass and took a swallow. "Stay a while," I said.

'No." She turned. "Enough is enough."

I had an impulses to throw her out the door or to pull off her clothes and fuck her, I couldn't tell which. "Are you going to help me choose paintings to show to Conti?" I asked her.

"You've decided to get in touch with Conti?"

"I'm thinking about it, yes."

"I think you should," she said.

"You'll come around to look at the paintings," I said. I offered her a drink from my glass of Asti, but she shook her head no.

"Some time when she's not around would be good," Alba said. So we left it at that.

59

LATE ON FRIDAY I DROVE OVER TO ZOE'S AND ARRIVED as she was closing her studio. "I'm going to the sailboat races at Marblehead this weekend," she announced. That was her way of saying that she was going to spend the weekend with Derek Mallow.

"Well. Good luck at the races," I said.

She turned off her computer and began to gather the scattered papers and file folders from her desktop. "Some of the excitement has worn off. No man's perfect, I suppose. We stayed in an expensive cottage on the Vineyard last weekend. Anyway, I don't think you and I should talk about it. About him, I mean."

"Right, you're right."

"Did you know he's younger than me?" she asked, jamming the folders into an open file drawer.

"That doesn't make any difference."

"It does if you're in the middle of menopause." She slammed the drawer shut with her knee.

"He doesn't expect to have more children, Zoe."

"He doesn't expect problems in bed, either."

"You're going to give him problems?"

She had turned away and was putting an armful of catalogs on a shelf. "Menopause is wonderful but I don't want to talk about it."

"All right."

She straightened out the catalog shelf and turned to me. "I'm drying out, Ren. And you know it. I'm dry everywhere. My hair is brittle. My skin is cracked. My lips are dry. My eyes are dry. I'm dry *inside*. Have you forgotten? Have you forgotten how it hurts when we do it, I'm so dry!"

"There are ways around that. There are—"

"This is nature's way of telling women they're finished."

"Come on, Zoe. You're in a mood. You're not thinking clearly."

"What has thinking got to do with it!" she said, flaring at me. "Thinking isn't going to change a thing!"

"Zoe, you're a good looking woman, one of the most interesting—"

"Is that the same thing as a good time in bed?" she cried. "I don't think so! A good time in bed is when you're fucking Avalon! Warm and wet. Right?"

"Should I leave?"

"No," she said. She sighed and glanced around the studio, one hand on the light switch. "Come upstairs for a drink."

"Come to dinner at my place."

"With that Avalon?" Zoe switched off the studio lights and we went up the stairs. "You want everyone to love everyone, but that's not the way it works, Renato."

I helped her open the large window in the sitting room. I told her Avalon was leaving, was going to be moving in with Sebastian Gabriel. Zoe listened and said nothing. "Why not come to dinner?" I asked her.

"What a strange-looking couple they'll make. —I'm going to wash up. Even if you don't want a drink you can get one for me. There's a fresh bottle of Australian Chardonnay in the refrigerator. I'm not fussy."

I went to the kitchen, uncorked the bottle and poured a

glass of cold Australian Chardonnay. Zoe came in from the bathroom, saying, "—Because I agree with her not only about baths and flowers but about touch, too."

I gave her the glass and asked what she was talking about.

"I agree with Alba about what happens when our kids grow up and we can't cuddle with them or even hug them when they're naked and kiss their necks. After twelve years old they keep their clothes on and don't want to be touched by their mothers. If I had a house full of four-year-olds I wouldn't need men." She walked through the sitting room and into her bedroom.

"Well," I said. "Maybe. But I don't think—"

"You know you're old when nobody touches you and you're not allowed to touch anybody. That's how they punish you for growing old. Then you wither and die, from lack of touch."

"Why are we talking about old age? Where do you get these ideas?"

"They're mine, my ideas. —I think I'll change," she added.

"I hope so. I'd be sorry if you had to live with that view of life."

"No, Renato. I'm going to change *this*," she said, plucking at her shirt. "I put this on for a business lunch. I'm getting into something more comfortable. I'll keep my ideas."

Zoe pulled off her shirt and skirt, hung them quickly in the closet, unfastened her bra and tossed it onto her bureau. The bra had incised the flesh beneath her breasts, leaving a cruel pink line which she now rubbed tenderly with her finger tips, as if to erase. "We're born in the flesh and we die of it, or from it, because of it. I haven't worked this up to a philosophy yet," she said.

"I hope there's more to me than flesh," I told her. "My flesh is betraying me. It's letting me down. It's failing."

"Well, so is mine," she said. "But that doesn't mean we have something else or something more than our bodies."

"You have to get beyond that, beyond flesh," I told her.

"Please, Ren, you're *not* the one to tell me to renounce my body." She began flipping through the dresses in the closet.

"I'm not saying renounce your body. I'm saying there's more to you than mere flesh."

"When I think of what you've spent your life painting—"

"Everything I've painted shows there's more. There's meaning. We crave meaning as much as we crave anything."

"Oh, we crave it all right," she said. "But is it there?"

"There's meaning or there's no point to painting or to living. By the way, I've just finished a group of paintings."

She drew out a dress, saying, "I'll wear this. No bra. What do you think?" It was a kind of thin white shift with big pale splashes of blue and green.

"Fine. It looks fine."

"As for your paintings, Ren, they show a lot of different things." She plunged her hands into the coiled cloth and lifted her arms, letting the dress slide down over her.

"There's more to a living body than flesh," I insisted.

"Maybe that's true for you and not for me," she said, looking into the mirror on the closet door. "I'd love for you to be a woman for just one month."

"What's *that* got to do with it?"

She drained her glass. "I'm hungry. Are we going to your place for dinner now or not? I can look at your new works." But she went to the mirror and began to brush her hair back, first one side then the other.

"Your hair looks fine, Zoe. Let's go."

"I bet you don't know the difference between a ketch and a sloop. I keep getting them confused. It's quite boring. Why is it that the more I get to know a man, the more I feel like I'm going to jail?"

"The door's over here, let's go."

"And my sexual fantasies bore me. Does that ever happen to anyone else? Does that ever happen to Alba?" she asked as we went out.

60

ONE NIGHT AVALON TOLD ME I OWED HER HALF a dozen photos, and I said Since when do I owe you photos? and she said Since I give you those photos of me, and I said What photos of you? and she said The photos I put up on the wall where you keep your other relatives.

"Oh, *those* photos," I said.

"Yes, those."

"I didn't know you wanted me to—I mean, I didn't know I could keep them."

"Yes. You keep those and you give me some of yours," she informed me. Then she flipped open her small square album, the glossy lilac one that holds one photo per page, and showed me the empty pages. "I've rearranged everything so yours can go in here. See?"

I saw. I went to the blanket chest at the foot of my bed, took out the cigar box crammed with unsorted photographs and brought it to the table. "Help yourself," I told her. Then I put on those tiny earphones she bought for me and listened to her music player while she sorted through the photos. She worked with a business-like frown of concentration and after twenty minutes she had chosen maybe four snapshots. She went off, came back with two water glasses full of wine, and plucked the earphones from my ears. "How about one of these olden-time photographs where your ancestors are dressed up like, you know, historical," she said. She went over to the cork board and studied the black-and-white studio portrait of my mother as a teenage flapper—cloche hat, bobbed hair, flat body. "I think that was taken in 1925," I told her.

"How old is this one?" Avalon asked, looking at the brown

photograph in the pressed cardboard frame.

"That was taken around 1917 or 1918. It had to be before the influenza epidemic. There was no money for fancy photographs after that. My father's about eighteen or nineteen. His sister is about fourteen."

"She was the wild one."

"So I've heard"

"Wild how?" Avalon asked.

"She got pregnant at seventeen, I think, and—"

"She didn't *get* pregnant. Some man *got* her pregnant," Avalon informed me.

"Right, some man *got* her pregnant. In fact, his name was Zampa. They got married about six months before the baby was born, and the baby lived only a few days. I heard a lot about that. After the baby died, Zampa went to Las Vegas and Vivianna went back to live with her brother—that's my father—in the apartment over the store. Zampa deserted her, is what I was told. Maybe he went off before the baby was born. I don't know."

"You never met her, the wild one."

"She was long gone before I was born."

"She died?"

"All I know is that my father got her a job with my mother's father, in his store. That was when my father and mother were engaged to be married. After the wedding, they sailed off to France and Italy, mostly Italy, and when they got back Vivianna was gone again. She was always taking off. Then she'd send a postcard from wherever when she got there. Maybe she hooked up with Zampa again. I don't think they ever got a divorce. Anyway, nobody ever saw her again."

Avalon had the photograph in her hand and turned it over —I knew there was nothing on the back—and now she had turned it face up and was studying the image once more. "I do like these old-time pictures," she said. It was clear she wanted that photo.

"That won't fit in your album," I said, which was the truth, after all. "I'll get you a different one."

I went back to the blanket chest and dug out the cardboard letter box that had the papers from my father's family. I emptied it onto the table. The biggest item, which was wrapped in tissue paper, was the tintype photograph of my father's mother's mother, Serafina's mother, who lived in Venice where, she liked to say, the streets were made of water. There was a lot of junk — a couple of canceled passbooks from the Shawmut Bank, a paid-off mortgage, my father's Social Security card, his old passport from their wedding trip — stuff like that, but of Vivianna there was only a baptismal certificate and a picture postcard, which I showed to Avalon. The postcard said, *Here I am but not for long. Leaving for San Francisco on Monday & will write from there. Love to all, Viv.* The picture on the other side was of the Hotel National which was shaped like a shoebox, had two storeys and maybe eighteen rooms, each window with a striped awning. "I wouldn't have stayed there a week either," Avalon said. "Why did she go to Las Vegas?"

"I don't know. Maybe her husband was still out there. Italians built Las Vegas. — I can't find any small size photos of her. I thought I remembered some, just little snapshots. Sorry about that."

Avalon said That's all right, I'll go get one I took of you and you can write on the back, and I said What do you want me to write? and she said Jesus, Ren, do I have to do everything?

61

ALBA CAME TO THE STUDIO ON A HOT WEDNESDAY afternoon to look at the paintings and to tell me whatever she knew about Leo Conti before I approached him about getting a show at his gallery. I had thought because of the heat she might arrive wearing that same dress with the slit up the side, opened higher this time—which would be a good sign—but, no; she was outfitted from an L. L. Bean sportswoman's catalog, a sleeveless top with a high neck and a wrap-around skirt that looked to be sewn shut. To relax us I asked did she want something to drink, maybe a glass of wine over ice, but she said No, it's too early in the day, and she even said No to a glass of water with a sprig of mint in it. I asked did she want to take a look around the place, meaning I had nothing to hide, but she said No, she'd just look at the paintings, and she walked over to the canvases. I discovered Avalon's bottle of shampoo glitter on the kitchen counter and shoved it under the sink with the soaps and sponges.

"These look good," Alba said.

"Yeah. Well. Maybe. Some of them. I hope."

"They're really good, Ren. Mind if I move them around?"

"Move anything."

While Alba looked at the paintings, I ducked into the bathroom to see what else Avalon might have left out and, in fact, found an apple-green thong hanging from the shower-head. I put in my pocket, drifted into the back room and slipped it into the plastic box where she kept her underthings, then ambled back to the studio and, because I didn't want to stand there looking at her while she looked at the paintings, I told her I was going out for a minute. "Good idea," she said, not turning from the painting she was gazing at. I went downstairs and walked through Ashcan Alley to the John Sloan realism backyard where Kim was playing with Jamal and the Gupta kids. For a while I watched them scooting around, oblivious to the heavy heat, then I went back through the alley and climbed upstairs to the studio. Alba greeted me with, "These are really great, Ren. These are the best things you've done yet. They're marvelous."

"You think so?" I was sweating from the climb.

"Yes. And if you take photos or slides to Conti, these over here are the ones I'd show."

"What's wrong with those others?"

"Nothing. But these are the ones I'd show him, that's all."

"You don't like the others?"

"That's *not* what I said, Ren. You asked me to pick out the ones I'd show Leo, and I've picked them out."

"I thought you were going to pick out the ones you liked."

"I like them all. But these are the ones I'd show him."

"What about the ink-brush nudes or semi-nudes or whatever, what did you think of them?"

"The ones you did of Avalon?"

"All right, the ones I did of Avalon, if you want to think of them that way."

"I don't think they'd show up well in a big gallery with these other paintings on the wall."

"Oh, sure! You're saying that just because it's Avalon. They're good and, in fact, they're very good. I got a vigorous line in there and not a starved thin anemic line, but a good thick powerful line that's fluid at the same time. That's something I can do."

"You asked for my opinion. You got it. All I'm saying is that they'll get overwhelmed by the canvases." The humidity had caused some loosened tendrils of hair to curl against her temple. "Believe me."

I went to the window and looked out, not to see anything but to think about what Alba had said and to calm down.

I recognized that she knew more about Leo Conti and his gallery than I did, and I knew that after she left here I'd sort through the canvases to see how I felt about the ones she had chosen, and I figured I'd mostly agree with her choices, as usual. I was still at the window with my hands in my pockets, brooding on these things, when Alba came up. "What are you thinking?" she asked. I caught the fleeting scent of her perfume, not the cologne she sometimes dabbed on herself before going out, but the perfume she reserved for the evening and, more precisely, for the two of us, a light scent with a hidden muskiness someplace down there. "Are you sure you wouldn't like a drink?" I asked her. "Cinzano over ice?"

"I could do that, yes," she said slowly, apparently thinking it over.

I hurriedly groped into the back of the cabinet and retrieved the bottle, then pulled the ice tray from the refrigerator, letting Alba take two water glasses from the cupboard shelf.

"I haven't had a Cinzano for a while," she said.

"Nor have I." Alba remembered as well as I did the dead day we had a Cinzano. There was a growing silence as I broke the ice cubes from the try, dropped them into the glass, and poured the Cinzano. "So," I said, handing her a glass.

"So," she echoed.

"What have you been up to?"

"Not much." She put her finger against one of the ice cubes and swirled it around in the glass, studying the eddies of the wine. She looked up and I glanced away, then came back.

"What are you doing Sunday morning?" I asked her.

"I don't know. —You could come over for brunch," she added after a pause. "If you want to," she emended.

The drink was complex, smooth but with a heavy tart edge that all but obliterated its own sweet solace. "I could come over the night before, then I'd be there when morning came around."

She took a drink. "That might work."

"I'm willing, if you are."

We were standing close and the day was hot and I could see the tiny drops of perspiration on her forehead at her hairline. I didn't know what I was feeling, but I knew it was best just to keep going. The obscure evanescent scent rising from her mingled with the odor of the wine and I could feel my flesh begin to stir, which itself was pleasant and made it easier not to think of anything, not to recall anything. If Alba's eyes had changed in forty years I couldn't see the difference, one eye invisibly larger than the other, the dark sea-green irises flecked with uneven rays of lighter green and blue. Kim burst into the room, the door crashing behind him while he pulled himself head first to the sink, twisted sideways under the faucet and turned on the water, his skateboard racketing across the floor to whack into my bunk. He gulped at the stream of water, then eased himself down from the counter to stand beside us. "It's burning hot outside and I'm burning up!" he announced. "Can I have an ice cream?"

"Do you remember Alba?" I asked him.

"Yes. She's your wife. —Can I please have an ice cream bar? We have some in the refrigerator, chocolate-covered."

I told him to say hello to my wife, which he did, and I opened the refrigerator to get out a chocolate-covered ice cream bar.

"Do you like skateboarding?" Alba asked him.

"Of course. But Jamal is the best. Renato gave me the skateboard. It's mine."

I unwrapped the ice cream, gave it to him, and he went off with it, saying, "I have to go to the bathroom now." Alba said she had to get back to her place, and we agreed that I'd go over there on Friday evening.

62

L EO CONTI BUILT A SUCCESSFUL ACCOUNTING FIRM
(Conti, Cronin, Stein & Bradford) and then sold his
share to his partners in order to open a gallery in East Cambridge—that's all I knew about him—and here he was in
my studio, a short, jovial man with a round face and a head
of thick curly dazzling black hair. He wore a white cotton
jacket with broad rose stripes, a pink necktie and—*clump*,
clump—platform shoes with thick heels and soles to boost
himself two inches more. He studied the paintings I had set
out for him and when he was through he turned to me and
announced, "I love your work. You have a fresh way of looking at things, of seeing them. I don't know why you're not
better known." I gave a short laugh and told him it baffled me,
too. He flung out an arm toward the canvases and said, "You
have a genius for color. This is great work." I thanked him. He
grabbed a fistful of his own hair and tugged, peeling off the
wig that had fooled me. He mopped his glistening tanned
scalp with a handkerchief and said, "Too hot. Come around
to the gallery tomorrow morning. We'll talk."

I don't know how Leo Conti succeeded as an accountant because, frankly, I wouldn't have trusted him with an
old laundry list, much less with bills or receipts, but I went
around to his gallery, a smudged brick shoebox among all the
tall, shining structures being built in what used to be dumpy
East Cambridge. Today he was wearing sneakers and a bright
yellow polo shirt, no wig. "You still want to exhibit my work?"
I asked him.

"Of *course* I want to exhibit your work," he replied, apparently astonished I would doubt him. We were standing in
the middle of the gleaming gray, uneven concrete floor; the

windows were made of old-fashioned glass blocks, and there was enough space around us to display a dozen automobiles or play a game of tennis. "But after this current show I'm closing the gallery. Everything comes down tomorrow," he said, nodding toward the paintings on the wall. "I'm forced to move. The building has been sold."

"The building has been sold?"

"Sold," he said. "And they want me out of here."

"Why are we talking?"

"Because I'm opening a place in Boston this fall and I want to exhibit you there. —What do you think of these?" he asked, spreading his arms toward the wall of paintings.

"I haven't really looked at them."

"Tell me anyway. What do you think?"

"There's something a little wrong with every canvass, Leo. But the work isn't all bad. In fact, some of it's all right. Somebody has energy and half a style. The painter's going to be good in ten years."

Conti laughed joyfully. "Five years. I'm betting five years or less. She's not thirty and she's already selling."

"Where are you going in Boston?"

"Not Newbury Street. There's too many galleries there already. It's glutted. I'll be in what you might call off-Newbury. Off-Newbury, but not too far off."

"When would I get a show?"

"I'm booked up for a year. I can't show you till a year from now. That's my dilemma." His face grew very sad, his head drooped a bit and he looked up at me, waiting.

I recognized my cue. "Don't take it so hard, Leo. You can put up one more show right here. I like this place."

"You deserve better than this, Renato. And there's no time. This place has been sold. It gets demolished eight weeks from today. I know you deserve better than this."

I was elated because I understood him now. "I *like* this place, it has a nice echo. We'll have to work fast."

Leo shook his head vigorously, no. "There's no time to get the word out about a new show. And I'm going on vacation. I've got *plans*."

"You can get the word out. Send invitations, glossy color prints. You can have a great party. The last, the best show. Invite everybody. My work is big and I have lots of it. I can fill this whole concrete ballroom."

"I haven't got a penny!" Like a successful pickpocket, he flung out his hands with his palms up to show me how empty they were. "I put everything into my new gallery. I've got nothing left. Your invitations, your announcements, getting the word out about your wonderful paintings — that would take money. The food, the wine — the cost of it all! I'd need help."

"We'll sell lots of paintings. I'll make you rich."

"I hope so. But I'll need help," he added.

"You used to be an accountant, Leo. Tell me how much help you'll need."

He laughed. "I want to talk art, you want to talk finances!" Then he sighed and said, "Well, all right, if you insist. Come into my office."

Leo led me to his office, a glass-walled cube which jutted into the exhibition space and, with the drapes pulled aside, gave a view of everything in the long gallery, much like the mechanic's office in an automobile repair shop, but here the floor was thickly carpeted and upon the carpet there lay a wine-colored rug with an intricate Afghan or Persian design, and a small teak desk with a matching teak file cabinet waited at the side. The place was comfortable and quiet.

"Leo," I said, "I keep sixty percent of the selling price."

"You read my mind!"

"No. Leo doesn't keep sixty. Renato keeps sixty."

"Oh." And after a pulse beat, he said, "Absolutely! Now, please take a chair. We have some things to talk about if we're going to sell paintings and we have to work fast."

63

AFTER TALKING WITH CONTI I FELT GOOD AND decided not to go back to the studio, but to stay in Cambridge and plow through traffic to Alba's place. "Well, this is a pleasant surprise. I hope. Come in," she said. Her hair was pulled back tight and she was in white shorts and a black swimsuit top. "Sorry I'm sweaty. Just got back from the gym," she said. "And I thought you were coming tonight," she added, not quite frowning.

"I just finished talking with Leo Conti at his gallery," I said, following her into the apartment. Loose tendrils of her hair, damp and curled, hung above the nape of her heck. I told her I was getting a one-man show. "Hey, that's wonderful," she said, going down the hall toward the bedroom. I told her I was getting sixty percent of each sale. "*Very* good," she said, lifting her voice against the splashing rattle of water pouring into the tub.

"I'll be paying for the advertising, the announcements, the invitations, the food, the wine. Which is not so very good or wonderful." The water was making too much damn noise.

"You'll sell lots of paintings, Ren," she said, turning off the water.

I had halted outside the bathroom and was trying to figure out how she was feeling toward me today. I said, "Conti tells me he has ways of getting the word out to his regular buyers, as well as a few hundred others. He's got lists." Alba stood with her hands on her hips, her face a pleasant mask, still lightly flushed and completely closed. "I think I'll let you take your bath."

"The bath can wait. Tell me more." She folded her arms and leaned a shoulder against the door jamb, not inviting but waiting, expectant.

"I'm bringing canvases to the gallery on Monday. We'll hang the show in two days. The rest is up to him," I said.

"Skye and family might be back by the time the show opens. That would be great."

"You're right," I said. "That would be great. —Take your bath. I'll take you out to lunch. —If you want, I mean."

"Yes. A quick shower." She turned away and shut the door and I started back up the hall. "What do you think of the gallery?" she called out.

"The gallery?"

"Yeah. What do you think about it?" she asked, raising her voice against the opening hiss of the shower.

"It's ten times bigger than I thought it would be," I said.

I couldn't make out Alba's reply.

"*What did you say?*"

"*I said, he fills it. He gets a good crowd.*" Alba's voice was blurred under the rushing cataract.

"*I'll need a crowd, a very big crowd,*" I said.

Alba said something, but I couldn't make it out.

I stepped into the bathroom that was now cloudy with steam and everything there nebulous, humid, close and private. A few moments later she calls out: "*What did you think of the man himself?*"

"I don't know what to think."

"Oh! You're in here!" she says, startled.

"Should I leave?"

"Whatever you want."

"When Conti was an accountant he learned who had money and who collected paintings," I say, unbuttoning my shirt. "He knows a lot of the right people. He may be better at the artbiz than he looks."

"I heard he was moving the gallery to Boston," Alba says, her body fluid and elusive, dissolving and reappearing in the tall pleats and hollows of the shower curtain. "Renato? Are you there?" I step out of my falling clothes and into the stinging hot downpour. She says, "Oh! Here you are. —Well, well, hello."

It's never that easy, actually. I mean, it's easy for us to begin in the shower and end on the bed, but it's not that easy to talk or, more precisely, go back to sort things out. It's as bad as it gets when you've been wronged, and worse if you did wrong—don't ask me how that's possible, all I know is what I know. I prefer to go forward, prefer her warm slippery flesh in the shower or moist on the sunny bed cover and hot inside, prefer the weight and crush and being able to say, *She's mine.* We can talk another time, we always do, not on the bed and not now but some other place, talk about that event, what really happened, essentially happened, which was not what it might appear to be, but less, much less—though wrong, yes, wrong and stupid and vain and foolish. We have spent more than half our lives together, for which I'm grateful. We won't talk of forgiveness, not this Alba, not *my* Alba, for which I'm also grateful, because I've never loved or got aroused amid forgiveness.

64

A LETTER ARRIVED FROM INDONESIA (BADLY DE-signed stamps) from Skye, saying they were getting ready to leave, were already beginning to pack, would be flying from Jakarta and arrive, after a stop in Los Angeles, in Boston around the time the exhibit opened at the Conti Gallery. Meanwhile, Alba had received an e-mail from Brizio, telling her no more than what he had written earlier to me, that he was coming to visit us and was bringing his friend Heather with him; I had a photo of Brizio and Heather taken at a picnic two years ago and knew about her only that she had a college degree, ran in marathons and grew herbs for a living. I didn't have time to think long about these things as I was at the gallery every day that week to work with Leo Conti and his associate Ms Monday, hanging the show. By the way, Leo was surprisingly efficient in spreading information about the exhibit—little hand-written notes, e-mails, the Conti Gallery newsletter and his gallery web site, a few last-minute ads—and he even persuaded a printer to do rush job turning out a tri-fold brochure which showed three of my paintings. "What do you think of this?" he asked, taking off his new glasses and using them to point dramatically at the brochures on his desk. I told him they looked great and had very good color reproduction. "What? No, no, not the brochures. These, *these*," he said, waving the glasses. "Do you think they make me look authoritative and smart, or just bookish?" I told him authoritative. He looked at the glasses skeptically—gigantic lenses with thin black frames—and said, "It's just window glass, but I thought they might help with the image." I told him he absolutely didn't need any help with his image. He studied the glasses a moment longer, then tossed them aside on his desk. "Image is everything," he told me.

After leaving Conti's I wedged into the traffic and drove around to Alba's, thinking of lunch, but she wasn't in so I got back in the car and joined the traffic over the river into Boston and swung down to Zoe's. I parked and walked into her studio, but before I could open my mouth she had clutched my arm, saying, "Galaxy phoned a minute ago. She's pregnant."

"Wait a minute—"

"She and Weston want to get married in a couple of weeks."

"She's thought she was pregnant before. Twice before. What makes her think—"

"She's pregnant, Ren. Galaxy says they plan to get married in a week or two. Or three."

"What's the rush? How pregnant is she? And what does she—"

Zoe had clapped her hands over her ears and walked away, but now she dropped her hands and turned, saying, "We haven't even met this man, this Weston! I *told* you we should have gone down to New York. We should have gone down when she told us she wanted to marry him. I *told* you."

"I've been trying to paint. I've been trying to get a show. Not to mention, I've been—"

"This is your *daughter* we're talking about," she cried.

"And isn't she supposed to bring him to us? Isn't that the way it's done or have they changed the rules?"

Zoe stopped walking back and forth and looked at me. "She'll come to your exhibit, I'm sure, so we can tell her to bring Weston along. Right? And she will, I'm sure. Right?"

"Absolutely."

"And then she'll get married," she added, sounding as if the idea had struck her so hard it left her dazed.

"You could look a little happier. Listen, let me take you out to lunch."

Zoe looked at her wristwatch. "How did it get so late?" She went to her desk, shut down her computer and gathered up a dozen large square envelopes in her arm, then she stopped. "What's going to happen to me after she gets married?"

"You're going to be fine," I said. She had remained standing there motionless, so I touched her shoulder and murmured, "Come on, Zoe. We'll have lunch."

Her eye had started to glisten and, as she turned to get a tissue from the box on her desk, the envelopes slipped from under her arm and slid to the floor. She sobbed. I picked up the envelopes while she wiped her eyes, blew her nose. "I've had a bad week," she said, her voice shaky. "Things haven't been going well for me."

"We'll talk about it over lunch." I put my arm around her shoulders.

"I don't want to talk about it. —Have you seen my keys?" she asked, peering into her purse. "Where are my envelopes?"

"Your keys are there and I've got the envelopes. Let's go."

Over lunch we talked some about Galaxy and Weston, but more about Zoe herself— "Because if Galaxy is married well, and I hope she does marry well, she's going to love him more and more and me less and less." I told her that's not the way love works. "That's what you think because you've been lucky. And when Galaxy's safely married you'll have less reason to see me, too." I told her that's not the way I work, but she simply turned her face away and stared out the café window. On the way back to her studio she told me she had broken up with Derek Mallow. "You never liked him, anyway," she added.

"That's not why you split."

"I split because we didn't have anything to talk about. I'm not interested in boats and he's not interested in anything else. That's why we spent too much time, you know, fucking. And one weekend was all it took to exhaust his repertoire in that area."

When we arrived back at her studio she asked me what I thought of Emerson Ripley, and I said I thought he was a good guy and I liked him. "He asked me out to dinner tonight and I said yes, but he's so poor I don't know where we'll eat." I told her he was a nice guy and that was enough. "But what does he do?" she asked. I said he sold books and wrote book reviews. "You can't make a living that way," she said. He lives simply, I said. "I've decided to become celibate," Zoe said.

65

LATE ONE NIGHT — IT WAS OUR LAST NIGHT — I BE-gan hunting for those little photos of Vivianna which I remembered seeing, because it was so clear in my mind, my finding them some years ago among a sheaf of old letters and documents. I went back to the chest at the foot of my bunk, got down on my creaky knees, and fished out the letter box which had all the Stillamare papers. I emptied it onto the floor and then looked at each scrap as I put it back into the box, but again there wasn't any photo of Vivianna. "You look like your praying over there," Avalon informed me. I dug my way down into the chest, lifting layers of sketch books, photo albums, art reviews, book lists handwritten by uncle Zitti, my high-school yearbook, down through a strata of bank statements and tax returns, then sideways past a sealed bundle of Polaroids (Alba and me fooling around) to the big business envelope with the label *P. Cavallù & Co.* I got to my feet, opened the envelope and poured everything onto the table. It was junk.

"That's not junk," Avalon told me. "Those are family documents. They're valuable. You should treat them with respect, carefully."

"It's junk. I'm looking for some old photos."

"Let me—"

"Damnit, Avalon—"

All the letters were carbon copies, some about a shipment of shoe machinery to Sicily and others about a commercial building in Palermo, plus there were six pocket calendars running from 1925 to 1931, each advertising P. Cavallù & Co., stock certificates totaling forty shares of Stanley & Mac-Gibbons, Co., sheet music for "Cosa Ne Hai Fatto Del Mio Cuore?" (What have you done to my heart?), some receipts from a typewriter repair company, a couple of invoices and— Ha!—five little snapshots of Vivianna in her mid-twenties.

"Hey, maybe we're rich," Avalon said, studying the worthless stock certificates.

Two of the snapshots were taken indoors and they're dark; in one, Vivianna, her hair fashionably bobbed, sits in a heavy swivel chair beside a broad black desk, and in the other she's by a window where the light leaves almost half her face in shadow. Frankly, they're lousy photos. The remaining three snapshots were taken out of doors on a breezy summer day. Her pale blouse opens wide at the throat and her hair blows across her cheek in a short dark crescent. The sun is bright and there's no blurring, even though she's turned her head and is laughing. In this other snapshot she represses a smile, trying to hold still for the photographer, and in this last one—caught unaware, her skirt flapping in the wind—she's stepping down from a boulder to a beach, most likely the same rocky beach that shows in the background of the other outdoor shots.

"So that's her," Avalon said. "The wild one."

Vivianna appears to be twenty-five, but there's no date or writing of any kind on the back of the photos.

"You should put them in an album," Avalon said. "Why do you keep them in the envelope with all this business stuff?"

"That's how I found them, sandwiched in between all this business stuff."

"How much do you think these stock certificates are worth?" she asked.

"I think they're worth zero."

Avalon set aside the certificates and took up one of the little photos. "She's good-looking. If you ask me, your grandfather took these snapshots and kept them hidden at his office where no one else would know, that's how come they wound up in this envelope, because your Pacifico and your Vivianna were close, real close, and nobody else knew. That's what *I* think."

"That's what *you* think. Actually, she was still working for my grandfather that summer while my parents went on their wedding trip to Europe. That's what *I* know. That's probably his office over the store."

"And this is probably the beach they played on together. They were lovers, is what I think," said Avalon

"That was 1929. My aunt Vivianna was about twenty-five. My grandfather must have been at least fifty. And you think they were *lovers*?"

"Of course it wouldn't happen nowadays," Avalon said sarcastically. "Not now. Not here. Not in this room with you and me. But maybe back then young women and older men weren't so choosey who they went to bed with."

"Well, she was out of the picture when my mother and father got back in September. That was 1929 and nobody ever heard from her again, except for that one solitary postcard from Las Vegas my father got."

I went back to the chest, found the Stillamare letter box and fished out the postcard from the Hotel National.

"That lousy hotel," Avalon said. "But look when she sent it. See?"

"She didn't say when she —."

"Up here, see?"

The faded postage cancellation mark was a circle with **LAS VEGAS NEV**. printed around the inside and **APR 3 1930 P.M.** down the middle. "So Vivianna didn't go to Las Vegas until the next year," Avalon said. "Before that, she was still around here. If nobody saw her, she must have been hiding."

"She could have been anywhere. Why would she be hiding?"

"Don't tell. Let me guess."

"I have a long day tomorrow. I should go to bed."

"Don't you want to hear the rest?"

"I want to give you this. Here. It's for you." I gave her the portfolio I had put together a couple of days earlier — big ink-on-paper works done with a calligraphic brush, each one of her, and damned good ones though I say so myself.

66

ALL I NEEDED TO DO WAS SHOWER AND PULL ON some fresh clothes, but I was distracted by the lonely emptiness of the studio, my big canvases gone, all that life and color gone, and especially Avalon and Kim gone, because for three days Avalon had been cleaning our place, scrubbing the kitchen and bathroom and back room, then packing up her stuff, all her cheap things—every jersey and blue jeans, every pair of shorts, all the cut-offs, sweatshirts, fishnets, vinyl, all the wire rings, black leather bracelets, chokers, chromium chains, spikes, studs, lipsticks, eye pencils, hair sparkle, all her books, postcards, bottle caps, corks, seashells, and all Kim's toys—every goddamned rag and scrap, left nothing behind except the door key, which lay so lonely on the kitchen counter, though I had emphatically told her she could keep it.

The back room felt especially lonely with that bare floor space, the sleeping bag and backpack gone, the mattress up on edge over here and the bookcase pushed back over there, and she'd swept all her little things from the shelves and returned my books in neat rows, arranged—why not?—by height. There wasn't anything for me to straighten up or put away or save, so I took a shower and when I pulled open my drawer to get a shirt there was a letter addressed to me, two folded sheets of lined notebook paper covered on both sides with Avalon's jagged handwriting. It was a thank-you note. *Dear Renato, As you see, I am writing a letter now that I have somebody to write to. There's many things I want to thank you for and I have been making a list, it's incomplete but here it is—"* Frankly, I was pleased that she appreciated those things, but as I read I began to weep and I don't know why. She was thankful for so many little, little things. Now, let me say this about Avalon—the multicolored hair, the jewelry stuck to her face, those were distractions and I've spent too much time talking about them, because if you ever knew Avalon you'd know she was beautiful and good. She was beautiful not like those women who are so pretty they think they don't fart, but beautiful when she was smeared with coffee dust from hauling sacks of coffee beans or when she was quietly watching Kim draw one of his maps, or when she tossed her head back and laughed or simply whenever. And she was good and true.

Anyway, I got myself together, got into fresh L. L. Bean chinos and a pair of paint-spotted running shoes, which shoes I felt were enough, a kind of signature at the bottom of the image to assure the buyer that I was the painter. I tried on the white wash-and-wear jacket which I had worn to get married in and which Galaxy had returned to me a year ago; it looked good, so I kept it on. I trotted downstairs, got in the wagon drove through the rain to Cambridge and Conti's gallery. The reception was scheduled from six to nine and I was almost an hour late.

There was a good enough crowd in the gallery, but before I could take a step Leo Conti popped up, whispering, "Where have you been? All these paintings and no painter!" I told him my daughter and her family had flown in from Indonesia this morning and that I'd been running late and that—. But Conti had thrust his arm through mine and was pulling me on a long diagonal across the floor. Tonight he was wearing black trousers and a black jacket over black turtleneck jersey. I said, "Leo, why are you dressed like a mortician? You sold three paintings before we even opened." He tugged my arm, tilted me down toward him to speak into my ear, saying, "Listen, buyers come to receptions to see the *painter*, not the paintings. Some of these people have money to spend and you've got to *help* them." He told me who they were and what they were, so I could perform properly as an artist, which is to say like a trained circus lion, all wild display and no bite. I chatted in a surly yet respectful way with these potential buyers, then merciful Alba came up to hand me a glass of soda water, so they withdrew, after which she took my arm, saying, "Galaxy's over here."

And here's my daughter, her face luminous and her eyes dancing, as if the room is filled lighted candles, coming to give me a hug. "Dad, this is Weston," she tells me, conjuring out of the empty air beside her a thin young man with an amiable angular face. We shake hands and agree it's time for us to meet, since we've heard so much about each other, and I turn to Galaxy to say, "I heard some news about you, I heard—" but before I can finish, she says, "Yes, I'm having a baby, really, truly, a baby," and I said, "That's wonderful, that's great, that beats all."

At first there were only people standing together in islands, a long archipelago which began at the food table and curved gently across the glassy gray concrete floor, but when I next had the time to look around the place was full. Vanderzee had come wearing what I thought was a backpack but which turned out to be a baby carrier with a little kid peering out. "These are really great. This is a great show. I love it," Vanderzee said, looking around, apparently quite pleased at what he saw. "It's a great party, too. Which reminds me," he added, turning to me, "I play Dixieland with a jazz group and I can get them over here to play a set, if you want." And before I could ask Vanderzee was he joking or simply crazy he had swung into an energetic talk with Leo, their heads together. Then a couple of gallery patrons engaged me in conversation, but sometime later I saw Vanderzee's Winona and Gail, she with a sleepy toddler in her arms. I asked the women if Vanderzee played in a jazz group. Oh, yes, they assured me, he plays the clarinet, and he's good at it.

I'm happy to say I didn't know most of the people who came, but friends did show up and I was grateful for that, too. From Copley College came Azarig and his wife, and loyal

Nils Petersen, whose Pixels show I had attended, and Nils's wife Hanna, and five of my former students or, to be precise, three former male students and a couple of their women. Karl Kadish came, as did Tom Hay and his wife, and Cormac with Karen McCormac drove in from the middle of Massachusetts, the Scanlons from Connecticut, and Zocco came, and Michkio with a tall fellow named Quincy, and Gordon Levy and Garland from the café—Gordon, bless him, bought a small painting—and to my surprise boyish Peter Bell, Sonia Strand's assistant, turned up and introduced me to his companion, David Somebody.

I was talking with a twenty-something internet entrepreneur (blue jeans, yellow cotton jersey) who fancied himself a collector of contemporary art when I saw Zoe approaching. After the kid left, Zoe asked had I talked yet with Galaxy and Weston, and I said, "Yes. And they make a good-looking couple. Galaxy knows what she's doing." We could see them over by the wine table, chatting with Cormac. We watched as Galaxy, gesturing in a great zigzag, said something to Cormac, then Cormac smiled and said something in reply which caused Galaxy to laugh. While she went on talking, her hand at her side brushed against Weston's hand and returned, fingers outspread, seeking it again. Zoe turned to me and said, "We all did all right with Galaxy. I know we made a few mistakes, but we did good." And I said, "Yes, we did." Zoe had come to the exhibit with Emerson Ripley who had been at the wine table to fill two glasses and was now maneuvering through the crowd toward us. "Emerson's actually good company," Zoe told me. "But I need more time, lots more time, before I let myself—you know—get involved. Deeply," she added.

"I thought you were going to be celibate," I said.

"I am. I've been celibate for days. I'm celibate right now."

Our Avalon and Kim came with Sebastian Gabriel and his daughter Kate, making a family. Avalon was in a fanciful dress, a colorful paper confection which Sebastian had probably made for her, and Sebastian himself was wearing a sky-blue jacket decorated with gold braid, and bogus military insignia, including a shoulder patch from Sgt. Pepper's Lonely Hearts Club Band and a breast-pocket crest from Monty Python's Flying Circus. "I don't know which one of you looks more magnificent," I said. As a matter of fact, Avalon had a beautifully weird aura about her, perhaps because of the strange dye job she had done on her hair, the tips being pale pink which shaded into a glorious rose as it neared her scalp.

Zoe took my hand and turned me around, telling me, "Look who's here," and here was Alba and our traveling daughter, Skye, who gave me a long, long hug. "We're all jet-lagged!" says Skye, holding both my hands. "Eric's at the apartment looking after the kids or he'd be here too." You look wonderful, I tell her, and behind Skye comes our son Brizio, taller than I remembered, so tall he seemed to hunch down to give me a hug. Then he swung his backpack to the floor and brought forward the young woman at his side—clear green eyes, no lipstick and a plain silver clip in her smooth chestnut hair—his companion for the last two years. "You remember Heather," Brizio says. I say, Yes, of course. "We're getting married," Brizio says. "And having a baby," Heather adds, shaking my hand.

I don't know exactly when Vanderzee's Dixieland band began to play, but by then the evening was coming to a close so there was open space on the floor and people began to dance, turning my paintings to wallpaper. Frankly, I thought the exhibit had been too damn much of a party all along and I was sore at Vanderzee and angry with Conti or, actually, I would have been if I had been sober, but because of the wine in my veins, or because I could see Brizio and Heather and Galaxy and Weston talking together, I felt elated, expansive and warm-hearted toward everyone. I had started to tell Scanlon my plans to paint frescos in a barn, but he interrupted to tell me his theory that artists shouldn't move to the country, that painting should never be done out of doors, that it's essential to paint indoors and under artificial light, otherwise the colors will look off key, because paintings are destined to be seen in the artificial light and canned air of galleries. I told him we had already signed a lease to rent a country place for a year with an option to buy.

My conversation with Scanlon was interrupted by a writer from the *Boston Phoenix* who leaned in to confide that the exhibit was the best bash he'd been to all summer, and then his tall blond companion, who said she wrote for *Art New England*, remarked on Conti's having made a killing when he sold this piece of real estate to a builder eager to put up another office building. I went looking for Conti, the man with empty pockets who had induced me to pay for all the advertising and half the wine, but he found me first, catching my arm and turning me round to meet a man whom I'd seen chatting idly with Conti when I began delivering my paintings to the gallery, a middle-aged pear-shaped man with a soft, formless face and gentle eyes. He had looked over my work a couple of days ago and was buying one of my paintings—a huge canvas, *Charles River Basin*, delicious licks of ultramarine and green and black, velvety black, and gray and blazing white—on which Conti had slapped a handsome high price. We three stepped into Conti's and the buyer told me, "That painting is better than any Kokoshka," and I agreed, said it was a hundred times better (though it was a brainless comparison) and we exchanged other such pleasantries, after which I gave him my studio address and we shook hands.

I returned to the gallery floor feeling very good; the band was swinging into "Sensation Rag," and that's when Avalon came up, telling me, "I have an idea about your aunt Vivianna."

"Another one?" I said Hi to Kim who was beside her.

"We agree that your grandfather got her pregnant and then—" she says.

"I don't remember agreeing." We were standing in front of the band and it was hard to hear. I asked Kim how he liked his new place.

"—She went into hiding but didn't go out to Las Vegas until after the baby was born," Avalon says, lifting her voice above the music.

"That's your idea."

"No, Ren, those are more or less the facts. My idea is she left her baby on your grandfather's doorstep and bought a ticket to Las Vegas a couple of weeks later."

At first I didn't understand her. All around us people were dancing and laughing and Vanderzee's clarinet was making neon-colored scribbles that hovered in the air, entangling everything, and I began to laugh, shaking my head, partly to clear it and partly to say no, not at all, never. Alba had come up and was talking with Avalon. Kim said he guessed his new place was all right and asked when was I coming to visit him. "When would you like?" I asked him

"Tomorrow," he said.

"Not tomorrow," I said. "Tomorrow I'm going out to the country."

"I could get a ride out to the country. You could show me water bugs," Kim said. Alba looked at him a moment and then asked him, "Would you like to come to a picnic tomorrow?"

By the end we had invited not only Kim but, naturally, Avalon and, of course, Sebastian and his daughter Kate, and Cormac and Karen McCormac and, though Scanlon and his wife had to return to Connecticut, we did get Vanderzee and his kid or kids and whoever. And then—because I didn't want to see my paintings as backdrop to a near-deserted ballroom where every chair and window displayed a handful of used plastic glasses and waded paper napkins, and the caterer's table was littered with mangled piles of fruit, cheese wedges and cracker bowls with only crumbs in the bottom—I said to Alba, "Let's get out of here." We had dinner with Brizio, Heather, Galaxy, Weston, Zoe and Emerson, after which we said goodnight to everyone and, because Alba's place was crammed full with Skye and her family, plus Brizio and Heather, and my studio quite empty, we bedded down there.

67

*G*OD MADE US MORTAL, AND ALL WE HAVE TO ASSUAGE us is this perishable art and human love. At one of my exhibits I was greeted by a woman pushing a wheelchair from painting to painting—Nancy Lorette she was, whom I had last seen sprinkling confectioner's sugar into her navel, and in the wheelchair sat her little old mother Avril, bright-eyed and completely puzzled. While I was writing these pages I got word that my enduring friend Max, who brought me food when I was sick in the city, had died of prostate cancer, and a couple of days ago I learned that bright Odine, who let me draw with crayon on her beautiful long back, had died of congestive heart failure.

Looking back, I'm baffled that I haven't done better. I don't mean painting; I've done all right painting even if nobody knows it. But I could have given more time to my friends, could have listened more and complained less, could have been more generous to everyone. And I could have taken Avalon more seriously, including her notion that I'm the child of my aunt Vivianna and my grandfather Pacifico—which might be true, but Avalon is always trying to tie loose ends into a family. I've loved greedily and not with perfect chastity and I don't even know why I love the people I do. I know only that I love them. Montaigne, speaking of his dead friend Ètienne, could never explain the depth of their friendship, could say only that such friendship came because "he was he and I was I"—which is another reason to think Montaigne was Italian. I miss Mike Bruno.

I saw my first actual painting high on the wall of our Post Office, where Paul Revere galloped through the blue moon-lit morning of April 19, 1775, to warn us villagers that the British were coming, galloped on the road just outside our Post Office door, his arm flung out as he thundered past. Ever since then I've always wanted to paint a mural, and may still get around to it. I wake up in the morning—flex my fingers and toes, stretch my legs—and I'm delighted to find that my body still works, that I can paint at least one more day, and especially happy I paint better than anyone else. I paint to give viewers solace for being human. A couple of years ago I drove down to Hartford to see the paintings of Pieter de Hooch (1629–1694), because he was having his first solo show. So maybe like him I'll have a retrospective three hundred years from now, or maybe, like my friend who worked by torch-light in those caves above the waters of the Ardeche, I'll wait thirty-one thousand years.

68

NEXT MORNING THE SKY WAS CLEAR BLUE, WASHED by the drenching rain of the past few days, and the deep grass around the old white farm house shimmered in the sun like shallow sea water. We unlocked the doors, threw open the windows, carried a couple of crates of wine from the wagon, and I was lugging a pair of sawhorses when Brizio and Heather pulled in, bringing food they had bought from a local farmer who, they said with satisfaction, used only natural organic fertilizers and natural organic pesticides; then Skye and Eric and their four kids drove up in a rented van with a carton of paper plates, cups, napkins, loaded from Alba's concrete storage box in Cambridge.

Later, Eric and I unhinged the board door from the kitchen closet and carried it outside where we laid it across the sawhorses for a makeshift table. We set it up by the house and figured we could spread some tablecloths on the grass a ways beyond it, under the apple branches that faced out across the hay fields toward the woods — our own paradise, though, as I pointed out to Alba, all of the apples were flawed and some had worms. As we were standing there surveying the landscape I asked Eric where his anthropology was going to take him next, which I believed was a better way of asking a son-in-law was he ever going to get a goddamn job with a decent goddamn wage and settle down within a five goddamn hundred miles of here. He took my meaning and smiled, a likeable man, I believe, though it's hard to know him well when he's always at some distant edge of the map. He told me he had a letter from a friend at the University of Massachusetts about a job opening there, which he thought would be convenient for all of us, and he guessed he should write back and ask for details; on the other hand, he said, squinting at the horizon, there was some good research being done up in Toronto and some really fascinating work being talked about at a place in Saskatchewan. He looked at me and smiled, saying, "Something will turn up, I'm sure," and, after rolling that around in my head for a while, I agreed, as there was no good my doing otherwise.

I went looking for my grandchildren, last seen disappearing around a corner of the house, and along the way I bumped into Brizio's Heather who was carrying a crate of wine into the shade of the apple trees. I took it from her and we began talking about how hot the sun was and how it was too bad no one had thought to bring ice, and all the while I was taking pleasure in her clear eyes and, I confess, in the knowledge that she was carrying Brizio's baby. We were discussing the herbs she was growing for gourmet restaurants when Skye walked over to us — this athlete in a flowing batik dress, my daughter. "I didn't have time to tell to you yesterday," Skye says to me. "So I want to tell you now — I'm pregnant." She watched me expectantly, then while I'm gathering my wits, she says, as if to help me understand, "We're having another baby, Dad," to which I think I said Oh and But and Well, and then as Alba came up I told her, "Everybody's pregnant," and Alba says decisively, "Yes, it's *wonderful*."

"Yes, wonderful," I chimed, giving Skye a belated hug and a kiss. Skye and Heather went off to explore the fields, their voices diminishing in the distance as Skye told her about some kind of Asian or Indonesian sling, a kerchief knotted to make a sling, which women, someplace, use to carry a baby. I turned to Alba. "Everybody's pregnant at once. Is that possible?"

"Apparently so," says Alba.

"She already has *four* kids."

"I'm sure Skye realizes that. I'm sure they both do."

"How are they going to support *five*?"

"That's not our worry."

"It isn't?"

Then Emerson Ripley's beater hove into view, carrying not only Emerson and Zoe, but Galaxy and Galaxy's Weston, too. They had brought bread — Tuscan rounds and rolls and long baguettes — plus a couple of bottles of wine. Later I told Zoe that Skye was pregnant. "Yes. Isn't it wonderful?"

"You knew?" I said, stopping so abruptly that Zoe, who was holding the other end of the table cloth, was yanked to a stop. "Why, yes. I think Galaxy told me," she says, opening her arms to stretch the cloth tight between us.

"When?"

"Last night. Or maybe before then. I don't remember," she says as we lowered the billowing cloth to the grass where we anchored it with a small stone at each corner.

Vanderzee and Winona and Gail and their kids arrived with more food, and so did Cormac and Karen McCormac, so we had at least three baskets full of grapes, a bushel of peaches, a dozen ears of early corn, several freshly baked loaves, a bag of tomatoes, three fried chickens (sliced and cold), sardines, more tomatoes, a couple of cucumbers, a couple of crates of wine, some bottles of Moxie if you didn't want wine, and water from the kitchen faucet if you couldn't stand the Moxie. And at last came Kim and Avalon plus Sebastian and his daughter Kate, bringing cheeses, black olives and figs —chosen, I'm sure, by Avalon.

"Isn't she beautiful?" Sebastian said to me. Anybody else might have said Avalon looked bizarre, for she was wearing a dress again, as she had last night, but this one was composed of filmy white material with burnt umber trim and its huge sleeves were pleated like fans, so when she lifted her arms they looked like angel wings. "Oh, did you ever see anyone so beautiful?" he said, his voice hushed with awe. We were standing in the shade and Avalon, letting Kim go off to the barn with the other kids, turned and walked toward us, the sun shooting clear through her dress. She must have re-dyed her hair this morning, because it was darker than last night, the luminous rose color being closer to her scalp, the tips now reddish gold, and as she walked past you could see the backs of her hands were hued like peacock feathers, her nails like emeralds and sapphires, radiant as her own mother when she was pregnant with Avalon. "She thinks the world of you," I told Sebastian.

I supposed Avalon was pregnant, too, seeing as how all the other young women were, which prompted me to tell Cormac I was going to include pregnant nudes in the frescos I was planning to paint in the barn. He laughed. "Great! But *frescos*? Don't you need special plaster for that?" he said.

"I can get it from Rome. It's ground up limestone mixed with volcanic sand. It's great stuff. I'll use powdered pigments, the kind you mix with oil to make oil paints, but I'll mix them with water and paint directly on the intonaco, the damp plaster. It'll be great fun." We got to the barn just as Kim and my two oldest grandchildren came popping out. The open side of the big sliding door, though still jammed into the earth, had pulled itself away from the barn and was standing at a crazy angle, giving bearish bulky Cormac almost enough room to step inside—a further shove on the door did the trick. We walked down the long interior to the big square of light at the far end where the floor was still spongy from rain water, took in the view of the green horizon, walked back to the place where we could stare up between the naked rafters to the sky —"Well, you could put in a skylight," said Cormac—then came out to bright sunshine.

"First I'll get the roof patched," I said. "And I'll put in big, big windows on both sides, high up, like clerestory windows. The barn is just the frame for the blank walls. I'll fill in the blanks, paint everything and everybody—it will be amazing, it'll be wonderful."

We got back to the others—"Hungry! Starved! Famished!" they cried—who had been waiting for Cormac and me, we raised a toast to the company, clinked our glasses and drank. In that moment of quiet we heard a very loud *CRACK*— sourceless as a thunderclap, but sharp—and a loud grinding groan came to us, we realized, from the barn, then a popping and crackling and we saw the old structure had swayed toward its back end where the land slanted steeply down so you could walk a horse in under the barn. Avalon came shooting past, holding Kim by the wrist, while Skye cried, "Where are the kids? Are any kids over there?" I must have started to run toward the barn, because I was almost there when up came a rippling snapping sound with an undertone of CRACKS and BOOMS as it began collapsing, slowly heaving itself down over its back cellar wall to crash and smash on the ground until there was only the silence of the hot sun and a long sloped tangle of broken beams, rafters, joists, shingles, planks and clapboards, over which hovered a cloud of dust, specks of straw and seed and wood a hundred and fifty years old.

No children had been inside, everyone was safe and there was nothing we could do about the barn, but the day wasn't going to last forever the way it used to when we were kids and, since the wine was uncorked and the food ready, we began to eat and drink and loaf in the shade, talking about what we were going to do next, like building a better barn, better for frescos.

The Author

Eugene Mirabelli lives in upstate New York and contributes to an alternative newsweekly and an online journal, criticalpages.com. He is a professor emeritus (State University of New York at Albany) and was a founder and director of Alternative Literary Programs in Schools, a nonprofit arts organization to bring poets and storytellers into the classroom. In addition to his novels he has written short stories, articles and essays.

The Typeface

William Caslon began to design typefaces around 1734 in England and his work quickly became popular throughout Europe and the American Colonies. Benjamin Franklin admired Caslon's work and rarely used any other and, indeed, the first printing of the Declaration of Independence was set in Caslon. The letterforms are properly unobtrusive and maintain a subtle balance of broad and thin strokes.